SECRETS OF THE DEAD

Also by Murray Bailey

Singapore 52
Singapore Girl
Singapore Boxer

Map of the Dead

Black Creek White Lies

I Dare You
Dare You Twice

SECRETS OF THE DEAD

Murray Bailey

Heritage Books

First published in Great Britain in 2019 by Heritage Books

123585321

copyright © Murray Bailey 2018

ISBN 978-1-9997954-7-4
e-book ISBN 978-1-9997954-8-1

Printed and bound in Great Britain by Clays Ltd, Elcograf S.p.A

Heritage Books, Truro, Cornwall

For my friends, fans and family.

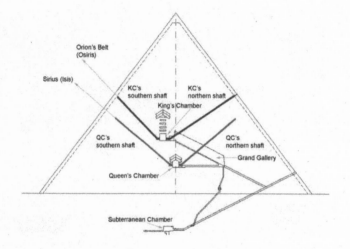

Cross section of the Great Pyramid of Giza

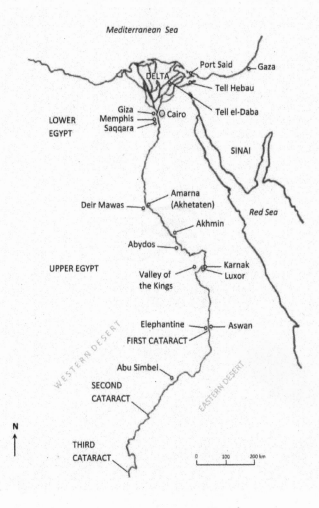

The First

ONE

When he first saw flesh in the dog's jaws, Eddie didn't think much of it. His two hounds were often finding bones. Only this time it was different. The dogs had been running out by the church. And when he took the human hand from Deion's jaws, Eddie worried he'd be in trouble.

JJ was nowhere to be seen and didn't come when called, which concerned Eddie too. But first he decided to find where Deion had been digging and just replace the hand. No one would ever know.

Then he spotted his second dog, far too intent on his bone to respond to calls. But this one wasn't a bone, it was an arm. And that wasn't all. Eddie watched a lot of TV but he'd also seen the posters. This arm was distinctive with a Maori sleeve tattoo.

Eddie didn't think he was in trouble any more. He knew he'd found the latest missing boy.

1

Special Agent Charlie Rebb watched FOX News. She finished blending the super-greens smoothie and used it to wash down a couple of Advil. What was worse, the green gloop or the thumping headache?

Her phone rang. It was her partner, Peter Zhang.

"You watching this?" he said.

"Morning, Peter."

"Yeah, morning. Have you got the news on?"

"If you mean, am I watching the media circus at the church, then yeah. It's crazy."

"Five bodies they've pulled out of there."

"Hold on," she said. The pastor of the church was being interviewed. The display gave his name as Reverend Piccard. Behind him was a cluster of doleful members of his congregation.

"We are all deeply shocked," Piccard said. "The community is in shock. But at the same time, we must have faith in the risen Lord. The Son of Man must be delivered over to the hands of the sinners, be crucified, and on the third day be raised again." Piccard reached out and the people behind closed in and held hands.

Peter said something but she cut him off. "Wait, I want to hear this."

The reporter said, "Reverend, Mark Simmons had been missing from Georgia State University for forty days. There's been a state-wide hunt for him. And now we discover he's been under this church—under your church. Forty days under your church." She paused, adding weight to the statement. "Tell us how you found out about the body. How you learned about the other bodies?"

In Charlie's ear, Zhang said, "We don't know Simmons was under there for forty days! He could have been someplace else and been moved."

"Shush!" Charlie put the phone down on the counter so her partner couldn't interrupt.

Reverend Piccard repeated the story that everyone knew by now: a local man had found "the poor boy" while out walking his dogs. He said, "The man called the police and I got a call from them at home yesterday at around 10am. Of course, I came straight here and we have been praying ever since. This is a wake-up call." Reverend Piccard looked into the camera, speaking to the TV audience. "The human race is out of control and corrupt. Evil is abound. Greed and self-gratification have replaced God and godliness. We are being punished for turning our backs on the Lord. Only by accepting Christ can we hope for salvation."

"Has he said the words 'fire and brimstone' yet?" Charlie heard her partner scoff.

The reporter had managed to get a word in: "—and this morning the police issued a statement about there being multiple bodies under your church."

The reverend swallowed and nodded. A woman beside him closed in as though for comfort or protection.

The reporter said, "What can you tell us about those other bodies?"

Piccard looked like he was on the verge of tears. "Those poor boys... I've been told there are four more that the crime scene people have found. Five poor boys. We should all take a moment today and pray for their souls..." He paused. "I am sure we will learn in due course who they were, but for now I say, Father, into your hands I commit their souls. Christ our saviour rose on the third day. He will rise again. He will lead us from damnation and the serpent of evil will be driven out once and for all."

"This is crap," she heard Zhang shout. "Listen, I'll be there in fifteen to pick you up." He disconnected.

Twenty minutes later she was in his car and heading for the church in Dunwoody, north of the city.

He caught her rubbing her forehead.

"Headache, Chicago?"

She didn't respond. He knew the nickname wound her up and he kept using it. Just because she'd previously lived in the suburbs of Chicago. It'd been where her husband's job had taken him—before it all went wrong. Before she discovered what a two-timing little douchebag he was.

Zhang said, "That headache. Marcie says it's because you drink too much coffee."

Special Agent Zhang was a few years younger than Charlie. Maybe just the wrong side of thirty, although sometimes he could seem much older. He'd been married to Marcie for five years, and she always had an opinion. Or maybe it was just his way of expressing his own opinion. Charlie hadn't figured out which it was yet.

What she had figured was that Peter was struggling. Marcie didn't work and had health problems. At least that was what she claimed. Hypochondriac was what she appeared, and yet Peter would never say it. Her treatments for mystery illnesses were eating away at Zhang's savings. But worst of all were the sleepless nights.

Peter used to talk about her symptoms and insomnia. But not lately. It was like he'd resigned himself to the situation. It was never getting better.

As a good partner, Charlie knew she should be more understanding. But it was hard. Zhang was a difficult guy. Aggressive and sarcastic, he wasn't the person you let cry on your shoulder.

"Too much coffee," he repeated.

"Actually, it's because I need a goddamn coffee," she said. "I'm trying a health kick and there's more kick than health at the moment."

"Wow! So no coffee?"

"That's what I'm saying. Not for two days now. If this headache doesn't quit in another then I'm back on the caffeine."

They went through the centre of Dunwoody and took Mount Vernon Road before turning left.

He said, "Headache ain't so good for you know what."

Charlie thought, I guess you should know.

"And speaking of which," he said, "how is the new guy, Pablo?"

"Paolo."

"Close enough," he said. "About time I met him, isn't it?"

"No."

"Oh come on, Chicago!"

She pressed her thumbs to her temples. "Quit calling me that."

He chuckled. "Just winding you up. Getting under your skin. It's what partners do. Psych 101, that's all it is. Just be grateful you're not from some hick state like Kansas. Then I could have some real fun."

She turned to him, feeling a wave of despair. "For fu—"

"We're here," he interrupted.

The church stood proudly on a slight rise, with sunlight glinting off white shutters and a steeple. A giant white cross dominated the cut grass frontage. As they turned into the driveway, Charlie read the gate sign: "Church of the Risen Christ—New Beginnings". Beneath that was

Reverend Piccard's name. Charlie noted that it was on a removable strip. Maybe they didn't expect him to stay here long. Maybe after this he wouldn't anyway.

"I've not heard of this church before," she said.

"Fairly new," Zhang grunted. "They seem to be springing up all over the state."

"Doesn't look new," she said as they badged a uniformed cop and were waved through.

Behind and to the right were the media crews. They were penned off and well controlled. Ahead of them was the church parking lot. There were two police cars, an unmarked, an ambulance and a coroner's van.

Zhang stopped in the entrance.

"There are parking spaces," she said, but she knew why he did it, why he stopped here. It was like a statement: we're in charge because we can park where we goddamn like. She knew he played the same games with her. She was the senior and yet he liked to act like he was in control. It was the little things, like the nickname to wind her up. She'd come across it all the time from men in her career. But she suspected there was more to it from her partner. Maybe it was his way of compensating for problems at home.

They got out and both put on their FBI jackets. Zhang put on sunglasses, retro ones that he always wore for the image. She spotted the officer-in-charge, but for a moment Zhang was going nowhere. He surveyed the scene and then pointed at the church.

"You said it doesn't look new," he said. "You're right. I think they take over older churches. You know, ones that aren't doing so well. CRC seems to be doing all right."

Her brain took a moment to realize what CRC meant. Church of the Risen Christ.

She said, "You seem to know an awful lot."

"The internet." He smiled pointedly. "While you were watching TV, I was doing research."

They walked around the side towards the detective-in-charge. Charlie showed her ID and introduced them both.

The detective sighed like he'd been waiting for them to arrive and was a little pissed that he was losing the case.

"Detective Nick Garcia," he said. "Atlanta Homicide." He nodded towards the rear, where the uniformed officers were standing behind a media screen. "Just pulled out another one."

They quickly confirmed that all of the bodies were of young men. So far, only Mark Simmons had been ID'd, on account of his distinctive tattoo.

Number six was lying on the grass naked and on his front. The body was smeared with black mud.

"Caucasian male, probably early twenties," the detective said. "Obviously no identification. My gut says it's another missing guy."

Zhang beckoned the investigating coroner over. He introduced them both before saying, "Preliminary cause of death?"

"Of course, hard to say, but for the moment this one's strangulation. Ligature marks on the neck and wrists. A few lacerations on the body but they appear post-mortem. Looks like more than one animal got under there recently. Probably wild animals broke in before the two dogs found the hole." He nodded towards the church. The base had boards running around it, and at the rear they were broken.

"Would you flip him over?"

The coroner signalled to the uniforms and they carefully lifted number six and turned him onto his back. The whole procedure was smooth and respectful.

From the torso it was hard to tell the guy was white, there was so much muck. Charlie guessed they'd pulled him out by his feet, face down.

The ligature marks were less obvious on this side. His eyes were closed and his face looked peaceful, like he was just resting.

Zhang asked, "Had a look at the others?"

"Still only preliminary. This is the only one with obvious ligature marks. I'd say it's the second most recent."

"Mark Simmons being the most recent?" Charlie asked.

"Yes. He was also the only incomplete body. I don't think the two dogs tore off the hand or the arm. I can't be certain. The damage is all post-mortem, but probably a different animal or animals."

"Let's take a look at the site," Zhang said.

The detective and investigating coroner joined them as they knelt by the broken panels and looked under the church. Spotlights lit the otherwise enclosed area that was about twenty yards by six. It wasn't much more than an uneven crawl space—which explained why the body had been dragged out—maybe as much as three feet high in some places and almost nothing in others. Two investigators were at work, probing the space for more bodies.

Detective Garcia said, "None of the bodies were more than a few inches under the soil."

"So far," Charlie said.

Garcia grunted agreement.

She said, "There will be more."

Zhang said, "You can count on it."

He touched her arm and indicated they should move away. When they were out of earshot he said, "Did you notice?"

8

"Yes," she said quietly. Not because she didn't want the homicide guy to overhear, but because her stomach was knotted. It had been three years since they'd found anything else. Found any more bodies.

He said, "Looks like the Surgeon is back."

TWO

Charlie and her partner pretended to be in deep discussion but in reality they were checking out the crowd. A perpetrator often came back to the scene of the crime. Many of them fed off the attention as much as the act of killing itself.

Besides the media people, there was Reverend Piccard and his flock. They were holding candles now. There must have been over fifty other onlookers. There was also a gathering crowd on a hill behind the church.

"Spot the guy who found the first body—the Simmons kid?"

Charlie had seen a man with two dogs. He was hanging around the reporters. "Hoping for another interview," she said. "Fifteen minutes of fame. No matter how awful."

"What kind of dogs are they?" The way he said it told her that he knew and was just testing her. He was a dog person; she didn't have any pets. Never had, never would. Didn't see the point of it.

He said, "Treeing Walker Hounds. Great hunting dogs. Doesn't surprise me those dogs sniffed out the fresh meat under the church."

"Nice."

"Hey, I just say it as it is. All I'm saying is they're a good dog. Whoever chose this site as a body dump didn't figure on a hunting dog sniffing around."

She glanced back at the church and the wooden panels. The killer may not have allowed for hunting dogs but it was a smart location. Smarter than last time. This was akin to hiding in plain sight. Where else would you expect dead bodies?

Detective Garcia came over. "I thought I recognized you," he said to Charlie. "You were the lead on the Panola Mountain murders—the Surgeon, wasn't it?"

"I was on the case and yes it was," she said without encouraging further conversation.

Garcia didn't pick up on her tone. "This isn't linked, is it?"

Without looking at him, Zhang said, "Probably not."

Charlie said, "Let's avoid using that name. OK? You see anyone suspicious in the crowd?"

"Apart from the creepy pastor and the stupid dog guy?"

"Why stupid?"

"You've seen the interviews, right?"

She had. His dogs were called Deion and Julio Jones—JJ for short—famous Atlanta Falcon players. When he recounted what had happened he kept using football terms. Unless you followed football—and Charlie didn't—most of his sentences made no sense.

She said, "He's popular though. The media love a character." She rubbed her temples. The ache was back.

"Detective, anyone around here get me some water?"

"Sure." Garcia moved away.

"I'll have a cappuccino. Three sugars," Zhang called after him. Then to Charlie, he said, "Make an effort with the guy. He's on our team, so keep him sweet."

"Three sugars? Sounds like you're keeping yourself sweet."

"Bad night," he said.

"Isn't it always?"

He was studying the crowd again, looking for anyone familiar, anyone who looked out of place, anyone taking too much interest.

A young officer came up with a bottle of water and a cup of coffee.

She thanked him and gulped down three Advil tablets.

"Yuck," Zhang said, lifting the lid of the cup. "White coffee. I asked for a goddamn cappuccino." He replaced the lid and took a sip. "Nice and sweet though. Anyway, where were we? I think you were just about to tell me about Pablo."

"His name was Paolo. And no, I wasn't." She realized her mistake—she'd said *was* Paolo.

He looked at her from the corner of his eye and cocked an eyebrow. "So Pablo is no more?"

She shrugged. Whereas Peter liked to talk about his marital problems, Charlie didn't like to air her dirty laundry. She'd had a handful of relationships since moving to Atlanta and none of them had lasted more than a couple of months.

Zhang nodded towards the officer who had brought the drinks. "He was cute, though perhaps a bit young for you."

She ignored him. Greg, her ex, had been a Chicago homicide detective. Good-looking in a rugged sort of way. Unfaithful in a douchebag sort of way. When she walked out, she'd picked Atlanta. It hadn't been a random choice. Greg often referred to Atlanta as worse than Chicago—not in the number of murders but the murder rate in terms of population.

By moving here, she felt like it gave him the finger, although she couldn't explain it. If she'd seen a shrink, they'd probably have a different assessment. But she didn't give a damn. She was here. The weather was better and the crime was different. In Chicago, the gang crime meant she'd always been afraid. One day, she'd thought, I'll get that call to say Greg has been killed. Down here, she didn't have that concern. One, because Greg wasn't here, and two, because she wasn't afraid for her own life.

Yes, the murder rate was high, with about a murder every other day. But these were one-offs and a lot were domestic disputes. They were the purview of the police department. What sort of a crazy first world country thought that a murder every other day was OK as the norm?

"What you thinking?" Zhang said.

"The Surgeon," she lied. "Let's get back to the office and pull the Operation Deep Cut files."

The Surgeon was the name used by the media for the Panola Mountain murders. It had been Charlie's first job only weeks after moving to Georgia. She hadn't been the lead in that investigation but she'd received media attention after covering on a press conference. She knew she was photogenic, which was fine most of the time. But not so good when the media hounded you for pictures and quotes. Especially when the murders went unsolved.

Unusually heavy rainfall had caused a mudslide in the state park. Trees had fallen at the top of a hill and ploughed a wide furrow down the slope. More rain had washed away the loose stuff and the bodies were just there on the surface.

After being called in, because of the multiple homicides, the FBI called it Operation Deep Cut. It was in reference to the incision between the fourth and fifth ribs on the left.

It took the media no time at all to come up with the name "the Surgeon". Somehow they found out about the incisions. Each cut was one inch wide and without a jagged edge. They were looking for a scalpel or something similar according to the pathologist.

But the autopsies showed that in each case the incision had passed just to the side of the sternum, passing through the skin, subcutaneous tissues, pectoral muscle, intercostals and then avoiding the lungs through the pericardial notch, through the pericardium, to reach the heart. What the media didn't know however was that the heart was never penetrated. Death had either occurred as a result of the incision or close to. What puzzled them was the incredible precision resulting in minimal blood loss. It was as though the blade had delicately stopped the heart rather than cause massive blood loss.

Three years ago they had found eight bodies. All Caucasian males aged between twenty and thirty-five. All were eventually identified as missing persons.

There was no obvious connection.

The agents now had the pictures of the original eight on the board with personal details beside them. Charlie stood; her partner was on the edge of his desk.

Homicide Detective Garcia was with them, sitting in Charlie's chair. It irritated her but she'd resisted kicking him out. Entente cordiale, the supervisor, Mike Smith, kept reminding her.

Actually, Detective Garcia wasn't too bad, she'd decided. In fact, he was less annoying than Zhang.

There was a second board alongside the Panola Mountain murder board. It had the photos of eight more bodies, all of them from under the church. Three were still unidentified. All of them matched the same MO and profile. But there was still no apparent link between them.

Zhang said, "Why the body dump in the park?"

"Out of the way. Hidden."

"Not easy though. The Surgeon would have had to lug the body up there and dig a pit—"

"A shallow grave."

He rubbed his neck. "Yeah, see, that was stupid. Animals up there could have dug them up like they did under the church."

"Maybe that was the plan." She knocked back a double espresso—she was back on the caffeine big time. The case had done it. At least that was what she told herself. She added: "Maybe he wanted the evidence destroyed."

Zhang said, "So we go three years and then eight more bodies."

Garcia shook his head. "He didn't stop. All he did was switch sites."

"He's right," Charlie said. "When the mountain body dump was discovered he started using the church. The oldest body from there has been dated back over two years ago. He was using the mountain and we found the dump so he started burying them under the church." She knew she was repeating herself but she was thinking as she said it.

Garcia said, "So it looks like there was a lull. Maybe the Surgeon was scared for a while. The first eight appear to be over a period of two years. Three years later we find eight more. Makes sense."

15

Zhang nodded. "Eight then eight. Does that number mean something."

"Maybe four a year," Garcia said. "One a season. Maybe seasons are relevant."

Charlie was still thinking. "What if the church wasn't the next dump site? What if he used somewhere in between."

The guys looked at her and frowned.

"Possible," Garcia said. "Panola was three years ago and the oldest one at the church is two years. A gap of a year."

"Four a year," she said.

Zhang filled his chest with a deep, slow breath and exhaled loudly. "Shit, there could be more bodies."

Charlie said, "There's another possibility."

"Yeah?"

"Maybe he used multiple sites at the same time."

"Shit," Zhang said again.

Charlie said, "And what's worse is, Mark Simmons may not have been the last. This guy—"

"The Surgeon," Garcia said.

Charlie shook her head. "Let's not call him that. It could distract our thinking."

Garcia shrugged. "Come on, everyone calls him the Surgeon. It's natural with the name all over the news."

"Not yet," she said. "The media don't know this is the same killer."

"Are you also going to question the profile? You going to say it might not even be a man?"

"Of course it's a man."

"I don't know," Zhang said, and she couldn't tell if he was being sarcastic. "Most serial killers are men, I'll grant you, but then most victims are women. There's usually some kind of sexual motive, whether it's obvious or not." He winked at her. "Psych 101, Special Agent Rebb."

"It's a man," she said to Garcia. "He's strong because he had to carry the bodies. At the original site he lugged them up a hill. And some of the men have ligature marks, so he physically overpowered them."

Garcia said, "I think it's a man."

Zhang grunted. "To assume makes an ass of you and me."

Garcia ignored him. "What do your Behavioural Analysis guys say?"

"Most likely older than his victims," Charlie said. "Aged thirty to fifty. In every case the eyes are closed. That normally suggests the killer knew his victims, but it may not be. The lack of mutilation or abuse of any kind suggests either sensitivity or remorse."

Garcia said, "As far as we know, only one of the victims was gay, so it's not that."

Zhang rubbed his forehead. She knew he did that when he was frustrated. Hell, they were all frustrated, but his attitude wasn't helping.

Then he surprised her by saying, "Doesn't mean the Surgeon isn't gay."

"It's Operation Deep Cut," Charlie said.

Garcia and Zhang exchanged looks like they'd discussed this already. Then the detective said, "Charlie, let's call him the Surgeon, it's easier that way."

"Agreed," Zhang said.

Charlie shook her head in frustration. "Fine."

Garcia grinned. "OK what else we got?"

Charlie said, "The precision of the cut, along with no abuse, suggests control. It's very unusual, which therefore suggests a highly intelligent individual, maybe a professional. Someone who is used to controlling their emotions, maybe highly dextrous too."

17

Zhang said, "Which means it could be a goddamn surgeon. I'd hate the media hacks to be right."

They stared at the boards for a while.

Garcia rubbed his eyes. "Let's wind back. Why did you say there might be multiple locations?"

Charlie said, "Because Simmons had been missing for forty days. The John Doe prior to him has been dated to three months ago. That's not one a season."

Zhang said, "It could be, just not exactly ninety days between."

"Or he's accelerating," Garcia said. "They do that, right?"

"Yeah," Zhang agreed.

Charlie was thinking. She went up to the boards and tapped a picture of the church and then the park photos.

"He knows these locations," she said. "Let's say the church means something to him."

"Maybe he's a member of this church. Maybe he was one of the people with Reverend Piccard," Garcia said, expressing Charlie's own chain of thought. They were still out there with their candle-lit vigil. Although they had joined the group on the hill.

"Let's get a list," Charlie said. Garcia nodded.

"Do we want to talk to Piccard?" Zhang asked. "I don't like the guy."

Charlie shrugged. Officially she was the lead but he normally tried to take charge. Not now. The dynamic was shifting. Probably because she had the only real serial killer experience from her past in Chicago.

The phone rang and Zhang picked it up. He listened, swore and put the receiver back down.

"Shit," he said again.

"What?"

"Good shit," he said. "The pathologist missed something the first time. He thought they were animal

18

scratches but he's spotted a consistency between a few of the bodies."

The other two waited as he took a breath.

"There's a mark, like a signature maybe."

THREE

Charlie pinched the bridge of her nose to ease the eye ache. She'd spent the evening handling calls from the media. Someone had leaked details and the Surgeon's name was in the headlines again.

In between calls, she'd reviewed all the TV footage of the two crime scenes, looking for anyone who appeared in both, anyone who looked out of place, anyone who just seemed suspicious.

They'd also zoomed in on the hillside group. Some of the people wore simple white robes. Give them pointed hats and they could be the KKK, she thought. However, one character had attracted her attention. He was always central, like a focal point of the group, and in some shots he appeared to have his arms out, like a cross.

The cops had been through the photos with Reverend Piccard. They'd wanted names of all the members of the church who'd attended vigils and checked how long they'd attended the church. They'd followed up and interviewed all the men but nothing seemed untoward.

They found the man with his arms out. He was a young preacher called Robert Kingren. Quietly spoken, originally from Boston and gone straight into the church following school were the only points of note from the interview.

They'd also made no progress with the mark on the bodies in the last three days.

If it had just been the one body, then it could have been a scratch. But the same mark had been confirmed on three. Charlie thought it looked like a snake, whereas Zhang insisted it was a lower-case Z.

They'd studied the autopsy photos of the original eight bodies from the Panola Mountain case and found nothing. Then again, they hadn't been looking for it back then. Maybe it had been missed.

There were some marks that hadn't been explained but nothing consistent. Not a signature like the snake-Z.

Her phone rang. Her sister, Liz, from Kansas City. Why did she always call so late?

"Liz?" Charlie answered.

"It's Dad again," Liz said. The despair was thick in her voice, or maybe that was the alcohol. Her sister tended to overdo the drink when their dad was acting up.

"He's been arrested this time."

"For?"

"Shoplifting. I can cope with him turning up in places he shouldn't be, but shoplifting is... well, I just don't know how to handle it."

Charlie wanted to say, "You took him on, you take the responsibility," but she bit her tongue. It wouldn't help but it was annoying. Her sister had been all too willing to have their dad move to Kansas and help buy their house. It seemed like she wanted the money more than provide the care.

"He needs full-time supervision," Liz continued. "Rob and I work all day. I can't keep an eye on him twenty-four seven."

Charlie said nothing. She knew what was coming next. It always did. Liz was looking for Charlie's approval, but there was no way she was giving it. Not just like that anyway.

Liz said, "He needs to be in a home."

"Tell me about the shoplifting."

"Dillard's. He had his pockets stuffed with ladies underwear."

Charlie couldn't help herself. She snickered.

"It's not funny!"

"No, it's not."

"He's constantly disorientated and doesn't know what's going on. The police said he was surprised that he had the stuff in his pockets. He kept talking about Mom as though she was with him. He said she was doing the shopping and he just did what he was told."

Liz kept talking but Charlie found her mind wandering. *Did what he was told.* Could it be someone was hearing voices? The church would make sense then—maybe the perpetrator was being told by God to kill these men.

"You still there, Charlie?"

"Yeah, sorry, this case is hurting my head."

Liz didn't immediately comment, and when she finally spoke, Charlie was surprised by the switch away from the previous subject.

"Making progress?"

"Not really."

"Oh, Channel 5 news said there'd been a break-through."

"Not really. We found a small unusual mark on three of the bodies, but—"

"What like?"

"Like a snake, I suppose."

"They're calling him the Surgeon, aren't they?"

22

"Right."

"Surgeon... snake. You know, the medical symbol of a snake around a pole... I never did understand that."

"Me either, but it's more like a Z than a curly snake. Anyway, I think that has two snakes."

"Can be one. Message me a photo."

Charlie ended the call, sent a photo, and a few minutes later, Liz called back.

"Dad's best friend, when he can remember, is Mandy Silverman."

"A woman? Is that who the underwear was for?"

Now it was Liz's turn to laugh. Maybe the alcohol had relaxed her a little. "Not a woman, you idiot! Mandy is a Jewish man's name."

"OK?" Charlie said slowly, trying to make sense of her sister's comment.

"So, Mr Silverman is Jewish, and I've met him and I'm familiar with Hebrew."

"You are?" Now Charlie was suspecting that her sister was the one who needed the help rather than their dad. Maybe she was the one who'd been caught stealing underwear from Dillard's.

"Charlie, I think I'm looking at a Hebrew letter. I'm not a hundred per cent sure, but I think I'm looking at the letter L."

Charlie thanked her sister, promised to call soon and ended the call. She immediately went on the internet and looked up Hebrew letters.

Excited, she called Zhang.

"It's late," he grumbled.

"Not that late."

"I dozed off on the sofa. Anyway, it's late for me."

"The scratch on the bodies—it looks like the letter called Lamed"—she pronounced it lah-med.

"I never did think it looked like a Z. What's your point, Charlie?"

She bit back her frustration with him. He was the one championing Z. She took a breath.

"Maybe it's relevant. You know what the original symbol for Lamed was—in old Hebrew?"

"Enlighten me."

"A shepherd's crook." Now he was interested. She could tell by his breathing.

"Shit," he said.

"That's right. Shepherd's crook equals Christianity. The Good Shepherd was Jesus, right? The church—"

"Let's go and speak with the good Reverend Piccard."

She was about to end the call when he said, "And Charlie…"

"Yes?"

"Next time save it until the morning, OK?"

Reverend Piccard couldn't see them until midday, and when they were shown into his sumptuous home office, there was another man standing by the wall-to-ceiling bookcase.

Piccard introduced them to Governor McCubbin.

"Governor?" Charlie asked, not recognizing the name or face. He looked in his sixties, with neat grey hair and watery eyes. He had a smart suit and tie, and when he smiled she saw perfect teeth.

"Not a state governor," he said. "I'm the head of the General Assembly of the Church of the Risen Christ. Silly title, I know, but someone at some time agreed the titles and I'm stuck with it."

Charlie thought the church hadn't been going very long, but the name didn't matter.

She said, "Excuse the direct question, but you're here because…?"

McCubbin smiled kindly. "No offence taken, I can assure you. In fact, I prefer the direct approach, Agent… Sorry, I've forgotten your name already."

"Rebb," Charlie said. "Special Agents Rebb and Zhang. And this is Detective Garcia."

"Atlanta Homicide," Garcia explained.

Piccard offered coffee and they all declined. He then showed them to the sofas. He took a bucket chair while McCubbin remained standing at the bookcase. Just observing, Charlie told herself.

"Right…" Piccard rubbed his hands together, flat, like he was praying, before he held them together in front of him. "Always happy to help in whatever way I can."

"Thank you," Zhang said. "You've been very helpful so far with the photos."

"That's right," Garcia chimed in.

Unplanned, Charlie said, "Tell me about Kingren."

Piccard said, "Rob's one of us."

"From Boston."

"Originally, I understand."

Charlie was looking at a painting of Christ on the wall. There were similarities between Robert Kingren and the painting: a tall fair-skinned man, bright blue eyes, long hair. Of course, the painting was total fantasy, she knew that. Jesus had been a Jew from the Middle East.

McCubbin smiled kindly. "You've noticed how he dresses."

Charlie nodded towards the painting. "Looks a bit like Jesus."

"It's intentional. We choose a preacher to represent Christ. At the moment it's Rob. It's one of our practices.

25

Our modus operandi, if you like. He visits all the churches and performs sermons in the same way Jesus did. Of course, he isn't Christ, but it's just a recognition that Christ is risen. He is among us. He could be any one of us."

Charlie was going to ask more, but she could see Zhang was itching to speak so she nodded at him.

Zhang said, "So we wondered if there was any Jewish connection with the church."

Charlie glanced over at McCubbin, but the man showed no reaction.

Piccard shook his head, thoughtfully. Then he also looked at his superior, before saying, "No. I can't think of any. Why d'you ask?"

Zhang said, "What about the Hebrew letter L?"

Piccard shook his head. "Why?"

Zhang handed the pastor a picture of the letter.

Piccard studied it, handed it back and shook his head.

"There's a possible link to Christianity," Zhang said. "In old Hebrew the letter is a shepherd's crook. Crook... flock. See the connection?"

"All right, but what's the relevance to the case?"

Charlie said, "We think the letter was scratched onto some of the bodies."

Piccard shook his head again.

McCubbin stepped forward. "This is all very distressing for us, you realize?"

"Yes, sir," Zhang said. "But—"

"But we need this whole thing resolved. It's damaging the church. Congregation numbers are down fifty per cent on what they were before the incident."

"Incident?" Charlie said.

The older man shook his head. "You know what I meant, Agent Rebb."

Charlie said, "We are looking for a serial killer and eight young men were murdered and stashed under your church." She paused for emphasis and directed it at Piccard. "No way was your church randomly selected."

Piccard looked uncomfortable.

The agents and detective said nothing and Charlie became aware of a ticking clock, quiet and sonorous. She couldn't see anything in the room. Maybe there was an antique grandfather clock marking time somewhere in another room.

McCubbin took another step forward and held out his hand. "May I see the picture, Agent Zhang?"

Zhang passed him the picture of the Hebrew letter.

McCubbin held it in his hand. It shook slightly and Charlie wondered if it was the early onset of Parkinson's disease.

The clock ticked.

Eventually the governor handed the paper to Piccard. "Tell them about the trouble," he said.

Piccard looked at the symbol like it was for the first time. Then he handed it back to Zhang.

"Three years ago," he began. "At least I think it was about then. There was a man who caused us a little trouble. He didn't like that we'd taken over the old church. At least, that's what he said at first, but then it was clear he was just a troublemaker."

"What was his name?" Zhang asked.

"I don't know if I ever knew his name."

27

Charlie said, "What has the symbol got to do with him?"

Piccard flicked a glance at McCubbin like he was looking for support. Then he said, "He was a Satanist, Agent Rebb. That letter may be something to do with him."

FOUR

Deir Mawas, Egypt

Although he wasn't staying in Amarna, it seemed appropriate that Alex MacLure had a room in a hotel called Nefertiti. She'd been instrumental in the construction of Pharaoh Akhenaten's incredible city and culture that had once been there.

The town of Deir Mawas was just across the river from the ancient site. Although the Nefertiti wasn't the best hotel, in places you could see the pillars and ruins of the old palaces and temples.

As the lead archaeologist, Alex knew the season was coming to an end. It was getting too hot to work out there and it would soon be time for a break. They had found more clay tablets and constructed most of the encoded secrets of the old man called Meryra and the story of a peasant boy called Yanhamu who grew up to be a scribe and soldier. However, Alex had a sense that something was missing.

"I still feel there's more to be had," he said to his girlfriend, Vanessa, as he joined her in the hotel after a long day.

"More of the story?"

"Yes. There are bits I can't fathom, sections I'm sure are in code but don't match the encryption of the others."

"Or maybe it's incomplete. How likely is it that after more than three thousand years, all of the tablets are here?"

He kissed her and they took their coffee onto the veranda. Their loungers faced the Nile, with Amarna beyond. Alex liked to picture the city of Akhetaten as it used to be: a glorious acclamation to the one god, Aten. Was Pharaoh Akhenaten a heretic who rejected all other gods or was he a visionary who merely promoted a form of the sun god Ra above all others?

It was said that there had been a tower so high that people from the old capitals in the north and south could see the pennants fluttering from the top. Alex knew the vast distances made this impossible but it was a nice idea.

Akhenaten had encouraged art and inventiveness, and his city had been both modern and creative for its time. Alex envisaged bright colours and awnings that shielded the streets from the sun's blaze.

Vanessa stretched out on her lounger. "Fancy a holiday?"

He looked at her. She had a lovely curve to her figure and her middle-eastern skin looked almost golden in the late afternoon light. They had been together now for over a year. Although "together" was a stretch by anyone's definition. Vanessa was a traveller and a writer. She left him for months at a time looking for a story. And when she came back it was with exotic tales from lands he'd only dreamed about.

He, on the other hand, seemed to be in a rut. In the early days they'd made amazing discoveries and Vanessa had helped write Alex's stories. The truth about

Akhenaten's wife, Nefertiti, had been picked up and reported globally. For a short time Alex had been a celebrity, and yet here he was still tugging away at the same thread, hoping something new would emerge.

Archaeologists live for that moment when they uncover something, whether it be a physical object that has lain undiscovered for hundreds or thousands of years, or seeing a previously discovered object and understanding its purpose for the first time.

Alex had had that experience immediately. Now it seemed like the next wow moment would never happen.

"A holiday?" he said after a sip of coffee. "Whereabouts?"

"Mexico."

"Really? Like regular tourists you mean?" The idea of Vanessa being on a package holiday seemed impossible, laughable even.

"Not the Caribbean coast. I'm thinking Puebla. It's pretty central and out of the way."

The name rang a bell but he couldn't place it. "What's there?" he asked intrigued.

"You'll know it when I tell you—the Great Pyramid of Cholula. It's fifty-five metres tall."

"A third of the height of the Great Pyramid of Giza."

She pouted. "You are so... so picky!"

He laughed. "Picky? Is that the best you can come up with? I thought you were a writer!" He leaned over and kissed her as an apology for mocking her. "Seriously though," he added, "I'm interested in three thousand years ago. In fact my real interest is before that. You know my original thesis began with Predynastic Egyptian culture."

"How old is the Great Pyramid of Cholula then?"

"Just a few hundred years BC."

"But the Mayan's were building pyramids much earlier, right?"

"I'll give you that," he said. "They were around at the time of the early Egyptian dynasties."

"So doesn't it make you wonder?"

"What?" He was intrigued again.

"How civilizations on opposite sides of the world were building pyramids at the same time."

"This sounds like a conspiracy theory."

"Not really, I just mean it makes you wonder."

"Whether ancient Egyptians ever travelled to South America?"

She shrugged. "So how about Machu Picchu? I've always meant to travel there."

"Inca civilization, and again much later."

She playfully punched his arm. "As a holiday! Forget archaeology for once."

"All right," he said. "We'll go in a month—providing Andrew is better. I would hate—" He couldn't finish the sentence as his voice caught in his throat, and Vanessa wrapped her arms around him.

Andrew was his younger brother and suffered from Duchenne muscular dystrophy. At twenty-seven, he was totally dependent on their mother. But he was a brave kid. He'd accepted that the typical sufferer only made it until their mid to late teens. And here he was, proving the doctors wrong, heading for double the life expectancy.

But his condition was rapidly worsening. He could no longer raise his arms more than a few inches, and the doctors were worried about his pulmonary system. He'd had a cold virus recently that had made his condition much worse.

Alex decided he would have a holiday with Vanessa, but he would go home first and spend some time with his little brother.

Vanessa said she'd join him in England, and that made it exciting. She'd meet his mother for the first time. Something which surely took their relationship to another level.

After dinner they browsed the internet on the super-slow hotel Wi-Fi and talked of holiday plans. Whatever they chose wouldn't be a beach and pool holiday, it would be an adventure.

And then in the night, Alex awoke to the vibration of his phone.

Caller number withheld.

He slipped out of bed and into the bathroom so he wouldn't disturb Vanessa.

"Alex MacLure," he whispered.

"Can you be overheard?" a man whispered back.

"Who is this?"

The man hesitated. "How about you call me Agent J?"

"How about I end this call right now?"

Alex heard an intake of breath, like the caller was controlling annoyance.

The guy said, "I've found something."

Alex waited.

"It's like the truth you discovered... only maybe this is bigger."

Was this guy some kind of nutjob? "How did you get this number?" Alex demanded.

"Listen," the guy said. He sounded earnest, possibly desperate. "My life's in danger and I need to tell someone what I know."

FIVE

Atlanta, Georgia

The letter Charlie had was the first in the Hebrew word leviathan. Although often thought of as a sea monster, it appeared that the word actually meant "twisted serpent". Which was ironic, since they had first assumed the mark was a snake.

The word leviathan featured on the Satanic church's logo. Two concentric circles around a pentangle. Inside the pentangle was the head of a goat. Between the circles and at each point of the star were the five Hebrew letters making up leviathan. L was at the bottom.

There was an Atlanta chapter of the church with a Satanic temple on Euclid Avenue in Little Five Points. Charlie had never considered the relevance of the district's name before. Now Five Points seemed a deliberate reference to the pentangle of the devil.

They drove up and parked where Google Maps said the temple was. They didn't have a full address, just the zip code. On one side of the road was a factory converted into lofts. It was set back behind trees and looked much more affluent than the opposite side of the street. There was a short row with the same zip: two buildings with a donut shack between them. The right-hand building was the Variety theatre. There was a door then two blocks of windows. One was called BBQ DAS and the other was a Mediterranean restaurant.

Zhang looked through the window of BBQ DAS. He pointed to the red writing on the window.

"What the hell is 'Champion Quality'?"

The theatre was locked up, a big chain and padlock on the door.

The Mediterranean restaurant was called Alibaba. Charlie glanced in and thought it looked all right. Not as rough as the rest of the block. She opened the door and a bell rang.

A man came from the back, smiling broadly. "Help you?"

"Satanic temple?" Charlie said. The words tasted funny in her mouth, like it was wrong to say them.

The man pulled a face, raising his eyebrows like he was saying "weirdos". Then he nodded right. "They meet next door at 7 Stages."

Charlie thanked the man. When she stepped outside, Zhang had a bag of donuts.

"Want one?" he said, handing one to the detective and sticking another in his mouth.

"No thanks. The temple is next door—in 7 Stages."

The place called 7 Stages was like the theatre. It had sublet two units in the front. On the right was a coffee house. On the left was a pawnshop. Both were shut, and despite the fact that Charlie could have knocked back a double espresso, she didn't like the look of the coffee house.

Detective Garcia was already at the 7 Stages' entrance, talking to a woman at the door. Charlie could see her shaking her head.

Garcia came back. "The Satanists rent a stage here for what she called 'events'. But they've not been back for a few months. Said that the main man—the high priest, would you believe it?—has been arrested. Xavier Larouse."

"Rings a bell," Zhang said with a mouthful of donut. He had sugar powder and jam on his chin.

Garcia got on the phone. He said Larouse's name and listened. Finally, he said, "Right, right" and ended the call.

"He's being held downtown, at Grady Detention Centre."

Zhang wiped his mouth with his sleeve. "OK, let's go. No time like the present."

Larouse looked like a regular guy, except for his wild eyes and pointy eyebrows maybe. Garcia told them that the Satanists had been outside elementary schools trying to convert the kids, until an injunction was slapped on them.

He said, "They tried to get school district approval for after-school clubs. When that got rejected, Larouse protested by putting on a goat's head and standing naked outside a school."

"Nice image," Zhang said screwing up his face.

Garcia led them inside, where they were shown to a room, glass walls at either end, a guard standing outside.

Larouse was already there, waiting for them, sitting at a table. He lounged in the plastic seat, legs protruding on the far side of the table.

Charlie and Zhang pulled out chairs and sat either side of Larouse's feet.

Garcia leaned against a sidewall. He looked uncomfortable but was trying to hide it. He had his phone out and Charlie wondered whether he was recording the interview unofficially. If he were they wouldn't be able to use it in court later.

"Thanks for seeing us," Charlie said.

Larouse raised his fists to show manacles. "Not a problem," he said. "Always try to help as best I can."

"Do you know why we're here, Mr Larouse?"

"Specifically, no. Generally, I guess so. I recognize you from the TV. You're investigating the Surgeon killings."

She nodded.

Zhang said, "Could you enlighten us about the Church of Satan?"

"We're misunderstood," Larouse said as Charlie thought she saw a twinkle in his eye. "People think we're about worshipping death, but we're not. We're about appreciating life. Our lives are short and we should live life to the fullest."

"Sounds reasonable," Zhang said, encouraging him. "What about the devil-worship bit? How does that fit in?"

Larouse snorted a laugh. "We aren't devil-worshippers, Agent Zhang. We don't abuse children or sacrifice animals."

Charlie sat back and folded her arms and she wondered why Larouse had said that, why choose to deny such specifics?

He continued: "Satan is simply a word that means adversary or opposition. It's a recognition that we are the opposite of traditional religions that stifle and restrict. Karl Marx called religion the opiate of the masses. It's there to control and prevent free thinking."

"And you are a free thinker?" Charlie asked, trying to sit more relaxed. She unfolded her arms.

"Look," he said, smiling with his eyes again, "Ninety-five per cent of it is theatre. You enjoy Halloween, don't you?"

Actually she didn't, but she said, "Sure."

"Dressing up is fun. And by reflecting death we feel more alive. *Día de Muertos* is just good healthy fun and people enjoy scaring each other."

"As long as it's harmless," Garcia said from the wall.

"Of course," Larouse said without looking at him.

Garcia said, "Tell us about the temple's commandments."

"The commandments..." Larouse twitched his shoulder. "Which rules are you referring to, Detective?" Now he looked up and his eyes hardened for a second. He switched back to Charlie and winked.

"We like sex," he said and paused, probably savouring her involuntary revulsion. Then he shrugged, "But we do not make sexual advances unless given the mating signal." He paused again. "Are you giving me a mating signal, Agent Rebb?"

She said, "What about killing other people?"

"What about it?"

"Have you ever killed anyone, Mr Larouse?"

He shook his head and smiled, "Oh dear, Agent Rebb."

Garcia said, "Tell us the eleven rules, Larouse."

Larouse cleared his throat and sat up. "Do not give opinions or advice unless you are asked. Do not tell your troubles unless others want to hear them. Do not complain about anything to which you need not subject yourself. Do not harm little children. Do not take that which does not belong to you. Acknowledge the power of magic."

"Go on," Garcia said.

"When in another's lair, show him respect or else do not go there. It's another reasonable rule that the police would do well to adhere to, Detective. What do you think, Agent Rebb?"

Charlie said nothing.

Garcia seemed to be reading his phone. He put it in his pocket and stepped closer. "What about if someone annoys you?"

Larouse didn't hesitate. "Treat him cruelly and without mercy."

Wow! He said it in such a cold way that the hair on Charlie's neck prickled.

Zhang said, "Did you kill those men?"

"Don't be ridiculous," Larouse said. "We are considerate. Where was I? Do not kill non-human animals"—again a strange choice of words, Charlie realized—"unless you are attacked or for your food. When walking in open territory, bother no one. If someone bothers you, ask him to stop—"

Garcia completed the rule. "If he does not stop then destroy him. Isn't that right, Larouse?"

Larouse shrugged. "Yes. But it is an expression."

"Destroy him!" Garcia repeated.

Zhang said, "Sounds unequivocal to me! Destroy him? I've heard you say you don't kill non-humans. The implication is obvious. You will destroy, you will show no mercy, you will be cruel."

Garcia said, "Did those men annoy you, Larouse? Did they disrespect you?"

For a moment Charlie thought he was going to confess, but then Larouse laughed long and hard. "You have no idea, do you?"

Charlie said, "Help us then, Xavier."

"Why did you assume this was me?"

"You or one of your flock," Garcia said. He emphasized *flock*. Maybe he was thinking about the symbol.

Charlie said, "A few of the bodies had a mark on them, like the Hebrew L in leviathan."

"Could I see?"

Zhang showed him the picture of the Hebrew letter.

"I know what Lamed looks like, Agent Zhang. What about the actual mark on a body?"

Zhang held back and exchanged glances with Charlie. So what if Larouse gets an obscene pleasure from it? But no harm, she decided. Not if it leads somewhere.

She gave a slight nod.

Zhang dug out a picture from his jacket pocket and put it on the table.

Larouse's chain rattled as he picked up the photo. He said nothing for a moment as he studied it, before looking up and smiling at Charlie. "Interesting," he said.

"What's interesting?"

He nodded slowly, his eyes on Charlie. "So this led you to me. What about a Jew? It's Hebrew, so surely that would make more logical sense."

Charlie softened her tone. "Please, think. We're bound by conventional thought. You're more creative and… intelligent."

He smiled again.

She said, "They were all men between twenty and thirty-five. They were found under the Church of the Risen Christ in Dunwoody. There was a precise incision by a blade that pierced the chest cavity and stopped the heart."

He raised his pointy eyebrows. They'd so far kept that piece out of the media. Then he smiled at her. "You are very sexy, Agent Rebb. The way you talk..."

She said, "Can you think of anything? The precision, the symbol, the church?"

"Oh yes," he said, "I can think of someone. Tony Zart. Why don't you ask him?"

"Why him?"

"Because he's evil."

Zhang scoffed. "But you're—"

"Don't get confused," Larouse said, cutting the agent off. "I am a Satanist. That is not the same thing. We relish life and living. We are not evil. Got it?"

"We get it," Charlie said. "Tell us more about this Zart guy."

"He's nuts and he's dangerous. He claims to be religious but he's scary. I don't scare easily, but I'll admit to being scared of that weird fucker. He runs a tattoo studio and you'd think he'd do whatever the customer wanted, right? Wrong! He went ballistic when he realized my tattoo was Satanic. I had to get it finished elsewhere, refused to pay him. Then, afterwards, he stalked me for a while." He looked hard at Detective Garcia. "You'll find a few reports about it three to four years ago. Well, I hope you'll find them. Wouldn't surprise me if they were dropped straight in the trash. You know, I deserve the same civil rights as the next guy."

Charlie nodded. "Yes, you do. What else can you tell us about Zart? Why else suggest him?"

41

"The symbol you showed me," He said. "You'll see when you see his office." He wouldn't explain further but gave them an address in south Atlanta.

"Thanks," she said as they stood to leave. "And thank you for your time."

"No problem," he said. "And when you realize you want me for carnal pleasure, Charlie Rebb"—he flashed his eyes at her—"you know where I am."

SIX

Charlie shivered. "Larouse made my skin crawl."

"Oh, I thought you liked him," Zhang joked.

From the back of the car, Garcia said, "I can't get my head around it. Sixteen murdered young men. There's never been anything like it."

"So far as we know."

Garcia said, "God I hope there aren't more. The Feds were the first to recognize serial murders, weren't they?"

Zhang said, "Although we originally called them series murders. Meaning one after another. Now we call them serial because of the pattern. Because of the link. Normally we see a development over time. The murders become more elaborate as the killer searches for gratification."

"Right," Charlie said. "And that also bothers me, because there's no progression here. He's been doing it for a long time, and as far as we can tell, it's always the same, or pretty much."

Zhang parked outside the address Larouse had given them. A shop with a sign: "Tony'z Art". Underneath, it said: "Tattoo Artist Extraordinaire".

They stared at the sign. The Z was like the symbol.

"Not a Jewish L," she said. "Maybe it really is a Z after all."

"Which is what I've been telling you," Zhang said with total conviction. "One day you'll listen to your partner."

Charlie shook her head.

The windows were covered with tattoo art. The lights were on inside but the patches of glass that weren't covered in posters were obscured.

A buzzer sounded somewhere as they stepped across the threshold.

They entered a reception area with chairs, green leather cushions, and a vacant reception desk. A green velvet curtain hung across a doorway to the rear. There were hundreds of pictures on the walls and books of tattoo designs on a coffee table.

"Good job it said tattoo artist," Zhang said. "Otherwise I never would have guessed they did tattoos here!"

"With you in a minute," a woman's voice called from behind the curtain. "Take a look at the books. See if there's anything you fancy."

They waited five minutes then ten. Zhang paced the room, restless.

Eventually Garcia exchanged glances and nods with them and called out, "Police, mam. Just a minute of your time."

Another minute passed and a purple-haired young woman emerged.

"What?" she said in a tone that was anything but friendly. "I'm in the middle of a job."

Garcia badged her. "I'll just be a minute, mam—providing you are helpful."

Zhang said, "We're looking for Tony."

"He's not here."

44

Charlie held out her hand. "Hi, I'm Charlie. And you are...?"

"Tammy."

"Surname?"

"Dike."

Charlie saw Zhang roll his eyes. She said, "I'm a bit confused, Tammy. Is Tony's surname Zart?"

The girl grinned. "Yeah, clever, isn't it? Tony Zart—Tony'z Art."

Zhang muttered, "Pure genius."

Charlie said, "And where will we find Tony?"

"Don't know." The girl shrugged and looked up like she was frustrated at not knowing.

"When did you last see him?"

"About three weeks ago. Didn't tell me he was off, just didn't come down one morning. He'd better be back soon. Payday is just next week. I don't get paid then I'm outta here."

Garcia said, "What do you mean by he 'didn't come down'?"

"Lives upstairs, doesn't he."

"Right," Charlie said. "Does that happen often—he not turn up for a while?"

"Tony's unusual," she said. "Doesn't normally bother me with his behaviour. He's creative. Sort of comes with the territory. And I know he'd protect me if there was any trouble. People don't mess with Tony, which is funny because he's also the best damn fine artist I've ever met."

Zhang said, "But he does tattoos."

"Yeah, but he could have been famous. It's who you know, right? He couldn't break in to the fine art world. You know, this was an art gallery to start with but he made no money so he packed it all in and started doing

45

body art." She looked at a clock on the wall. "Are we done now? I have a customer back there."

Garcia said, "One more minute, mam. We need to find him. Could we take a look upstairs?"

She looked uncertain.

Charlie said, "You're concerned about him, aren't you, Tammy?"

"Well…"

They worked her for another minute and she then willingly led them through the back to an apartment door. She unlocked it.

"Thanks, Tammy," Charlie said.

"Yeah, OK, but don't mess with anything. I need this job."

The flat was totally different to the tattoo studio. Oil paintings adorned the walls or were stacked on the floor. Most of the art seemed to have a religious theme and many featured Christ.

"Definitely a whack job," Zhang said studying one. "Picasso meets Rembrandt."

Charlie said, "I didn't know you appreciated art, Peter."

"I don't," he chuckled. "In fact, if you can unappreciate art, then that's me."

Garcia had gloves on and was looking through papers on a desk. Charlie took a look through a bookcase that had multiple books about religion. She put on gloves and picked one up. It was entitled *Mission to God's Kingdom*. She flicked through it but didn't take anything in. Same thing with the next few. Then she pulled out a book on ancient cultures, which surprised her. There was no logic to the arrangement, and she now saw there were art books as well as ones on the civilizations of Sumeria, ancient Egypt, the Mayans and one she'd never heard of: Harappan. She picked up one on ancient Egypt and flicked through the pages. In some of the images, the symbols had been circled. She picked up another book and saw the same again.

"He's putting ancient symbols in his pictures," she said half to herself.

Zhang looked at her open book and then at a painting of Christ on the cross.

"Are these tattoos?" he asked, pointing to the marks on Christ's body.

Before Charlie could respond, Garcia let out a whoop.

"Whoa! Take a look at this." He held up a piece of paper.

Charlie took it and gasped. There was a series of letters and symbols.

"What?" Zhang said, peering closer.

Charlie pointed to the third set of initials from the bottom. MS.

"Mark Simmons!" Garcia said.

"Holy shit," Zhang said. "And the one above that is PT. Paul Toolie."

Paul Toolie had been identified as another body from under the church. He was probably the next most recent murder.

Zhang said, "The media know about him now, don't they?"

"Zart hasn't been seen for three weeks," Charlie said. "Either this is a weird coincidence or he's psychic or—"

She didn't finish, and Garcia was holding up a bundle of papers. "What?" she asked.

He said, "How many bodies do we have?"

"You know," Charlie said, "counting the Panola Mountain murders, it's sixteen."

Garcia shook his head. "These papers are full of initials and symbols. If Zart's the Surgeon and initials equal victim then this is much bigger than any of us imagined."

SEVEN

There were thirty-six sets of initials with symbols. Zhang suggested that maybe the list wasn't complete, maybe there were earlier pages. Maybe this was double thirty-six. Maybe even a hundred.

The other two shook their heads. Charlie struggled to comprehend the enormity of it.

Zhang voiced her thoughts: "There's never been anything on that scale before. Surely that's it."

"Not necessarily," Charlie said. "This guy just hasn't been caught. Thirty-six suggests maybe six years. Maybe he's been doing this for ten years."

"What?" Garcia said as she ran her finger down the list for the third time, thinking.

"The lamed/Zart symbol isn't here."

"So this is something different?"

"I don't think so," Charlie said and pointed to the symbol next to the MS initials. "Simmons was covered in tattoos but I think this one was on his chest. If the lamed/Zart thing is a signature, then these tattoos mean something else."

"Like what?" Zhang asked.

"I don't know."

"OK," Zhang said, "At least thirty-six bodies. Where do we start looking for the rest? Dig under all the churches?"

Garcia shook his head. "I'm not sure what you do next, but first things first. We get a warrant and do this part properly."

Charlie agreed but understanding this list of symbols also seemed vital. Had there been tattoos on the other bodies?

In addition to the sheets of initials, there was an old laptop in the apartment and the computer division set to work pulling files and history from it. Forensics came back with a negative on any of the victims' DNA.

The only other interesting thing they found was a stash of henna tattoo ink. Which, in itself wasn't suspicious, but with it were a notebook of symbols and religious iconography and an ancient-looking Bible. They were together in a leather-bound box that looked precious.

Charlie called the pathologist's office. "Henna washes off, doesn't it?"

"You're speaking to the wrong department," the pathologist said and then chuckled. "Why do you ask, Agent Rebb?"

"I'm wondering whether the bodies from the Church of the Risen Christ could have had tattoos."

"We're not calling them the Surgeon murders anymore?"

"We never did," Charlie said. "Would you have spotted a henna tattoo on a body?"

"Probably under forensic light, providing the skin hadn't decomposed too much, and the only two who hadn't were Toolie and Simmons. And both of them had tattoos."

Charlie said, "On his chest, Simmons had a triangle with a circle inside it with a line down the middle, right?"

"Just left and up from the sternum."

"Could Toolie have a tattoo in the same place?"

"The same place exactly?"

"Yes."

He said nothing for a beat and she could hear him breathing, maybe thinking.

Charlie said, "What is it?"

"I think I know where you're going with this. But Toolie and Simmons had black henna tattoos, which is different to regular henna. Which is actually good news. Tattoos may not show up ordinarily, but I can try an IR light. I remember reading about a surfer who was identified by his tattoos after being mostly eaten by a great white. Infrared light might work on a couple of them. Do you think you're on to something? This won't be a waste of time?"

She told him about the list found at Tony Zart's place. "So I think that the symbols by the initials could relate to symbols tattooed on the body."

"Send me the list," he said. "Let's see what comes up."

It took the pathologist a day. He reported that there appeared to be a symbol over the third most recent body's heart. He sent a picture. It matched the symbol on the paper found in Zart's apartment: a cross with three horizontal lines.

"Confirmation that the guy before Paul Toolie has the initials RT," Zhang said on the phone. Garcia was in the office with him.

"Right."

"We probably have the initials of the last thirty-six murdered guys."

"Right," Charlie said again but she was distracted by the symbol.

She called the pathologist back. "Russian Orthodox cross."

"That's what I think."

"How about the other bodies?"

"Would you like me to check them?"

"Yes."

He chuckled. "Already have, Agent Rebb. Already have. Unfortunately most of their skin is too decomposed, however I got an image on three more."

A second later, her phone pinged with three more images.

She called Zhang.

"Peter, five of them had a tattoo over the heart. They're all on the list. Not all of them are complete but I think we have a match to the eight bodies from the church. Which means we have the initials of the three unidentified ones now."

"OK," he said, "but my news trumps yours."

She waited.

"I'm with Nick Garcia and we're looking at a data dump from the Surgeon's—"

"—the subject," she interrupted, "or Zart." Her partner's adoption of the media's name for the killer irritated her. And Zhang knew it.

"—the Surgeon's PC," he finished. "Do you want to hear or not?"

"Sure."

"The last activity on the computer was three weeks ago and he was looking at airline flights."

"Where to?"

52

"That's the problem. We have a bunch of locations. From Kabul to Cairo. Paris to Pakistan."

"No definite booking?"

They must have been on speaker because Garcia shouted, "We think he must have researched on his computer but booked on his phone."

"Could be a misdirection," Zhang added.

Charlie pondered that.

She said, "No. If he was misdirecting he'd have booked a flight on the computer."

"True!" Garcia called.

Charlie said, "We need to get his description to Interpol and—"

"Already ahead of you, Chicago. Also got airlines checking manifests for his name."

She said, "Great. You know what bothers me? Mark Simmons wasn't the last name. There were two more initials on the sheets after him. There were two more murders after the bodies under the church. Two more in the forty days since Simmons." She took a breath. "Hell, if Zart disappeared three weeks ago, that may be two more bodies in less than twenty days."

"Don't sweat the small things," Zhang said. "There's at least twenty other bodies out there from before and after the Panola Mountain murders. This mother was prolific. Maybe we should celebrate that he's gone?"

Over the following week they discovered that Tony Zart had been born Anthony Zarakolu, second-generation American, family originally from Turkey. Detective Garcia also provided his date of birth. Zart was forty-one and had attended the Art Institute in San Francisco. According to them, he'd excelled and specialized in make-up before pursuing a career in the film industry.

The police had traced him to various companies until, at the age of twenty-nine, he was fired.

Still in the name of Zarakolu, he had a record for causing disturbances. Multiple times. It appeared that he had become a Christian religious zealot. He'd been an active Jehovah's Witness until he fell out with them. He'd been convicted of arson—burning down one of their halls. No one was injured. He got ten years, reduced to four in the Twin Towers Correctional Facility, LA. After that, he changed his name and returned to Georgia.

Initially he sold a few paintings to galleries and then tried to establish his own in Atlanta. It lasted a year before going bust. That was four years ago, when he turned to body art and was doing well enough to employ Tammy.

Although Larouse, the confessed Satanist, complained about Zart, they found no police record of the complaint. They also found no evidence of Zart being part of any church.

The other progress they had made was to match up most of the initials on Zart's list to missing persons. Of the thirty-six they thought they'd found thirty-one. DNA and dental records had confirmed the sixteen bodies they'd found.

Zhang had taped a map of Georgia to a wall in the office they were now using. There was a yellow pin for each missing person, identifying their last-known locations. The thirty-one photographs had their names, dates of birth and date of assumed abduction underneath. Red string linked each photo with its associated yellow pin.

There were a further twenty-five unsolved missing-person cases involving a young male. Each of these was marked with a white pin.

"They could be victims," Zhang said. "After all, we could be looking for at least thirty-six more if we only found the second page."

Charlie said, "Which means others were out of state. God, I hope you're wrong." However, the more she looked at the map, the more she felt that Zart wasn't confined to Georgia.

"Why's he doing it?" she asked. The conundrum kept her awake at night.

"Because he's a sick mother-fucker. Simple."

She shook her head. He wasn't mentally ill. His killing technique was too clinical. His abduction technique was also precise. No witnesses, no trace, no obvious pattern. This guy knew exactly what he was doing.

"Why's he doing it?" she asked again.

They were going through the missing-person files trying to spot a link. So far they'd found nothing consistent.

Charlie's email pinged and she opened a file she'd been waiting for: the analysis of the tattoo symbols. She scanned the email and sent the attachment to print.

Her phone rang. Detective Garcia.

She put him on speaker.

"Any progress?" he asked.

"Nada," Zhang called out. "Except for a lot of holes in the wall."

The line was quiet for a moment.

"You've got something for us, Nick?" Charlie said.

"D'you know Finchley's downtown?"

"Art gallery? Fairly new."

"That's the one."

"Know who owns it?"

Charlie took a gulp of cold coffee. "You're kidding!"

"That's right: Tony Zart. Only, the records have him down as Anthony Zarakolu. DOB matches so it's definitely him."

That didn't make sense, did it? Zart didn't have much money. You couldn't make a fortune in body art.

Garcia said, "The pictures all have religious icons, although there aren't any pieces in his name."

"Using a pseudonym?"

"That's what we figure. Sales are pretty poor, so it's like a vanity thing—only, it's rich kids who normally go in for that game, don't they?"

"Unless this is another bankruptcy waiting to happen."

"Why would he—?"

"On behalf of someone else?" she suggested.

"Maybe, but he has two staff and it doesn't look like it's about to fail."

"Do they ever?" She didn't really know, and he didn't answer.

He said, "We've run all the artists' names and Anthony Zarakolu through the airline manifests and not had a hit. So, unfortunately we still don't know the name he travelled under."

"If he really went."

"Yeah, sure. If he really went."

She picked up the print-out. The Crypto boys had written an explanation against each of the tattoo symbols from the list. There were obvious Christian signs like the cross and a fish, St Peter's cross, a Christogram—they explained that the initials IHS were an abbreviation of Jesus—and something called a triquetra which was also known as a Trinity knot. There were Hebrew letters representing names of God and, surprisingly, there were Islamic symbols. The email had explained that there were cyphers from multiple religions and cultures.

What's the link? Charlie was thinking, but then the next group made her brain spin.

"Charlie, are you still there?"

She'd forgotten Garcia was on the line. She looked at her phone in her hand and then back at the paper.

"Hieroglyphs," she said. "Those last two tattoos are ancient Egyptian: a scarab and an Isis knot. He'd looked at flights to Cairo on his PC."

"Right."

"Then he's gone to Egypt all right, Nick. He's damn well in Egypt."

EIGHT

Cairo, Egypt

Alex got off the train at Ramses Station in Cairo. The guy calling himself Agent J had insisted that he come alone, so Alex had explained to Vanessa and left her in Deir Mawas. The guy also said that Alex had to make sure he wasn't followed.

"If they find me they'll kill me for sure," the guy had said. "If you want to know the truth I've found, then you need to be damned careful. Like *your* life depends on it."

Alex hailed a cab and asked to be taken to the Cairo Egyptian Museum, but this wasn't his true destination. When they started to go around Tahrir Square he told the driver to go around twice. And then again. He watched the other traffic. The gyratory heaved with cars, buses, lorries and motor scooters. Was anyone following? It was so hard to judge.

At the last moment, after passing the road towards the museum, Alex pointed to the next exit.

"Take it quickly!" he said and then looked behind for anyone copying the sudden manoeuvre.

They crossed the bridge to the island on the Nile, and again Alex instructed the driver to turn at the last minute. They came off, passed the Cairo Tower and went under the 6th October Bridge. He then had the taxi go around the circular Al Gazira twice as he checked other traffic.

Finally, satisfied that he wasn't being followed, he asked to be dropped outside the tower and tipped the driver handsomely for his trouble.

This was where Agent J had said to meet. On the tower's viewing platform.

Alex looked up at the enormous column, taller than the Great Pyramid. It was reputedly giving the finger to the US because in the 1960s the US had given President Nasser $6 million, which he saw as a bribe. He spent the whole amount on this folly, visible from the US embassy and a symbol of Arab resistance to Western influence and control.

After the 2011 revolution and the rise of the Muslim Brotherhood, it looked like Egypt was heading the same way as some of its extreme neighbours. However the government was becoming more secular. It was still a dangerous place and Islamist terrorists still murdered non-Muslims but there was hope for the future. Light at the end of the tunnel, people said. Which was ironic, he thought, looking up. Maybe there was just a light at the top of the tower.

Nerves screwed up his stomach as he waited in the long line. Who was this man he'd agreed to meet? Agent J. Cloak and dagger. Who was the guy afraid of?

Then the laughter of school children relaxed him a little as the climbed the steps to the vast entrance. He paid the foreigners' entrance fee—six times more than a local—and continued to shuffle forward and wait.

When it was his turn, he was crammed into the single elevator and shot up to the restaurant floor. He spilled out with the others and took the stairs to the observation deck.

The panoramic views were stunning although the amount of pollution he could see made him realize what a health risk the city's air must be. But he wasn't here for the views. There must have been thirty people on the floor, excluding the kids. From his voice last night, Alex figured Agent J was white and possibly German.

That reduced the number significantly. There were only six white males. Alex walked around and eventually made eye contact with each of them. There was no reaction, no recognition. He walked around once more trying to look casual and saw new people had arrived. Again still no reaction.

He checked his watch. He was half an hour late because of the queue. Had Agent J also been delayed or had he been and gone?

After another half an hour he decided to look in the restaurant. There were white males but no one on their own. So Alex asked for a table and ordered peppermint tea.

Most people looked out at the revolving view. Alex sat with his back to the window and watched people coming out of the elevator.

Another hour and three cups of overly sweet tea later, he paid the bill. It was extortionate and he wondered whether there were two rates for food and drink here as well as the rate for entry. Probably.

It was only as he lined up for the elevator that he noticed the bill had writing on the back. Not really writing, it was a series of arrows and numbers.

He stared. It couldn't be! The waiter must have known who he was and slipped him the paper. To anyone else, the marks would have looked like nothing, maybe a doodle. But to Alex it was a message and he knew exactly how to decode it.

NINE

Atlanta, Georgia

Charlie called her sister. "How's Dad doing?"

"No more women's underwear issues if that's what you mean?"

"I mean generally."

"He had a fall last week and hurt his wrist—"

"You should have called me."

"What? Every time he has a minor injury?" Liz scoffed.

"I worry about him."

"He misses you. You should call him more often."

"I'll try," Charlie said.

"How's the case? The media's been quiet for over a week."

Charlie sighed. It occupied her mind day and night, but the progress had stalled. "Busy," she said. "Just plodding on. Slowly, slowly. You know how it is."

"You are coming for the holidays, aren't you?"

Christmas was just a few days away and Charlie knew she couldn't switch off. "I can't—"

"There you go."

"What?"

"You need a break, Charlie. I can hear it in your voice. You're stressed."

"This guy has murdered at least thirty-six people, Liz. I can't just ignore it and walk away."

"I'm just talking about a vacation! You could be at this for a year and still make no progress. Then where will you be? You're stressed now for Christ's sake! And you're single. How do you expect—"

"I've got to go," Charlie interrupted, annoyed that Liz didn't understand the importance of the job. Angry with herself for letting her sister wind her up.

She didn't take a vacation and the weeks turned to months. They scanned hours of CCTV footage, checked passenger manifests against passport photographs but nothing. The case seemed to be stalled. But then they got a hit on a press report: a body with a similar incision to the heart. When Charlie received a photograph, she immediately spotted a tattoo on the victim's chest.

Charlie, Zhang and their boss, Mike Smith, were in Jim Gould's office. He was the special agent in-charge of Atlanta and you only got invited to a meeting in his office if they were onto something big. Charlie could barely contain her excitement. They'd finally found their connection.

"Where was the body found?" Gould asked again.

"Egypt," Zhang said.

"Specifically?"

"In temple ruins near a place called Dashur, south of Cairo," Charlie said. She drummed her fingers, desperate for Gould to bite.

"Same MO?"

"Precisely."

Gould said nothing for a minute, processing.

Charlie said, "We need to go. This is way too important to leave to the locals."

Gould still said nothing. She couldn't read his face either.

Smith said, "We're sure Tony Zart travelled to Egypt."

Gould sighed. "You didn't find any evidence except for the searches on his computer."

"No," Charlie said. "He must have changed his name and changed his appearance. Must have. But he is the subject. I'll bet my salary on it."

Gould looked hard at Zhang. "And you?"

"I can't go," he said. "Marcie's not well."

Charlie knew it was true, but she suspected her partner would have found an excuse anyway. He didn't want to go whereas she just had to go.

Gould's eyes narrowed. "We're not talking about anyone going."

"Sir—" Charlie started.

"What's the MLAT situation with Egypt?" Gould asked. He tapped on his computer presumably looking for the answer.

An MLAT was a mutual legal assistance treaty, for the arrest and extradition of suspects. Charlie already knew but Smith spoke first. "It's been in place with Egypt since ninety-eight," he said.

Gould nodded. "Then we let the LEGAT coordinate with the authorities." He looked at Charlie. "That is the attaché's job after all."

"Sir—"

"That's it, Agent Rebb."

But it wasn't. Charlie didn't understand the politics but their LEGAT—their legal attaché—in Cairo said he'd welcome the assistance. And two days later, Gould called Charlie back into his office.

"The media know about the signature and Tony Zart. They're asking if he the Surgeon."

She was about to comment but Gould continued. "That's not why I've called you in here."

"It's not?"

"You have two weeks to find concrete evidence that it's our man," he said. "Our LEGAT has asked for you. I know Egypt and it's not a safe place—situations can get sticky—and it's worse for a woman. You'll liaise with him and I'll get you joint agency support. You'll also work with the local law enforcement. I don't want you doing or being involved in anything problematic. Understand?"

"Thank you," she said.

"Don't thank me," Gould said, standing so that she knew the meeting was over. "Just stay safe and find me that bastard Surgeon."

TEN

Cairo, Egypt

The man who now thought of himself as the Surgeon, sat in his secure place, and put aside his sketches and sucked up water from his bottle. There were literally thousands of possible combinations and he didn't even know for sure that a hieroglyph was the answer. That bothered him. That and the damned heat. But they weren't his biggest problem.

He'd made a mistake and the cops had found one of his victims. And the Egyptian papers had picked up on it. Not because they suspected a Surgeon murder. No. With all the missing people and murders in Egypt, and the damned press gave it prominence because of the location.

Execution in the Temple was the headline's translation. They'd even shown a picture of the body. The incision was clearly visible, as was the tattoo.

It was only a matter of time before the Master picked up on it.

The Surgeon logged into the secure website and provided his daily update.

He waited. Despite the air conditioning in the converted office, sweat still prickled his face.

He checked his watch. Dead on time. Why wasn't the Master responding? It happened sometimes. He'd be delayed by some important meeting, although it was rare.

An hour ticked by.

He started to wonder whether something was seriously wrong. He desperately wanted to send another message but he knew his place. He was to wait and he'd receive no explanation or apology. It was his job to do what he was told.

The Surgeon looked at the canvases arranged around the room. He'd partitioned it into three: space for his living area and bed, space for his painting and space for his work.

His painting and gallery were his unofficial reward for what he did for the Master but they both knew this was more. Much more. This was a calling. The main reward was the spiritual satisfaction. The knowledge of being the one to solve the oldest mystery in the world. The mystery of life itself. The key to life beyond the mortal realm.

The message board light flashed. The Master was typing.

They know it's you.

The Surgeon started to respond but the Master beat him to it.

The media says you left a signature

The Surgeon hesitated, thought about denying it, but then responded: **It was a stupid mistake**

The message light didn't flash. The Master was angry, the Surgeon knew, but instead of a reprimand, the Master wrote, **We can talk about it another time,** the next message said. **For now I have a more pressing issue.** There was a pause before the Master typed again. He wrote, **We've been monitoring traffic.**

The Surgeon knew he meant communications. There was some big monitoring unit somewhere funded by the organization. This was a big project and money wasn't an issue. They'd funded his rapid evacuation, his changed identity and they'd set him up here. All he needed was to find the answer for the Master.

The light blinked and then the Master continued. **Ansar is tracking someone else. Not just MacLure. You need to move quickly.**

Where?

Directions being sent. Remove threat and extract. Extreme caution

The Surgeon was about to log off and jump into his vehicle when the flashing started again.

And message me when done. We need to talk

ELEVEN

Alex studied the napkin. The code was the same as Yanhamu's code on the clay tablets. Whoever had written this had read his paper on the interpretation of the ancient Egyptian's secret messages.

Alex held the paper tightly in his pocket as he left the queue and located a toilet. Once the door lock clicked into place, he took out the note and literally read between the lines of the cuneiform symbols. The message was: EZA.

What does that mean? Alex checked his interpretation but there was no doubt about the three letters. There was also no doubt in his mind that the message was meant for him. Who else would expect a code hidden within cuneiform letters? So it must mean something and it must be relevant.

Using the browser on his phone he searched for the term. Eza was a record label. They were also the initials of a company on the South African stock exchange. There was a twitter account and a brand of batteries. Nothing jumped out as relevant. He checked two more pages and gave up.

He tried EZA Egypt and then EZA Cairo. He followed links to movies with EZA in the title and some Facebook pages. None of the hits leapt out at him.

Giving up, he stuck the phone in his pocket and exited the bathroom. He waited in line for the elevator and enjoyed another crammed journey.

Outside once more, he hailed a taxi.

"Where to, mister?"

On impulse Alex replied, "Eza?"

"Ten pounds," the driver said with dead eyes.

Alex figured this was an inflated figure but he had no idea. He established it was Egyptian rather than English pounds and got in the back.

The driver crossed the bridge heading west and through an affluent sector and Cairo University with its impressive domed central building and grand avenue. Then the roads narrowed and became more congested. He guessed the buildings were tenement blocks and the further they drove, the grubbier they became.

Alex kept glancing around but had no idea of his exact position or whether they were being followed. Then the driver said, "Where on Eza, Mister?"

"Keep driving, please. At the end, turn right."

The driver kept going.

"Now left."

When the driver took the next left Alex asked him to stop. He paid the man and watched him drive away. Then he walked back towards the road called Eza. All the time he kept a look out for anyone acting suspiciously.

The road wasn't busy. It was lined with parked vehicles and had a fruit shop on the corner. A van came down the road and stopped, blocking the way. Another car came up behind and sounded his horn but the van didn't move. After a minute the driver of the van jumped out and posted a parcel. Another car queued up and both vehicles blared their horns. The van driver ignored them, casually walked back, got in and pulled away.

There was a paramedic vehicle stopped midway along, half parked, with enough space for other vehicles to get around.

Alex watched as two men came out of a door twenty yards away and walk towards him. Alex ducked in the shop and bought a bag of apples, all the time with an eye on the door.

The men walked past.

Alex came out of the shop. For a moment there were no cars on the road. The paramedic had gone and there were no pedestrians along the hundred-yard stretch.

He took an apple from the bag, dropped the rest in a rubbish bin and casually walked down the road.

Which property?

Alex had been in Egypt long enough to speak a few words and recognize numbers. He walked the whole length of the road and munched his apple thinking, why didn't Agent J provide a number?

Was he a numbers guy? Did he expect Alex to convert the letters to numbers? The most obvious would be 5 for E, 26 for Z, 1 for A. Number 32 then? Or flat 5 of number 27? There were other options too since there were…

He stopped and looked at the door beside him. While his conscious was processing numbers, his back brain was seeing the obvious. The property had a name: University Residence A block.

Alex quickly ran along the row. Yes! There was a J block. He noticed that he was about where he'd seen the paramedic car earlier.

The door of J block was wooden with peeling brown paint. It had two thin frosted glass windows that he could see nothing through, and the door was locked.

Alongside the door was a metal panel of buzzers and a speaker. Each one had a letter. There was a mix of

71

names, some in Arabic some in English. One in particular caught his attention. MI Black. Oh my God, he thought. It's a *Men in Black* reference. He recalled that the 1990s film had an Agent J. Will Smith maybe? J was the block and MI Black was the apartment.

It was the fifth buzzer down. He pressed it and waited.

There was no response. He pressed it again.

After a third failed attempt, he pressed the bottom most button. A buzzer marked "Service". The door clicked.

He was in.

Inside, there was what he guessed to be a communal storage area with ten bins, five bicycles—none of which looked ride-able—a stroller and a single mattress.

Doors marked 1 and 2 in Arabic were side by side: one flat at the front one overlooking the rear.

He climbed a flight of concrete steps to the first floor and found doors 3 and 4. Another flight and he was looking at door 5.

It was slightly ajar.

Alex knocked. The door moved and he could see a hallway beyond. Doors to the left and one to the right. None of the doors were shut. There was a door at the end of the hall and this was also open. The room looked like a lounge.

He pushed the front door wider and called out, "Hello. Anyone there?"

He stood on the landing for a moment before deciding. He may as well enter. He'd come this far, he'd worked out the address, so what did he have to lose?

The guy had probably left the door open so that Alex would go inside. Once there, he'd find another cryptic note. This Agent J was probably a crank playing games after all.

Alex knew all about the oddballs out there. Because of his research papers and Vanessa's articles, he'd attracted a group of followers. Sometimes they sent sensible messages on Facebook or by email. Sometimes they sent crazy ones.

He stepped into the hall.

The apartment smelled of food and he imagined falafel. His shoes made a squeaky noise on the linoleum flooring. To his left was a small bathroom and then a linen cupboard. On the right was a bedroom.

The bed was unmade and clothes were strewn about.

"Hello?" Alex called out again, suddenly feeling like he was intruding. Hell, he was intruding!

The apartment seemed lived in but empty. Maybe the guy had left in a hurry. Maybe he'd just nipped out and that's why the door was on the latch.

Alex pushed open the door at the end of the corridor. The living room.

He stepped forward and froze.

There was a man on the floor. And he was definitely dead. Blood was pooled around his head and upper body. So much blood! There was also a spray of scarlet up the wall.

Alex's first thought was: My God, his throat's been cut. And then the shock was replaced by the realization: Get out! Get out now!

He turned to run, stepped into the hall and gasped.

In the doorway was a man. And he had a gun.

TWELVE

The Surgeon was relieved to be back in his safe house. The student hadn't been in the apartment there but the Arab had been. Given more time maybe the Arab could have become another guinea pig. He was the right age and he was fit. Maybe. However, it was too late now.

He typed, It's done. Clean

The response was immediate, which surprised him.

Tell me what you have done, the Master wrote.

The Surgeon looked at his hands, moist with sudden perspiration. Honesty was the only policy, he knew. I made a mistake, he replied after a long breath.

The light flickered but nothing appeared. Maybe he'd started and deleted it.

The Surgeon wrote, I was interrupted. A body has been found.

You mean *another* body

Not like before, the Surgeon wrote. I was in a temple. I was disturbed. I was only half-way through.

And this means?

It's in the papers. I fear...

That the FBI will find out you're in Egypt?

Yes

Of course they will. You need to be more careful. No more slip-ups

I will, the Surgeon wrote. He knew this was his last chance. First there had been the stupid urge to leave his own mark—his signature Z. And now this. The US media knew he was responsible for the murders and he figured they'd soon realize he was in Egypt. No more mistakes

We need that symbol, the Master wrote.

I'll get it

Don't approach him—he was referring to MacLure—not until he's ready. Not until he knows the answer

THIRTEEN

A policeman pointed his carbine at Alex. At least one more policeman stood behind the first, and they were shouting.

Alex thrust his hands into the air.

"I just got here!" he said, but his voice was lost in the stream of Arabic that the cop was shouting. The gestures were obvious. They wanted Alex down on the ground.

As Alex went down a knee immediately went into his back. His arms were jerked behind him and handcuff ties bit into his wrists. The two cops didn't stop shouting at him. Then he was pulled to his feet and pushed along the hallway. Outside in the stairwell, the man who had hold of his arm levered him forward so that he stumbled towards the stairs.

Down and down they went. Unbalanced with each step, Alex realized the guy could let go at any moment and he'd fall. His face would smack into concrete and there would be nothing he could do to stop it.

But the cop didn't let go, he just kept lifting and pushing and Alex was soon going past the detritus of the entrance hall and out through the front door.

A white minibus was parked at an angle outside. For a second, Alex panicked.

What if these guys aren't real cops?

Then he spotted the vehicle behind the minibus. It had "Police" written on the side. He breathed with relief at the same time as he was unceremoniously flung into the minibus. He gave a quick glance back at the apartment and saw an army of policemen going into the block.

Once inside the vehicle he was forced to the floor and a foot placed on his back to keep him in place. The driver gunned the engine and the siren made a terrible screech. The minibus jolted and sped down the road.

Alex said, "I'm innocent. You've made a mistake." But his outburst was met with a stamp in his back. He lay still and waited for what would happen next. Surely someone reasonable would talk to him?

The journey lasted less than ten minutes so he knew they were still in Cairo, probably in the centre. As soon as he was pulled out, he looked around. His first view was of a citadel and mosque. He recognized it as the iconic Mosque Madrass; although clearly Islamic with its minarets and dome, the sandstone structure with its detail reminded him of ancient Egyptian temples.

His view of the beautiful building was short-lived because he was swung around and marched into the building opposite. This was the El Khalifa, a police station. A notorious police station.

It too was built of sandstone, but it looked more like a modernist take on a pylon from a Karnak temple. Alex knew it had been bombed in the 2011 revolution but there was no sign of the burnt walls now.

The policemen hurried him up the steps and into a room with a man behind a bench. A desk sergeant, Alex figured. One of the policemen spoke in rapid Arabic and Alex heard the words: murder and guilty. The desk guy wrote in a large book and then glared at Alex.

He looked like he was about to spit in Alex's face, but instead he said, "You speak Arabic?"

"I understand a little," Alex replied in Arabic.

The guy switched to English. "Nationality?"

"British."

He wrote it down and then asked for his name and address in Egypt. As soon as Alex answered, the man called out and two men appeared.

They had black uniforms with no markings and carried long batons. Guards, Alex suspected.

"B twelve," the desk guy said in Arabic, and then "twelve" again in English.

The cop behind him pushed him sideways into the hands of the nearest guard. A vice-like grip took hold of his biceps and he was frog-marched down a corridor. When they came to a room he was pushed inside. The nylon ties were cut and he received a whack on the thigh with a baton.

He turned and glared but the men's faces showed nothing.

"Strip!" one barked.

Alex hesitated a second; a moment of defiance before he complied.

They took his watch, wallet and phone and put them in a tray. There was no form to sign. No check of the contents of the wallet. His shoes were placed on top and the whole lot was stuck in a plastic bag.

Alex was told to get dressed again and was led out of the room. This time there was a baton in his back. He looked down and saw black writing on his shirt. It looked like a line and an inverted tick. The Arabic number twelve, he figured.

They went down a flight of stone steps and the light diminished. The air smelled rank. It was hot and got warmer as they descended into the basement.

Alex heard the moan of other men as they reached a corridor at the bottom. They went through two locked gates and then passed a block marked "A". They stopped outside the next one. After a turn, Alex saw the metal bars of a big cell. There were maybe thirty men inside all looking weak and lost. Some stared at him with dull eyes. Others just looked at the floor.

The guard banged his baton against the bars and screamed at the prisoners to get back.

They shuffled away until there was enough room to open the gate. Alex was shoved inside and took a blow to the back of the head.

He staggered and saw stars for a moment. He would have fallen if not for the bodies that pressed against him as the men moved back to fill the space by the bars.

He could smell their bodies but there was worse. A strong stink of sewage made him gag.

The only light came from a dim bulb outside the cage. There were no windows and he wondered if they pushed to the bars like some sort of instinctive behaviour. Perhaps, psychologically, there seemed to be more air here.

"You OK?" the man beside him said. He was grubby with dark blond hair plastered to his scalp with sweat. He had "18" on his T-shirt.

"I shouldn't be here."

"Of course not. Me either."

"American?"

He shook his head, exaggerated disgust on his face. "Canuck."

"Sorry, I've—"

"Canadian."

"Oh, sorry. I'm Alex."

The other guy hesitated then smiled. "You Brits—always apologizing. Welcome to the shithole, Alex."

Alex waited for the other guy to give a name then said, "So what do I call you?"

"Eighteen," the guy replied. "Best that you don't share too much in here. We can cover each other's backs but don't expect anything more. And—a word of advice—don't go talking about your crime. Got it?"

"OK. Can I ask you how long you've been down here?"

"Sure. Ten days."

"Hey!" Alex complained at a push in his back.

The Canadian moved beside him. "Stay calm, buddy. Just go with the flow and you'll survive this."

"You make it sound like people don't... survive this, I mean."

"Some don't," he said.

FOURTEEN

The Canadian cocked an eyebrow.

"It's bad here but Qena is worse." They were moving slowly around the cell, not a deliberate walk, just a "flow" as the Canadian had described it. Alex recognized the name Qena. It was a city about an hour north of Luxor. There was a large temple to Hathor on the opposite bank of the Nile but he figured the Canadian wasn't talking about monuments.

"You mean the prison?" he said.

"Sure."

They were nearing the back of the cell now, and the stench made Alex hold his shirt to his mouth and nose. A man had pulled back a cloth and revealed a short trench in the concrete. He dropped his trousers and squatted for a minute. When he finished, he covered the toilet and washed his hands under a tap at the end of the trench.

The Canadian nodded towards it. "That's the only drinking water. It tastes foul at first but you'll get used to it after a couple of days. You'll get so thirsty that you'll think it tastes like nectar."

Alex doubted that. He watched another man use the toilet. There was no paper to wipe with. No soap to wash with. Disease must be so easy to catch and spread, he thought.

When he looked around, he was still at the back, near the toilet. The Canadian had moved and looked like he was forcing his way to the front. Not going with the flow after all. And then Alex realized why. A couple of guards were at the cell, pushing food through the bars.

Alex tried to get to them. At five deep it was like attempting to order at a crowded bar. Arms and elbows jutted out, bodies tensed, but eventually Alex made it to the Canadian's side.

It was too late. The guards had stopped handing out food and they whacked the cell bars to deter men from reaching through.

Most of the inmates had chunks of bread. Those who didn't seemed to accept their fate, and Alex was surprised that no one fought—openly at least. He didn't feel like fighting but then he'd eaten lunch on the train and an apple a short time ago. Maybe by tomorrow he'd be more driven to ensure he got food.

Nearly everyone squatted to eat. Alex hunkered down next to the Canadian.

"Gotta be prepared, buddy," the other man said. "You don't get food and you won't survive this." He handed Alex a small piece. "What didn't you do to be here?"

Alex took a moment to realize what he meant. "I didn't murder someone."

"Woah!"

"I mean it. I really didn't!"

"Wrong place, wrong time?"

"I suppose so. I just need a chance to explain."

"They're not so good at listening down here. You call out, they'll either ignore you or beat you. Either way you'll only talk when they want you to. Hear those screams earlier?"

Alex had heard muffled cries on and off since being in the cell. He nodded.

"Interrogation," the Canadian said. "If you're lucky, you won't get to talk to anyone."

"But then... how long will we be down here? What happens next if I can't explain?"

He shrugged. "The longest I'm aware of is about thirty days. But who knows? Most people don't talk. In fact, if you want to survive Qena then you should probably follow that advice."

They were up and moving again. Alex said, "How do you know this stuff?"

"I had a buddy. He was in Qena." He shrugged. "Plus I've been down here before. I did ten days last time before I got released. My buddy got out too. I heard it was just a gesture of goodwill towards the new prime minster. Plus it helps that I'm not American. Or maybe there was some underhand deal done. You know this stuff goes on all the time behind the scenes. Anyway I'm not complaining. I got released."

"But you're back."

He shrugged again. "Yeah, pretty dumb of me."

The light never went out and no one had a watch, but a bell signalled a time for prayer. Everyone except for Alex and the Canadian got on their knees. Afterwards they began to settle, preparing for the night.

Alex sat with his back to the bars. Most men lay on the concrete, legs bent or legs up. A few used another man as a kind of pillow.

It was a long night and Alex heard someone from another cell calling for help. Something about a man dying. No guards came.

Alex must have dropped off because he awoke with a stiff back and neck. He needed the toilet but the floor was a solid morass of bodies so he focused on the positive things in his life as a distraction. He thought about his brother and the poor kid's struggle against the cruel and debilitating disease that was muscular dystrophy. Andrew was strong though. He could have spent his life miserable and aggrieved but he'd never once said, "Why me?" He was positive and happy. He saw each day as a blessing, to enjoy the wonder of life. How do people manage that?

Alex thought about his dog, Topsy. The thirteen-year-old cocker spaniel-cross couldn't come to Egypt of course. Nor would she have wanted to. He pictured her enthusiasm, jumping up at him, chasing a Frisbee in Regent's Park. She lived with his mum and Andrew while he was away. Perhaps it was time to give up archaeology and go back home?

He thought about Vanessa, his girlfriend. How was she? She must be worried as hell. He hadn't called or messaged since arriving in Cairo. Would she ring the police? Would they tell her he'd been arrested? Alex had no idea about how things worked here, except for what he'd learned from the Canadian with the number eighteen on his top.

Eventually, men started to stir, and those at the back used the toilet. As soon as he could get through, Alex joined the orderly queue. They used the trough then washed their hands. At least men in here try to be hygienic, he thought.

The floor was sticky-wet under his bare feet, and he couldn't help pray that it was just water. After using the toilet he used the tap and splashed his face. Then he cupped his hand under the trickle and tested it. He knew he couldn't last long without drinking but the first foul taste stopped him for now.

A bell sounded and everyone else knelt and began their morning prayers. Alex could hear the muezzin, muffled through the walls.

The Canadian raised a hand and Alex squirmed through to him.

"Hold onto the bars," the other man whispered.

Alex did as instructed and later shrugged off the pushes from the other men encouraging him to move. Within what felt like an hour, a claxon sounded and the guards arrived with bread.

Alex snatched a large chunk and smuggled it under his shirt. He then wriggled away from the front to let others get their turn.

"Thanks!" he said when they sat down to eat.

"I'd like to know your name so I can thank you properly. It can't hurt."

"Fine," the Canadian said shaking his head. "If you must then call me Wills."

"Then thank you, Wills. I needed this. My stomach was starting to turn inside out."

The Canadian shook his head. "Better prepare yourself for worse. But you've gotta eat when you can," he said. "If you want to survive this, that is."

When they finished, the routine of shuffling around the cell began again. Alex found his mind going blank, maybe with the monotony, maybe the tiredness was kicking in.

Sometime later, the guards came back and banged their batons on the cage. One of them shouted, "four," and a man was pushed forward by the others. He had "four" written front and back on his shirt.

The gate opened, the man was pulled through and the gate clanged shut again.

"Poor bugger," Wills said. "Interrogation."

Alex was wondering at everyone's behaviour. They had been quick to identify the man that the guards wanted.

Wills must have read his mind. "If we don't give them up straight away, they would come in here and beat the shit out of us. A lot easier for everyone to just comply."

When the man was brought back, Alex was relieved that he seemed all right. Maybe Wills was just paranoid. Maybe he enjoyed worrying people. Alex hoped that was the case and he'd get his chance to explain the mistake.

Soon after, another man was taken, only this one was dragged back semi-conscious.

"Told you," Wills said.

Men seemed to be taken regularly after that, either from their cell or one of the others.

"How many cells are there?" Alex asked.

Wills was about to respond when a large number of guards came in led by two in riot gear. Everyone pressed to the rear of the cell, no longer concerned about the latrine. Alex found himself pressed back with the others and just avoided stepping into the trench.

It was a quick operation and eight men were called out. Instead of dragging them away one at a time, they were chained together and marched off.

Alex looked at the Canadian.

"Off to a hearing," he said.

"Which is good, right?"

"Good and bad. Good that this part is probably over. Bad because you can end up in Qena. That is if the transportation doesn't kill you. They take twenty at a time in a van with no ventilation. It gets parked in direct sunlight in a military compound. They don't give you water and ignore the cries for pity."

Alex said, "You're buddy told you this too?"

"I experienced it last time. I could see the guards sitting in the shade drinking tea while we were part-steamed to death. You can't treat a dog like that! There's no humanity in this system."

"What happens next?"

"They take you four or five at a time into the court house and you get put in a long thin cage. I think I got legal representation but I can't be sure. A man claiming to be my defence lawyer spoke to me through the bars. He didn't ask much and didn't say anything when I faced the judges. You get called to the front of the cage and listen to a whole load of Arabic. There wasn't a translation so I have no idea what was said. If it hadn't been for the political situation—whatever it was—I have no doubt I'd be rotting in the Qena hellhole right now."

Alex didn't comment. He was partially thinking about finding himself there and partially realizing Wills was going to Qena this time. No way would the Canadian government step in twice for a drug dealer. Caught once and it could be a mistake. Twice and Wills looked guilty as hell.

"Twelve!"

Alex didn't register what was being said. The first time he realized his number had been called was when the crowd parted and hands pushed him towards the gate.

It opened and a guard grabbed his collar.

FIFTEEN

Charlie's limo driver met her in Cairo airport Arrivals. She introduced herself to the Egyptian who nodded deferentially. He took charge of her trolley and led her towards the parking lot.

"Tired?" he said once they were underway, travelling fast in the dark.

She blinked her eyes and realized he was looking at her through the rear-view mirror. She had been travelling for over twenty hours with a four hour layover in Germany. She'd drunk coffee to keep herself going and only dropped off briefly on the first leg—the classic mistake of thinking a movie would help her to sleep. Two movies later and breakfast was being served.

"Long journey," she responded and looked out of the window at the speckled, rushing lights, hoping it was the end of the conversation.

"What time is it now in America?" her driver asked.

"Pardon?"

"The time difference? You will suffer from jetlag."

She looked at her phone. Six hours difference. "Almost nine in the evening," she said in a flat tone. Surely he'd get the message that she didn't want to chat.

But he talked all the way until he stopped outside an apartment block.

She hadn't really thought about the arrival time and had expected to meet SSA John Graham, the LEGAT, straight away.

"I'm staying here?" she asked as she got out and looked at the building. Despite the street lights, she couldn't determine how good a neighbourhood this was. However the apartment block looked clean enough. In fact she was pleasantly surprised once inside. It was small—a living room with a kitchen on the side, a bedroom with a bathroom beyond—but it looked new or newly decorated. She'd expected a hotel room, but this was much better.

The driver handed her a packet of documents including a set of keys and a fob.

He said, "The door operates with a code or the fob. The instructions are inside as is the code. Use the code or fob to lock the door too."

She held up the keys and looked at him, a question on her face.

"You have use of a small car. There's a garage in the basement," he said with a strange smile. "But for short journeys I recommend a taxi. Cairo is not like Atlanta. Imagine New York but with more cars."

She nodded. "And when do I meet John?"

"I don't know. I was told that Mr Graham will call you." He pointed to the telephone on a side table. "Until then, make yourself comfortable. There is food in the refrigerator and cupboards."

She thanked him and was surprised that he didn't look like he expected a tip. She gave him a few notes anyway. Once alone, she hunted through the cupboards and was delighted to find a Lavazza coffee machine. She plugged it in, made a drink and settled down in her temporary home with the pack of documents.

She quickly sussed the door locking system, changed the code and reset the fob. Then she tested it, locking the door with the code and unlocking it with the fob on the outside. Inside, turning the door handle unlocked it.

After resetting the lock with the fob, she tested out the multiple jet shower, then lay on the bed in a luxury bathrobe.

Two weeks, she thought. I'm going to enjoy this.

Despite the great coffee, sleep came quickly and it was late morning when she awoke with a start. She checked the landline phone for a ringtone and hoped she hadn't been woken by its ring.

The pack she'd been given included the LEGAT's office number so she called it and asked for John Graham and apologized in case she'd missed his call.

His secretary said he hadn't called and had been in meetings all morning. She thought he would be tied up for some time.

Charlie waited another two hours and called again. This time the secretary sounded cross at the imposition. "He'll call you when he's free," the woman said. "No rush. I suggest you let me have your cell phone number and explore the city."

No rush? Charlie put the phone down with frustration. She just wanted to get going.

The last time Vanessa had heard from Alex was when he'd sent a text saying he'd arrived and she could join him in their favourite hotel. She knew he'd gone to meet a stranger and warned against it. But Alex had been too intrigued and too headstrong. She also knew that he was a terrible communicator. Although she never mentioned it, she figured he was somewhere on the spectrum because of his tunnel vision, his ability with numbers,

90

and his social awkwardness. He often forgot to message or call her, but this was different.

Arriving in Cairo x, was all he'd texted and nothing since.

He also hadn't picked up when she'd phoned him, and that had worried her.

I'm just being foolish, she admonished herself. He's ignored me before and I'll probably find him in the pool at the hotel, oblivious of my concerns.

But he wasn't at the hotel, nor had he checked in.

Vanessa couldn't find him at any of the main hotels she rang, and that's when her worry turned to serious anxiety. She called his number again and left yet another message.

"Alex, call me back straight away. Whatever you are doing, let me know you're all right."

Another hour later she called the Cairo police and reported Alex as a missing person.

After providing his description and what she knew, she ended the call feeling no less concerned. Would the police investigate or was that just a form-filling exercise? She feared the latter.

And so she jumped on the overnight train to Cairo and as the train pulled into Ramses Station, she called the Marriott hotel again. He still hadn't checked in.

From the station she caught a taxi to the British Embassy.

It was a single storey property that looked more like a bank than an embassy although the royal crest above the black door, gave her some confidence.

The speed with which an official saw her was also a relief, and despite his relaxed demeanour, Vanessa sensed that things would happen.

"Have you spoken to his family?" the official asked.

"No. I don't want to worry his mother—not until..."

91

He tilted his head. "I understand. Don't worry. It's early days and there may be a simple explanation for his lack of communication."

She was going to speak but he raised his hand.

"But that doesn't mean we won't get moving on this. As soon as I leave this room, I'll call the Egyptian authorities." He nodded reassurance. "Don't worry. The police will take this seriously once I've stirred things up a little."

SIXTEEN

Alex was forced into a chair and chained to it. A stern-looking man sat across a table from him. There was nothing else in the room except for the two guards, now out of sight, directly behind him. There was nothing on the table and no visible recording equipment.

The man raised his chin, stretching his neck. "I am Detective Shafik," he said in clear, though flat, English. "You murdered a man in apartment five, J block on Eza Street."

"No, sir," Alex said trying to sound calmer than he felt. "I did not kill anyone."

"You are Alex MacLure, British, and working as an archaeologist on behalf of Macquarie University, Australia. Here on a one-year permit with three months left."

Although it was a statement rather than a question, Alex responded, "Yes, sir."

"Why did you kill the man in the apartment?"

"I did not."

"Who was he?"

"I don't know."

Detective Shafik inclined his head and Alex yelped as a rubber baton struck his arm.

"Who was he?"

"Honestly I don't know."

Shafik inclined his head and Alex was struck again.

"Please listen to me first." Alex took a shuddering breath. "Let me tell you what happened."

Shafik said, "You'll answer my questions, Mr MacLure."

"I'd like to call the embassy."

"All right."

Alex went lightheaded with excitement. "I can make a call?"

"No." Shafik glared. "Tell me what happened."

Alex composed himself, closed his eyes and tried to think clearly. He continued: "I had a phone call in the middle of the night from someone who said their life was in danger."

"Why call you?"

"I don't know. I agreed to meet him."

"A man?"

"Yes."

"What was his name?"

"I don't know."

"The dead man who spoke to you—how do you know him?"

"I don't."

"So you went to meet a stranger on a whim?"

Alex shook his head. How could he explain? "Look, I bought a bag of apples from the shop at the top of the road. I haven't got a receipt but the shop owner may remember me being there. Maybe he can confirm the time and you'll know I couldn't have murdered that chap. Someone must have known about the murder—what?—ten or fifteen minutes earlier? Long enough for your men to drive to the street and find me."

"Enough of telling me my job! Why did you go there?"

"Like I said, I don't know. Because he asked me to."

"I don't believe you."

"It's true."

Shafik nodded and Alex received a blow to the back of the skull. His eyes watered.

"I went there because I got a message."

"You dropped what you were doing in the middle of the night and travelled from Deir Mawas to Cairo to visit a man who told you someone was out to kill him."

"Yes."

Alex realized that the German-sounding guy had actually said his life was in danger. Which didn't necessarily mean someone would kill him. But it was a likely assumption.

"Or you were told to kill the man."

"I'm not a killer."

"Anyone can be a killer, Mr MacLure."

Alex shook his head.

"Who is the dead man?"

Alex shook his head.

"Tell me something and I will let you make that phone call."

"I was told to meet him at the Cairo Tower. Only he didn't show. He left me a note on a napkin."

"What did the note say?"

"It was in code—a code that I know from my research."

"And he knew it?"

"I'm published. I've explained how the code works... it's hidden—"

"What did the note say?"

"EZA."

"And from that you expect me to believe you found his apartment."

"Yes."

For that he received an unexpected whack. Alex felt moisture on his cheeks. Tears dripped onto his lap.

"Yes," he said again quietly. "It was because he'd said Black and Agent J. I realized it was block J and the MI Black was too big a coincidence. Men in Black."

"And you just went inside the apartment?"

"The door was open."

"You didn't kill the man and you don't know his name?"

"No."

Shafik raised his head and two arms lifted Alex to his feet.

"Take him back. Perhaps he'll remember more next time we talk."

Wills shuffled over and they circled the cell together.

"You OK?" the Canadian asked.

"He didn't listen."

"But you weren't beaten?"

"Not too badly. Not as bad as some I've seen."

"Did he offer you a phone call?"

"Yes."

"That's the reward for a confession. Of course it'll do you no good once you do confess."

"I'm innocent."

"Oh yes, I forgot."

The rest of the day became a blur of bodies moving through the clammy, smelly cell. Round and round. The monotony was only broken by the prayers, the arrival of inmates and removal of others for interrogation.

The fourth of the five calls to prayer had already passed when eighteen was called. Wills nodded and smiled like it was his time to leave the hell hole.

"Good luck," Alex muttered as the Canadian was pushed into the arms of the guards.

Alex realized what was happening just in time. He pushed as close to the bars as he could and then the claxon sounded. Bread was coming.

Chunks were passed through, snatched up and then the men moved, shoved so that the person behind could reach the food.

Alex got to the bars early. He took one chunk for himself, smuggled it under his shirt, managed to squirm around and got a second.

The furore was over as quickly as it had begun and Alex turned his back on the crowd and took a mouthful.

A jolt in his back made him move away. Then a second, harder push made him turn. Two skinny men glared at him.

There was another man behind them. Alex recognized him as having arrived only a few hours ago. He was number thirty-two and his shirt looked clean and pressed. He was also plump and without the exhausted eyes of the other inmates.

"Please," Thirty-two said. He made a welcoming gesture with his hands. "Nice to meet you, my friend."

Alex said nothing.

The skinny men had moved either side of him and one poked him in the ribs.

"Hey!"

At this point, Alex noticed that other inmates had moved away. They continued their shuffling ritual but there was a clear boundary two paces beyond Thirty-two.

The plump man smiled and made the same gesture with his hands. "Let us break bread together."

"Share bread?"

The disarming smile again. "Your bread."

Alex clutched his chunk of bread harder. "Another time," he said.

The plump man shrugged and stepped closer. "I understand," he said quietly.

A blur of movement and Alex felt a sharp pain in his neck. The three men backed away and were lost in the melee.

Alex had his hand to his neck. It stung like hell. He looked at his fingers with horror. They were wet with blood.

SEVENTEEN

Charlie had returned to the apartment when she got the call from Graham's secretary.

"He will see you soon," the woman said. A car will pick you up in ten minutes.

Twenty minutes later, Charlie was sitting outside an office which had SSA John Graham's nameplate on the door.

The officious secretary hadn't smiled. She'd simply looked up and told Charlie to wait. And wait she did. Another half an hour ticked by.

Finally, Miss Personality answered a call and said, "You can go in now."

Charlie opened the door and walked into Graham's large office. He flashed a warm smile.

"Welcome to Cairo," he said, his voice softer and more charming than she'd come to expect, partly from his reputation and partly because of the ice-cold secretary.

"Thanks for letting me come," she said accepting his handshake and taking a sofa.

"I apologize for making you wait." He sat opposite and raised his hands like he was saying *what can you do?* "Always a lot going on. Meetings, paperwork, more meetings. This job is ninety per cent bureaucracy."

She nodded. "And the other ten per cent?"

"Politics." He smiled again. "How are you feeling? Jetlagged?"

"I'm fine and had a nice afternoon as a tourist."

"The pyramids?"

"And the Egyptian Museum."

"Good," he said. "Again, sorry for keeping you waiting, I had to take some calls about a missing Brit. Anyway, you must been keen to get on."

"I am."

"Tell me about your case."

She figured he must know the details, but humoured him anyway. When she finished she repeated, "Thanks for letting me come."

Again he made the hand gesture like he had no choice. "I've enough to do," he said. "However, I will insist—ask—that you keep me informed of any developments."

Charlie nodded.

He said, "How's the apartment."

"Great."

"You can get most of the channels on the TV. Should feel like home from home."

She cleared her throat. "With respect, sir, I'm not intending to watch much TV. I'd like to meet the homicide detective—"

"It's the Murder Division here, Charlie. The guy you want is called Shafik. I've requested you get access and now it's just a matter of time."

"A matter of time?"

"Waiting. It's part of the game, I'm afraid. You'll get access, but in their time."

She shook her head, her heart pounding with pent up frustration. "Sir, we may not have much time."

Alex touched the cut on his neck again. Yes, it was bleeding, but it was just a nick.

With his back to the wall, he ate his bread. The majority was stale and the fresh part had become squashed.

He looked for Thirty-two and saw a few men splitting their bread and handing it to the plump man.

Thirty minutes later, Wills came back. He hobbled in and Alex saw that each step caused him pain.

"They beat the soles of my—Jesus, what happened?"

"A guy wanted my bread," Alex said.

He turned his back on the group and pulled the chunk from beneath his shirt.

"I saved you some."

The Canadian's eyes bulged with gratitude. "Thank you," he said, cramming a handful into his mouth. "But next time you're better off giving it to the other man."

"But…"

"I'll explain later," Wills said.

They moved around the cell with Alex providing support until Wills said the pain had eased.

The bell sounded, the Muslims prayed and then an hour or so later everyone settled for the night.

Wills whispered, "I'm going to Qena. If they don't kill me in here first."

Alex looked at the Canadian. "There's always hope."

Wills scoffed. "Some people really think like that. Life is all raindrops on roses and whiskers on kittens."

"I'm just saying—"

"Listen. This is only your second night. After a few more, your spirit will be broken. That or your bones."

"But I'm innocent."

"Doesn't matter. Just listen to me."

Alex held his tongue.

Wills said, "The longest I'm aware of anyone lasting down here is about thirty days. And on the other side is most likely Qena. In case I don't make it I want to prepare you for what's to come."

"You keep talking about Qena."

"It's hell man. If you want to survive Qena then you should learn to keep your mouth shut. Don't tell anyone your name or your crime or anything personal."

"Like you said when we first spoke."

"Yeah, I was stupid. A white face and ten days suddenly seemed a long time. But it wasn't."

"OK," Alex said.

"There will be a cell boss. You know Thirty-two, the fat guy. Like him but worse. There'll be sixty or seventy in a cell not much bigger than this. Here we have space compared to there. If you're unlucky you'll find yourself in the shitter. Or worse. Disrespect anyone and they'll use a razor blade on you like Thirty-two did today. First time it'll just be a cut. Second time... well, there won't be a third time."

Alex shook his head in disbelief. How did he get here?

Wills said, "The cell boss will control the food and the drugs—yeah, apparently the guards will sell you drugs."

"Where does the money come from?"

"Family. They can visit and bring food. That's the only food that goes in. No visitor and you either starve or accept charity. One good thing though, there's air in Qena prison. They have windows and they're kept open. Which is also a bad thing in winter because it can get very cold."

"Sodomy is also a crime. Which is another good thing, right? However remember the cell boss is in with the guards. So the advice is spot the cell boss early on and keep well away from him. Being white won't help though."

The Canadian went quiet for a while and Alex wondered if he was imagining himself in Qena, confronted by a cell boss.

They didn't talk for a while. Then Alex said, "Who used to say raindrops on roses and whiskers on kittens?"

"My sister." He stared into the distance. "It's from *The Sound of Music*."

"You miss your family."

"I have regrets."

Alex waited a while and said, "What happened?"

"Drug dealing. Egypt was easy money plus I'd already been in trouble back home. My sister tried to sort me out but I guess I couldn't take her rose-tinted view of the world." He shrugged. "Yeah, so I am guilty. I got in with a Russian and made a lot of bucks. Also had access to the good stuff."

"And you can't confess? But if you're going to Qena anyway, Wills…"

"Charles Williams," the Canadian said and held out his hand.

"Not Wills?"

"I prefer Charles, but it's not a cool name for a drug dealer, right?"

"You didn't answer my question."

Williams's eyes looked hollow and desperate. "The Russians… The cops want me to give up the mob. I do that and I'm dead. At least Qena delays things. At least there's a chance that we'll get another new president that will delight our Egyptian friends and I'll get parole."

"There you go," Alex said. "There is hope."

Williams snorted. "Do something for me?"

"Yes."

"If you get out, would you write my sister? Would you remember if I told you what to write?"

"Yes," Alex said again.

And so Williams dictated a letter to his sister, Melissa in Ottawa, Canada.

EIGHTEEN

The morning began in the same way as every day: toilet, prayer, bread.

Alex and Williams avoided the fat man and his cronies and circled the cell. Men came and went. Two more bells and two more prayers followed. And then the guards called "Twelve" again.

Alex was manhandled back to the same interrogation room as before. The same hard-looking Arab sat opposite him. Behind him were the guards with their punishment sticks.

"Tell me what happened," Shafik said.

Alex began and told the same story. The detective challenged him after every sentence and Alex tried his best to be clear and concise. He took a blow to the neck and watched the room swim.

"You're tired," Shafik said.

"Yes."

"You haven't slept?"

"No."

"Tell me the truth and you can have a comfortable bed. You can sleep." He reached below the table and retrieved a bottle of water. Opening it slowly, he proceeded to take a long drink.

Alex watched, his eyes bulging.

When Shafik finished, he slid the bottle across the table. Despite the manacles, Alex managed to pick it up and drink hungrily.

Shafik smiled.

"Who was the man in the apartment?"

"Black?" Alex said, but as the words came out he knew it wasn't. He quickly added, "But whoever it was wasn't the man on the phone. The dead man looked Arabic."

"And the man on the phone?"

"He spoke English well, but I think he was probably German."

"Why did you kill him?"

"The man on the phone?"

"The man in the apartment."

Despite his exhaustion Alex had spent his lucid moments trying to understand the problem.

"I couldn't have killed him."

For that, he received a blow to his left ear. He felt wetness on his neck and hoped it was from the cut rather than a new one from his ear.

He took a shuddering breath.

"Please, I can explain," he said.

Shafik looked at the guards and shook his head.

"Go ahead," he said, "but any nonsense and you *will* be hit."

"Firstly," Alex said, focusing hard, "there wasn't any blood on my clothes. If I'd slit that man's throat I would have been covered with blood. Wouldn't I?"

The guards should have taken his clothes when he came in, for testing. The fact they hadn't had seemed like a positive thing. Now he worried it was merely incompetence.

Shafik looked like he was thinking and maybe realizing their mistake.

And then Alex had an epiphany. Had he been set up? Was the German who rang him luring him to the scene of the crime? "The police got there too soon," he said.

"What do you mean?"

"I'd only just arrived. Who called in the murder?"

For that, Alex received a blow to the arm and Shafik barked his disapproval at the guard. Then he stood and hurried out, leaving Alex to stare at the wall behind the detective's empty chair.

Maybe ten minutes passed before Shafik returned. He looked more concerned than stony-faced now. He had a piece of paper in his hand. "Why is your name on this piece of paper, Mr MacLure?"

Alex leaned forward an inch. "Could I see it?"

The detective turned it around and smoothed out the folds. It was A4 with different font sizes. Alex thought it looked like a word cloud.

Shafik pointed to "MacLure". It wasn't central, nor was it particularly large.

"I don't know," Alex said. "Is it linked to Black?

"Who called you?"

"I keep telling you I can't be sure." Alex prepared himself for a blow but nothing came. He continued: "The man on the phone just used the code name Agent J. Agent J was a character from *Men in Black*—the movie. The name on the apartment bell was MI Black. That's how I knew to go up there. Maybe his real surname was Black. He sounded German." Alex realized he was going over the same ground, probably babbling now. He took a calming breath. "I was there only a couple of minutes. I saw the body and then the police charged in. I didn't have a weapon. I didn't have blood on me."

The detective held up a hand.

"Tell me again from the start. From the phone call."

Alex repeated the whole story, trying to be clear although his head swam. He could hear the blood in his ears, like cymbals crashing again and again. Was he not making sense? Maybe the words in his head weren't the words coming out of his mouth? Sleep deprivation did strange things to the mind.

Shafik looked like he was listening intently and, when Alex was finished, the detective rubbed and stretched his neck.

"You can go," he said.

Alex couldn't believe his ears. "What?"

"You can go. I think you are right about the blood, although whoever did it was an expert. I don't think they got any blood on themselves." He nodded at Alex. "Like you, but you aren't a trained killer, are you Mr MacLure?"

"No, sir."

"I also accept your argument about the timing. I have learned that we took twenty minutes to respond to a phone call about a murder happening."

"Do you—" Alex stopped when Shafik glared at him.

"You still don't get to ask questions. And you don't get to investigate this, understand?"

"Yes, sir."

"Go back to the Nefertiti Hotel and your pretty girlfriend, Mr MacLure, and forget all about this." He paused and fixed Alex with bloodshot eyes. "Am I making myself clear?"

"Yes, sir."

The detective nodded at the guards and one second Alex was sitting in cuffs, the next he was standing, a free man. Well almost.

The two guards escorted him upstairs. He was given a towel and soap, and shown to a toilet room with a sink where he cleaned himself up. He also gulped down water until he thought his stomach would burst.

When he came out, they gave him back his personal items, and he was soon outside in the blinding sunlight.

The first thing he did was switch on the phone. There were twenty missed calls from Vanessa, beside herself with worry. She had come to Cairo looking for him and was staying at the Marriott. No one knew where he was and she'd reported his disappearance to the police and British Embassy.

He called her and gave her the briefest of explanations.

"I can't believe it," she kept saying. That and "Thank God!"

"I'm all right," he said. "I need to pick up some fresh clothes and I'll be with you soon—within half an hour. Promise."

She was waiting outside the hotel when he arrived and she hugged him long and hard.

"You stink!" she said.

"Thanks, baby."

"Let's get you cleaned up and you can tell me the details," she said leading the way to the elevators. "If you're up to it, that is?"

"Oh I'm up to it," he said. "The detective doesn't want me to investigate, but I'm involved in this now."

She stopped and shook her head, with concern etched on her face. "Alex—"

He said, "My name appeared in a word cloud."

"So?"

"I read some of the other words on there and I really am involved. There's a mystery here and I need to get to the bottom of it."

NINETEEN

Detective Shafik watched as Alex MacLure left the interrogation room. In a few more minutes the Englishman would be free. He wasn't guilty of the murder, Shafik was certain of it. But he had been in the apartment—effectively broken in. He knew something and was involved, and Shafik wasn't a man who just let things slide. He had a drawer full of unsolved murders, but most could be explained.

Extremists attacking other religious groups was the department's biggest issue, but he tended to pick up the specialist cases, like the slitting of a man's throat in another man's apartment. The apartment was being used by Tomasz Schwartz, a German student studying computer science. But he wasn't the murdered man and he was missing. Neighbours said they'd seen a man answering Schwartz's description climbing down the fire escape about the time the police had received a panicked call.

"A man is in my apartment. I think he's going to kill me!" was the anonymous message.

Schwartz was white-skinned with blond hair. The dead man was Arabic and about ten years older than the student. No, Schwartz had escaped from the Arab and then someone else had come in and killed the first intruder.

The murder had been professional. It took skill to slit a man's throat, and MacLure wasn't the sort. Somehow he'd stumbled across the murder and the bad timing had made him appear guilty. Like he'd said, he didn't have any blood on him. He was right that they should have bagged his clothes and tested them for blood.

Shafik had already made a complaint about it, but it happened so often he knew things were unlikely to improve. Detective work in Egypt was sometimes like having one arm behind your back and a patch over one eye.

The Arab from the apartment was still unidentified. He'd had nothing on him. No phone. No wallet. No ID. But Shafik wasn't thinking about the Arab. There must have been another man. Four in total. There was Schwartz, the man MacLure called Black. There was MacLure himself—the hapless archaeologist. Then the dead man, and the murderer.

Four men.

So who was the murderer?

Witnesses reported nothing useful. People came and went all the time: residents, visitors, doctors, postal workers. There was no CCTV inside or outside.

Shafik had two hopes. The first was that Schwartz would resurface and explain. The second was that MacLure knew something either consciously or subconsciously.

A junior detective knocked on the door and entered.

"She's here, sir."

Shafik looked up and sighed. "What, the American? Already?"

"She's upstairs, waiting."

Special Agent Rebb was looking out of the window at the mosque opposite. Shafik watched her for a moment before opening the office door. She looked small, maybe just over five foot, with short dark hair. She was dressed in a navy blue trouser suit and, from her appearance, he could imagine the letters FBI stencilled on the back.

Shafik knew the FBI's legal attaché, John Graham, an ineffectual man, more concerned with surviving his posting to Egypt than doing any actual work. The man had readily passed the buck to the case agent from Atlanta. But whomever he had to deal with, the Americans would just get in the way.

He took a breath to compose himself and show as little irritation as he could.

"Special Agent Rebb," he said as he entered. He nodded rather than offer her a handshake. "I am Detective Shafik, Murder Division."

She turned and stood in one smooth movement. She's fit and has a pretty face, Shafik couldn't help thinking. Then he immediately admonished himself for the attraction.

"I am to be your liaison here," he said. "I apologize for the formality, but could I see your papers first?"

She handed them over like she had expected it.

He pointed to the chair she'd vacated. "Please take a seat, Special Agent."

"Call me Charlie."

He sat opposite and read through the paperwork. After a while he looked up. "You have a gun, I see."

"Yes."

"Please don't use it unless—"

"I've already had a lecture," she said, cutting him off.

"I see. But whether you've heard it before or not, my own rules are that you don't go off on your own and you don't carry the gun unless with me."

She said nothing.

"You agree to my rules now or this meeting is over."

"I agree."

"Good." He handed her back the papers. "And did you have a lecture about our culture? This is not the US, you will appreciate."

"I know that it's predominantly a Muslim country—"

"The state of women's rights in my country has never been so poor. We have women police officers but they are in the minority. You should be prepared for prejudice and disrespect. Do you understand?"

"Yes."

"Then why are you dressed like an FBI agent, Miss Rebb?" He saw sharp eyes glare back and expected a bitter retort, but when she spoke she was calm.

She said, "What do you suggest, Detective?"

"As a minimum, a head-scarf. Better still, you should wear looser fitting clothes."

She nodded. "I'll get it sorted as soon as we're done."

"Good."

"You know why I'm here?"

He wanted to say something like "Because my government wants to show an olive branch to your stupid president", but he didn't. Instead, he forced a smile. "You think one of our cases looks similar to yours, I am led to believe."

"The body at the Abusir temple. The cut to the chest that doesn't pierce the heart and a henna tattoo over the heart. We have a serial killer believed to be a man called Tony Zart." She handed Shafik a photograph before adding a description: "Caucasian male aged forty-one.

Height six-four. Weight estimated as between two hundred pounds and two-twenty."

"A large man," Shafik said. "I see no distinguishing marks on his face."

"Right, and we think he's changed his appearance as well as his name."

If it weren't for the tattoo on the victim's chest, Shafik would have thought this was a waste of time. He knew they had no evidence of Zart entering the country but the MO suggested it was the American serial killer.

He said, "How many did you say he had murdered?"

"I didn't, but the number is at least thirty-six of which we've uncovered sixteen."

"Thirty-six," he said, raising an eyebrow. "Similar to your Ted Bundy then."

"That's what Bundy was convicted of. We're sure there were many more."

"Of course, there are always many more. I was involved in the Al-Tourbini case. He raped and tortured boys mostly and threw their bodies from trains. I will admit to you that I still have nightmares about it. There are sick people in the world, Special Agent Rebb."

She nodded, and her eyes betrayed that she had been affected by their evil in the same way.

He said, "This man is different, no? He does not kill children or women like most. He kills young men, but not for sexual reasons it would seem."

"Correct, he appears to show them respect." She handed him a piece of paper—a photocopy—with initials and symbols. "These are the marks he has left on the bodies. The initials highlighted are those we can identify."

"In order—oldest first? Does this mean you haven't identified the last two—the two most recent murders?"

"We haven't. We've also tried to spot a pattern and can't see one. He may be speeding up, because the last two were within forty days of the third from the bottom."

"MS," he said.

"Mark Simmons. He was the first we found this time, and we think Zart left the country around the time Simmons's body was uncovered. Which means—"

"—That Zart killed two in just over a month. This was three months ago, no? And we have just one body."

She repeated what he'd said earlier and it made him smile. "Of course, there are always many more."

He said, "If he's not speeding up, then he's killed at least six since he's been here."

"At least."

"If this is your man. If this is the Surgeon."

"Everything suggests it is."

"Except yours were all buried. My victim was left in the open in a temple."

She said, "A deviation."

Shafik nodded as he studied the photograph of the man. Zart didn't look like a monster, but then they rarely did.

She said, "Could I see the file?"

Five minutes later she had a murder file in her hands. He figured she'd have already seen the photograph of the victim. It had been in the papers. But there were many more here.

Shafik kept the notes and read the Arabic report. "The victim was five ten and estimated as between twenty-three and twenty-six years old. He had the one-inch cut between his fourth and fifth ribs, just to the left of the sternum. He was naked, eyes closed, arms by his side. Unlike your cases, he was not Caucasian. We think he may be a local man. The tattoo is unusual—"

She held a close-up photo of the tattoo. "Unusual because you can still see it. On our victims, we think the Surgeon had washed the bodies which removed the tattoo."

Shafik shook his head, "No, I mean unusual because of the hieroglyph. It appears to be the vulture—possibly meaning the goddess Nekhbet representing protection. However if it's from the New Kingdom it could be Nephthys or her sister Isis. Both goddesses could be vultures and associated with death. We can't know for certain because the tattoo is incomplete."

"He was interrupted."

Shafik looked at the FBI lady. She was quick. Maybe American's weren't all dumb and lazy.

She said, "My guess, he was preparing the body for a ritual. The tattooing is part of that. How long had the victim been dead?"

Good question. "Maybe three days, maybe less," Shafik said. "It's hard to say because the body may have been kept cool."

"Zart—the Surgeon—kills them before the tattooing. That's could be something new. He placed the body in the temple and started tattooing the chest but was disturbed. Rather than be caught, he fled and left the body." She raised her eyebrows. "What do you think? Zart didn't have time to finish and clean the body?"

"I think the location must be important. If this is your Surgeon, then we should consider what it means. Why he is doing this."

She said, "You still aren't convinced that this is my killer?"

He shrugged. Professionally, he would like it to be. Practically, the last thing he needed was a serial killer. The backlog of work was bad enough as it was.

He was about to comment when his phone rang.

"Excuse me," he said, answering it. He listened and thanked the caller then put the phone away.

She was looking at him.

"You asked whether I am convinced. What would convince me is another body." He swallowed. "Well, Special Agent Rebb we appear to have our evidence. They have just found two more."

TWENTY

Vanessa's face remained stern. They sat in the luxury hotel room overlooking the Nile drinking tea. Alex had showered and scrubbed and felt human again. He had told her the complete bizarre story while she just listened.

At the end she said, "So what was on the paper, apart from your name?"

"There were loads of words and the font was mostly small and I only saw it for a few seconds."

"You're making excuses."

"I saw British Museum and Amarna Letters, all of which relate to me."

She nodded.

"I also saw Queen's shaft items, Masons, Great Pyramid and flood."

"Flood?"

He shrugged. "That's what it said. No explanation, just the word. Along with my name there were others. I recognized a famous local Egyptologist called Dr Hawass, but most interesting to me was the term Keeper of Secrets."

She frowned.

"The Keeper of Secrets," he repeated, thinking she'd recognize the title. "It's one of the things I translated from the clay tablets. It's one of the things I don't understand."

"Who is the Keeper of Secrets?"

He shrugged. "I have no idea."

"So what next?"

"That holiday you offered."

She looked guilty.

"What?" he asked.

"I can't go yet. I was meaning in a few weeks or so. I have some deadlines to meet before that." She reached out and held his hand. "Sorry, Alex."

"It's fine. I just need to get away. I can't be here, not after what I've been through."

"All right," she said. "Go home for a while—like you planned—and as soon as I can get away, I will. Then we'll have that holiday. We'll go wherever you want. I'll even do sun worshipping by the pool if that's what you fancy."

In the back of the car, Shafik handed Charlie a scarf. "You don't have to cover your hair, but it would be respectful if you did."

She thought about it for a second before deciding to comply. Better to have this man as an ally. Without his support she may as well get back on the plane.

The scarf was black and didn't suit her but she tied it over her head and was sure she looked like an old washerwoman.

She'd tried to make conversation in the car but he was either preoccupied or indifferent. She'd yet to see any sense of the real man behind his stony expression.

John Graham, the FBI LEGAT, had warned her about Shafik. He'd said the detective was no more or less misogynistic than any of the others but he especially didn't like to share information. Graham had told her she'd have to wheedle information out of the man and keep a close eye on him.

Charlie watched the traffic go by. Graham had been charming but he was a consummate politician. He'd been in Egypt for more than the standard three years, so despite his complaints he must enjoy the job. And yet he'd been happy for her to come, happy for her to be the liaison. Was he overworked or lazy? He seemed one big contradiction. Despite his apparent warmth she'd decide to treat him with caution.

Shafik, on the other hand, was as straight as they came. There was no warmth there whatsoever.

"Where are we?" she asked as the car stopped. They were still within Cairo but she had no sense of the distance or direction they'd travelled in.

Shafik said, "When we get out together, I want you to stay close."

"I can take care of myself."

"I've no doubt that you can, Miss Rebb, but I don't want you to get into any kind of trouble."

They got out by a tenement block with a police cordon ribbon around the door, closing off the pavement. There were police cars and men with guns all around.

Shafik didn't show any ID as he ducked under the cordon and marched to the entrance. Inside, there were more police. One of them pointed to the rear and the detective continued.

There was a flight of stone steps leading to a basement. The light was dim, and Charlie saw thick dust swirl in the warm air. She smelled soap and oil.

Another plain-clothed man met them at the foot of the steps. He and Shafik exchanged rapid words and they were led into a dark recess behind a bank of washing machines that were old and dented like they'd been rescued from a rubbish tip.

Two naked men lay in a pool of congealed blood.

Shafik took a quick look and stepped back so that Charlie could see.

She bent down, studied the scene, stood and looked at Shafik.

He nodded upwards, like he was saying, "Let's go outside."

She nodded back. The smell of the bodies was no longer masked by the washing and it cloyed, dry and sticky in her throat.

Upstairs, Shafik said, "A mistake."

"Yes," she said.

"These men were executed, stabbed in the heart. Not the same MO."

"I agree."

He looked at her and she wondered if he didn't care whether she agreed or not, his explanation merely a courtesy.

He said, "I said I needed more bodies to be convinced that your serial killer is here. This is not the evidence."

"Doesn't mean he's not here. It took us three years between finding the body dump in the Panola Mountains and the Church of the Risen Christ in Atlanta."

He looked at her. "You can't stay here three years, Special Agent Rebb."

"No," she said. "But we have more to go on now. We know who he is. We know he's using tattoos—some of which are hieroglyphs. And we know he abducts young men—probably less than two weeks apart."

He shook his head and opened the car door. "We know nothing," he said.

She climbed in beside him. "Then we start by looking at missing-person files."

TWENTY-ONE

Alex called Professor Steele, his dig supervisor, and let him know what had happened. The professor was very understanding and even said he'd arrange for Alex's things to be sent to the UK if needed. There was no need to return to Amarna.

Alex booked a flight home for the following day, exchanged messages with his mother and arranged to be picked up from the airport.

He also wrote the letter to Charles Williams's sister Melissa. He said everything that the prisoner had asked him to write: an apology for not listening to her advice, and for screwing up again. He also reminisced about good times they'd had, simple things like playing in the park or solving puzzles together.

It was basically a good-bye letter and Alex was touched by the sentiment. However, by the time he'd finished what Williams had requested, Alex had an idea. He wrote a second letter from himself. The Canadian hadn't wanted to describe the awful conditions in the prison, but Alex provided some detail. He also said that her brother expected to be sent to Qena prison, which was worse. He explained that Charles was holding out because of the Russian mob. If only he could provide names then he would be treated more leniently.

However, his dilemma was that such a disclosure was likely to get him killed.

Alex wrote: **Perhaps you can find a way to protect him. I understand you've been campaigning for his release, but extradition to Canada in exchange for what they want might work.**

At the end of the letter, Alex provided his contact details in case there was any way he could help.

With his remaining time in Egypt, he decided to enjoy his stay in the luxury hotel. An outdoor pool seemed the perfect way to relax. After lying in the sun, he swam fifty lengths, although he was conscious that his stamina in the water wasn't what it had once been. He rested after each ten lengths. Only a few years ago he'd have swum all fifty without a break.

Afterwards, he got in the elevator and went back to his room. As he pressed the button, another person scooted inside. The guy wore an Arab head-scarf, like he was heading for a sandstorm. If he hadn't immediately turned away, Alex might have worried.

The man punched a button and just stood close to the door. The lift went up a single floor and stopped. As the doors started to open, the guy spoke in a hushed voice.

"Lobby. Third table, facing window. In thirty minutes." And then he was gone.

"Are you OK?" Vanessa asked when she opened the bedroom door. "You look pale."

He told her what had happened.

"We need to get out," she said. "We should pack and go. Now." She was already moving to the wardrobe and grabbing a bag.

"No," he said. "It'll be fine. I need to know what's going on."

"But what if—?"

"It's not the killer from J block, if that's what you're thinking. The guy in the lift was nervous. Clandestine. He wants to talk."

"Then I'm coming too."

Alex shook his head. "It would be better if you could watch. Video it if you can. But don't let him see you. Don't scare him off."

So that's what they agreed, and when he sat at the third table from the window he could just about see her reflection. She was reading a newspaper at a table behind him.

Half an hour passed. Ten minutes later, Alex heard a buzzing sound. It was coming from under the table. He looked and found an old-style mobile phone taped to the underside.

He answered. "Hello?"

"Now I want you to go outside and walk—"

"No," Alex interrupted.

"No, what?"

"I'm not going on any more wild goose chases. We talk now or not at all."

The other man said nothing for a moment, his breathing harsh.

Alex said, "I'm putting the phone down now."

"Can you be overheard?" the man said.

"No."

"Fine. We'll do it your way but no more questions."

"Tell me one thing. Are you Black?" Alex asked despite realizing the voice sounded different.

"No. His real name is Schwartz. Tomasz Schwartz. I'm his friend."

Alex got it. Schwartz, German for black. He asked, "And what's your name?"

"Stop asking—"

125

"What's your name?" Alex demanded.

"Brown. Call me Brown." Alex heard the frustration in the man's voice. The guy said, "Now listen."

"Is that your real name?"

"Of course not."

"What happened to your friend? I went to his apartment and—"

"I know. Tomasz got out just in time."

"Who was the dead guy? And the killer?"

"Stop asking questions. We need to keep this short. Ready?"

"For what?"

"Tomasz has developed an AI program that scans internet traffic for messages."

Alex had the sense that the guy was now reading from a script. He wanted to ask more questions but held his tongue for now.

Brown said, "The darker the web, the more importance the program allocates. It sifts through billions of snippets of information and compares them. Basically, it's looking for patterns." He paused. "The starting point is a subject. Tomasz thought the software could be used by intelligence agencies to identify terrorist plans but he wanted to prove it first. He wanted to show it could work so he set it running with the phrase 'pyramid conspiracy'. We know there are conspiracy theories about the pyramids so thought it would be fun."

Alex suddenly got it. "The output is a word cloud, isn't it? I saw it."

Brown seemed thrown for a second by the interruption. "Yes," he said after a breath. "It produces a series of word clouds. It refines and refines."

"My name was on one."

"Yes," he said, irritation edging his voice. "Let me talk, please. The first few word clouds made no sense and then Tomasz saw your name and read your research. We knew this was something different. Not the ordinary conspiracy stuff. But Tomasz realized someone was hacking into his program. Someone had detected his spiders and was tracing them back. He contacted you, but they got to him first."

"Did you call the police?"

"Tomasz did. He got out when he saw the first man arrive. He went down the fire escape, but a camera recorded what happened next. A man broke in and started to search the apartment. He went through everything. He was going to take Tomasz's laptop and found the early word cloud results. He made a phone call and said what he'd found."

"Was he an Arab?"

"I would guess so."

"And then another man came in," Alex prompted.

"This was a big white guy, wearing a white coat. Tomasz said he was scary. He only appeared briefly, grabbing the Arab from behind and slitting his throat. Tomasz said he was a professional. Quick and clean. No blood on that white coat. An assassin probably looking for Tomasz."

Alex nodded to himself. It made sense. "And you think he's after you now?"

"Probably."

"Where do you fit in?"

"I'm just his friend. I'm the conspiracy nut who suggested he type in 'pyramid conspiracy'. It's my fault." His voice quavered now and Alex had the sense of a very nervous young man, probably a student.

"Why tell me?"

"Because Tomasz trusted you."

"How do I get in touch?"

"Promise that you will destroy the SIM card and throw the phone away as soon as we end this."

"OK."

"Get the Telegram app." He gave Alex a username to register with. "I'll be in touch through that."

"And what's your username?"

But before Alex finished the sentence, he was already listening to dead air.

"You're crazy," Vanessa said after Alex updated her.

"What do you mean?"

"You've just spent three days in a stinking prison because some stranger suggested you meet. And now you're talking to another stranger and getting involved again."

Alex stared out of the window for a couple of beats. "But this is about me," he said. However his tone didn't even convince himself.

"They're making it about you," Vanessa said. She put her arms around him. "You've been through a hell of a lot in the last few days and you need a break. The last thing you need is getting involved with some conspiracy nut and a murderer."

He nodded and kissed her. "You're right. I'll go home and wind down, and after you join me we'll take that holiday."

And so Alex put the conversation with Brown out of his mind and focused on buying a gift for his mother and his brother, Andrew.

Over six thousand miles west and a day later, the man known as the Master checked the calendar. There wasn't much time left but they had never got this far before.

He realized that the move to Egypt may have been premature, but the Surgeon's access to young men had been greatly increased. There had been a much greater risk of discovery in the US despite the Surgeon's talent for identifying, tracking and abducting his targets.

On the other hand, Egypt created its own problems. The Surgeon wasn't a typical acolyte. His view of the world was a warped one and he enjoyed the killing. For the Master it was a necessary evil. For the Surgeon it was a delight.

He'd been foolish with the signature. He'd been careless with the bodies. And there was a frisson of madness or uncontrollability in his nature.

The Master had his organization set everything up. All the Surgeon needed to do was stay out of trouble and keep testing. The latest research, the latest theory on the symbols, had been messaged to the Surgeon. Perhaps one of them was the sign, the mark.

And if it wasn't then maybe Alex MacLure could find it. Schwartz's AI program had found him and the student was now safely ensconced in the place built for the Surgeon.

The Master picked up his treasured papers and read the passages of the scriptures that had driven him for half of his life. The truth was just out of reach. Maybe, until now.

Thirty minutes later, the Surgeon checked in.

Symbol eighty had no effect, the message read.

You have someone in play? the Master asked, wanting to know whether the Surgeon had picked up anyone else yet.

Not yet. Two targets identified. Other distractions.

What?

The student is being awkward.

Do we need him?

No.

Then you have another subject.

A pause from the Surgeon, before: **Yes Master.**

What else?

MacLure. He's left the country. Gone to the UK. Can we try Hawass?

The Master groaned inwardly. **Not Hawass,** he replied. They had previously got information that Dr Hawass wouldn't help. Maybe he was involved. Maybe he was too afraid. The Master continued: **Is the FBI agent a problem?**

No. Charlie Rebb from Atlanta. From the TV. This is no different than before.

The Master nodded to himself. Yes, a lone agent in a country like Egypt wouldn't create a problem. But MacLure leaving could be. He typed, **Seti came to prominence in the word cloud.**

I saw. Is it Ansar?

Got to be. Look at MacLure's team. There must be someone else there.

The messages ended and the Master picked up his own notes, taken from cross-checking the early versions of the Bible with other documents from antiquity. Seti, he thought to himself. Of course, the Egyptian god made sense. But did that mean the ancient order—those who wanted to keep the secret—were on to them?

And did MacLure, or someone in his team, know the secret already?

The Second

TWENTY-TWO

Surrey, England

Woking is in the commuter belt of London. Lots of the City crowd, with money but no desire to be city-based, chose the picturesque villages nearby. That's why Alex's father had chosen the area and moved them from Aberdeen.

In the early days, the business had been thriving and his father had an important role. As it turned out, the role was to be the fall guy for years of malpractice.

Alex knew he'd never get over his father's suicide, but it was just one of those dark things that you had to live with. At least the mortgage had been paid off and his mother coped.

Although, for the past six months she'd had Topsy, Alex's dog, to look after as well as his brother, Andrew.

Andrew sat in his wheelchair and played on the Xbox; some shoot 'em-up game that Alex found pointless. At least it made Andrew happy and there were dozens, if not hundreds, of other online gamers he interacted with.

Alex had just come in from walking Topsy when his brother logged off from his game and buzzed his motorized chair around.

Alex smiled at him. The musculature had degenerated more than Alex had appreciated. Knowing isn't the same as seeing it up close. At least he was over his cold and his breathing seemed fine. Andrew's mobility had deteriorated—although he liked to exaggerate it by restricted arm movements. For some reason he found it amusing.

They'd talked about the latest research, and apart from football and gaming it was the only thing that got Andrew excited.

Hope is what drives us, Alex had told himself. Andrew's condition was way beyond any remedy, and yet the hope of a cure kept him going, kept him smiling. The human spirit is an amazing thing—most of the time.

As Alex looked at his little brother, the thought made him consider his own hobby: ancient Egypt. So much they still didn't know. So many mysteries.

Was it the hope of the next big discovery that kept him fascinated?

"What are you thinking about?" Andrew asked as Topsy licked his legs, her tail wagging furiously.

"Have you heard of the *ha* and *ka*? The ancient Egyptians believed in multiple parts of the body. The *ha* was the physical body. The *ka* was the spark of life, the spirit."

Andrew frowned, maybe projecting Alex's thoughts.

"Just looking at you… You have that spark. It's easy to believe there's more to this life."

Andrew stopped frowning. "Of course there is. It's what gets me up in the morning, dummy. The body is just a husk, a vessel for the soul."

Alex felt uncomfortable. He tried to understand what it was like for his brother, tried to empathize, but how could he? Alex was disappointed at swimming only ten lengths at a time, when his brother could barely splash in the water.

"So how's the latest game?" he asked, changing the subject.

"Forget that! We need to talk." Andrew nodded towards the sofa and Alex obediently sat down.

His brother said, "Two things. First off, I need you to stop pussy-footing about around me."

"What—?"

"Stop patronizing me!"

"I don't mean—"

"Stop treating me like I'm different. You of all people can treat me like I'm just the same. I don't need you to be awkward and sensitive."

"I didn't think I was being."

"Well you are. And secondly, it's about time you got off your lardy arse and did something about that conspiracy."

Alex shrugged. He'd told Andrew all about the incidents in Cairo and he'd sworn him to secrecy. The last thing he wanted was for his mother to worry about him. She knew nothing of the murder or jail time. All she knew was that he'd finished his dig early and needed a holiday.

"Like what?"

"The word cloud."

"I promised Vanessa, I wouldn't get involved."

Andrew laughed. "You are involved, dummy."

It was a fair point. He'd tried not to think about it and put it out of his mind like he'd promised but it was impossible. It was a niggle in the back of his brain.

"OK," Alex said. "What about the word cloud?"

"You mentioned the Masons."

"Yeah, everyone knows they trace themselves back to the pyramid builders. Nothing too surprising there."

Andrew smiled. "What do you think I do all day?"

Alex didn't answer. He suspected that watching TV and playing computer games wasn't the answer his brother was driving for.

"I use my mind, Alex. I can think, you know?"

"OK."

Then Andrew laughed. "Actually I know what you were thinking—I play computer games—and you're almost right. I also communicate with hundreds of gamers. Getting an answer from them is faster than browsing the internet. You know that the big search engines like Google filter and prioritize based on their own algorithms? You don't get a true series of responses from them."

"Unlike when you ask random people?"

"Fair point." Andrew laughed again. "Truth is subjective."

"You were going to tell me about the Masons…"

"Oh right. There's all this conspiracy stuff around the US and Masons." Andrew scrolled through something on his gaming device. "On the reverse of the Great Seal of the United States are an eye and a pyramid. Roosevelt put it on the dollar bill in the 1930s."

"Everyone knows about the pyramid on the dollar."

"Know what the inscription is above it?"

"No."

Andrew leaned forward. "Annuit Coeptis."

"Latin? What does it mean?"

"He favours our undertakings."

Alex shook his head, not getting his brother's point.

"Undertakings," Andrew said with heavy meaning. "Undertakers. Masons believe that God favours them as undertakers."

Alex scoffed.

"Seriously!" Andrew said. "Masons become funeral directors by first directing whose body will be at the funeral, and where that life will be taken. If a life is taken close to the northern 33rd Parallel, this fits with the Masons' demonic mythology in which they demonstrate their worldly power by spilling human blood at a predetermined location."

Alex scoffed again. "It's gobbledegook."

"The 33rd Parallel. Know where that is? Egypt. In the US, know where Cairo is?" Andrew didn't wait for a response. "Below Atlanta on the 33rd parallel."

"I still don't get—"

"The numbers 3 and 33 have mystical significance." He referenced his screen again. "On the third of March 1933—three, three, thirty-three—the US Federal Reserve Board and the New York Reserve Bank's governor agreed there would be an emergency bank holiday in New York. Then when Roosevelt was inaugurated on the following day he announced a three-day bank holiday. FDR was a member of the Ancient Arabic Order Nobles of the Mystic Shrine, or Shriner. Shriners are 33rd degree Masons."

Andrew pointed to his screen. On it was a symbol.

"It's called *Aoum*, what mystics chant," Andrew said before making the resonating sound. "It's also called the third eye. It's the third force that allows you to see your true self or essence."

137

"Which connects back to Masons?" Alex said unconvinced.

"Yes, but let's go back to the Great Seal. The inscription below the pyramid is *Novus Ordo Seclorum*. It means *The New Order of the Ages*."

"And that relates to Masons?"

"Oh yes," Andrew said with passion. "Take the first and last letters of each inscription: A and S from *Annuit Coeptis*, N and M from *Novus Ordo Seclorum*. Then take the first letter of the middle word, *Ordo*. You get A-S-N-M-O. Ordo means order so, like a cryptic crossword puzzle, reorder those letters."

"M-A-S-O-N," Alex said after a moment. "It's Mason!"

Andrew nodded and grinned. "You may think it's farfetched, but when you join up those letters you can fit the Star of David to them."

TWENTY-THREE

Alex was helping prepare dinner when Andrew called him into the living room.

His brother seemed agitated, and Alex rushed to see him.

"What's up?"

"Got something more for you."

"More about the 33rd parallel? Look, Andrew, I have to tell you it's just conspiracy nonsense."

"Maybe it is, but I've got something that will make your head spin."

Alex sat on the sofa and waited for his brother's explanation.

"Well, you used to work at the British Museum," Andrew said. "There's a connection with Masons."

Alex shook his head, unaware of such a link.

"The items found in one of the mysterious shafts of Khufu's pyramid. Know about it?"

It sounded familiar, although Alex couldn't remember any details.

Andrew said, "Late nineteenth century, two brothers called Dixon poked a metal rod into the northern shaft of the Queen's Chamber and pulled out a metal ball, a hook and a piece of wood. The Dixons allegedly put them in a cigar box and gave the box to the British Museum."

"OK," Alex said, realizing what his brother meant. "The hook was copper. The ball wasn't. It was granite and the equivalent of a ball bearing. Ball bearings would help explain how the pyramid builders could move huge stones with fine precision. Explaining the stone ball was the subject of my first paper."

"Whatever," Andrew said, clearly not impressed. "It's the piece of wood that's important. It was allegedly about five inches long. Made of cedar and broken off, probably due to being pulled through the hole they made. Anyway, it disappeared. And that's convenient, right?"

"Why convenient?"

"Because, unlike the ball and hook, it could have been carbon-dated. Dating it would have dated the pyramids."

Alex nodded. He knew the conspiracy theory that the pyramids were thousands of years older than the official view. Khufu was a pharaoh of the Fourth Dynasty.

"You said this was connected to the Masons."

Andrew said, "Firstly, the Dixons were Masons, and secondly, one of the brothers laid a cigar box under Cleopatra's Needle when it was erected on the Embankment."

Their mother interrupted them with a call for dinner.

"It's nice to hear you boys talking so animatedly," she said when they sat at the table. "Especially for Andrew. It's so good to have you here, Alex. What were you talking about?"

"Ancient Egypt," Alex said.

He was about to say more when Andrew chimed in: "Conspiracy theories."

"Oh, sounds interesting. What in particular?"

"Masons and the British Museum," Andrew said, and he repeated the story about the missing wood.

140

"Sounds like you should spend a day at the museum." She looked at Alex but he suspected she was including Andrew.

"Already sorted," Andrew said. "We're going tomorrow."

Alex frowned. "We are?"

"I've been in touch with the Freemason Hall on Great Queen Street. We've got an appointment with their director of communications. Seems like a nice guy. That's at twelve o'clock tomorrow, so I thought we could visit the British Museum first. Sound OK?"

Alex was stunned for the second time that day. Not only was his brother interested, he had also arranged a trip for them.

"Yeah, sure," he said. "I think I'm looking forward to it."

TWENTY-FOUR

They took the train into Waterloo and then the underground to Tottenham Court Road tube station. Alex felt guilty that he had never thought about wheelchair access before. They were lucky that the tube station had been refurbished and had a lift. Very few other tube stations seemed able to accommodate wheelchairs.

Andrew preferred to use the motor rather than be pushed as they travelled the short distance to Bloomsbury Square.

When they approached the front of the museum, Alex was surprised by how it had changed. Barriers had been erected, directing people to the left. The gate where Old Eddie had sat for decades was now manned by two men. Their black uniforms with high visibility bands made them look more like security guards. Maybe they were.

The barriers took them to a marquee where more security people checked bags. A scanner was waved over Andrew's wheelchair before they were allowed through.

There were steps up to the entrance of the museum and Alex had wondered where the wheelchair access was. And then he saw it: a single wheelchair lift beside the steps. He wondered if it'd always been there; he just hadn't been looking before.

Andrew had been distracted on the train, playing a game on his phone. As they went through the museum foyer, his phone pinged.

"Jesus!" he complained.

"What is it?"

"Some new player keeps messaging me—stupid messages. They don't make sense."

Alex was barely paying attention. He was at the main information desk and asked whether Professor Lloyd—his old boss—was in today.

"Great," he said turning back to Andrew. "She is here... What is it?"

Andrew looked concerned. "That guy I just mentioned just used your name!"

"What? Let me see."

Andrew handed him the phone and he read the series of short messages, some just single words. AM. Tell AM was the first one.

"I thought he meant me," Andrew said, "But the last one says Alex."

Alex read the others. **Open T. Accept me. S.**

He unlocked his phone and opened Telegram. There was an invite waiting. Username: agent_k.

Andrew was looking over his arm. "Agent K. That was Kevin Brown, right? It's your *Men in Black* guy. You didn't have the notifications switched on, numpty!"

"I decided against it." He put the phone in his pocket. "I promised Vanessa I wouldn't get involved."

"You are involved!" Andrew said.

"But—"

"What's the harm in seeing what he has to say?"

Alex hesitated. Would it hurt to just see what the guy had to say? That wouldn't be getting involved, would it?

143

His non-response prompted Andrew to spin his wheelchair. "I'm going no further until you accept that invite!"

"Fine." Alex pulled out the phone, unlocked it and accepted agent_k's request. A message immediately popped up.

Latest from the AI: Seti has suddenly jumped in prominence. Also FBI and the name Rebb.

"It's from the guy I mentioned, the one who's a friend of Tomasz Schwartz, the one—"

"—Who developed the AI program and word cloud with your name on. I know, dummy."

Alex read out the message.

"Seti? There was a Pharaoh Seti wasn't there?" Andrew asked.

"The Nineteenth Dynasty, son of Ramses I and father of Ramses II—the Great. There was also a Seti II."

"Or does it mean the SETI Institute. You know, as in the search for extra terrestrial intelligence? Now that would be interesting!" Andrew did a little movement with his chair that Alex had learned was like a little dance, his equivalent of a fist in the air.

"OK, we did what you asked," Alex said. "Now let's take a look around, shall we?"

They went through the long ground floor hall on the left that contained all the large Egyptian items, like the statue of Ramses II and the Rosetta Stone.

Alex waited patiently because he'd seen it all before whereas this was Andrew's first visit. As Andrew read information about the giant false door from the tomb of a high priest called Ptahshepses, Alex took a look at the King List from Ramses II's tomb. The partial list of previous pharaohs deliberately excluded Hatshepsut and some of the Eighteenth Dynasty rulers from Akhenaten to Aye. But Alex was most interested in Seti's cartouche.

It was obvious by the name, but although broken at the top, it also stood out as different. Nearly every other name reflected the worship of the sun, Ra, or Horus. Their Horus name. Seti's cartouche included a staff. The head looked like Anubis rather than the Seth creature, as it was known: an anteater with square ears.

It took almost an hour to cover the entire hall, which meant they had limited time for the main exhibit upstairs.

Alex took his brother up to the top floor and left him to explore. In the meantime, he went down the east stairs to the Egyptian Study Room.

On either side of the innocuous-looking door was a plaster cast from a temple. Alex hadn't paid much attention before but now he stared. The one on the right was from Pharaoh Merenptah's tomb. The one on the left was from Seti I's. He studied it for a moment and saw nothing unusual. It depicted the pharaoh with Horus by his side, presenting himself to Osiris and Isis. Perhaps the only questionable thing was the lack of any representation of Seth. After all, the king had named himself the son of Seth and here he was acting like the son of Ra, a manifestation of Horus on Earth.

All thoughts of the contradiction left him as he entered the room and saw his old professor, Sian Lloyd.

She seemed genuinely pleased to see him despite his past.

"I'm legit now," he said.

"I know." She gave him a warm smile. "Macquarie University, Australia, under Professor Steele."

"You know him?"

"Only by reputation. So is this a professional visit, Alex, or something else?"

"I'm not sure," he said, and asked about the items from Dixon.

"Waynman Dixon," she said. "I know the story. The cigar box was brought here and was recorded as containing three items."

"So all three are here?"

"Allegedly, although the cedar wood—which was categorized as part of a ruler—subsequently went missing."

"Is that suspicious?"

"Maybe." She winked. "However, we've had two world wars since, and during that time many of the items were taken into storage for their preservation. Some things got lost. Whether mislaid, misfiled, or misappropriated, I couldn't say."

"Do you have a theory?"

"Like what?"

Alex didn't want to make it too obvious. "Like a deliberate act or something?"

"You know he was a Mason, don't you? There's a theory that his brother, John Dixon—also a Mason—buried it under Cleopatra's Needle."

"But it was given to the British Museum. That doesn't make sense unless…"

She smiled again. "Yes?"

"The ruler was originally longer."

Lloyd clapped her hands. "You got it! And there's a reason for believing it was longer than five inches. It was clearly broken, and subsequently no search of the northern shaft has revealed more." She paused, then: "Not only that, but another man present at the original discovery of the relics was Dr James Grant. After his death his private collection was donated to Aberdeen University. There were nine items listed, and it included a stone-mason's ruler, noted as originating from the Queen's Chamber."

"So it could be carbon-dated after all!" Alex exclaimed.

"It could if they knew where it was," Lloyd said. "Unfortunately, apart from the letter accompanying the items, the university can't locate that piece either."

TWENTY-FIVE

Cairo, Egypt

Charlie spent three days reviewing the missing-person files. Cairo alone had over a hundred missing in the past six months. She'd learned that it didn't literally mean they hadn't been found. Detective Shafik explained that there were also many John and Jane Does in the morgue. Too few resources to match the missing with the dead.

"If we're to make progress," she said, nursing a cup of strong coffee, "then maybe it becomes our job."

She saw him smile at that. But not in a good way. She'd learned to read his facial expression, and this one meant he wasn't going to disagree, but equally he wasn't going to help. If she wanted to check the missing in the morgue, she'd be doing it alone.

She spun the page full of initials and images on the table and he placed a hand on it.

"Tell me about the ones with hieroglyphs," she said.

"They are all associated with death. The ankh, the scarab, the Isis knot."

"I thought the ankh was the life force, or something."

He shrugged. "Of course. It is precisely what a dead person would need."

"So why these? What's he doing?"

148

"Perhaps it is something like the ancient process, giving the deceased the gifts associated with eternal life." He shook his head. "But then surely it would be all of them and not just one at a time."

"He's trying them out," Charlie said. "It's as though he's searching for the right symbol. He started with all sorts of religious images and has progressed to the ancient Egyptian ones. And now that he is here—"

"I wish I had your confidence, Special Agent Rebb. I really do. Now if you'll excuse me? If you would like to go to the morgue..."

"Maybe after I've made a call," she said.

After the detective left the room, she dialled Peter Zhang.

"Can you tell the time?" he said, answering after the sixth ring.

"You could have let it go to voicemail."

He grumbled. "What have you got for me?"

"Nothing," she said. "I just wanted to hear a friendly voice."

The line was quiet for a moment.

She said, "We have lots of missing young men, all of whom could be victims of Zart."

"OK," he said uncertainly. "So you've started a board like ours? Names, dates, times?"

"Too many. Looks like I'm going to have to find out who's already turned up dead."

"Nice." He paused. "Check for tattoos."

"Good idea," she said sarcastically. "I hadn't thought of that, Peter."

"Just trying to help, Chicago. Sometimes the obvious needs pointing out."

"Right."

"How you getting on with Shufty?"

"Detective Shafik."

"Yeah, him."

"I—" She stopped. Shafik burst into the room. "Peter, got to go. Call you back."

"Let's go," Shafik said as she put the phone down. He was breathing hard, excited.

"What is it?"

"This time," he said. "I think we've got real proof this time."

They raced to the detective's car and she got in beside him. Within five minutes he turned into a road blocked by a marked police car. It was a short road and she could see two policemen with assault rifles about half-way along.

"Where are we?" she asked as he passed a garden and then stopped by a tall ochre wall.

"Old Cairo. The cemetery section." He glanced at the armed men and then back at Charlie. "Head scarf."

She got out into the heat and adjusted the scarf.

Shafik walked quickly with Charlie a couple of steps behind. Without a word, the policemen opened heavy-looking wooden doors and they were through into a cemetery.

"Ironic," he said, slowing. "An American killer and an American cemetery."

She looked around the walled enclosure and figured it to be just shy of fifty metres wide and thirty-five deep. The entrance gates were midway. There were palms and eucalyptus trees and it had probably looked attractive at some time, but not now. Between the packed lines of graves were weeds. Years of weeds.

"A bit of a mess," she said.

"Since the revolution I'm afraid." He started walking again, turned left and walked to near the end. There was an overhead white sheet and another policeman. Under the cover stood two men she took as being crime scene

150

investigators. They wore the typical white plastic suits, gloves and overshoes.

They were standing over an open grave. A stone slab had been moved to one side revealing the hole. Not six feet deep, shallower and filled with bodies.

Shafik spoke to the crime scene guys in Arabic and then turned to Charlie. "We have five minutes. Take a quick look and then we'll let these men get these bodies into the cooler."

Charlie stepped closer. The bodies were packed in two on top of two, naked, and all appeared to be male. On one, she could see the clear cut to the ribs where the Surgeon had pierced the victims' chests to reach the heart. She could also see a tattoo on his chest.

"What is it?" she asked. "The tattoo."

"It's an ankh and djed combined. Both symbols of the afterlife."

"So he used the ankh before. Now it's in combination with another."

"Anything else you notice."

"Apart from the obvious? As far as we know all his prior victims were white. Pure white. These men have darker skins."

"Yes," he said, "they are probably Egyptian although none is especially dark. They could be well-tanned foreigners."

"And something else," she said, stepping back and letting the crime scene guys take over. "He's been here three months. Those bodies don't look three months old. They look days old to me. I think the Surgeon's stepping things up. Big time."

TWENTY-SIX

London, England

The brothers arrived at the Masonic Hall on Great Queen Street. They'd discussed the missing ruler or rulers and agreed it was suspicious. It looked like someone didn't want the wood carbon-dated.

"Queen Street," Alex said thinking out loud.

"That's right. The Queen's shaft in the Great Pyramid. Coincidence?"

"Probably," Alex said. "Once you're looking for conspiracies, you see them everywhere." He went up the stone steps into the building while Andrew took a wheelchair lift tucked to the right hand side.

Tom Dillon, the director of communication, was already in reception waiting for them. He greeted Alex with a handshake and Andrew did a finger wiggle thing.

"Can I give you a tour?" Dillon said before immediately leading them into a lift without waiting for a response. He began a well-practised spiel about the building, how it was finished in 1933 and not damaged in the Second World War despite being one of the three largest buildings at the time. He chuckled. "I know you're interested in conspiracy theories, and people think Hitler deliberately avoided bombing this building."

"Did he?" Andrew asked.

"No!" Dillon chuckled again. "Firstly, because the Luftwaffe used it as a marker to target the City and secondly, why would Hitler do that when he hated Masons? It's estimated that as many as two hundred thousand Masons went to the gas chamber—although it's hard to determine exactly because many of them could have been Jews. Hitler, like Stalin and Franco, persecuted Masons because of a belief that we are all Jews. Which is nonsense of course."

"What are you then?" Alex asked. "If you'll excuse the bluntness?"

If Dillon was affronted by the question, he hid it well. They were now standing by a memorial, a large chest with a very Christian-looking stained-glass window behind.

He said, "Let me first explain that this is a Peace Memorial. There is a scroll inside containing all the names of Masons who died in the First World War. Sixty-four Masons were awarded the Victoria Cross which is seventeen per cent of all VCs awarded. It doesn't mean we're any braver but is more a reflection of our sense of duty." He turned and pointed towards gates that ran across what Alex now viewed as a giant foyer. "Now to your question: Freemasonry is a pure system of morality, validated in allegory and illustrated by symbols."

Andrew said, "What does that mean?"

Dillon smiled politely. "It means we are not bound by the confines of religion, young man. I'll explain more."

They walked through a second gate and into a great hall. Alex noted that the giant copper doors were embossed with pictures just like he'd expect in an Egyptian temple: workers and oxen with building blocks.

On the opposite side Dillon showed them something much more modern.

"It represents ascension to Heaven—although there is no specific religious Heaven meant by it."

There were rows of blue chairs to the left and right. A man was tidying around them. Looking up, he exchanged glances with Alex, maybe intrigued at why the brothers wanted the tour.

Ahead were golden pillars with three throne-like chairs. A blue night sky painted ceiling arched into a mural. Alex and Andrew stared in awe.

Dillon was still talking. "There are three grand principles of Freemasonry: brotherly love, relief and truth. These principles imbue everything we do."

Alex said, "Would you mind explaining the ceiling art?"

"On the four corners we have the four cardinal virtues."

Alex noted these were represented as angels.

"Ahead, to the east, we have Solomon and Hiram beside Jacob's ladder," Dillon continued. "The symbols on the ladder"—a cross, an anchor and a heart—"represent faith, hope and charity."

"What's that above them?" Andrew asked. "It looks like the sun with a slanted S inside."

Dillon said, "That represents the Grand Geometrician of the Universe."

"But specifically?" Alex asked.

Dillon turned and looked at the west ceiling edge, ignoring the question. "Here we have Euclid and Pythagoras. You'll recognize the triangle illustrating Pythagoras' Theorem. We also see it as a symbol of three."

Andrew said, "Three is important to you."

"Yes because it represents the Holy Trinity."

"Isn't that Christian?"

"Not only Christian. We consider ourselves beyond such religious classifications."

Again with the *no religion*, and yet Alex saw Christian and Jewish symbols everywhere.

The mosaic to the north was of Saint George and a dragon. Above a royal crest that Alex didn't recognize was the Star of David.

"The Mark of Solomon," Dillon corrected when he said it. "On the south it's the all-seeing eye, which I think is common to many religions."

The mosaic showed a charioteer driving two white horses. Between pillars, below the eye, was another geometric star.

"What does that star represent?" Alex asked.

"Another form of the Mark of Solomon."

It didn't seem right, but Alex didn't want to pursue it. He had specific questions about the relics and ancient Egypt. But before he could ask, he realized Andrew had moved over to the thrones.

"What's the symbol on the back wall?" he asked.

Alex joined him and saw a geometric design the outside of which looked a bit like an omega.

"Alpha and omega?" he said.

"It could be," Dillon said stepping over. "We have a circle which represents the continuum. Inside that is an equilateral triangle which represents the Trinity and then we have the Three Taus."

"Tau, as in the letter T?" Alex asked, looking at the strange symbol that looked like two horizontal Ts joined up with an upside down one in the middle.

"That's right. It also represents the Trinity."

Andrew said, "I see triangles and diamonds everywhere—like pyramids or a pyramid and inverted one joined."

Alex said, "Like Blake's famous painting."

"*The Ancient of Days*," Dillon said, and then shook his head. "I don't know anything about pyramids or ancient Egypt I'm afraid."

Alex was disappointed.

"What about the Dixon brothers and the wooden relic from the Great Pyramid?" Andrew asked, and Alex winced at his lack of tact. He'd wanted to be more subtle in the lead-up, but Andrew had just gone straight for it.

Dillon shook his head again. "Sorry."

Alex told him the story but Dillon showed no interest.

When Alex had finished, the director said, "Perhaps email me with the details and I'll ask the historians here."

He tried to sound convincing but Alex thought they'd be wasting their time.

Andrew said, "I thought Masons claimed to be descended from the architects of the pyramids."

Dillon smiled. "Stone masons," he said. "We can't trace our origins back beyond the seventeen hundreds."

Alex mentioned that the obelisk on the Embankment had been funded by Masons. And that one of the Dixon brothers may have buried a ruler taken from the Great Pyramid.

Dillon shook his head. It was becoming his default response. Then suddenly he seemed to come to a decision. He said, "I know you're looking for conspiracies, but we have nothing to hide."

"Really?" Alex said. He pointed to Latin on the nearest throne. "What does this mean?"

"Ah. That inscription means listen, observe, and say nothing."

Alex nodded.

"It sounds like we're secretive, doesn't it?" Dillon said smiling. "But it's not the case and that's why we're happy to provide tours like this. And if we seem a bit secretive it's to maintain a little mystique and protect ourselves."

Dillon's phone rang. He answered it and listened. Then he apologized to the brothers. "Would you give me a couple of minutes? You're welcome to look around."

They watched him scuttle away.

"Bloody hell!" Andrew grumbled. "We've learned nothing."

"Except that Dillon's story is full of contradictions. He's here to spin a story that disguises the true meaning."

"You want the truth?" an Eastern European voice said behind them. The cleaning guy hustled over. "You want the truth?"

"Yes!" Alex and Andrew said at the same time.

"Starbucks in fifteen minutes. See you there."

The brothers found a Starbucks coffee shop close by. Fifteen minutes passed without the guy showing.

"We should have checked which Starbucks," Alex said.

"Or maybe he was joking."

Alex was about to agree when the cleaning guy hustled in.

"So you are interested in the conspiracy?" he said.

"Yes—anything relating to the pyramids."

The guy nodded sagely. "It will cost you."

"How much?"

"One hundred."

Alex despaired. "I'm not paying you a hundred pounds for a conspiracy theory."

The guy gave a little shrug. "Then you don't want to know badly enough."

"What's your lowest price?" Andrew asked.

The guy looked from one to the other. "Seventy."

"Forty." Andrew said without checking with Alex.

"I'll tell you what. Give me forty and I'll tell you enough. If you want the rest it will cost you twenty more. Agreed?"

"Agreed," Andrew said, and signalled for his brother to pay.

Alex reluctantly handed over two twenty-pound notes. He sensed this was just a con.

"Good," the man said, stuffing the cash in his jeans. "Now let's have coffee."

Alex was sent to buy three drinks. When he returned, Andrew and the other man were talking like conspirators.

"Started without me?" Alex said, sitting at the table.

The man shook his head. "No. Your brother was just telling me about what happened to you in Egypt. You are a lucky man."

"I don't feel lucky."

"You could have been killed in that apartment. Meeting someone you don't know and without backup." He shook his head. "Very dangerous."

This all seemed like a delaying tactic, so Alex prompted the guy to tell them the truth he'd promised.

"You have been looking into the wrong Masons. The Brits are too secretive—unlike the Americans."

"Is that it?" Alex said, anger starting to bubble up in his chest.

"No!" the man said and glanced around. "Who controls the research and disclosure for Egyptian antiquities?"

Alex said, "It's the Ministry of Antiquities—the Egyptian government."

The man raised his eyebrows and smiled.

Alex didn't get it. It had been the same since Carter and Carnarvon's time, although called the Ministry of Public Works then. They had clamped down on the large-scale pilfering by the archaeologists of the time, controlled access to sites and ensured accurate recording of finds.

"What's your point?"

The man said, "What do you know about the ScanPyramids project?"

"They've used muons and detected apparent voids in the Great Pyramid."

"Who's running it?"

"I don't know?"

"The authorities. Take a look at who's on the project team. Any genuine archaeologists? Anyone who might actually know what they are looking for?" He was still smiling but Alex saw cynicism in the other man's eyes. "And take a look at the investigation of the Queen's Chamber shafts. It was the same thing."

Alex got it now. "And the research only seemed half finished."

"Right. Red hieroglyphs in the shaft were dismissed as architects' measurements. Take a look. They don't make sense. Then take a look at what they found in the southern shaft but didn't investigate further."

"But why?" Andrew asked. "Why do the research and then stop it."

"Public interest," the man said. "Feed the masses titbits, just enough to maintain the mysticism—and tourism of course. But not enough to tell the truth."

Alex said, "So what is the truth?"

The man with the Eastern European accent held out his hand. "Twenty pounds."

Alex handed it over.

The man smiled. "I don't know, but I sure as hell do know the authorities want to keep it that way."

Alex clenched his fists. Tricked out of the last twenty pounds. But then the man spoke again in a whisper.

"Like I said, you are looking at the wrong Masons. Not the British nor the Americans."

"Who then?"

"The French." He tapped his nose. "You may know that the French placed a golden cap on their obelisk to celebrate the bicentenary of their revolution. It was a Masonic symbol and the event was attended by hundreds of Masons."

"Of course," Andrew said. "The glass pyramid at the Louvre. The French are even more obsessed with ancient Egypt than us."

"Not just obsessed," the man said. "They have a secret order whose mission is to keep the secrets of the pyramids." He paused and drank coffee, letting his words hang in the air before he spoke again. "Did you know they had plans to cap the Great Pyramid for the Millennium? It would have been amazing, with a planned laser show to highlight its former glory."

The brothers shook their heads.

"It would have been gold foil and light as a feather. But the plans were thwarted."

"By?" Alex prompted.

The man smiled. "The other group with a similar objective, but who hate Jews and, by association, all Masons."

"Who?" Andrew asked.

"None other than the Ministry of Antiquities."

TWENTY-SEVEN

On the journey home, Alex and his brother spent time on the internet reading about the ScanPyramids project and the two projects to explore the shafts in the Queen's Chamber. The cleaning guy from the Masonic lodge was correct about the project teams. They were scientists coordinated by the Egyptian authorities. The initial exploration of the northern shaft and discovery of a doorway in 1993 was halted on the grounds that the robot was marking the limestone.

A second exploration wasn't started until 2011. This also stopped with incomplete findings.

Alex said, "I can't find out why the second robot exploration was abandoned. The death of one of the team is mentioned, but—"

"What about that self-styled Indiana Jones guy?"

Dr Hawass. He had been the Minister of State for Antiquities Affairs at the time and project leader. "What about him?" Alex asked.

"He seems to have continued the project in secret and—" Andrew gasped. "My God, he also claimed to have found the rest of the wooden ruler!"

"What?"

"The cedar wood—"

"I know you mean the Dixon relic, I just can't believe it. Dr Hawass found another piece. So there is still something to carbon-date!"

"No," Andrew said, "that's the point. I can't find anything else on it. And that seems to be the last thing Hawass reported before he went quiet."

"What are you suggesting?" Alex searched for Dr Hawass on his browser. "It says he's still around—an international lecturer."

"It also says Hawass has been accused of domineering behaviour, forbidding archaeologists to announce their own findings, and courting the media for his own gain after they were denied access to archaeological sites. He was controlling, just like Dillon said." He read a bit more. "It also says he denies a Jewish conspiracy. Which is odd, right?"

"Protesting too much?"

"Odd because he really means an anti-Jewish conspiracy. And the Masons are connected to the Jews because of their Hebrew rituals related to Solomon's Temple in Jerusalem."

"Which Dillon denied."

"He would though, wouldn't he?" Andrew snorted a laugh. "But that tallies with what the guy from Starbucks said."

They continued their research later. Andrew messaged his gaming friends about conspiracy theories and the pyramids. Alex sent a Telegram message to Brown.

He said that the Masons seemed to be at odds with the Egyptian authorities. He wondered whether that was why two men had been in Schwartz's apartment. Was one a Mason and another representing the authorities?

He went on to mention the missing wooden ruler and carbon-dating, which meant the pyramids couldn't be dated.

Brown responded with. **Interesting. The AI word cloud. Pyramid and conspiracy still most prominent. Seti has jumped in size. As well as your name, it's clear the FBI agent is Rebb. Charlie Rebb.**

Afterwards, Alex was thinking. "If it's true about the piece of ruler found in 1993 then there probably was only one original five-inch piece. Which means that Grant somehow got it after it was given to the British Museum."

"Sorry. Remind me who Grant was."

"Part of the original team who discovered the ruler," Alex said. "He must have got it somehow, but it didn't arrive when his wife donated all his Egyptian relics to Aberdeen Uni."

"Or someone there took it and covered their tracks."

Alex nodded. "Maybe. Do any of your gamer friends comment on that?"

"No, the biggest thing they talk about is the age of the pyramids—which is linked, right? The five-inch piece is missing and the rest is only mentioned in passing by Hawass."

"So they can't be aged. But there's plenty of evidence it's Khufu's pyramid, which dates it back to around 2,500 BCE."

"Really?" Andrew said, cocking one eyebrow.

"Really what?"

Andrew tapped his nose like it was a secret. "Why do you say it's Khufu's?"

"Because everyone knows…" Even as he said it, Alex realized he was making a mistake. Despite this, he resumed: "Khufu's cartouche is on the walls and his solar barques have been found in the pits beside it."

"Well, first off, the boats could have been buried at any time. They have been carbon-dated so it's like validation but without direct proof. That ruler would have been proof. The boats are not."

"OK, I get that."

"Next, there's the cartouche—which isn't actually. As you know, royal cartouches were in an oval. Khufu's name wasn't. It was also more like graffiti in the King's Chamber. There's no other mark confirming his ownership."

Alex considered this. "You're right, it is unusual. There's no Book of the Dead on the walls. Nothing."

"And someone mentioned the order the pyramids were built. Each of the three main Giza pyramids is smaller than its alleged predecessor. I've thought about it and the argument does make sense."

"What argument?"

"If the next generation builds something, surely he outdoes his father? He doesn't build something smaller. It's like he's admitting to be a lesser man."

Alex nodded. "So what's the theory?"

"That the three pyramids were adopted by each pharaoh in order. The first king—Khufu—made the Great pyramid his. Then Khafre adopts the next largest and his son...what's he called?"

"Menkaure."

"He takes the smallest one... the only one left." Andrew paused and raised his eyebrows. "And if that's not convincing, then think about the other pyramids. According to my sources, the bent and stepped pyramids were earlier"

"Yes, Sneferu's—he came before Khufu."

"They're less advanced."

164

"As you'd expect," Alex said. "And Sneferu's Meidum pyramid collapsed during the build. But that just shows they were learning how to construct them."

"But the Giza pyramids are so much more advanced with some foundation blocks of over 200 tons. And then you look at the pyramids 100 years later and they are more simplistic—based on the step design and much smaller stones and cut more roughly than the Giza ones."

Alex nodded thoughtfully. "So what do they say this all means."

"That the Giza pyramids are much, much older. Some people say 10,000 years old, others as much as 25,000 years."

They bounced the ideas around a bit and confirmed a lot of what Andrew had been told by his contacts. Andrew was convinced but Alex was not so sure. He was reading about water damage found behind the door at the top of the Queen's northern shaft when Andrew whistled.

"Look at this!" He showed Alex a picture of a fossilized sea urchin. "Guess where."

"Tell me."

"A block fallen from Menkaure's pyramid. Dismissed by the *authorities*"—he emphasized authorities like it was a bad taste in his mouth—"as from the original quarry. But quarrying cut the stone and didn't leave sea creatures on the surface."

"Flood," Alex said, thinking about the word he'd seen on the word cloud.

Andrew nodded. "There's a lot of flood damage. Particularly of the Sphinx."

"Erosion."

"It's too much for simple erosion." Andrew checked his computer screen. "At least sixty feet underwater."

So flood and pyramids seemed to fit into some kind of conspiracy possibly involving the Masons and the Egyptian authorities. Perhaps the Masons were the good guys. Maybe the Arab in Schwartz's apartment was there to kill him but was stopped by the second man—working for the Masons.

Alex messaged Brown and got a reply an hour later.

FBI Agent Rebb is in Egypt. She was in the news investigating some bodies they found at Mit-Rahineh. They say it's connected to a US serial killer case.

Apart from regular text messages, Alex spoke to Vanessa every day. He was trying especially hard since the prison episode, making sure he communicated, making sure she knew he loved her.

On that evening's call she started with, "I have news, but tell me yours first."

She already knew about his trip to London with Andrew, so he told her about the water damage to the Sphinx and pyramids which might be linked to flooding.

"The Biblical flood?" she asked.

"I don't know," he said. "Once you start looking for conspiracies you see them everywhere. Like the wooden relic that was donated to Aberdeen University. We're originally from Aberdeen, so maybe…"

"You're secretly Masons!"

For a second he thought she was being serious but then she laughed.

"I miss your laugh," he said.

"Oh, but you don't miss me?"

He was about to deny that when she laughed again.

Relieved, he said, "When will I see you?"

"I've one more assignment to complete. I need to go to Israel but it shouldn't be long. Maybe three days. No more than a week. Any other developments before I tell you my news?"

"Brown says that an FBI agent is in Egypt, although I can't find any reports on the web. Apparently there's an American serial killer and there's some connection to an Egyptian case."

"Alex."

"Yes?"

"You said you wouldn't be involved."

"I'm not. I'm just interested."

After a pause, she said, "Are you sure that's all it is?"

"Andrew's interested too," he said, having planned his explanation earlier. "We're bonding on this thing like never before. He's really excited by the conspiracy stuff. It's great."

"I'm pleased, but, this guy who's messaging you, how do you know he's genuine?"

"I..." Alex stopped, as he realized he had no idea about the man he'd never met.

She said, "He's a friend of the one calling himself Black—the one who fled his apartment..."

"Yes."

"The one who wrote the AI program that's creating a word cloud that included your name."

"Right..."

Alex was just getting there as Vanessa finished the thought.

"How does this Brown guy know what the word cloud is saying?"

TWENTY-EIGHT

Alex said he'd call Vanessa back and then messaged Brown.

How do I know you're genuine?

A reply came back a few minutes later: What do you mean?

Alex watched the note self-destruct before he typed, When the AI program updates, how do you know?

Brown replied, The program is cloud-based. I've got access to the output

That sounded reasonable. Alex called Vanessa and told her.

"Just be careful," she said.

"Don't worry, I'm not really involved."

"I know you, Alex MacLure. You're fascinated about this and about your name appearing in the word cloud."

"And my research."

"That's my news for you." She paused and he wondered what she was building up to. "I was at the Nefertiti Hotel packing up your things and bumped into a member of your team. Actually it was a bit odd. I think he'd been in the room and he said he'd been told to pack your things."

"Professor Steele offered, but—"

"Anyway," she said cutting him off, "it seems they've discovered more of the clay tablets."

"What? No one's told me anything."

"Farid said there were almost seventy of the letters and to tell you they seem to continue Yanhamu's later story, the one about Ramses' Keeper of Secrets—if that makes any sense?"

It did make sense. Every tablet had a hidden message but there was so little on each one. All they had so far were three tantalizing snippets.

I offered to be Ramses' Keeper of Secrets

On my advice he renamed his son, Seti beloved of Ptah

My wife was the genuine Lord Khety and they took her

Alex said, "Who's handling the decoding?"

"Farid said it was your assistant, Mahmood."

"Damn!"

"What's the matter, Alex?"

"I don't trust him. I'm suspicious he's a spy for the Ministry of Antiquities and, after what we've been finding out about conspiracies, that puts him firmly in the Egyptian authorities' camp."

"Alex?"

He realized he hadn't spoken for a minute, his mind racing ahead with the possibilities. He said, "That'll be why the Amarna Letters and my name appear in the word cloud. I can't leave this to Mahmood. This really is linked to the research. I may never know the truth, may never get the whole story."

"You're coming back, aren't you?"

"Yes," he said. "As soon as we finish this call, I'll check flights."

★ ★ ★

Mahmood called the number he'd been given. It was a conference line that told him to wait for the chairman to join the call. He gave his codename, pressed hash, and waited.

The line clicked.

"You have news?"

"You were right," Mahmood said. "I thought I better report straight away."

"And?" There was impatience in the man's voice.

"Immortality." Mahmood swallowed. "It connects Pharaoh Ramses to the Great Pyramid."

The following evening, Alex's Egyptair flight touched down at Cairo airport. It might not have had the comfort of British Airways, but it was cheaper and arrived on time—before nine o'clock.

He'd booked a taxi to the Marriott hotel and stayed the night. Vanessa had hoped to join him but the timing didn't work out. She'd already left for Tel Aviv.

Alex exchanged messages with Brown and Andrew, and hired a car for the morning.

"Stay calm," Vanessa said when they spoke the next day after breakfast. "Maybe Mahmood was acting with the best intensions."

"You don't really think that."

"No, but we only have Farid's word for it. Think positively. More tablets have been found, which is exciting, right?"

Alex had to agree, but he was on edge the whole drive south in his rented VW Toureg. He crossed the Nile on the flatbed ferry to Tell el-Amarna and reported to the police station at the other side, showing them his credentials.

After driving through the modern town he soon arrived at the archaeological dig site in the desert. The team were sheltering from the midday sun and he strode purposefully over.

Mahmood was the first to jump up and greet him.

"How good to see you back, my friend!" the assistant said, although his smile didn't include his eyes.

"I hear you found more tablets, Mahmood."

"Yes. Sixty-six, and in fairly good condition." He must have read Alex's face, because he pulled him to one side and started apologizing. "Please, I am sorry. I thought I could translate them and have some glory. You understand?"

"Just show me what you've found," Alex said.

Mahmood took him into one of the tents and there, lined up on a table, were rows of the biscuit-sized clay tablets.

Alex's heart missed a beat as the excitement struck him. It was like being transported back over three thousand years. He put on surgical gloves and picked one up. He immediately saw the code within the cuneiform.

"My God!" he said. "This is it. This is the rest of the story."

"I've managed to translate part of it."

"Let me see."

Mahmood went to a satchel and removed some papers. Alex glanced at them and then put them in his pocket.

"Hey!"

Alex ignored the assistant. He was in charge and any translations should be done for him. He took out his phone and worked along the row, taking photos of each individual stone. When he'd finished he said, "I'm leaving these here. When I've copied your translations

171

I'll let you have the notes back. However..." He paused and fixed Mahmood with a cold stare. "You are not to release anything without my permission or that of Professor Steele. Understand?"

"Of course."

"Not, of course! You were duty bound to inform me of this find. If you ever want to work a dig again..."

Mahmood lowered his head in contrition. "You can count on me," he said. "You can trust me."

Mahmood felt sick as he watched Alex drive away. He knew he should call his contact and let him know. But that sounded like failure. And he was so close to success.

No, Mahmood decided, if I tell them what's happened, they will take matters into their own hands and they won't need me.

Much better to handle this himself. Their objective might be to destroy the evidence. And if they thought Alex had it on his own, they might remove him. And that wouldn't be good. Mahmood knew that Alex was the best person to interpret the codes. And although the assistant had to report to the authorities, first and foremost he was also an Egyptologist.

TWENTY-NINE

Alex returned to his old hotel and went back to his notes. The stories he'd previously deciphered from the clay tablets had mostly made sense. They had recognized that there were at least two narratives: one about Meryra, the scribe, and the second about the boy Yanhamu. Meryra's was more hidden and partial and about secrets. Yanhamu's was the story of his life and appeared to be in two parts, the latter referring to Ramses and Seti, many years after the original story.

He read Mahmood's translations:

Die or become the Keeper of Secrets.

Pharaoh's tomb stories not complete.

Held by? Ramses.

Only a priest of Horem-Akhet or the pharaoh go?

Find all the secrets for eternal life.

Like water and the colour of gods.

Apep defeated during Ra's journey.

Underworld where Apep plotted?

Tutankhamen and Ay equals the truth.

Half the gold for my wife.

Seth has two heads.

Immortality is through something?

Pyramid is the Field of Reeds.

Alex noted the reference to Seth and immortality but the translations didn't make sense. The starting point had to be to get the tablets in order. Only by getting their sequence right would Yanhamu's story be told.

He worked long into the night arranging and rearranging the photographs until he was satisfied that he had it. Now he could begin.

1315 BCE, Badari

The large crowd fell into an expectant hush as they awaited the judgement. Magistrate Yan-Khety sat in the shade of the awning and adjusted his purple sash.

"Sir, they are waiting," his assistant whispered.

Let them wait, Yanhamu thought. Make the guilty man sweat.

He cleared his throat. And, as was the custom, he summarized the case before pronouncing judgement. "The defendant, Theshan, was commissioned by the accuser—a minor nobleman called Rudjek—to build an extension to his house. The defendant obtained agreement to the design and construction and built it in accordance with requirements. In fact, he finished the building ahead of the three months he promised. The accuser paid for the build—although we heard that this was paid a month later than agreed. However, we also visited the site and found that part of the structure has moved and appears unstable. The accuser therefore demands repayment of the money and reparations for the problems and anxiety caused."

Yanhamu stopped and glanced at the slave, Yuf, who was listening so hard he'd stopped waving the ostrich feather fan. The slave realized his error and immediately began fanning again.

"The case would appear straight-forward," Yanhamu began.

"As is the Law of the Two Lands," Rudjek said with a smirk. The crowd muttered their agreement, perhaps hoping for a severe punishment.

"Quiet!" Yanhamu shouted, knowing that most of the people were there to see blood rather than justice. He was weary of the show that such cases often became. He was in the insignificant eleventh nome, where the wine was bad and the accommodation worse. It made him irritable and he knew he needed to remind himself that he was here to do the right thing, however unpopular.

"I have heard witnesses speak as to the character of the defendant. I have heard other customers express satisfaction with his work. I have also learned that the original price he quoted was rejected and that the accuser, Rudjek, insisted on a lower price and sourced the building materials himself.

"Theshan, the defendant, says that he expressed concern regarding the materials, although Rudjek denies this." Yanhamu looked at both men's faces and could now see the truth. "My judgement is that Theshan should rebuild the extension so that it is sound and of good quality and so repair his reputation." The defendant lowered his eyes in acceptance. But Yanhamu wasn't finished. "However, I find the accuser guilty of bringing this case when it is his own fault. He provided substandard materials and insisted that the construction should go ahead despite Theshan's concerns. He will therefore not only provide any additional acceptable quality material required for the rebuilding, but he will also pay the defendant for those repairs. This is my judgement."

Rudjek clenched his teeth and then muttered something. A guard stepped forward.

"Don't disrespect the judgement," he growled at the minor noble. "Or you'll find yourself in prison."

Rudjek slunk away without another word and two guards brought forward the next defendant. It was a Nubian, as black as coal, although he was small for a man from that country. He was accused of using pig meat in his pies. Pig was only eaten by the peasants, because it was blamed for the plague that had killed hundreds over the years. Yanhamu knew this all too well since his mother had died this way. It was a serious crime to pass off pig as another meat. In another nome, under another magistrate, the crime might have been punishable by death. Yanhamu prayed there was no evidence of such a crime.

He listened to witnesses' statements and then had twenty pies opened and inspected. Yanhamu himself prodded at the contents with a stick.

"What is this?"

"A mixture, my lord. Beef, chicken, goat and..." The Nubian swallowed hard, as though the words wouldn't come out.

The crowd remained tense.

"What is it?" Yanhamu bellowed.

"Dog, my lord." He nodded with contrition as he said it quietly

There were gasps in the crowd and a woman fainted.

"Not pig?"

"Oh no, my lord! Never!"

Yanhamu waved his assistant to bring him a pie. He stuck a finger in and tasted it.

"My lord?" the assistant whispered, alarmed. Nobles would never eat dog meat.

Yanhamu repeated the procedure. "It's not pig, it is indeed dog," he announced a moment later.

He asked for the witnesses again and questioned whether the pie seller had made any claims as to the contents. All of them admitted that he had not. They were sold as meat pies and that's what they were.

Yanhamu dismissed the case, saying, "The pie seller is not guilty of including pig meat. However, I suspect he will never sell another pie in this nome."

As the defendant was led away to the hisses of the crowd, the assistant leaned in.

"My lord, how did you know it was dog meat? You could have risked your life if it had been pig."

"I'll explain later. What's the last case?"

"A man accused of selling dates past their best."

Thank Thoth, Yanhamu thought. He dreaded the thief who would need to lose a hand or a rapist who would have his testicles crushed. But this was a simple case and Yanhamu quickly passed judgement. The man received five lashes, much to the satisfaction of the crowd.

Even before the assistant began to dismantle the stage, Yanhamu was up and heading for their accommodation. The eleventh nome tribunals were over for another month and he was ready to go home.

As he packed the magistrate's things, the assistant asked about the day's lesson.

"First of all, Sadhu, I believed the man when he said it wasn't pig."

"How could you read anything in that black face?"

"His eyes told the truth," Yanhamu said. "And I know that most towns-people have never tasted pig so could easily mislabel something different. Second of all, your lesson for today was observation."

"I observed you tasting either pig or dog. Neither of which is appropriate for a noble such as yourself, my lord."

"No! The observation was that I inserted my middle finger in the pie but licked my index finger."

When he arrived at his home in Akhmim, old Paneb opened the courtyard door and bowed. He took his master's coat and washed his feet.

"Is Nefer-bithia here?" Yanhamu asked the slave.

"In the drawing room, master."

Yanhamu noted hesitancy. "What is it, old friend? Did she have a difficult case?"

Paneb dropped his head and held his hands wide. He wasn't going to say, so Yanhamu walked into the house with trepidation.

"Bith?"

His wife rushed to him and kissed him hard.

He laughed. "I'm grateful, but why the extreme affection? I thought you'd had a bad day."

Nefer-bithia pointed to a scroll on a table. It had an unbroken royal seal. She said, "Have you done something wrong, Yani?"

"Probably!" He laughed again, although this time it was forced.

Two strides took him to the table and he snatched it up. It wasn't Pharaoh Horemheb's seal but the vizier of Thebes'. He hesitated and then broke it open.

"What does it say?"

"I'm being summoned by Vizier Paramese."

She looked pale so he put his arm around her. "It's not about one of my judgements. This is a call-up."

"But..."

He quoted: "In the name of Pharaoh Horemheb, rightful ruler and descendant of the great Ahmose, one who reunited the Two Lands, Mighty Sword, destroyer of her enemies the Nine Bows, King of Upper and

Lower Egypt, you are ordered to present yourself for duty—"

"Why?"

"Because I was once an officer, second class. This is a call-up because I am a veteran officer."

"To fight?" She still looked pale.

"It can't be, sweetheart. I was in communications and special missions in the last war. Perhaps I'm needed for training or advice."

"When?"

"Tomorrow." He held her tight until the shadow of the sundial told them it was time to pray. "One good thing," he said as they went to an upstairs room where they could witness the setting sun. "If this takes more than a month, I won't need to do the tribunal at Badari."

"Great," she said. "That means I have to do it. And knowing your wayward judgements, I'll probably have to retry your old cases."

But it wasn't for a month. When he arrived at the garrison outside Thebes, Yanhamu found himself in a queue of thirty other veterans. They were destined for Canaan, to take back Egyptian land. And they were going there as an army.

THIRTY

Cairo, Egypt

Charlie had set up a board on Shafik's wall. It was like the one in Atlanta but a map of Cairo and the surrounding towns. So far she only had the cemetery and the temple marked. The temple was connected to the initial body discovered before she arrived. The American cemetery had lines to the photographs of the four men recently discovered. She'd included photographs of the tattoos but had no names for any of the victims.

Shafik had been on the telephone and she waited for him to finish before using the phone to call Zhang.

"You're a celebrity again, Chicago," he said straight off. "I'm glad you called."

"Good morning to you, Peter."

"You're in all the papers," he said, ignoring her sarcasm. The media here is loving the Egyptian connection. Your photo is all over the place. It's a good one too—from a few years ago."

"I was about to give you an update."

"I've seen the photos. Four bodies from an American cemetery. Four Egyptian symbols." He laughed. "Ha! The Metro has a cartoon of you versus the Surgeon.

They've called you Cleopatra Charlie. Ever thought of dressing up as—?"

"Zhang!"

"Just an idea." She could hear more chuckling in the background and guessed others had seen the same cartoon. He continued: "So, is there more to this? You have an update?"

"Not really. Sounds like the news has preceded me. We've got the bodies but no IDs yet. That's the next job: finding out who they were and where they were abducted from. You said you were glad I'd called. Has there been a development or were you just glad because you could rib me about the Cleopatra thing?"

"Both." He chuckled. "Seriously though, I took an interesting call this morning. Got past the screening— not one of the million cranks we've had call with bogus information. Professor Suza from San Francisco. Like I said, sounded interesting."

Charlie waited, knowing he was deliberately drawing this out.

He said, "So this Suza says this is a religious thing. Says the Surgeon is choosing churches and temples and cemeteries for a reason."

"OK, Peter, what's the reason?"

"I don't know. She wouldn't say over the phone."

Charlie sighed. It did sound like another crank call. Most callers said they knew the Surgeon or had seen him. Some claimed to be psychics and knew where the bodies were buried. Some even claimed to be the Surgeon himself. And then there were those who claimed to have information but couldn't share it. Usually because they feared for their lives.

Zhang said, "I know what you're thinking, but we checked her out. She really is a retired professor of theology. She seems legit, Charlie."

181

"Then go see her."

"Flying out in an hour," he said. "Will let you know what comes up."

"Great."

"Charlie?"

"Yes?"

"We've had John Graham call here asking for an update."

"Really?" The LEGAT had called Charlie when he'd seen the news of the American cemetery bodies. He'd asked her to keep him informed of developments. She'd left a message with his robotic secretary when they found the bodies, but didn't think there was much else to report yet. Maybe he suspected she'd forgotten.

"OK," she said. "I'll keep him informed—as much as I have to."

"Good," Zhang said with a chuckle, "because I'm not discussing the case with him. That's your job."

"Got it," Charlie said. She was watching Shafik talking to another officer. He looked concerned.

"What's up?" she asked the detective after she ended her call.

"Another case," he said. "Not connected. An Englishman has returned to Egypt. I thought he wasn't responsible for a murder and he left the country straight after being released. Now he is back—less than a week later. Now I am thinking he wasn't so innocent after all."

THIRTY-ONE

1309 BCE, Akhmim

The courtyard was strangely dusty and silent. On the last leg of his journey, Yanhamu had witnessed a barge capsize. It had been carrying salt. His crew immediately prostrated themselves and prayed, requesting protection against the bad omen. Yanhamu didn't believe such silly superstitions. He knew the gods were above petty warnings like spilled salt. Even though their only son had been still-born, he didn't believe it was a judgement by the gods. It was life. Good things happened and bad things happened. The gods were far too busy making sure the heavens moved, the annual flood occurred and the harvest was bountiful.

As a boy he'd worried about Het's judgement the day he took too many duck eggs. Foolish childish fears, that's all they were. It's what separated the intelligent from the commoners. It's why they needed good magistrates like him and Nefer-bithia.

That's what he told himself, and yet, as he stood in his desolate courtyard, he wondered whether his world-view was mistaken. Had the spilled salt really been a bad omen?

It took him just a couple of minutes to confirm that the house was deserted. Nefer-bithia had gone and there was no message, nothing telling him why she wasn't there. He sat down on the edge of the well and thought.

He'd been away for almost six years. The armies had moved north. They took land and retreated. They built garrisons and fortifications. They policed the lands and then fought. They overcame the Caananites, they fought skirmishes with the Ibru and finally drove the Hittites out of Ugarit.

He'd started as officer, first class and ended up leader of Three Osiris—the Blues. They weren't as respected as the Reds or feared so much as the Blacks, and that suited Yanhamu. He'd been strategic and survived. Unlike his old colleague Thayjem.

In the last war they'd been simple communication officers, translating and scribing. Thayjem wasn't a fighter. Neither of them was. But his old friend had found himself in the front line officer, second class in a Red unit that had been ambushed by Ibru. That enemy did not understand or abide by the rules of war. They attacked in small groups and thought nothing of dirty tricks.

Transporting wagon-loads of dead Egyptians back to Egypt was the closest Yanhamu had come to returning home during those six years. On that mission he discovered that the dead officer in his care was none other than Thayjem.

It was a long, arduous journey and the bodies stank before they were half-way home. But they were to be buried in the soil of the Two Lands. That was all that mattered. Then the dead could find their way to the Field of Reeds. It was the promise made to all Egyptian fighters no matter how lowly.

"My Lord Khety, is that you?"

The voice snapped Yanhamu out of his reverie. He sat up and looked at the young man standing in the courtyard doorway. Sadhu.

"By Sobek, it is you!" Sadhu gasped. "May I come in?"

Yanhamu beckoned the young man over. "You've grown up," he said.

Sadhu smiled wanly. "And you have grown grey, master. I hardly recognize you."

"Where's my wife? Do you know?"

Sadhu lowered his eyes. "I have returned everyday hoping to find you so that you might know. So that you wouldn't come here and think the worst. Not after you have fought for our safety and defeated our enemies."

"I see you've got no better at coming to the point."

"A lot has changed since you've been gone. Egypt—at least Upper Egypt—has changed."

"Where is she?" Yanhamu bit back his frustration with the man. "Just tell me."

"She's gone." There were tears in Sadhu's eyes now. "She was taken away."

Yanhamu stood up. His heart, though weak, thudded against his chest. "Where?"

"I don't know."

Yanhamu could see the young man was losing it so he calmed himself and led him into the house. In the kitchen he found a bottle of unopened wine and poured them both a cup. They sat at the table and drank two before he spoke again.

"Now, start at the beginning and explain what you do know."

"The vizier of the south…"

"Paramese?"

"He's just calling himself Ramses now."

"Go on, what did Vizier Ramses do?"

"He has been Pharaoh's voice here in the Upper lands and he has been making new laws. Although he says they are old laws of the First Ones. He says they are the Law of Ra."

Yanhamu knew about the Law of Ra. He'd sought it his whole life after his first encounter with Meryra the scribe after his sister disappeared—taken by the gods because of her beautiful soul. And when he had found the law of man he had found it sadly lacking. So, he thought, perhaps Vizier Ramses has addressed the disparity between justice and law.

However, Yanhamu's hope was soon dashed.

Sadhu continued: "There are many changes. We must now all worship Amun and Ra, whether we are from the north or south. Only the men are permitted inside the temples. Women must pray separately. Married women must cover their heads and mouths so as not to encourage infidelity. Any married woman found to be acting lewdly will be stoned. And lewd behaviour has been interpreted as just looking at a man a certain way!"

Yanhamu shook his head. This was a strange interpretation of the Law of Ra. He feared the worst when he asked, "So are you telling me that Nefer-bithia has been stoned?"

"Oh no! What I haven't explained is that the new law also precludes a woman from certain jobs. Of course, women must work and satisfy their husband's needs, we all know that, but Vizier Ramses said something new. He decreed that no woman could take high office."

"Like being a magistrate?"

"Yes."

"So my wife stopped acting as a magistrate and went where?"

Sadhu poured himself another glass and glugged it down. "No, my lord. Your wife refused to accept the ruling. She wasn't so foolish as to refute it in public but she carried on. She wore your beard of office and—although clearly a woman—said she was a man. After all, she explained to me, Pharaoh Hatshepsut was a woman. She also said other pharaohs were originally women too. She said a person could, by their office, change their sex."

"And she carried on."

"In the name of Lord Khety. After all, you weren't here and it had been her father's name."

"What happened?"

"They came for her. Three moons ago, they let her open the tribunal in Abydos and then the local Nomarch stepped forward as the first case and accused her of being a woman and breaking the law. The crowd would have stoned her to death if it weren't for the guards. I was hit on the head and body, and your wife took some stones too. But the city guard encircled us and the prefect tore off her beard and gown. The last I saw of her was as they marched her out of the square. I was too much in shock…"

Yanhamu placed a calming hand on the young man's arm. "You could have done nothing. Where is everyone else? Where are the slaves?"

"Taken by the state."

"Poor Paneb."

"My lord, the slave Paneb is dead. The soldiers killed him." He started to cry. "And I am sorry, my lord for your wife is surely dead too."

"No!" Yanhamu stood, his hands clenched. "They wouldn't dare. Despite this new law, she was still a noble of high birth and they would not spill her blood. If they wanted that then she could have been fed to the mob.

No, they wanted her alive." He thanked the young man and marched out of the house.

"Where are you going, my lord."

"To find her!"

"Good," Sadhu said, hurrying beside him. "Then I'm coming with you."

THIRTY-TWO

San Francisco, California

The house had a great view of the bay and looked maybe a hundred years old. Special Agent Zhang was impressed. Maybe if he moved Marcie out to a place like this, she wouldn't be so sick. California weather and a picture postcard vista—couldn't hurt could it? Time to consider a move from Atlanta, he decided.

Professor Suza looked almost as old as her house but much less attractive. She was under five feet tall with a face like a crumpled bed sheet. But she was friendly enough and offered him iced tea.

He sat in her study and looked out across the gardens and bay view.

She said, "Second-generation Chinese, Agent Zhang?"

"I was born in China," he said, tasting the tea and deciding it wasn't to his liking. He put it down and returned her kindly smile.

"So you came here for school?"

"I studied econometrics at Peking University," he said. "I came to America for an MBA. I thought I'd become a business tycoon."

"And now you are in the FBI."

"Special entry scheme," he said. "Life rarely works out the way you plan."

"Man plans and God laughs," she said.

He nodded, pleasantries over. "Professor, you said you might have information that could help with the Surgeon case."

She pushed back her white hair, and although she was still smiling, he could see something darker in her eyes, some kind of sadness.

"What do you know about the resurrection, Agent Zhang?"

"Please call me Peter," he said. Then: "Christ was resurrected. Is that what you're referring to?"

"Was he?"

Zhang frowned. "Well that's… I guess it's a matter of belief, isn't it? The Bible tells us he was resurrected."

Professor Suza leaned forward. While he spoke, she had a finger hooked over her upper lip. Now she moved her hand. "What I'm about to tell you may come as a bit of a shock. It's controversial and has garnered me a great deal of hate mail over the years." She sighed. "Let's start by discussing Christ. The name comes from the Greek for the Messiah, and the Abrahamic religions—"

"Sorry, the what religions?"

"Judaism and Islam stem from Abraham. They both believe that the Messiah will be the saviour. In Judaism he is descended from the line of King David. He will only come once and will unify the tribes of Israel and return them to the Promised Land. He will rebuild the Temple in Jerusalem and usher in the Messianic Age of global peace."

Zhang nodded.

She continued: "In Islam the Messiah will return to Earth at the end of times, along with the Mahdi, and defeat al-Masih ad-Dajjal, the false Messiah."

190

Zhang must have looked nonplussed because she explained further.

"Not the Messianic Age of peace but the final judgement. In this there is annihilation of all creatures, including mankind, and the judgement of all sentient creatures. It is a time where everyone would be shown his or her deeds and actions with impartiality. At this point everyone's deeds and actions are judged and those found worthy are resurrected. However, this is about the on-going life of the soul and doesn't refer to bodily resurrection. Christians, on the other hand, believe that Jesus was the Messiah and was resurrected on the third day. He fulfilled the prophesies of the Old Testament, being the Son of God, dying for our sins and the resurrection to prove that life is eternal."

"Right," Zhang said, becoming uncomfortable. The old lady was a religious zealot and wasting his time. "Professor, excuse the bluntness, but could you get to the point?"

"The point, Peter, is that only Christians believe in bodily resurrection and a Second Coming. Before I talk about this I want to explain why my work received so much vitriol and why I went into hiding many years ago. There are fundamental flaws in the gospels—and bear in mind the meaning of the word. It's supposed to be the undeniable truth. Literally. And yet there are four accounts of the resurrection in the New Testament and they all differ. According to Paul, the entire Christian faith hinges upon the centrality of the resurrection of Jesus and the hope for a life after death."

Zhang nodded. He knew that much.

She continued: "Mark and Luke agree three women find the open tomb. They both agree on two Marys but Mark says the third was Salome whereas Luke reports someone called Joanna. Matthew on the other hand says it was only the Marys whereas John says it was Mary Magdelene alone. He goes on to say she saw two angels. Luke says the women saw two men. Mark says they saw a young man whereas Matthew says there was a single angel. He also mentions an earthquake. You'd have thought the others would have noticed an earthquake! Anyway, then we have the discrepancy over what happened next. What do you think happened, Agent Zhang?"

Zhang felt a cold sweat as if he were under a spotlight. "Er... I'm not sure I remember. Doesn't he speak with the disciples and then ascend to Heaven?"

Professor Suza smiled kindly, her face crinkling even more. "Mark says that the women tell no one. Luke says they tell the disciples but only Peter believes them and goes to the tomb to find the shroud. Jesus then appears to two strangers who then go and convince the disciples. John says that Mary only tells Peter who then finds the shroud. In his version, Jesus then appears to Mary Magdalene. And finally, we have what I believe to be the most likely from Luke. He says Peter goes to the tomb, finds the shroud and believes the body has been stolen. Interestingly he also mentions that soldiers guarding the tomb saw the angel, they tell the chief priests who then spread the story that the disciples stole the body. Agent Zhang—Peter—the fundamental tenet of Christianity is a befuddled mess."

"And that helps me how?"

"I'll come to that, but the person who could have cleared all of this up was your namesake—Peter the disciple. After all, he founded the modern day church as the first Bishop of Rome—or Pope."

"And you're saying he didn't."

She raised her eyebrow and her crinkled forehead folded over even more. "He would not discuss the resurrection. In fact he privately quarrelled with Paul—who after all hadn't been there. Paul was just a convert not a witness to any resurrection."

"OK," Zhang said uncertainly.

"So I'm telling you this, because I want you to understand how millions of believers can accept what is clearly nonsense. They believe what they want to believe and that delusion is the problem your so-called Surgeon is suffering from."

"You're saying he's a Christian?"

"Undoubtedly, but he's much more than that, Special Agent. Let me tell you about a cult called the Seventh Hour."

"I've not heard of them."

"That's not surprising because they masquerade as common or average Christians. Just a few people at the top of their organization know the precise nature of their beliefs." She paused for effect. "You've heard of Millennialism?"

"Possibly," he said unconvincingly.

"The belief that the Messiah will reign for a thousand years. This was later interpreted as successive thousand-year periods. These epochs will culminate in the final destruction of evil by a triumphant messianic figure, the Saoshyant, at the end of the last millennial age. There was a specific group who were convinced that the year 2000 was the end of the last epoch. I needn't remind you about how much unfounded hysteria there was at the time."

"No." Zhang remembered the expectation of computer catastrophe, not to mention the expectation of some apocalyptic flood caused by the alignment of planets.

"And of course the Jehovah's Witnesses prophesized that the Second Coming would be in 1878, which was revised to 1914, and they also believe in the literal thousand-year reign. But I'm not talking about either of these groups. The Seventh Hour probably refers to the time at which Jesus died on the cross."

"OK," Zhang said. His phone pinged but he ignored it.

"And the crucial moment for this group is the piercing of Jesus's side by a lance. John doesn't record much detail but just refers to a Roman soldier checking that Jesus is dead. Allegedly blood and water escape from the cut. The Seventh Hour believes that this cut penetrated the heart and therefore caused Jesus to die at that time. I don't know why, but they appear to believe the timing—the seventh hour is significant. Furthermore they believe that the cut is vital to the resurrection."

Zhang blinked. "The soldier pierces the dying man's heart—like the Surgeon."

"Precisely!"

"What else can you tell me?" Zhang said as his phone pinged again.

"According to the Gospel of Nicodemus—"

"Who?"

"Also known as the Acts of Pilate and one of the many gospels not included in the New Testament, possibly written in the fourth century AD." She laughed. "Which in itself is a ridiculous reason to reject the account, since none of the gospels were written until at least fifty years after Jesus's death."

Zhang's phone pinged again and he glanced at it. His wife wanted him to call urgently.

"Something important?" Suza asked.

"My wife wants me to call."

The professor stood. "I'll fetch some more iced tea, Peter. Please go ahead."

He nodded his thanks and dialled Marcie's number. "I'm working," he said when she answered.

"I thought you'd care to know," his wife said.

He took a breath. "What, dear?"

"The results have come back. I've spoken to the consultant and he's diagnosed POTS."

"What's that?"

"It's a heart condition that's affected when I lie down. It's why my heart rate and adrenaline go sky high. No wonder I can't sleep."

"OK…" he said uncertainly.

Marcie told him how it linked to her other problems, that they'd been looking at symptoms all this time rather than the cause.

"Which is this POTS."

"That's what I'm telling you. It's not very well understood, but there's one expert who's based in California. The consultant says this specialist can help me."

Zhang could visualize the dollar signs. This had happened before. A different diagnosis, but another so-called expert who'd charge the earth.

The professor returned with two recharged glasses.

"Great news," he said trying hard to sound genuine. "Let's talk about this when I get back."

Suza smiled at him kindly as he put away his phone.

"Where was I?" she said. "Ah, yes. The gospels. Not all of them made it into the New Testament, you know?"

She continued before Zhang could answer. "Anyway the Gospel of Nicodemus provides us with some missing detail of the crucifixion. It says that the Roman was a centurion from Cappadocia named Gaius Cassius Longinus. However the name is likely to be derivative since Longinus is probably the Latinized version of *lonche,* which was Greek for lance." She paused again before continuing. "I know I go around the houses, young man, but I'm coming to the point. The centurion not only pierces Jesus's side but also cleanses his body afterwards. I understand that the Surgeon is thought to wash the bodies. Is that right?"

Zhang nodded. Channel 7 had recently discovered that information. It did seem to fit, but he wasn't sure how it helped. Apart from deciding it was time to relocate to California—if he could still afford it—this looked like a wasted trip. He took another sip of the iced tea before he remembered how bad it was.

"Well thank you for your time, Professor," he said.

She looked at him quizzically.

"What?"

"I think you've missed the point."

He shook his head, uncertain. "Which is…?"

"This may have happened before. Cain and Abel?"

"I'm aware of the Bible story; Cain killed his brother."

"And was given a symbol. The Mark of Cain. Allegedly so that everyone would know him."

"And what is that mark?"

"No one knows. Not only that, but it's another misconception. Because the story originates from ancient Egypt."

Now Zhang leaned forward, intrigued. "I didn't know that."

"Osiris and his brother Seth."

"Seth, as in the devil?"

"Not the devil. More the yin to Osiris' yang. The opposition but also a force, an energy. Osiris was stabbed by Seth. Able was stabbed by Cane. We don't know what happened to Cane, but Osiris was effectively resurrected. He also fathered a son, Horus."

"Wow!"

"So you see the connection?"

"Not really," Zhang said, wishing his brain wasn't too tired to follow the professor's logic. "Summarize it for me, please."

Suza repeated the explanation of the questionable resurrection, the belief that someone else played a part: a Roman in Christ's case. The stories from ancient Egypt being similar to the Biblical story of Cain and Abel. The cleansing of the body, the piercing of the heart and the Mark of Cain.

She concluded with: "The Surgeon is re-enacting the role of Longinus, of Seth and of Cain."

"Wow!" Zhang said again, his head spinning.

"The church where you found the bodies. The Church of the Risen Christ."

"Yes?"

"Risen Christ. Resurrection. Too much of a coincidence, I think. Young man, you need to find out whether the church has a connection with the Seventh Hour group."

THIRTY-THREE

Deir Mawas, Egypt

Alex had lost track of time. He'd been working all night and all of the next day, absorbed by Yanhamu's story, when Telegram pinged on his phone.

He opened Brown's message.

Where are you?

Alex replied: **Near Amarna.**

His message self-destructed just as another arrived from Brown.

There are three prominent words now. Resurrection and Seth. Is there a link?

Not that I know of. Although my assistant translated immortality and Seth.

Your assistant?

Alex explained that he was from the dig with access to the find. He added: **We're OK now. I got rid of him**

Good. He could be the source of the words we're seeing.

OK. What was the third thing? You said three words.

Ansar. Mean anything?

Alex thought it meant "supporters", but he guessed Brown wasn't asking for a literal translation. No, he fired back. You?

Meet tomorrow at Sphinx? Something that might help.

Alex didn't immediately respond. He thought about his conversation with Vanessa. Mostly she didn't want him involved, but she also warned him about Brown. Could he be trusted?

Alex didn't know, but there was a way to find out. It would be good to know he could trust someone on this.

He went back to Telegram and agreed a time and place to meet.

Alex finally switched off the light, but Yanhamu's story continued to play in his head.

1309 BCE, Akhmim

Yanhamu beat hard on the Nomarch's door until a guard opened it. He was still wearing the insignia of a Blue army officer and the guard immediately saluted.

"Where is Nomarch Amethu? Tell him Lord Khety, past magistrate of the eleventh nome, officer of the army of Horus, has returned from the northern wars and demands an audience."

The soldier saluted once more and hurried away. Yanhamu didn't wait to be asked. He marched through the courtyard to the Hall of Records. He was met by a gaggle of scribes and was reminded that this was an administration centre. The Nomarch was just an administrator.

"Where is he?" Yanhamu bellowed.

The panicking men in white robes drew back and then one stepped forward and bowed.

"My lord, the Nomarch is not here. Lord Amethu is at the merchant's quay."

Yanhamu didn't wait for any more information. He turned on his heel and raced out of the Nomarch's office, through the town towards the river. As soon as he reached the quay, he spotted Amethu stepping off a barge. The soldier from the office had beaten them here and was already speaking to the Nomarch.

Yanhamu waited for Amethu to approach him. The Nomarch bowed, not low, but enough to show respect.

"Where is she, Amethu?"

"It's funny how quickly the people turn."

Yanhamu grabbed the other man by the tunic. The soldier stepped forward but Amethu waved him down.

Yanhamu said, "Funny how quickly the people turn? You turned on us, Amethu!" He pulled the Nomarch closer and glared into his face. "We once called you friend."

"I was just following orders."

"Where is she?" he asked again.

"I don't know. I honestly don't know."

"Did you cast her into the Pit of Repentance?" Yanhamu found the words hard to say. It was a dungeon close to the desert where the convicted were dumped. Food and water was passed down but no one ever came up. The stench of death was said to be more foul than the waters of the underworld where Apep plotted against Ra.

The Nomarch held up his hands in horror. "Oh no, Lord Khety. I could never... No, I was just acting on orders from the vizier. I merely carried out his orders. He arranged for her to be taken from here."

"Vizier Paramese?"

"He's calling himself Ramses these days."

"So I hear. Well, I don't care if he thinks he's Ra himself!" The men within earshot gasped but Yanhamu continued: "Will I find him in Waset?"

"That's where your wife was taken."

Moored close by was a single-sailed small boat. It looked sleek and fast.

"For hire?" Yanhamu said as he boarded her. "I need to get to Waset quickly."

The pilot bowed and quoted an extortionate price.

"He'll pay," Yanhamu shouted, and pointed to Nomarch Amethu. "Isn't that right?"

The Nomarch looked uncomfortable but nodded agreement, and within seconds the sail-boat cast off and began tacking against the Nile current. Sadhu sat on cushions at the rear while Yanhamu stood on the prow. He leaned forward as though urging the boat on could make it go faster.

At the palace of the vizier, Yanhamu was forced to wait for an appointment. However, when he was finally called forward for an audience, it wasn't the vizier but another court official who met him. It had taken the little boat almost two days and Yanhamu's rage had subsided. He was tired from lack of sleep but knew that calm would work better than confrontation.

"I asked to speak with Vizier Ramses," Yanhamu said after polite introductions.

"I am sorry but he is not here."

"That is a considerable shame since I have travelled so far." Yanhamu took a breath. "When will the great vizier return?"

"It is unknown."

"May I enquire where he has gone?"

"He now resides in Memphis."

"But his lordship is responsible for Upper Egypt."

The court official seemed to relax. Almost conspiratorially he said, "Of course you are correct... at the present. Who knows what Pharaoh has planned for the future?"

Yanhamu didn't know what this meant except that he would need to deal with someone else if he was to find out where Nefer-bithia was—if she was still alive. He took an offered drink and smiled. "Perhaps you have the power to help me."

The man smiled back. "If I have the power then it will be freely given. However, you should speak with Chancellor Memephat."

Yanhamu had another long wait before he was led through the halls into the Room of Judgement. Ordinarily, the vizier would have occupied the ornate chair on the stage. But the overweight man in flowing gown was the chancellor.

Yanhamu bowed as he was introduced.

"Ah, the great Lord Khety," the chancellor said and raised a hand. It was plump, like a plucked, overfed duck, and every finger had a gold or electrum ring.

Yanhamu stepped forward and pretended to kiss the hand. "You honour me," he said.

"It is an honour to meet the real Lord Khety." The chancellor smiled and Yanhamu felt an imagined knife to the gut.

"My wife was the genuine Lord Khety. I was in a foreign land fighting for Pharaoh, who is the Two Lands. My wife had every right to use my title."

Chancellor Memephat shrugged. "I'm afraid the law changed while you were away. It is now a crime to assume the office of a man. These were the old laws, passed down by the gods."

Yanhamu wanted to challenge the nonsense but there was clearly no point. There were guards behind the stage, and on either side sat two large cats with spots. Although docile, the threat was subtle. The chancellor must have seen his gaze.

"They are beautiful are they not? A gift. Faster and sleeker than a lion. More intelligent than a dog."

Yanhamu looked into Memephat's cold eyes. "My wife is beautiful and intelligent. I have been told she was brought to this city. Where would I begin to look for her?"

The chancellor held his hands wide, causing a ripple of fat under his arms. "I am afraid I do not know all cases or persons. Perhaps if you would like to take the Lodging of Nobles, I will enquire."

Yanhamu nodded. He tried to smile, although the knot in his stomach tightened with frustration. The man was telling him to wait for an indefinite period. "I would just like to know that she is alive."

"Oh, of course. I fully understand, Lord Khety. Please, take the lodging and we will send you a message as soon as an answer is available."

Five days passed before a messenger came to the Lodgings of Nobles asking for him. He'd spent the time in his room. Sadhu had visited him daily and brought food and wine. He spoke with enthusiasm about the excitement and gaiety of the city and the wonder of the temples in the adjacent City of a Thousand Gates. The boy had never been to the great third nome before. But his enthusiasm was lost on his master.

They travelled together with the messenger but it wasn't to the vizier's palace. They were taken to a small house in the artisan centre of town. Memephat was sitting under an awning drinking milk and eating cake when they arrived. He waved away his servant and pointed to Yanhamu. The message was clear. This was a private meeting and Sadhu was to wait outside.

"I trust you are well," Memephat began.

"I have found the lodgings to be most acceptable."

"And the entertainment?"

"Ah, unfortunately I have been unable to sample the delights of the city. However, my assistant tells me how much he has been enjoying the sights and pleasures."

The chancellor held out a plate. "Please try some of this honey bread. I have it imported from Punt." After Yanhamu took a small sticky slice, Memephat continued: "So, as I was saying, the women are very beautiful, no? Now that the married ones must wear a veil, it is easier to choose the available fruit."

"I am sure they are. However, my wife..."

The man showed a touch of irritation at Yanhamu's directness but didn't comment. Instead he tightened his lips in a faux smile. "My lord, I am saying that perhaps it is time for you to find yourself a young maiden."

"I am married."

"Ah yes..." Now the official grinned. "Aren't we all but the law allows for a man—"

"Where is my wife?"

Again the tight-lipped smile and then the shake of his head.

"A shame, I could arrange for an attractive mistress."
He held up a placatory hand as Yanhamu started to
stand. "Lord Khety, I see that you are determined, but I
can do nothing about it."

"Is she alive?"

"You would like to see her, yes? But it is impossible."

"How much will it cost me?"

Memephat turned up his nose like there was a bad
smell. "Please, there is no need for crudeness. Perhaps a
gift? Do you have any leopards?"

"I will give you my property in Akhmim. It has
twenty rooms, a courtyard ten times the size of this one
and has a view of the Great River."

"In the lowly ninth nome? How many slaves can you
throw in?"

"All my slaves were confiscated by the state."

Memephat's smile told Yanhamu that the man
already knew about the slaves.

Yanhamu said, "I have returned to claim what is
rightfully mine. I am Lord Khety, and when the slaves
are mine once more, I will gift them to you."

"Alas it is too late. Your slaves are gone. Sold or
dead." He smiled, although his small dark eyes stayed
cold. "Perhaps gold?"

"Half my salary in gold is yours, great Memephat."

The chancellor nodded slowly, as though considering
the bargain. "Half your gold for ten minutes with your
wife. All your gold for thirty minutes. I'm sure you
understand that these things must be arranged and
funded."

Memephat smiled naturally for the first time. He held
out the Rod of Agreement—an ivory bar with golden
scrolled tips. Both men gripped it, sealing the deal.
Between nobles it was as good as a signature or
independent witnesses.

"Come to the palace tomorrow," Memephat said. "Not the main gate. You will find a small door in the west wall. Be there at the hour of Sais, before sunrise, and you shall see your wife."

"Small door, west wall," Yanhamu said, his head light with relief.

"Yes," the man said still smiling. "It is the way to the vizier's private harem."

THIRTY-FOUR

Cairo, Egypt

Charlie kicked off her shoes and flopped onto her sofa. It had been a long day. She hadn't heard from Zhang and wondered whether he'd seen the professor in California yet.

A sharp rap on the door surprised her.

She peered through the peep hole and was relieved to see John Graham on the other side.

"John," she said, opening the door. "What...?"

He strode in and she realized his face was set with anger.

"What the hell?" he barked turning on her.

She took an involuntary step back. Without her shoes on, he towered over her. "Sir?"

"You're supposed to keep me informed, Agent Rebb."

She took a breath. "Can I fix you a drink, sir?"

"Why didn't you tell me about the other case?"

"What other case?"

"The one about the Brit."

She shook her head, not understanding. Yes, she was guilty of not feeding him her updates but they were tedious. What did a Brit have to do with it? And then she got it.

"You mean Detective Shafik's other case!"

"Of course," Graham said, his neck flushed with annoyance. "Of course that's what I mean. It might be connected."

"It might?"

"Find out."

"I will," she said, conscious that her heart was pounding. Graham had got himself wound up about a link between her case and the one he'd been involved in when she'd arrived. She shook her head. "I didn't know, but now that I do—"

"You'll update me at least daily," he snapped then spun on his heels and marched out again.

She shut the door behind him and stared at it for a moment before swiping the fob across the lock.

What an idiot, she thought to herself. Any idea of him being charming had dissipated. He was just a bureaucratic idiot. If he'd been so concerned then he should have done the job himself rather than ask her to do it.

She poured herself a large glass of red and dropped onto the sofa again.

Her phone rang.

"Liz," she answered.

"Is now a good time?" her sister asked.

"Not really."

Liz continued anyway. "Dad's been picked up down by the river. He was disorientated. Told the police he didn't know his way home. God, Charlie, we've been there a thousand times. He should know his way home from there."

Charlie sighed but said nothing.

Liz said, "He's suffering from dementia, Charlie. Early signs, but he's losing it. Why, only yesterday he thought I was Mom and he calls Rob, Mandy and other names all the time."

"Rob probably deserves it—the name calling that is," Charlie said. She took a sip of wine, half listening, half her brain still wound up by John Graham.

Liz said nothing for a moment. Then her voice changed and was edged with excitement when she next spoke. "I have news," she said.

"News?"

"I'm pregnant."

"Congratulations."

"You don't sound very happy for me."

Charlie clenched her teeth and then it all came out. "You want the truth? I'm not happy. This is why… why you want Dad in a home."

"He's a liability to himself, Charlie." She was defensive now.

"No, Liz. Dad is in your way. You used him to buy your big house and now you're starting a family. That's what this has all been about."

Liz began arguing but Charlie cut her short.

"I can't deal with this right now, Liz," she said and ended the call.

THIRTY-FIVE

1309 BCE, Waset (Luxor)

The nocturnal hour of Sais was the false dawn. It was said that at this hour, Seth would lead the four serpent goddesses to ward off the final dangers that might threaten sunrise. In the pits, the shadows, the ba-souls, and the heads of those to be punished are destroyed one by one.

As Yanhamu touched the grain of the tamarisk door he felt the same portent. Beyond this door was either a new day or the pits of eternal darkness. Of course, he hadn't slept. Memephat had said he would see his wife. It wasn't until after the meeting that Yanhamu had realized the chancellor had not been clear. When he'd asked if she was alive, Memephat had said it was impossible to see her and then he'd accepted the financial agreement. Yanhamu knew of such trickery and he kicked himself for falling for it. Nefer-bithia could be dead.

At the precise moment of the hour, Yanhamu knocked. He then placed his shaking hands behind his back.

The door was immediately opened a crack.

"You are Yan-Khety?"

It had been a long time since his name had been used without a title. But he wore a simple grey gown with no symbols of office or status. Memephat had said it was for discretion but Yanhamu knew it was a gesture of control. The chancellor wanted him belittled. He had taken everything that Yanhamu owned and now he was taking his pride.

"I am he," Yanhamu said, and the door opened wide. He stepped through into a courtyard. The man who closed the door behind him had a spear and a lifeless face.

Yanhamu swallowed. "I am here to see Nefer Khety."

"This way."

The path led under an arch into a garden. Even in the grey light of pre-dawn Yanhamu could see its beauty. There were circular beds of flowers and manicured trees that were like sleeping storks. They walked on and came to another arch over soil that had been freshly turned. There was a spade.

Oh Anhuris, strong and good protector! Yanhamu prayed. My Bith has been taken to the afterlife. His legs gave way and he fell to his knees. They were going to dig up her body so that he could see her. That was Memephat's trick.

He felt a rough hand under his arm pulling him back up.

"You only have thirty minutes, and you don't want to waste it sniffing the mud!"

Yanhamu staggered on, confused. "She's alive?" he managed to say.

The guard chuckled. "Of course, you idiot! Why would anyone in their right mind pay to come in here to see a dead girl?"

211

They went through another courtyard and, for the first time, Yanhamu saw the walls of the palace. Two storeys up was a balcony with an ornate screen.

"Wait and watch and be quiet," the guard said.

Yanhamu waited. Nothing happened for five minutes except the honk of unseen geese beyond the next wall. He was about to complain when a shadow moved on the balcony.

"Bith!" Yanhamu shouted. He would have shouted again but a rough hand clamped around his throat.

"Silence, or this is over right now!"

Yanhamu nodded and the hand was released. He could see more shadows and then the screens were pulled back. Ladies stood above him and stretched and yawned. One opened her tunic and showed perfectly formed breasts. The guard chuckled.

They glanced down, and Yanhamu suspected the show had just been for them. The women moved and more appeared, but he couldn't see his wife. And then she was there, as beautiful as the day they had married ten years ago.

"Bith!" he screamed. At the same time, he twisted away from the guard.

"Yani?"

"I'll get you out, my sweet. I'll—" but his words were smothered by a hand.

"Vizier Ramses," she called as he was dragged away. "Tell the pharaoh he's holding me!"

Ramses was no longer a vizier. He was now referred to as the Deputy Lord of the Two Lands, as well as Pharaoh's right-hand fan-bearer. He'd built a palace in Memphis bigger than the vizier's palace in the south. There was a great deal of construction going on, continuing the recognition of Memphis as the state's capital, whereas Waset and the City of a Thousand Gates was the religious capital. Amun in the south and Ra in the north. United as one god Amun-Ra, making Egypt great again. But all the wealth and power and joy were alien to Yanhamu. He'd spent a week travelling back after Sadhu had persuaded him to leave Waset.

His wife wanted Yanhamu to speak to the pharaoh, but that would be impossible and pointless. So, Yanhamu's initial plan was to raise an army and break into the vizier's palace. He was sure he could find ex-Blue soldiers who would follow him.

"And if you gain a victory, if you are reunited with your wife, what then?" Sadhu had said.

"It will be over."

"Yes it will," he had said with wisdom beyond his years. "You will be hunted down and destroyed. You cannot fight the state and expect to survive."

"But justice is on my side!"

"Tell that to Osiris when your body is dumped in the pit."

So Yanhamu and his assistant had travelled north to the capital and they had plotted. What does a man do when he has nothing? He creates something from that nothing.

Yanhamu requested an audience with Deputy Lord Ramses and within two hours was taken to the Great Hall.

Yanhamu almost stopped in his tracks as he approached Ramses' throne. The man could have passed for the pharaoh if he had worn the two crowns—the red and white of the Two Lands—rather than the lesser blue one.

The man squinted at him, and Yanhamu was reminded that he was not a young man. His eldest son—

now Master of the King's Horses—was at least Yanhamu's age.

"Is that you, Yan-Khety? I don't recognize you."

"Time has passed."

Ramses nodded.

Yanhamu said, "And you, my lord, have been recognized as a great leader. I remember when you were commander of the king's army."

"And you were once a translation officer in the Black and rose to the status of leader of 250, for the Blues." The way Ramses said it was with contempt rather than as an accolade. Then he smiled. "You bring a message. What's this I hear about secrets?"

"I have secrets to tell."

Ramses smiled again. "Yes?"

"I know what happened to Pharaoh Tutankhaten."

"Tutankhamen."

"And his father."

"So?"

"And Pharaoh Ay."

Ramses clapped his hands and bellowed, "Leave us!"

There must have been thirty men in the room, and within seconds, Ramses and Yanhamu were alone.

"Are you threatening me, Khety?"

"No, my lord, certainly not! I am offering you my services. The pharaoh must have a Keeper of Secrets and I know that since the royal line was broken, the secrets have been lost."

"I am a descendant of Ahmose who could trace his origins back to Horus Himself."

"You are Pharaoh Horemheb's cousin."

Ramses nodded, and Yanhamu saw something in the old man's eye. Something wasn't quite right although he doubted he'd ever find out what it was. The deputy said. "Go on, then. Tell me what you know."

So Yanhamu told Ramses what he had learned from Meryra, who had served Akhenaten and Nefertiti. He told the deputy that, after her husband's death, Nefertiti had ruled using the name Smenkhkare. She had married her own daughter to continue the blood-line and wait until Tutankhaten—as he was originally called—was old enough. They had enemies, not least of whom were the priests who saw themselves undermined and impoverished by the heretic pharaoh. With their support, Ay—the boy's paternal grandfather, and of no royal blood—took charge as regent.

"He poisoned Pharaoh," Yanhamu said. Even after so many years, he still found it hard to say. "He also performed the Opening of the Mouth incorrectly and made sure the pharaoh could not find the Field of Reeds."

"What else do you know?"

"I know about Pharaoh Horemheb, how he persuaded the usurper Ay to take the old way and die with honour. However"—now he spoke quietly because he knew that his words were tantamount to treason—"he desecrated the tombs of Akhenaten and Ay."

Ramses shook his head. "This is terrible."

"And they are secrets, my lord. I have said them to no other but yourself—" Yanhamu took a breath. Everything that he had planned now hinged on what happened next. He said, "Descendant of Horus, future pharaoh of the Two Lands, you must know the facts."

Ramses said nothing for a long time. He fixed Yanhamu with his eyes and Yanhamu tried to look like a trusted servant. Eventually the deputy said, "You have gambled with your life, Khety. Either you should be put to death immediately for your lies or you should become my Keeper of Secrets. Which should it be?"

"Keeper of Pharaoh's secrets," Yanhamu replied.

Ramses shook his head. "But I need more. The secrets you know are nothing and of no use. I need the true secrets of the past."

"You need to be assured of Osiris' blessing and of guaranteed eternal life," Yanhamu said. None of the rulers since Amenhotep III, Akhenaten's father had been given the appropriate respect and shown the way to the Field of Reeds by their successors. And eternal life was what it was all about.

"Then you must prove yourself," Ramses said with finality. "Find me the truth."

THIRTY-SIX

Atlanta, Georgia

Agent Zhang's flight back to Atlanta was delayed. He got a cup of coffee and called Reverend Piccard.

"It's been a long time, Special Agent. How can I help you?"

"Have you heard of Professor Suza?"

"Can't say that I have heard of her. Is this relevant to the case? Have you made progress?"

"That's why I'm calling, Reverend. I wonder if the professor knows something. I wonder if she's right?"

"About what?"

Zhang took a gulp of coffee and realized he was looking at his reflection in the window. It was like he was talking to himself. Beyond, he could see an American Airlines plane being manoeuvred to a gate.

"Have you heard of the Seventh Hour?"

No response.

"Reverend?"

Piccard said, "Apologies, Special Agent, I was thinking. It sounds familiar. Do you mean the eleventh hour. Of course, I find that a familiar expression."

"Not the eleventh. Specifically the seventh. It's an organization, not an expression."

217

"And you think this organization is relevant? How?"

Again Zhang looked at himself. He was getting old and tired. Maybe he shouldn't just move field office. Maybe it was time to use his actual qualifications and get a real job. Or maybe that was just Marcie's voice he was hearing in his head.

"Special Agent?"

Zhang realized he'd been silent for a while. This was a bad idea. He said, "I'll come and see you. I'll explain what Professor Suza said. In the meantime, perhaps you can think about Seventh Hour and whether there could be a connection with your church."

"You think this organization is responsible for the murders? I thought you were looking for the Surgeon. And haven't I just read that he's in Egypt?"

"I'll explain when I see you."

"When?"

Zhang looked at his watch. The Delta flight time was almost five hours. Half an hour delay plus three-hour time difference would mean he wouldn't land until nine thirty in the evening. By the time he got to Piccard's it would be after ten. "Tomorrow," he said. "Let's do it tomorrow morning at nine."

"All right, Agent Zhang. I look forward to seeing you then."

Zhang ended the call and dialled Charlie.

Cairo, Egypt

Charlie put her book down and answered her partner's call. "It's late," she said. "I was just going to bed."

"On your own or do you have a new Pablo? Or should I say Pabhamed?"

"Is that supposed to be funny?"

Zhang chuckled. "It was to me."

Charlie had drunk most of the bottle of red and was still annoyed by Graham's visit and her sister's news. She said, "Is that the reason for the call or are you going to tell me about your meeting with the professor?"

"She thinks this is about religion."

Charlie had been thinking the same thing. The book she had been reading was called *Temples, Tombs and Hieroglyphs*. "And that's it?" she said.

Zhang summarized what the professor had said about Christianity being founded on the belief of the resurrection despite there being conflicting stories and Peter's lack of support.

He said, "There are groups like the Jehovah Witnesses and Millennium who believe in the Second Coming. Maybe Christ has come multiple times and will come again. And then there's the Seventh Hour group who believe it can be precipitated by a Roman with a spear."

"A Roman?"

"I may have gotten that bit wrong. But they believe Jesus's resurrection was helped along by the centurion who stabbed him in the heart with a spear."

"In the heart? I thought it was supposed to be his side."

"Apparently that's a misconception. The professor also said that Cain and Abel was taken from an ancient Egyptian story about Osiris and Seth. Seth is also called Set and—"

"Are you saying Larouse"—Charlie shivered at the thought of the disgusting man—"and the Satanic church are involved after all, Peter?"

"No. This is about a group called the Seventh Hour trying to precipitate the resurrection or the Second Coming."

"All right," she said. "I'll see if that makes sense over here. What are you doing next?"

"Tomorrow I'm going to see Piccard from the Church of the Risen Christ."

"Oh my God!"

"Wow!" he said. "You got that connection quicker than I did."

She said, "Resurrection."

"Precisely. Maybe the Surgeon used that church for a reason. Maybe he's used more of their churches."

"Good work," she said.

There was a pause on the line, before Zhang said, "Thanks, Charlie. Have a good night."

Charlie put the phone down and smiled for the first time that day. Maybe Peter was softening. Maybe this case would end the stupid psychological games he tried to play with her. Maybe he wasn't so bad.

Or maybe she'd had too much wine.

She picked up her book again and tried to read a chapter about the religious wars between the followers of Osiris and those of Seth. But nothing jumped out as relevant and she couldn't concentrate. She kept going over what Zhang had told her. Something else bothered her about the church and the body dump but she couldn't quite grasp it.

His title was the Haris al'Asrar—the Keeper of Secrets. Few people within the organization knew he was the one. He'd been selected by the previous Haris al'Asrar, like *he* had been before. And before him, back thousands of years. Back to the reign of Ramses I. Back when the secrets were rediscovered and passed down the generations.

Only he knew that the biggest secret of all had been forgotten. Or perhaps lost or deliberately hidden.

He wasn't the official head of their organization, Ansar Beit al-Maqdis, Champions of the Holy Site, but he had the power. His position within the Egyptian establishment also gave him control. It always had been as it always would be.

They'd had problems in the past; the Muslim Brotherhood's militant activities had at first been useful, but they had a different agenda. They didn't know the truth. And so the affiliation had been ended. Which was good since they were on the decline while Ansar Beit al-Maqdis had to continue, had to maintain their subtlety and subterfuge.

A bigger problem was of course the Zionist pigs, their stupid arrogant beliefs that they tried to impose on the world. Their racism, which was somehow acceptable because of their tragic history, and the West supported their illegal land grabbing and persecution of Arabs.

And then there were the Masons, that foolish organization that pretended to be secular but were Zionists in disguise. If they only knew of the secrets, then they may have some real reason for their worship of the pyramids and all things associated with ancient Egypt. But they didn't. They just kept their silly secrets and their pathetic rituals.

And because of this, the Haris al'Asrar knew that their enemy was not the Masons this time. There was someone else. Someone else had killed his man on Eza Street. Someone else was controlling the AI program that threatened to expose their organization. Maybe even the Keeper of Secrets himself. And that could never be allowed.

Initially he had wondered whether Dr Hawass was involved. He could have been an important part of the organization, but he couldn't be controlled. He was too much of a self-publicist. Too risky.

And then there were the clay tablets. Those little biscuit-like records that hid Khety Yanhamu's messages. The leader had wanted them translated in case the lost secret was written there. But that too was too risky. MacLure or his assistant, Mahmood, might tell others before the story could be stopped.

So the Keeper of Secrets had come to a decision.

He sent a message to his man in Deir Mawas.

Kill MacLure and the assistant, it said. **Destroy all evidence of the clay tablets.**

The Third

THIRTY-SEVEN

Atlanta, Georgia

Zhang and Detective Garcia were outside Reverend Piccard's house.

"Why don't you ring the doorbell a fifth time?" Zhang said sarcastically. "He didn't answer his home phone so I think it's safe to assume he's not here."

Garcia pulled a tight smile like he was just tolerating the FBI agent. He'd already expressed concern over Zhang's phone call yesterday.

"You warned him," Garcia said. "He's taken flight."

"Then call a goddamn APB and let's get over to the church." They were in separate cars and Zhang was already walking back to his.

He got to the Church of the Risen Christ five minutes later and parked properly in a bay next to a dark blue Lexus. Garcia pulled up beside him.

"Cancel that APB," Zhang said. "That's Piccard's car."

"It's just his car. Doesn't mean the good reverend is here."

But he was. Piccard strode towards them as they opened the church door. He smiled like there was nothing wrong.

Zhang growled, "You weren't home."

"Was I supposed to be?" Piccard said shaking his head like he was confused. "I thought you wanted to meet here."

Now it was Zhang's turn to shake his head. "No you didn't."

Piccard smiled beatifically. "Really, gentlemen, there's no need for this atmosphere of animosity."

"You lied," Zhang said, his tone still sharp.

Piccard blinked rapidly. "I beg your—"

"I asked if you knew Professor Suza. You replied that you didn't know her."

Piccard looked innocent.

Zhang said, "Sit down."

When the reverend sat in the nearest pew, Zhang continued: "How did you know the professor was a woman? You said 'her'."

Piccard shrugged, still composed. "I guessed."

"Odd guess," Garcia said.

"You knew," Zhang said, closing in and standing over Piccard. "Now, tell us how you know her."

"She sent threatening letters to the church. At least I assumed it was her. At first I thought—"

"No more bullshit!" Zhang snapped.

Piccard continued with the innocent look, which Zhang found increasingly annoying.

"The Seventh Hour..." Zhang prompted.

"Like I told you yesterday—"

"I don't believe you. Try harder." Zhang tapped the wooden pew beside the reverend like he was tapping the man's shoulder. "Think and then think some more until..."

Garcia had a hand on Zhang's arm. He wanted to speak in private.

Zhang eased back and then some more. "What?"

"Steady," Garcia said. "You were shouting. And I thought you were going to poke him. Remember, he is a man of God and we've got no—"

"Hold on," Zhang said raising a hand. He pulled out his phone, which was ringing. The display said: Charlie Rebb.

"Charlie?"

"Hey Peter, I've been thinking."

"In the middle of the night?"

"It's the afternoon here."

"Oh, right."

She said, "Something bothered me about what you said—about the church. You need to get over there right now."

"Already here."

"Really?" She paused. "Then great. Well, here's the problem. The bodies were under the church, right? Shallow graves, and you could just about crawl under there. We should have thought about that. It was hard for us to get them out. It would have been harder still to bury them. So why bury them at all?"

"Where are you going with this?" He looked at Piccard who still seemed as calm as a dog in the sun. "What you thinking?" Zhang asked Charlie.

"That the Surgeon didn't crawl under there to bury them."

"Then what—?"

"Search the whole church. Check the floor. There'll be trapdoors, I'll bet my salary on it." Zhang knew she only said that when she was right. And this certainly felt right. He ended the call and smiled at Piccard.

"Detective Garcia, let's get some men down here. We're going to rip up the goddamn flooring."

THIRTY-EIGHT

Giza, Egypt

Find me the truth, Ramses I had told Yanhamu. What was the truth? Alex walked towards the Great Pyramid and wondered if it really was Khufu's and if it wasn't then whose had it been? Who had built it and why?

He'd driven down in the early hours of the morning to be at the Giza necropolis for the 10am meeting with Brown. The back of the VW was laden with three suitcases of his and Vanessa's things. They weren't going back to Deir Mawas. Not for some time anyway.

While he drove, Alex thought about Seth, god of chaos, storms and the desert. He had killed and dismembered his brother, whom Isis then reconstructed. She placed Osiris under the Tree of Life so that he could be reborn. Was that the resurrection referred to in the word cloud?

Brown wanted to meet at the Sphinx. Not the pyramids. He specifically said the Sphinx. What was it about the pharaoh-headed lion? Could that have something to do with the new word—Ansar—that had been found by the AI program?

Alex went through the barriers into the Giza necropolis. Before the troubles, there would have been crowds walking up the dusty slope towards the pyramids. Not now. He figured there were less than a tenth of the tourists than there used to be.

There was a sprinkling of security men, but no one seemed interested in him. Alex looked around at the tourists. He'd only met Brown in the hotel elevator—and hadn't really seen him. In his mind's eye he saw a tallish man in a black and white wrap-around scarf. Not much to go on.

Alex had passed the ancient, sunken valley temple and now the Sphinx was on his left. He shook his head at the damage caused by French muskets. Napoleon's men had used the astounding sculpture for shooting practice.

He walked around the back and looked at the weathered stone. It certainly didn't look like wind or sand damage. Could there really have been a deep, prolonged flood here? Andrew had been convinced, but that made the statue tens of thousands of years older than the official age.

Alex focused on the head: a pharaoh, assumed to be Khafre. The second pyramid was Khafre's. Below the Sphinx's paws was the Sphinx temple. To the right of this was Khafre's temple. A causeway ran from the temple by the Sphinx to the funerary temple in front of Khafre's pyramid. Since there was no one looking remotely interested in him, Alex decided to stroll along the causeway to the pyramid. Five hundred paces.

Once there, he turned and looked back.

The Sphinx hadn't been carved for Khafre. He was certain of that. The alignment was all wrong. The Sphinx faced east. The funerary temple faced east and was dead centre in front of the pyramid. Surely the Sphinx should have been in line too, but it wasn't. It was off at maybe twenty degrees south.

Alex looked around. The three pyramids—and even the smaller ones—were in the cardinal directions, allegedly positioned as the Earthly representation of Orion's belt. The funerary temple and valley temple of Menkaure's pyramid ran from east to west. It was just Khafre's temple and the Sphinx that didn't make sense.

Alex checked his watch. Brown was over an hour late.

After sitting in the shade behind Khafre's pyramid, he opened the Telegram app and sent a message to Brown asking where he was.

A guard walked past and looked at Alex... maybe assessing. Presumably he rarely saw anyone just sheltering from the sun. Or... could that be Brown? Had he said to meet here because he was a guard?

A minute later, the man was back again.

"I take your photo?" the guard said.

Alex wondered if he'd misunderstood. "Sorry? What?"

"Photograph. You with pyramid behind." The guard shrugged casually. "Just five pounds. I take the best photos."

"Brown?"

"Photo," the guard repeated, clearly not reacting to the name.

Alex waved him away.

But the guard lingered. "Twenty pounds for a special tour."

"No," Alex said firmly. The man shrugged again and ambled away looking for another tourist. Not Brown, Alex was sure.

He checked his phone and saw that his message hadn't been read yet. Where was he?

As he was looking, a message pinged though from Vanessa. She would fly back to Cairo tomorrow. Alex messaged back with an update.

I told you not to trust Brown, she replied.

Maybe something's happened

He's probably a crank

Alex wrote: But there's the AI program and Black's in hiding

According to the Brown guy. Seriously Alex give it up

They messaged some more and Alex headed for the exit. He'd meet Vanessa from the flight tomorrow, pack and then fly back to England.

And yet, something niggled in the back of Alex's mind. Yanhamu's secret notes talked about the truth, and it all seemed to point to the pyramids. Maybe a conspiracy. Maybe a hidden truth. And Brown seemed to be the link. If Black existed—and the police seemed to think so—then what had he stumbled upon?

A tourist in a Panama hat stood outside the ugly building that contained Khufu's funerary boat. He held a professional-looking camera with a large lens. Anyone studying him might have wondered why he'd need such a lens in the necropolis, but no one paid him any attention.

He moved the camera around as though looking for another great photo opportunity and then zoomed in on Alex MacLure.

He had white ear-phones, the ones with the discreet microphone for telephone calls. And he was speaking.

"The target is leaving," the cameraman said.

"And he spoke to no one?"

"Just a guard."

The man on the other end of the phone said, "Then he must be the contact."

"The conversation was brief. I don't think—"

The man on the phone barked, "Don't think, imbecile! When MacLure leaves, pick up the guard. Find out who he is and what he knows."

"And the target?"

"Someone else will follow MacLure."

THIRTY-NINE

1308 BCE, Valley of the Kings

Yanhamu and his assistant stepped off the ferry on the west bank. They drew strange glances from the other passengers dressed as priests and their acolytes.

"They're wondering why we are here," Yanhamu explained, but Sadhu wasn't listening. He was looking up at the pyramid-shaped hill, its peak glowing orange in the early hours of the day.

"It's wondrous," the young man said, slinging his heavy bag over one shoulder. "The closer I get, the more power I feel."

"Don't get too powerful!"

They walked over to a man with a donkey attached to a covered cart and paid him to take them up to the entrance of the necropolis. He didn't seem to understand.

"Not a temple, master?" He looked towards the ferry. "And no body for embalming?"

Yanhamu humoured the man. "Just the valley gates, if you please. And before this heat becomes unbearable."

Midway through the ponderous journey, as the donkey took the steady, curving incline, Sadhu said,

"Why are the pharaohs entombed here? Why not in pyramids like the First Ones?"

"Because this is the holiest of holy sites. This is the pyramid. This is where Horus was conceived, and after all, the pharaoh is the embodiment of Horus."

"Then why did the other pharaohs build replicas?"

"Perhaps they didn't think it right to disturb the holy place where our nation began."

"But then why did Pharaoh Thutmose decide it was all right?"

"I don't know, Sadhu."

"Really?" The young man laughed. "And yet you normally know everything!"

"I know that the life expectancy of a certain magistrate's assistant just got much shorter."

Sadhu was still laughing. "Thank Thoth that I'm no longer a magistrate's assistant then!"

At the gates to the Great Field, the wadi that carved through the heart of the magical hill, two Medjay guards stepped out of the shade and crossed spears.

"I am Lord Khety, here by order of Deputy Pharaoh Ramses."

Neither man blinked.

Yanhamu motioned for his assistant to step forward and Sadhu handed over the scroll bearing the blue seal of Ramses. The guard who took it glanced, recognized the seal and called out for someone.

An officer appeared and was handed the scroll. It was probable that only this man could read. He broke the seal, studied the contents and handed it back.

"You know it is forbidden for the deputy—or his representative—to see his tomb before the appointed day."

Yanhamu knew that both Horemheb's and Ramses' tombs were being excavated. The deputy's had only recently been started but Pharaoh Horemheb's was said to be near completion.

Yanhamu smiled and nodded. "Of course, I am not worthy. I am not qualified to see the secrets of the afterlife. No, my orders are to check on the tombs of Pharaoh Akhenaten and Pharaoh Tutankhamen."

He saw relief in the officer's face. Akhenaten was still hated by many and his son had been shown a similar lack of respect. Yanhamu had been allowed in their tombs before and now, with Ramses' blessing, he would do it again.

"It's cold," Sadhu said as they were led up the central path by one of the guards.

"What did you expect," Yanhamu said. "The souls of the dead are here."

"Just so long as we don't have to stay here after dark!"

They passed Akhenaten's tomb and Yanhamu said a silent prayer. He'd placed Meryra's coffin inside that empty tomb last time he'd been here. The guard hesitated but Yanhamu pointed ahead to the tomb on the right. Tutankhamen's tomb.

He paid a stonemason to chisel an opening large enough to crawl through. As they waited, he saw workmen in the left-hand spur. They were excavating, and he assumed they must be working on Ramses' tomb since it was early days. Yanhamu knew that the workers wore hoods when they came to and from work. It was a sign of respect to the gods as well as for security. There were heathens about who wouldn't think twice about breaking into a pharaoh's tomb and stealing the riches.

Further up the central wadi, Yanhamu spotted a priest and suspected he'd find Horemheb's tomb in that location.

When the hole was big enough to crawl through, the stonemason disappeared inside. They could hear him chipping away at the next door and half an hour later he re-emerged, dusty and grey. Yanhamu paid the man handsomely and tipped the guard. When they were alone, Sadhu lit two torches and they crawled one after the other into the darkness. They descended a short flight of stone steps before they came to a smooth passage. Moments later they were in front of the second blockage, the one to Tutankhamen's antechamber.

Yanhamu didn't hesitate. He went through the crawl space and Sadhu followed.

The light from the torches flickered around the room and lit the golden furniture. Sadhu gasped, awestruck.

Yanhamu went to his knees and prayed. "My Lord Tutankhamen, who wore the crowns and bound the Two Lands together, who pleases the gods and is the son of Ra, I have returned to honour you but also to ask for your tolerance and guidance."

When he finished, he realized Sadhu was shaking beside him. The young man stared up at the twin figures standing either side of the burial chamber door. In black and gold, the statues danced in the light as if alive.

"Vessels for Pharaoh Tutankhamen's ka," Yanhamu said in a hushed voice.

"Not real?"

"Representative."

The young man breathed heavily, although the air was bitter and dry. He stood and looked up at the face of one, held his torch close.

"Has anyone ever said you look like him?" he whispered.

"When I was a boy."

"You don't think...?"

"That I'm related? It's possible. My mother came from the harem of Akhenaten's court."

Sadhu's mouth dropped open.

"I'm joking." Yanhamu laughed. "My mother was a commoner and I was born a peasant." The tension eased and Yanhamu pointed to a dull wooden chest. He'd lugged it here an age ago with his old friend, Thayjem. It was Meryra's and it held the secrets intended for the boy-king. It told him everything Meryra knew about the villainy of Ay. It also included the Book of the Dead, because Ay had only included part of the instructions.

Yanhamu opened the chest and removed papyri. Sitting cross-legged in the confined space he dictated pieces of the documents to his assistant, who wrote them down.

They toiled for many hours stopping only to drink and eat fruit, and they lost the sense of time. In fact time did not seem to exist in this alien space beneath the pyramid hill.

And then they heard the three bells that signalled the end of the day. But Yanhamu kept translating.

"We should go," Sadhu said after an unknown period. "It will be dark soon and we don't want to be in the Great Field after dark."

Yanhamu kept reading.

"My lord?"

Yanhamu looked into the young man's eyes. "I'm afraid this is just the beginning. We need the darkness. We're staying."

"But—" Sadhu's eyes widened with alarm.

"But we aren't staying here. We're going into another tomb."

FORTY

1308 BCE, Valley of the Kings

Cool and refreshing air washed over his face and Yanhamu realized now how lightheaded he'd become from breathing the oil lamp fumes. He looked up at the clear sky, the Milky Way, the Great River of the Night. The pale light made the rocks white, and he wondered how many Horus-souls were here, awaiting the call of Ra, to assist him on his journey through the darkness.

"I'm scared," Sadhu whispered. "I'm afraid of the souls. I'm afraid of violating the sacred laws."

"Alright. I understand. You stay here with Tutankhamen's ka and I will go to Horemheb's tomb."

"On second thoughts..."

"Good. Now stop talking. If we are discovered by the Medjay, all this effort will be for nothing." Keeping close to the valley wall, he then led the young man west. They passed the spur where he guessed Ramses' tomb was being excavated and continued to the right. The opening was slightly higher than the valley floor and planks took them into the cave below overhanging rock.

Down a short flight of steps, they were soon in complete darkness, their footfall sounding loud. And something else. A sniff maybe.

"You aren't crying are you?"

"No, master. I thinking I'm getting a cold."

"Listen, there are no gods or spirits down here. This tomb is still being prepared, and I intend to learn the secrets of the high priests. Now light the oil lamp and let's see where we are going. Hopefully not very far."

They went down a steep tunnel, their sandals scuffing on little stones in the dust. After fifteen paces they came to a transition point where a door would be built, Yanhamu surmised. Another steep flight of steps confronted them disappearing into the gloom. There were recesses cut into the rock all the way down and Yanhamu wondered what these would be for. Maybe the statues of demons or shabti would be inserted.

An overhanging rock hid the bottom and the steps didn't go as deep as Yanhamu had feared. Here there was another transition that would probably be another door. Beyond this was another corridor. So far he had seen no decoration, no sign of the mystical preparation for Pharaoh's journey. Perhaps he'd been mistaken. They were already far deeper into the hill than Tutankhamen's tomb. He had heard about false tombs, passages that were intended to trap grave robbers rather than be the deceased pharaoh's resting place.

Wooden boards took them across a well shaft. It was about the depth of two men and again made Yanhamu think this was a trap. And then they stepped into a chamber. There were two pillars and the size was almost eight paces square—slightly longer than it was wide. But this still wasn't a burial chamber and the walls had no decoration.

"Master?" Sadhu held his light over the well, the way they'd come. "Perhaps we should leave now." But Yanhamu wasn't listening. He'd spotted a hole in the

238

floor at the rear and strode towards it. "More steps," he said.

Sadhu was quickly behind him and descending another short flight into another tunnel. And then another flight of steps.

"If we keep going we are bound to meet Anubis—or worse, the Devourer," Sadhu said.

"We're here." Yanhamu stepped past what would be another door and into a chamber. He raised his lamp and walked around. The room was the height of four men and scaffolding against the walls showed where the priests had plastered and painted sections. There were six pillars in pairs. Beyond them was a lower section. This was the burial chamber. Five small side chambers suggested these might be for Pharaoh's wives. None of these were of interest because of their lack of decoration. Beyond the last set of pillars was another stairway cut into the floor. Yanhamu realized his assistant wasn't following him as he descended to find another room. This was rough-hewn and reminded him of Tutankhamen's antechamber. Perhaps this was where the pharaoh's possessions would be stored. But again it was of no interest to Yanhamu.

When he re-emerged into the burial chamber he found Sadhu on the scaffolding drawing and writing.

Yanhamu began to measure the dimensions and search for magical bricks. He expected the ceiling to be decorated with Nut spanning the night sky but only the sides of the chamber were painted. It was still unfinished and Yanhamu expected the complete frieze would be painted before Horemheb was interred.

They worked for hours, sketching and taking notes. Yanhamu tried to judge the time based on the oil in his lamp because they had to be out before the gates opened and workers returned. Finally, he told Sadhu to stop because they had to leave.

It may have been the poor light but the young man's eyes were wide with excitement as they followed the long climb out of the tomb.

"There is so much mystery," Sadhu said after the second flight of steps. "I wonder if I should become a priest."

"Which god would you choose?"

They had seen so many in the chamber and the stories on the wall were different from the Book of the Dead that he'd transcribed from Meryra's documents. But the young man's next comment surprised him.

Sadhu said, "Some people believe there is only one god."

"I've heard such nonsense."

"Why is it nonsense?"

"Because it's obvious one god isn't enough. Ra is the life-giver, but he is also Amun."

"The hidden one."

"Because Ra still exists even when we can't see him. And then there is the son, Horus. Three gods who are one."

"Perhaps these people believe that this is their god—the Trinity."

"Perhaps, but then how were these gods created? The gods existed before the world." Yanhamu spoke the liturgy he'd learned as a child. "Ptah first conceived the world by the thought of his heart, and realized through the magic of his word."

Sadhu nodded. "And there was Nun, who was the water of chaos and Atum who stood on the Benben and sneezed out Ged and Nut." He nodded again. "So they were all there at the beginning?"

"It's the only logical conclusion."

They stood in the mouth of the tomb and listened but heard nothing. There were still hours before dawn and the opening of the gates. Yanhamu pointed down the wadi and led the way back to Tutankhamen's tomb. They waited there until daybreak and the morning bells. They ate and drank what was left of their beer.

After the stream of hooded labourers passed, they strolled down to the gates.

"What now?" Sadhu asked.

"Now we go back to Memphis and persuade Ramses to release my wife."

FORTY-ONE

Cairo, Egypt

Alex blinked away dry eyes. He'd been focused on decoding the tablets for three hours and his head was starting to hurt. He'd waited another thirty minutes for Brown before giving up and returning to the mid-priced hotel he'd checked into. Stay here a night and then head for the airport before Vanessa landed was his plan.

The translation was interesting but frustrating. Yanhamu had discovered something in the Valley of the Kings. He expected Ramses I to release his wife and yet Alex wondered what the truth could be and whether the pharaoh would consider it enough.

A Telegram notification pinged on his phone.

agent_k. Brown.

Alex was tempted to ignore it. But after a few minutes of staring out of the window at a dusty view of the city, he'd decided there was nothing to lose.

Sorry, the message started. **Really worried. Tomasz is missing**

Alex watched the message erase itself before replying. He was cross. **You're full of shit,** he typed.

No, seriously. The AI has been disabled and I can't get hold of my friend

You told me you didn't know where Black was. Now you know he's missing?

I didn't know if I could really trust you. I didn't know where he was but we have been in touch. His last message was panicked. He said they'd found him

Who?

I don't know

You don't know much, do you, Mr Brown?
There was a long delay and Alex tossed his phone onto the bed. But then it pinged with another message.
I know what it's about
Alex looked at his reflection in a mirror and shook his head. How do I know I can trust you?
Again a long delay, then: Meet same time tomorrow at the Sphinx. Meantime here's the address of the AI output. You'll see the latest and that it's now dead.
Alex replied: No, 9am. I need to get to the airport after.

Charlie was reading the missing-person file for Omar El-Hadary. Shafik had left her alone because of another case he was working on. She'd asked whether he knew about a case involving an Englishman, but he'd dismissed it as unconnected.
Omar El-Hadary had been confirmed as one of the bodies found in the American cemetery. He'd gone missing twenty-five days ago from El Obdour City, a low-rise concrete suburb of Cairo, just beyond the airport.

243

The body had the scarab tattoo, but nothing about him interested her. It was the report itself that caught her attention. He'd been seen leaving the packing factory where he worked. He left at nine-thirty most nights and this one was no different. However, his younger brother reported him missing after he never reached his home two miles away. Instead, there was a man matching his description who had collapsed in the street. Suspected heart attack, the witnesses said. They also said that they saw a doctor attend to him and then take him to hospital.

None of the hospitals had any record of receiving El-Hadary that night.

Charlie called Peter Zhang.

"I was just about to call *you*," Zhang said without preamble.

"News?"

"You were right about the church, Charlie."

She noticed he'd used her proper name, and it made her smile. That and the fact she'd been right.

She said, "Tell me. There were trapdoors with access to the space underneath."

"Exactly. Those goddamn bodies were put there from above. No way did the Surgeon do that without knowledge."

"What did the preacher—what's his name—say?"

"Piccard denies any involvement."

"Believe him?"

She heard her partner take a long breath. "I don't want to," he said, "but maybe I do."

"Damn."

"But then there's McCubbin."

Charlie recalled the older man from the study when they'd interviewed Piccard. "The man who called himself the governor."

"Right. Nick Garcia sent people to pick him up and he's disappeared."

"Where?" As she said it, Charlie realized it was a stupid question, but her partner didn't rib her for it.

"No idea. The whole house is locked up. There was a fire pit in the yard—looked like he'd burned some papers. Looks like he left in a hurry and destroyed evidence."

Charlie thought for a moment.

Zhang said, "You're wondering why he'd flee? Well, after I called Piccard yesterday—yeah, I know it was stupid to warn him—only he then called McCubbin. He's admitted as much. That's why I wonder if the good reverend really isn't involved. Looks like he inadvertently warned McCubbin."

"Thanks," she said. "There's something else I was thinking."

"Yeah?"

"The other churches in the group. How many are there?"

"Church of the Risen Christ? I don't know. Fifteen, maybe twenty."

"Get out there and check them all. Check for trapdoors."

"Christ almighty!" Zhang said without any hint that he got the irony of the expletive. She heard him speaking off-phone and guessed Garcia was with him.

When Zhang came back on the line, she said, "There was a reason I called you."

"Development there?"

"Maybe. Check the missing-person files on the victims we know about."

"What for?"

"Any that mention doctors or paramedics."

Zhang said he'd get right on it and then called back fifteen minutes later.

"Two cases," he said. "One mentioned a paramedic being the first on the scene after our guy collapsed with a suspected heart attack."

"And the second?"

"Similar. A doctor treated our man for a bang on the head. The witness thought the victim was drunk, although the PM showed only a low level of blood alcohol."

"What about after?"

"That's the thing," Zhang said. "Neither witness stayed around to see what happened next. We assumed both men continued on afterwards. And we never found the doctor or paramedic. You have something similar there?"

"I do," Charlie said. "I have a theory. The Surgeon pretends to be a paramedic or doctor, treats these guys then gets them into his vehicle."

Alex logged onto the secure site and found a series of outputs from the AI program. The word clouds were typically produced every three hours and there had been nothing new since yesterday evening.

The usual words appeared but also some sentences. It appeared that the AI program honed in on certain messages and made sense of the communications.

Alex's name appeared on all of the outputs. Phrases included: "MacLure's back in Egypt" and "MacLure has the letters".

The gods Seth and Ptah were listed and Alex remembered he'd just translated a section of Yanhamu's story that mentioned Ptah. Was he relevant somehow?

The pyramids featured on every output, as did the word Ansar, but the final two outputs had something new: The Tree of Life.

The final output had two clear sentences: "What do I do about the Tree of Life?" and "Kill the assistant".

If only I knew who was sending these messages and asking the questions, Alex thought.

Brown pinged him on Telegram but Alex ignored the message. He still hadn't decided what to do.

Vanessa wasn't available so Alex messaged his brother an update. Then he settled down and resumed the translation. At least that was a positive distraction.

When Detective Shafik came back into the room, he looked hassled before he looked from Charlie to the folders on the desk in front of her.

"You've found something?"

"Omar El-Hadary was attended to by a doctor," she said.

He shrugged. "And?"

"We have a pattern. Admittedly it's only two more cases back in the States, two of the missing-person witness statements have something similar. One reports a doctor and another a paramedic being the last they were seen with."

Shafik seemed miles away, staring at the desk.

"More than a coincidence?" she prompted.

"Paramedic," he muttered. From a filing cabinet he pulled a report and riffled through the pages. Then he placed it emphatically in front of Charlie.

"What?"

"Paramedic," he said, pointing to a page filled with Arabic.

"I'll accept your word for it, but what is this? Another missing person?"

"No," he said, fixing her with bloodshot, weary eyes. "It's another case... Not just another case. It's *the* other case I'm working on. You were right."

FORTY-TWO

1308 BCE, Memphis

The docks from Memphis to Heliopolis were closed to all except ceremonial boats, which meant Yanhamu's vessel had to moor at Helwan and wait for a day. Yanhamu and Sadhu walked the final eight miles. The celebration of the five Hidden Days before the New Year was in full swing, and at Deputy Ramses' palace they were told he was at Giza.

They were swept along with the crowds heading north, led by groups of priests and sistra players. By the time they reached the bank opposite the pyramids, the crowds were in the thousands. Royal barges with forty oars and colourful flags lined the river. On the far side, Yanhamu could see the priests gathering, ready for nightfall. Torches were lit and the chanting began.

He could hear the prayer to Osiris carrying across the water and people hushed as the sun descended beyond the horizon. A hush fell and the people moved as one, swivelling to face the west as the night swept up across the heavens.

A great bell sounded. The chanting began again and cheers erupted from the crowd. Across the water, the priests prayed with serious intent, but around Yanhamu everyone was in party mood. The dancing and drinking began in earnest.

Despite a heavy heart, Yanhamu found that he had to stay up all night. It was tradition. Witness the rising of Sirius and welcome the birth of Ra in the morning.

Two hours before dawn, people were flagging. Yanhamu and Sadhu had found a spot overlooking the river, and sat watching the priests and the lights across the water. As the eleventh hour came, the energy levels in the temple reached a crescendo. The people stopped partying and watched. Seemingly out of nowhere, a figure appeared between the paws of the Sphinx. A man rose up out of the ground until he stood just below the creature's head.

"Pharaoh," Yanhamu said.

Sirius rose for the first time in seventy days and then the first rays of sunlight appeared on the horizon. Horemheb raised his arms and began the *Litany of Ra*.

A day later, Yanhamu was back in the deputy's palace.

"Did you notice Pharaoh?" Ramses asked when they were alone.

"I saw him perform the ritual," Yanhamu replied. "Although I was too far away—"

Ramses nodded and Yanhamu detected a glint in his eye. "Yes, of course you were. And a good job too. Not just you, I mean all of the public. He's not well and hasn't been. It will not be long before I am the ruler of the Two Lands."

Yanhamu bowed—hands on his knees and then out— and hoped his obsequious behaviour wasn't obviously fake. "And Majesty, I will be your Keeper of Secrets."

"Let us hope so. Tell me, what have you learned?"

"I have learned the path of the solar barque through the night sky. I have seen the demons and the gates that Ra must overcome to be born anew."

"Good."

"I know the magical dimensions—the golden triangle and where the magic bricks must be placed within your tomb. Spells that speak to the gods must be written in red. I would also advise a red marble sarcophagus."

Yanhamu went on to describe the deities who should be addressed, the importance of the four sons of Horus, of Anubis and the four goddesses: Isis, Nephthys, Neith and Serqet. He talked about the Book of the Dead and the detail he'd seen in Horemheb's tomb, the Book of Gates.

Ramses nodded. "And these are what will make me immortal?"

"They are the instructions so that you will find your way to the Field of Reeds."

"What aren't you telling me, Khety?"

Yanhamu had been wondering whether now was the time to ask for his wife to be released. Instead, he said, "I don't understand what you mean, Your Majesty?"

"Don't think I can't read you! You are cynical about something. I need to know how I become immortal."

"You will live on forever providing your successor performs the Opening of the Mouth and prepares your body for the afterlife. Like Osiris."

"And yet? Out with it! If you want to be my Keeper of Secrets, then you must be honest with me."

"My absolute honesty comes at a cost, Majesty. You may not remember but my wife was a magistrate. The law changed, and by right—since I was abroad fighting in Pharaoh's army—she took my name."

"And pretended to be a man!"

"Majesty. She will repent. All I ask is that you release her into my care."

Ramses scrutinized Yanhamu before speaking. "Tell me the truth."

"I have seen the instructions on walls and on papyri. I have seen the twelve stages and gates. I have seen the names of the demons and the words that must be used to destroy them. But—"

"But?" Ramses leaned forward. Despite the man's advanced years he still had powerful muscles in his arms.

Yanhamu lowered his eyes. "I think there has been a great misunderstanding, Majesty. I think what we witnessed in the New Year's Day festival—the prayers to Ra as he passes through the night sky and the urging him to rise again now that Sirius has risen is what the books tell us. I think they are just a corruption of the important annual story."

Ramses said nothing.

Yanhamu continued: "The descriptions in Pharaoh Horemheb's tomb aren't instructions for his ba to reach the Field of Reeds. They are the instructions for Ra and his followers to rise each day."

Veins stood out on the deputy's neck when Yanhamu looked up. The man was momentarily speechless, and then he bellowed, "Guards! Arrest this man for blasphemy."

A phalanx of guards immediately appeared, running towards the platform where Ramses stood over Yanhamu, his staff of authority raised as if to strike downwards.

"Majesty," Yanhamu said, unable to quell the tremble in his voice, "all I tell you is that there's been a mistake. I will find the second truth for you."

Ramses stopped his soldiers with a twist of his wrist so that the staff became horizontal.

Yanhamu continued, thinking quickly: "Your heart is weighed by Anubis in the Hall of the Two Truths, correct?"

Ramses nodded, listening.

"Then we know that there are two truths. I believe the Book of the Dead is just the first of these truths and I promise that I will uncover the second."

Ramses sat. He beckoned for Yanhamu to come close. So close that the two men could smell each other's sweat.

The deputy whispered, "You have a year to find out the two truths. Tell me how to be immortal and I will release your wife. Fail me and I shall have you fed piece by piece to the crocodiles."

FORTY-THREE

Cairo, Egypt

Alex considered what Yanhamu had written. The Two Truths. His argument to Ramses made sense and yet Alex had the feeling that the man was desperate. The Egyptian would say anything to get his wife back, wouldn't he? Maybe this whole thing was a wild goose chase. Maybe there was no secret to be found.

Alex spoke to Vanessa before retiring to bed. She'd had a successful trip, which meant her boss was especially happy. Now, she convinced Alex, she was ready to switch off and enjoy that holiday.

He'd decided that he wouldn't tell her he was still going to meet Brown, because she'd disapprove. So he said he was ready too.

"What about Yanhamu's story?"

"I'm almost finished," he said. "If I can't finish in the morning, I should be able to have it done by the time we land in London."

During the call he got a Telegram message. He checked it as soon as he'd said goodnight to Vanessa.

Sorry about yesterday, Brown wrote.

What happened?

I got scared. Didn't go out
Alex didn't respond.

Brown wrote, I know what Ansar means. It's short
for Ansar Beit al-Maqdis. It means Champions of the
Holy Site

Who are they?

I don't know
Alex didn't bother replying. Brown didn't know much
but reminding him of the fact again wouldn't help. Then
he realized Brown's friend might know more.
He typed, Would Black know anything about them?

Possibly. But I haven't heard from him since
yesterday

Something wrong?

Can't get hold of him. I don't like it. That's why I'm
worried

They exchanged a few more messages and then Alex
called Andrew.
"Any news, bro?" his brother answered.
"Bro?" Alex said.
"Better bro than homie—always makes me laugh
when Americans say that."
"Brown didn't turn up at the Sphinx."
"Then he's full of shit."

"Maybe. His excuse was that his friend is now missing."

"Black? Wasn't he missing before?" Andrew asked.

"He was in hiding. Apparently, Tomasz Schwartz—AKA Black—has been in contact with Brown until yesterday."

"It sounds—"

"I made him give me access to the AI output," Alex interrupted. "So I could see for myself what it was saying."

"And?"

"Well, firstly he's been telling the truth. Secondly, my name is all over it. Tree of Life has now come to the fore."

"You do talk posh sometimes. *Come to the fore*," Andrew mimicked.

"Do you want to be involved or just piss me off?"

"Sorry, bro. What is this Tree of Life?"

Alex could hear his brother typing and guessed he was searching the internet as he spoke.

"You'll see most references to the Bible. The tree in Eden with the fruit for eternal life." As he said it, Alex realized the significance.

"Central mystical symbol of the Kabbalah," Andrew said, clearly reading. "Also known as the ten Sephirot. It represents a series of divine emanations of God's creation—"

"But what Wikipedia doesn't tell you is that you can map the archangels of Judaism to the Ennead of ancient Egypt."

"Ennead?"

"The nine main gods."

"Is Seth one of those?"

"Yes."

Andrew said, "It's funny that Satan was a main god."

"Satan is a Christian construct. However—"

"OK, interesting," Andrew said too easily, clearly not interested in Alex's explanation. "I'll see what the gaming guys think. See if there's any connection with a conspiracy. Anything else?"

"We know what Ansar means. It appears to refer to a secret organization called Champions of the Holy Site."

"Could the Holy Site be the pyramids at Giza?"

"That's my thinking. It fits with what that guy told us in Starbucks: an Arab organization, part of the establishment, anti-Zionist and probably anti-Mason."

"So this is looking like it's about the Masons versus these Arab Champions."

"I guess."

"So where do you fit in?"

"I don't know, Andrew. But I sure as hell want to find out."

The man known as the Haris al'Asrar—the Keeper of Secrets—excused himself from a meeting and checked the message on his phone. It was a report from his man in Deir Mawas.

It said, **Executed**. Nothing more, nothing less. But the Keeper of Secrets knew what it meant.

The ancient clay tablets had been destroyed and Mahmood, MacLure's assistant, would no longer be a problem.

FORTY-FOUR

Would Brown show this time or was he as unreliable as the quest for the truth?

It was almost 9am and Alex stood beside the Sphinx for the second time in two days. Yesterday had been still and cloudless. Today, a strong wind whipped up clouds of dust so that Alex pulled up his collar and turned his face away.

A few hardy tourists battled against the abrasive air. None of them looked like they could be Brown. They were either in groups or nowhere near the Sphinx.

Maybe it was the dust, but one minute Alex was alone and the next there was a man closing in.

"Keep walking," the guy said.

"Brown?"

"Of course. Who else did you expect?"

Alex didn't respond. They were walking up the slope to the left of Khafre's pyramid; both had their heads down against the wind. Alex glanced at the other man. He hadn't really seen him before, and he couldn't see much now since the guy had a scarf wrapped around his face. But he looked more like a local than Alex had expected.

"I thought you'd be white—you know, skin colour," Alex said.

The man snorted. "My friend is German. I'm Egyptian. Is that a problem for you?"

"Not at all. Any news of your friend?"

"No." Brown's voice seemed to catch and he said nothing else.

"I'm sorry."

They were beside the second pyramid now and Alex said, "Where are we going?"

"Just around. I want to make sure we aren't being followed."

They walked a little further before Brown said, "So what do you think about the Sphinx?"

"It's mysterious. Maybe majestic?"

"I mean physically."

Alex thought. "Do you mean, like the head?"

"Go on."

"The pharaoh's head is disproportionately small."

"Which tells you what?" Brown said, looking around nervously.

Alex said, "It wasn't the original head?"

"Look at the body and the erosion. Now look at the head."

Alex nodded. "The body is much more weathered."

"You'd expect weathering for a sculpture that's 4,500 years old. Right?"

"Are you going to tell me about the water damage theory?"

Brown looked at him. "Right! The weathering suggests it's much older. And if it's flood water, then that was at least 12,000 years ago."

Alex shook his head. "But that doesn't make sense. Firstly, respected Egyptologists date the Sphinx to the Fourth Dynasty, and secondly, it's Khafre's Sphinx, being associated with the mortuary temple at the end of the causeway and his pyramid."

"You are right, of course. The establishment has rejected any suggestion that the Sphinx is from an earlier epoch." Brown gave a derisory laugh. "We'll come back to that, but for now, how do we know it's Khafre's Sphinx?"

"Because of the stela between the paws."

"Correct. That plaque was erected by Thutmose IV—Eighteenth Dynasty, over a thousand years later—after a renovation and clearing away the sand. The plaque appears to refer to Khafre. The name is partial and not in the standard cartouche."

"So you're saying Thutmose was wrong?"

"Maybe, but it doesn't matter if the pharaoh's head is of Khafre or not. People have believed for thousands of years that it's his even when there's contrary evidence."

Alex waited to hear the explanation.

Brown said, "You may not have heard of the Inventory Stela found here at Giza."

"No."

"That's because it's been rejected by the establishment as a work of fiction. And the reason? Because it contradicts the accepted view. It states that the Sphinx was seen by Khufu."

"Khafre's father."

Brown raised his hands, palms up. "The Sphinx was already there. Khafre probably just restored it and had the head carved in his own image... if it is him."

Alex nodded. It seemed to make sense. This was much older than the Fourth Dynasty, but it raised another question. "Do you think the Ansar—the Champions of the Holy Site—are part of it?"

"Definitely," Brown said.

"So who carved the original Sphinx?"

"I don't know, but I do know that it must have been a tremendously significant act: the changing of what was probably a god's image."

"A god's image?"

"What is the body?"

"A lion."

"Really? How do you know that?"

"Because…" Alex thought of the other Sphinxes, especially those at Karnak. They were clearly a lion's body with a pharaoh's head or Amun's, the ram. "They all post-date the Fourth Dynasty, don't they?"

They were walking around Khufu's pyramid now. All the time, Brown glanced around. "All the other Sphinxes came after Thutmose uncovered the Great Sphinx. They thought it had had a lion's head. Basically they knew no better. Khafre had already erased the true nature of the beast."

"What is it then?"

Brown pointed to the pyramids. "Imagine for a minute that you have died. Who would you want to watch over you?"

Alex turned back to the Sphinx and tried to ignore the head. The posture of the body: alert, ready for a command. "Man's best friend," he said.

"It's a dog," Brown said with a grin. "It's a damned dog not a lion!"

"But you said a god. You said Khafre defaced a god."

"Seth," Brown said emphatically. "The Sphinx was Seth."

The man in the Panama hat yesterday had a baseball cap on today. Although his vision was marred by the clouds of dust, he saw someone approach MacLure. They spoke and began walking towards the left of Khafre's pyramid.

The man spoke into his microphone. "Another man has joined MacLure. No one I've seen before."

"What are they doing?" Detective Shafik said on the other end of the phone.

"Walking and talking. The second man looks nervous. Looking around."

"What are they saying?"

"I think it's the dust. I can't pick it up," the man with the fake camera said, trying again to adjust it.

"Keep trying and observe."

"And if they split?"

"Follow this new man. I'll get someone else to pick up MacLure."

Another man, dressed in a traditional gallibaya and a turban, did more than observe. He'd made his way over to the Eastern Cemetery and was listening to the conversation. He'd been tailing Brown and had dropped a bug into his pocket.

He heard the other man mention Seth and a conspiracy to hide the true nature of the Sphinx. He had an ear piece connected to a phone, but he said nothing. The man on the other end of the phone was also listening to the conversation.

FORTY-FIVE

1307 BCE, Elephantine

Yanhamu wore the robes of an official acting on behalf of the pharaoh. Before he'd left Memphis, Yanhamu had persuaded Ramses to give him a title and status so that he might challenge the priesthood and uncover all of the secrets. He'd also been given money to help elicit the truth.

They had found acolytes and priests who liked wine and plied them with much until their tongues wagged. And if that didn't work, then they found gold always loosened lips.

"I still have nightmares," Sadhu said. "I see the statues of Tutankhamen coming to life and chasing me."

"That's probably because you think I look like him. It's me chasing you."

"Ha ha!"

"I wish it was funny, Sadhu. We need to find something I can tell Pharaoh Ramses otherwise it really will be my spirit chasing you. All we have learned in these last eight months is how the priesthood knows so much. They use measurements of the Great River's level in special wells to predict the inundation—"

"Claiming it's the god Khnum."

"We have travelled from the Delta to Kush in the south. From Punt in the east to Gilf Kibir in the west. But I am afraid I don't have the second truth I promised him."

"We have a lot of stories. Perhaps he will be lenient if you can entertain him."

It was true they had learned many things from wise men who knew the past. They learned about the pyramid builders and the great astronomers who first mapped the stars and predicted their movements. They were told the story of Pharaoh Meni who reunited the Two Lands, the north and south of Egypt. He was given special powers so that he could walk on water and trapped by his enemies, and he escaped by walking across a lake. Someone else said he founded the city of Shedat and worship of the crocodile god Sobek for granting him the power.

Later, when they were alone, Yanhamu had said, "Even if he had special powers, it still doesn't help with immortality."

"Perhaps we should ask the gods directly," Sadhu had said, although he couldn't recall the conversation the next day due to the amount of wine he'd drunk. "There are temples where you can ask the gods questions and they answer!"

So they travelled to the Delta to an ancient town called Hut-waret and found the temple of Osiris. Other temples had oracle days where signs were used to provide yes/no responses. But not here. Sadhu had been right; there was a shrine to the god Osiris, hidden in a dark recess of the temple, in its inner-most sanctum, where Osiris could be heard.

It cost a considerable amount but Yanhamu bought an audience with the god.

"What is the secret of immortality?" he asked when the priest left him in the darkness.

He heard footsteps far away. He could hear the acolytes praying, but for a long time there was no voice from the god.

After a long time Yanhamu decided to try again. "Lord Osiris, great god of the afterlife, the king of eternity, the lord of everlastingness, who traverses millions of years in his existence, please answer your humble servant. What is the secret of immortality?"

And then a voice spoke quietly from the stone. "Truth and righteousness," Osiris said.

Yanhamu held his breath to hear better.

"Live your life according to Ma-at and I will hear your declarations. If your heart weighs no more than a feather, then your truth will open the gates and you will pass the demons. That is the way to join me in the Field of Reeds."

"And is my sister, Meretseger, with you, my lord?"

"She is here and wishes you happiness until it is your time and you join her in the Field of Reeds."

Yanhamu sat in the darkness, silent for five minutes thinking about his sister, desperate to meet her again in the afterlife. After he had composed himself and wiped away a tear, he walked out of the temple and joined Sadhu outside.

"I could feel the energy out here," Sadhu said in awe. "Did Osiris speak to you?"

"My question was answered."

"And you now know the answer of immortality?" He hesitated as he said it. "And yet you look disappointed, my lord."

"I am. Come on, we are going and I need a drink."

Sadhu hurried after him. "My lord?"

They found someone selling beer and sat in the shade. It was sour but Yanhamu drank his first flagon quickly. There were geese in the reeds nearby and again he thought about his childhood and taking the duck eggs. Worried that he had offended Het and upset Ma-at, he had returned to the village to find his sister taken by the soldiers. They had lied about her becoming a palace dancer.

He took another flagon. "Everybody lies," he said. "Life is a lie."

"Is that what Osiris told you?" Sadhu said, almost choking on his beer.

"Remember how we found out about the metal called B'ja?"

"The priesthood forbids anyone to collect it from the desert because it is sacred. Metal from the gods, they call it."

Yanhamu shook his head. "I didn't tell you what I discovered. When you were asleep I went back to that old priest and paid him to tell me the truth. It cost me more than speaking to Osiris just now."

Sadhu waited, his mouth open.

"We have seen the images of the gods paraded at festivals. And sometimes those mannequins are truly possessed by the gods' spirits. They are seen to hover above their platforms. They move and spin and yet there is nothing beneath them."

"Because gods can fly."

"Or is it because of B'ja?" Yanhamu sighed.

"I don't understand, my lord."

"B'ja has the special powers, not the gods. Some B'ja pushes other B'ja with an invisible force. Most B'ja attracts and can stick to other B'ja without binding, but it is the repealing B'ja that the priests use. They put some in the base of the statue and place more beneath it in the platform so that the statue appears to hover. It's a trick. That's what the old priest told me."

"What does he know? My lord, the very fact that the B'ja has these magical powers, does that not tell you that it is the metal of the gods?"

"No," Yanhamu said. "And Osiris speaking to me was also a trick. I think it was a man behind the wall. I suspect there is a passage under the temple that enables someone to crawl into a space, hidden in the inner sanctum."

Sadhu shook his head, clearly disbelieving. "What did he say to you?"

"His answer about immortality was fine, although nothing new. However, it was when he told me my sister Meretseger—"

"She who loves silence," Sadhu translated.

"—My sister Meretseger was with him and waiting for me in the Field of Reeds, I knew this to be another fake."

"Because?"

"My sister was called Laret."

They left Hut-waret without a plan. Everything they had set out to explore had been uncovered. And yet Yanhamu had no second truth to tell Deputy Ramses—unless that the truth was a fabrication. Somehow, he guessed, such an answer would not get Nefer-bithia released.

FORTY-SIX

Giza, Egypt

They had rounded the Great Pyramid and, through the dust, Alex could just make out the Sphinx.

He said, "No one knows what Seth was. Most say the Seth animal or an aardvark."

"The earliest image is from a Predynastic Period tomb—about 5,500 years ago," Brown said, still walking and glancing around. "But the animal is unclear. And they may not have even known, just like Pharaoh Thutmose didn't know what a Sphinx should really look like."

Alex shook his head. Brown seemed so confident, and yet by definition he couldn't know either.

Brown said, "I know what you're thinking, but we know that there were two kingdoms, one of which worshipped Horus and the other worshipped Seth."

"Red and White. The Two kingdoms that were united in the First Dynasty."

"Horus was the hawk, the hunting bird. When you are a powerful nation you want a powerful image. What you don't want is an aardvark—and by the way, others have said it's a donkey! Seth was the other main hunting animal—a dog. The Sphinx was a dog watching over its master. Plus I need not remind you of the importance of Canis Major, the dog constellation, and the Dog Star itself."

"It's rising heralded the arrival of the annual Nile flood."

"The dog, and by association the god Seth, were integral to the success and culture of an early Egyptian civilization. And yet it was expunged from memory and acceptability. Deliberately. And that censorship continues today."

"Why?"

"Because it doesn't fit with the accepted wisdom." He smiled. "But more than that, it's because it raises too many questions, not least for the three main religions."

Alex turned to the other man. "This is all very interesting. But why are we here?"

Brown looked uncomfortable. "I just—"

"You didn't just come here to say the Sphinx looks like Seth, now did you?"

"No."

"Then what?"

Brown pointed to the Great Pyramid. "There's something inside I need to show you."

"I've been many times..." Alex shook his head, frustrated.

Brown sighed. "Then let's talk about... Have you finished the translation yet?"

"No."

"You must... and quickly."

Alex frowned. "What's the urgency?"

"I need to know the answer—what the secret is."

"OK..."

Brown looked more uncomfortable.

"What is it? What aren't you telling me?"

"He has my friend," Brown said.

"Who has your friend?"

"The man who wants the answer. He's looking for a symbol that relates to Seth." Now Brown gripped Alex's arm. "You need to find the sign or he'll kill Tomasz."

The man in the gallibaya said, "Did you hear that? He's onto the secret."

"Do it," the voice on the other end of the phone said. "Do it now."

The undercover policeman saw the second man grip MacLure's arm. There appeared to be tension between them.

The policeman closed the distance, adjusted the fake camera, desperate to hear.

The wind whipped up and he closed his eyes against the tiny stones that stung his face. When he opened them again, MacLure and the other man were on the ground.

MacLure rolled away and staggered upright. The policeman pulled his gun and started running.

"Police!" he screamed.

MacLure turned and stared. He had blood over his shirt and hands, his face ghostly pale.

The man still on the ground twitched as blood spurted from his neck.

FORTY-SEVEN

On the phone, the Keeper of Secrets said, "Report."

"I was interrupted. There was a policeman," the man in the gallibaya said breathlessly.

"So they're still alive?"

"One taken care of."

"Who's alive?"

"MacLure. The police arrested him. I got away, hidden by a dust cloud."

The Keeper of Secrets bit his bottom lip. An imbecile. He was surrounded by imbeciles. One man had failed to get Tomasz Schwartz and now this one had done half a job. At least the man in Deir Mawas hadn't failed.

"Where is Alex MacLure now?"

"Like I said, sir, MacLure was arrested. They seemed to think he did it."

Alex was back in El Khalifa, the police station where he'd been held before. The man who'd arrested him had been an undercover policeman, and as soon as he'd screamed "Police!" guards had appeared from everywhere. Alex had been flung to the ground and pinned as his hands were cuffed.

He'd tried to talk but had received an assault rifle butt in the face for his efforts. He tasted his own blood where his lip had split, but that was the least of his worries. The police seemed to think he'd stabbed Brown.

He was thrust into cell B and glanced around hoping to see Charles Williams again. The Canadian wasn't there. Hopefully he's been released, Alex thought, although his subconscious said the guy was now in Qena prison.

Faces turned to look at him and turned away. They appeared to be locals. No white faces. However, having had his face shoved in the dirt, Alex suspected his own skin looked anything but Caucasian.

His hands were still covered with blood where he'd grappled with the man he knew as Brown. So the first thing he did was move through the stinking mass of bodies to the tap. He scrubbed at his hands and then splashed his face. Swilling bile from his mouth, he then took a gulp and swallowed the disgusting water.

There was a sickness in his stomach and he had to clench his teeth to stop his eyes filling with tears. How could this happen again? How could he survive this inhumanity, this insanity?

When he looked up, he saw a man close by, studying him. Number thirty-two. The cell boss. He was still here, and by the look on his face, he remembered Alex.

Alex slunk away and tucked his head down. He began the monotonous shuffle around the cage, joining the flow of the other prisoners.

He'd learned before to try and avoid thinking about the situation. Just focus on surviving, he told himself. And then he remembered Vanessa. She'd be arriving soon and wonder why he wasn't at the airport.

Would she guess? Maybe. However the despair welled up and he choked.

272

"Hello, my friend." The cell boss was beside him, a hand on his elbow. "Nice to see you back again."

"Thank you," Alex managed, because the man had stopped him stumbling.

The cell boss smiled. His shirt was still clean despite him being down here for more than a week.

Alex tried to move away, but the grip on his elbow tightened. He also felt a light touch on his thigh. The cell boss stroked his leg.

Alex shook his head vigorously.

"Oh come now," the cell boss said, and Alex was suddenly aware of the two other men—the body-guards or enforcers, whatever they were. They acted like a shield as Alex realized he was being pressed towards the back of the cell.

The cell boss' hand stroked higher, a little more pressure. "You owe me," he said.

"I don't—" Alex tried to say, but his quiet protest was lost in the clatter of batons on cell bars.

The three men eased away.

"Later," the cell boss said.

The guards came into the cell. "Twenty-two," one shouted in Arabic.

Alex looked down at his shirt. He was twenty-two! He'd only been in the cell a short time and he was already being summoned.

At the cell door, Alex's collar was grabbed and plastic cuffs snapped on his wrists. A frogmarch down the corridor and he was back in the interrogation room he'd seen twice before.

No, he was mistaken. This was different. This one had a mirror. A two-way mirror, he guessed, looking into it.

When Detective Shafik came in, Alex was relieved. At least this man knew his story. Knew he'd been wrongly arrested before.

And yet Shafik looked angry. His eyes were narrow and his body seemed tense with aggression.

"Alex MacLure. Englishman. Murderer," Shafik began. "The first time I thought you were in the wrong place at the wrong time. Now—this is too much of a coincidence. And this time you have the victim's blood all over you. You were caught red-handed, as you English say. It would be funny if this weren't so serious."

"May I speak?" Alex said, and waited for a blow on the head.

Shafik glanced at the men behind Alex and shook his head. "Tell me what happened, Mr MacLure."

"I was talking to a man."

"Mohamed Salam," Shafik said.

"I didn't know his real name. He said he was a friend of Tomasz Schwartz—, the man who—"

"I know who Tomasz Schwartz is. You were in his student accommodation, where you murdered the other man."

Alex shook his head. "I didn't mur—" A sting on his right ear from a rubber baton stopped him mid-sentence. He took a breath, tried to remain calm.

"We were talking. Brown... I mean Salam... said that his friend, Schwartz, had been in hiding. Only now he confessed that Schwartz was being held captive by someone."

"Why?"

"Because of his computer program. He was uncovering a conspiracy, he thought—or something."

"And what has that go to do with you?"

"You saw my name on that paper—the word cloud. That was the program's output. Someone knew I could find the answer. In the Amarna Letters."

"The what?" Shafik said. He was listening but his demeanour hadn't changed. Disbelief and anger was still written on his face.

"My research. It looks like my research is important in uncovering a sign."

For the first time, Shafik's expression changed. He was interested.

Spurred on, Alex said, "There's an ancient story about the search for a secret. Brown said there was a sign or symbol."

"Go on."

"That's all I know. I don't know why it's important or what it is."

Shafik got up, walked around and looked into the mirror. When he turned back to Alex, he said, "So why did you kill Mohamed Salam?"

"I didn't." Alex winced as a baton poked him in the back of the head. "I didn't," he said again defiantly.

The door opened and Alex heard someone come into the room. And then she was in front of him. A good-looking white woman in an ugly black headscarf.

"Then what happened?" she asked with an American accent.

Shafik scowled.

"Like I said, we were talking," Alex said quickly. "It was windy. The dust swirled all around. One minute it was fine, the next you couldn't see further than your arm. It was like that and then there was suddenly someone else there. Another man. Salam turned and the next thing I knew he was attacking me."

"Salam or this other guy?"

"Salam. Only he wasn't fighting me, I realized he was probably grappling because of the blood... his neck..."

"And you both fell over?" she said.

"Yes! That's how it happened. He was on top of me, bleeding. I rolled away and stood up. Although I didn't realize he was bleeding until I saw my hands covered in blood. The next thing I knew, I was being yelled at and forced to the ground."

"And the other man?"

"I only saw him briefly through the dust cloud."

"But you saw something?"

"Arab—." Alex shrugged. "Brown turban. Brown clothes."

The American and Shafik looked at one another. Alex couldn't read their faces. Did they believe him?

He said, "You're FBI Agent Rebb, aren't you?"

She blinked. "How the hell—?"

"The word cloud. You were mentioned. You're involved in this."

The American and Shafik looked at one another again.

Shafik inclined his head towards the door. "Wait here," he said to Alex. Like he had any choice.

FORTY-EIGHT

Vanessa stood in the arrivals area of Cairo airport's Terminal 1 and looked around. She hadn't heard from Alex but she still expected him to be here. He knew the flight details and she'd texted as the plane landed five minutes ahead of schedule. Could he have forgotten, assumed she was on the EgyptAir flight and gone to Terminal 3?

She called his mobile and got voicemail. For a moment she felt a creeping anxiety that there was something wrong again. But just as she was about to leave a message she spotted her name on one of those boards that taxi drivers use.

"That's me," she said uncertainly to the man— possibly Indian—in a cheap but smart grey suit.

He gave her a broad smile and bobbed his head.

"Yes, thank you. I have been asked to explain... Alex MacLure..."

"My boyfriend."

"Yes." The head bob. "He has been unavoidably delayed. So many apologies."

"Right?" she said uncertainly and a little annoyed. She felt like she deserved a better explanation, but realized it was unfair to expect it from a taxi driver.

She just had a carry-on bag but he insisted on taking it from her and led her to the car park. In contrast to the driver's smart appearance, the taxi looked over ten years old. The least Alex could have done was provide a limo if he was going to let her down.

She'd travelled the main drag into Cairo many times and found herself staring unfocused out of the window. What had happened this morning? Alex had met Brown at the pyramids. Brown can't have been a charlatan after all. He must have had significant information for Alex to miss collecting her—and not even leave a message. But it was so like him and she loved him despite it, loved his quirkiness.

When the taxi was clearly not heading for the Marriott, she groaned. Alex had chosen a cheap hotel on the other side of the river. And she was right. A few minutes later the driver turned down a side street and stopped next to a hotel called El Manar.

The driver opened her door and retrieved her bag. But he didn't hand it to her or ask for the fare. Instead, he walked swiftly across the road.

"Not the hotel?" she asked.

He turned and smiled. "Oh, apologies. My mistake. He's meeting here." Then he kept walking, knocked on what appeared to be an office door and opened it for her.

"Go straight in," he said and stepped back.

She obliged, walking up steps into a hallway. There was light from a room ahead, and she could smell something odd. For an office anyway. It smelled like an artist's studio: linseed oil and paint, she thought.

The front door closed behind her and she saw that the driver had just dropped her bag inside and left.

A noise made her turn back to the room ahead.

"Come in," a man said. "I've been waiting for you, Vanessa."

FORTY-NINE

Shafik said, "This is crazy. He's involved in two murders."

"But he seems innocent," Charlie protested.

"Seems innocent?" Shafik shook his head. "Is that how justice works in America?"

"No, but we don't hold witnesses just because we're suspicious of them."

"Suspicious? He had blood all over him!"

"But he had an explanation."

"An Arab dressed in brown!"

Charlie said, "He knew I was involved."

"Which makes perfect sense if he's involved with the Surgeon."

Charlie said nothing.

Shafik said, "The Surgeon can't do all this alone. Maybe MacLure is his accomplice. Maybe he sets people up. Maybe we've just been lucky to catch him and unlucky we've not caught the Surgeon."

Charlie shook her head. "What if the Surgeon is trying to kill MacLure?"

"Why would he do that?"

"Maybe to stop him finding out something," Charlie said, but it sounded all wrong. A hundred and eighty degrees wrong. She said, "What if this Salam guy was working for the Surgeon? What if they really do need MacLure to find the right symbol?"

"Then MacLure is a murderer. He killed Salam and there is no Arab in a brown turban."

Charlie frowned. Maybe. "What if there's someone else?"

"This is getting fanciful," Shafik said, snorting. "This is what we're—"

"No," Charlie interrupted. "Hear me out... please. What if there is another group?" She held up one palm. "We have the Surgeon, or a group called Seventh Hour on one side"—she held up her other palm—"and another group on the other side. The Surgeon wants the symbol but the other group wants to stop him."

"We want to stop him."

"But... think about it... We want to stop a serial killer. Maybe this other group want to protect something. Like this symbol. Like it's a secret or something." She brought her hands together. "And Alex MacLure is the luckless guy in the middle."

Alex breathed the warm stale air and closed his eyes. The two guards with rubber batons were still behind him but the FBI agent's involvement gave him hope. They'd left and hadn't sent him back to the cell; they were making him wait here. He figured they were debating how they should proceed.

Only fifteen minutes passed before the detective and the FBI agent were back in the room. Shafik looked troubled. Special Agent Rebb appeared relaxed. Maybe she'd won the argument.

Shafik leaned forward, his hot breath in Alex's face.

"Confess now. You're involved. Confess and help us catch a serial killer."

"The Surgeon?" Alex asked.

"How do you know...?"

Alex looked at Agent Rebb. "You're all over the media. You're the Panola Mountain murders agent. The lead FBI agent looking for the Surgeon."

Rebb said nothing but raised her eyebrows.

Shafik's face didn't change. "You know about the Surgeon," he said pointedly.

"All over the media, like I said." And then Alex got it: the tattoos on the victims. "He's looking for a special symbol," Alex said, directing his attention at Rebb. "He's tattooing the bodies and you think he's after the same secret symbol that I'm supposed to know."

"And do you?" Rebb asked. "Do you know it?"

"No. I promise you I don't. It might have been hidden in the Amarna Letters, but either it wasn't or I haven't found it."

"Or you aren't saying," Shafik said and he finally leaned away from Alex's face.

"The story hinted at a secret sign, but I don't know it," Alex said. "Honestly, I don't know."

"OK," Shafik said to his surprise. "You can go."

It was as abrupt as that, and ten minutes later Alex was standing on the street outside the police station. The call for prayer rang out from Mosque Madrass opposite. The wind continued to whip along the street but the air was fresh and Alex breathed it in deeply. He may have looked a state, with blood and dirt on his shirt but he was out.

He'd missed Vanessa by a couple of hours and he hadn't told her which hotel he'd booked into. After all, he'd intended to pick her up.

Charge the phone and let Vanessa know what had happened, he decided. But first things first: a shower and clean clothes.

282

The phone was only a third charged when he picked it up again. There was a message on Telegram and he wondered when Brown—Mohamed Salam—had left it. Maybe it'd been to say he'd arrived at Giza.

There was a text from Vanessa saying she'd landed and then a missed call but no message. She must have got a taxi into town. Was she pissed at him for not meeting her?

Alex rang her number and got voicemail. Despite her text, he double checked the Cairo arrivals. Her EgyptAir flight from Tel Aviv had landed five minutes early.

He tried calling again and sent a text message. Where the hell was she?

Telegram pinged with another message. Alex opened it.

Where are you? agent_k wrote.

Alex checked. The previous message said the same thing, sent two hours ago.

His head swam. *Who the hell...?* He paced the room and gulped down a glass of water as though it would help clear things up.

Who is this? He finally replied.

Your friend, Brown

He's dead

Ah, shame. I have Black here. He says hello

Who the hell are you?

Your worst nightmare, MacLure. I have your girlfriend too

Alex felt his legs give way. He sat on the bed, staring at the phone.

The other man typed, Vanessa would say hello but she's sleeping right now

What do you want?

You know what I want. The secret sign

"I don't know it!" Alex screamed at the phone as he typed it.

Then you'd better get working and find it, hadn't you?

The research didn't tell me what it was. Alex typed, wondering if the other man could sense his desperation. I just know it was the ultimate truth—the secret of eternal life given to Ramses I

Try harder was the reply. You have until sunset tomorrow. No symbol, no girlfriend

The Fourth

FIFTY

Charlie went back to Shafik's office. The detective was in a bad mood. He'd agreed to release Alex but only on the basis that he was followed. If he leads us to the Surgeon, Charlie thought, then it's all well and good. However, she felt sure MacLure was just the man in the middle. He needed protection rather than a tail. Whoever had killed the student, Salam, was surely after MacLure too. Maybe he'd also killed Salam's boyfriend, Tomasz Schwartz.

A note on Shafik's desk caught her attention. It was a message for her from her partner. She called him.

Zhang said, "My God, Charlie. My God."

"What is it, Peter?"

"There are bodies under most of the churches. The Surgeon was using the Church of the Risen Christ as his personal burial lot."

"How many," she asked tentatively.

"I don't know. A lot. More than on the sheet. My guess is... what? Eighteen churches in three states. Five bodies minimum per church."

"Ninety more bodies!" Charlie gasped.

Zhang blew out air. "To be honest we've only just started. Six for six. Every church had bodies. Maybe five is a lowball number. Maybe the one in Atlanta had only just started. Some of the guys are taking bets."

"They're sick," Charlie said. "Tell them from me, they're sick."

"I've got better news. At least I think it's better."

"What? I could do with some good news."

"Better, not good. We know where McCubbin went. He must have left in a hurry because he used his real name."

"Great. Where?"

"Tel Aviv."

"So he's in Israel."

"No. He immediately boarded a flight to Cairo. Since yesterday evening he's been in your neck of the woods, Charlie."

Shafik was still in a bad mood when he came back into his office. He sat in his chair like he was exhausted. Charlie gave him the news from the States.

"It's coming to a climax," he said when she finished.

"It looks that way. And Egypt is where it's happening."

Shafik rubbed his tired, watery eyes. "I have some news too. MacLure's assistant was murdered in Deir Mawas yesterday evening. The research was destroyed too. I think MacLure is covering his tracks."

Charlie shook her head. "But surely—"

"No," Shafik said. "He's involved. He knows what the secret is and he's destroying the evidence. He killed his assistant and then killed Salam."

Charlie couldn't believe what he was saying. She went to speak but he held up a hand.

"Enough of this bullshit. He's coming back in. I've ordered that MacLure be picked up again." He looked at her in the hard way she'd seen him look at suspects. "And the US needs to back off from this. You need to stand down, Special Agent Rebb."

Charlie walked out of the police station and hailed a taxi. She'd just about had enough of the way the Egyptian police operated. But who was she? One woman in a foreign country.

She couldn't recall the journey back, and when she got into her apartment, she flung her scarf on the floor like it was a rejection of the Egyptian constraints she felt. She flopped onto the bed and rang her boss.

"Mike Smith."

"It's Charlie Rebb. Sorry to disturb you," she said. There was a pain under both eyes and she pinched the top of her nose to ease it.

"Not a problem, Charlie," he said. "What's up?"

And so she vented her frustration on her boss. Smith just listened until she complained about John Graham.

She said, "Graham has got some diplomatic, bureaucratic issue going on, probably being pressured by the British Embassy but he keeps pestering me for updates. I'm trying—"

"Fuck him," Smith said.

"What?" she said surprised by his language though it made her smile.

"Just get on the next flight out," he said. "Graham shouldn't have backed out of the case to start with and the Egyptians—"

"No, sir. I can't."

"Charlie, listen to me. Like you said, there's nothing you can do now. Let's hope the Egyptians catch the bastard then we'll get an extradition order and fry his sorry ass."

"No, sir," she said. "Not yet. I just needed to talk."

"Don't do anything stupid, Charlie. You hear me?"

The truth was, Charlie didn't know what she was going to do, but while talking it out she knew she couldn't just walk away.

She'd been wearing the gun for the past few days. Shafik had relaxed his attitude but it felt heavy and useless. Now she flung it on the bed followed by her blouse.

She'd moved the coffee machine next to her bed, an indication of how her addiction had gone unchecked since arriving in Egypt. She started it up and turned on the taps in the bath. A huge amount of her favourite soak foamed under the torrent.

Back in the bedroom, she kicked off the rest of her clothes, waited for the coffee and then breathed in the strong aroma. This and a soak in the bath and she'd be transported to another time and place. A happier one. One before the murders. One before she'd discovered her husband's infidelity.

She noticed a missed call on her phone. John Graham chasing his update. Or maybe he'd also try and persuade her to go home. Not now, she thought. Now is not the time.

The water was starting to turn chilly when she realized she must have dropped off. Her remaining half-cup of coffee was stone cold. She climbed out, wrapped a giant, fluffy white towel around herself and headed for the coffee machine. Time to make a fresh one.

Charlie was half way past the bed when she noticed it. Was it just her imagination? Hadn't the holster and blouse been laid separately? Now the blouse covered the holster.

Definitely her mistake, she decided, and took two more steps towards the coffee machine. She turned back. Better check, she smiled to herself, remembering her dad's foolish old saying when she was a kid. If you think there's a monster under the bed, then you should look. Of course there never was, but how else could you go to sleep?

She flicked back the blouse, exposing the holster.

Her gun wasn't there.

That's when she registered that the door to the living room wasn't closed. She hadn't opened it.

Someone had taken her gun.

And that person was still in the apartment.

FIFTY-ONE

Alex sat in the living area, facing the bedroom door. He knew this was crazy but he had no choice. The worry and panic swelled inside him as he waited.

And then the FBI agent suddenly kicked open the door. She stood there, wrapped in a large towel, her hair wet on her shoulders, holding a lamp like it was a weapon.

She looked at the gun in his right hand and glanced at his empty left. Then back at his face. "You're not going to shoot me," she said, her calm impressive.

"No, and you're not going to attack me with a bedside lamp." He lowered the gun. "I took it because I didn't want you to shoot me."

She held out a hand. "Can I have it back?"

"Yes," he said, though instead of getting up and handing it to her, he placed it on a side table. "But for now I'll feel safer if neither of us have it."

She kept hold of the lamp. "How did you get in?"

"The door wasn't locked."

He could see her consider the possibility. She looked tired. Maybe that was why she hadn't locked it properly.

He said, "I need your help."

"How did you get here?"

He shrugged. "If you mean how did I throw the police tail? It was easy. I'd guessed Detective Shafik wouldn't just let me go without having me followed. After all, I figured he'd been doing it before. So I went out of my hotel the back way, hailed a taxi and kept switching. It's a crowded city you know. Easy to get lost. Easy to lose someone if you know your way about."

She nodded.

He continued: "I can't trust the police. You're the only one I could think of. The only one who could help me. You don't think I killed Brown—I mean Salam, do you?"

"No."

"And you don't think I'm working for the killer?"

"No."

He sighed. "Like I said, you're my only hope."

"Of what?"

"Saving Vanessa, my girlfriend. The killer has her!" His voice quavered as he said it.

"OK," Charlie said, raising a hand. "Give me a few minutes to get dressed and we'll talk about it."

She stepped back and started to close the bedroom door.

"Stop!" he said. Now she knew he was there, out of sight, she might raise the alarm.

Charlie said, "I'm not getting dressed in front of you Mr MacLure!"

"Call me Alex. Please."

"Alex—you need to trust me. Let me get dressed and I'll listen to your story. If I can help, I promise that I will."

"Leave your phone in here," he said.

She shrugged, retrieved her phone and tossed it onto a chair before disappearing into the bedroom.

While he waited, Alex looked at the maps on the wall. He noted there were markers showing the American cemetery, a temple in Abusir, a street in El Obdour City and Eza Street, the place where he'd gone to meet Black/Schwartz, found the body and been arrested.

There were piles of folders that he'd already glanced at: missing person and homicide cases from the US. He barely took anything in. A realization was a live thing inside him. One he didn't want to admit to himself.

He was looking at a sheet with initials and images on when the agent came back through the door wearing jeans and a T-shirt. Her hair was still wet but tied into a ponytail. She no longer held a lamp. Instead, she had a cup of coffee in her hands and perched on the seat opposite him.

She smiled. "See, I didn't call anyone."

"Thanks." He swallowed. "These are about the Surgeon, the serial killer, aren't they?"

"Yes." She looked at the wall and files then back to him.

"And I'm involved."

She took a sip of coffee before raising her eyebrows. "All right then, let's hear your story."

And so Alex told her about the messages he'd received telling him that Vanessa was being held.

"I think the Surgeon"—he struggled to say it—"the man who has my girlfriend is the Surgeon."

"He doesn't abduct women. Not as far as we know anyway."

"But this is different. This is because he wants the symbol." Alex waved the sheet of paper he was still holding. "The symbol is a secret and he thinks I know it."

"And you really don't know?"

"No. The ancient translation doesn't say." Alex rubbed his temples. The worry was now a growing pain inside his head.

She fetched a glass of water and two Advil. "Tell me what you know," she said, handing them over.

He said, "You were leading the investigation in Atlanta and you've traced him here. He tattoos his victims with different symbols. He's trying to find the right symbol."

"And what is the *right* symbol?"

"I think it's got something to do with eternal life."

She nodded. "That's our belief too. The Surgeon has been working with a church—the Church of the Risen Christ."

"Where the bodies were found in Atlanta."

"We've found more. More churches, more bodies. This has been an operation on an industrial scale. All for the sake of a symbol."

"The guy's a nut."

"Maybe. Probably. But he's not working alone. Others in the church are connected, not least the man at the top who calls himself the governor of the church." She finished her coffee. "Have you heard of the Mark of Cain?"

"Vaguely. Was it to do with the killing of Abel?"

"Yes. No one knows what the mark was and the orthodox opinion is that God scarred Cain so that others would recognize him for what he was."

"Orthodox?"

"There's a minority opinion that the mark was Cain's sign. The symbol of his power. His secret."

"OK," Alex said connecting the dots.

"They also believe that when Jesus was on the cross, a man in the form of a Roman centurion ensured that Jesus would be resurrected. He was carefully speared so that his heart stopped. They also think Jesus was tattooed with the Mark of Cain."

"Is there any evidence?"

"Of course not," she said. "It's the unfounded belief of either the Church of the Risen Christ themselves or a group within the church. They're believed to be called the Seventh Hour."

Alex stared. "You're kidding!"

"Why?"

"The seventh hour is significant. It's the point at which the god Seth spears Apep, the serpent. Seth became demonized—the one the Christian church call Satan—and yet he ensured that Ra progressed through the most difficult stage of the night. Seth ensures his..."

"What?"

"The resurrection of the sun. Seth is the one who causes the resurrection."

Charlie closed her eyes and nodded. "So the Seventh Hour group think that the centurion was Seth and the Surgeon is trying to find the Mark of Cain—the symbol—so that he can play the role of Seth."

Alex was also nodding. It was starting to make sense. "The Sign of Seth."

"The same thing," she said.

"There's just one problem," he said. "I need to give the Surgeon that symbol, and even having this information doesn't get me any closer to knowing what it is."

FIFTY-TWO

With only a month remaining, Yanhamu stayed in his lodgings in the city less than thirty miles north of Memphis. Sadhu was clearly becoming more and more concerned about his master's disposition. He believed Yanhamu would give up hope. And at times Yanhamu wondered if he already had.

Each day the young man would visit and talk of the exciting things he'd done. It transpired that Heliopolis was even more thrilling and definitely more liberal than the capital in the south. He'd spoken of bull runs and fights in stadia. He also loved all the temples, especially the newest: the Mansion of the Phoenix. He said it was a huge courtyard with a giant pillar in the middle.

"It's Ra's phallus," Sadhu explained. "And couples go there to aid fertility—you know…"

"Not really."

"To copulate, I mean, and what's so fantastic is that there are girls there too who don't mind if you copulate with them."

"Lovely," Yanhamu said without feeling. Is this what religion came down to? Was it all about sex?

From the window of his small room he could see the Great Pyramid. He stared, hardly able to believe the thought that had just come to him. All about sex! That was effectively the point of the pyramid: to bring together Osiris and Isis and create the new Horus. The wisdom texts spoke of the Second Coming of Horus and that is where it would happen.

Sadhu was watching him and must have guessed he was suddenly invigorated.

"What is it, my lord?"

"I'm going to do something, but, my friend, you mustn't be involved. I do not want to gamble with your life as well as my own."

Sadhu argued but finally agreed. As soon as he was gone, Yanhamu changed into a black robe. Then he left Heliopolis and found transport across the Great River. He needed to get to Giza but couldn't go there directly so he purchased a donkey and rode west before he turned in the wilderness and headed south.

It was night by the time he had circled back and could see the three pyramids ahead against the starry sky. Setting his donkey free, he travelled the remaining distance on foot. He could see the lights of the Sphinx temple and, as he passed the first pyramid, he began to hear the chanting. It went on all night every night, but he wasn't interested in the temple.

Making sure he wasn't observed by temple guards, he snuck around the second pyramid and waited by the foot of the Great Pyramid. He'd never been here before and only a select few could step onto this hallowed ground, the outcrop that had been determined as Orion's place on the Earth. The Duat. The counterpart of the night sky, where the Great River below reflected the Great River of stars above.

Only a priest of Horem-Akhet—the Sphinx—or Pharaoh himself could come here. He hoped the black clothes and a cowl were enough of a disguise. With a pounding heart he began to creep around until he was over the tunnel that led from the Sphinx to the pyramid. He'd paid good money months ago to be told about this tunnel, the one Horemheb would have used at the summer solstice. But he had also been told about the ventilation holes, and he located one now.

The space was narrow but Yanhamu managed to squirm through and drop the few feet into the tunnel. Now his hands were shaking as well as his blood pounding in his ears. But he had no time to waste because a guard could still find him.

In the pitch darkness, he walked quickly west, using his hand on the limestone wall as a guide. When the stone steps started, he stumbled into them. The flight was short and he knew that he was now directly under the pyramid. He counted twenty steps before they ended. There was a crawl space to his right and after a short distance he found himself in a chamber. This he knew from his informer was the first station. Pharaoh had to wait here and pray before continuing.

But Yanhamu wasn't the pharaoh and he had no intention of waiting. Only now did he take out an oil lamp and light it to see a throne in the centre of the room that was chiselled out of the rock without decoration and about the height of two men. He looked back at the crawl space from whence he'd come and then at a similar hole at the other side of the room.

Blowing out the lamp he began to crawl onwards. At first it was flat, but after four feet it angled, steep and smooth. Another six feet and he was below the well shaft. Rather than continue up the slope, Pharaoh now had to climb a rope. Yanhamu's informant had called it the umbilical cord. A challenging climb to test Pharaoh's strength and devotion.

Again the walls were rough, and Yanhamu used his feet on the catches as he pulled himself up, hand over hand. His laboured breaths seemed to fall like stones into the darkness below. An eternity passed before he reached a resting place known as the second station. But he pressed on. In places the shaft was almost vertical, but now his feet found notches like steps.

Finally, sweating from the exertion, he emerged into an alcove and lit the lamp again. Now he was in the main passageway, running down to the left and up to the right. He stepped forward and gasped. Despite his growing cynicism about religion, the sight of Osiris made him quake. Of course, it was just a statue, but power seemed to emanate from it as the god stared down at him: an unworthy commoner.

Yanhamu shook the negative thoughts away and saw a high and narrowing ceiling above Osiris, stone overlapping stone like reverse steps. He knew this was the main route to the Tree of Life, under which a deceased pharaoh would be placed. Even a living pharaoh would not visit that chamber, so instead of taking this path, he chose the lower road to the chamber below this. He could walk now and the walls were smooth like water. Then the limestone floor turned to red marble. The colour of the gods, Yanhamu found himself saying.

He was now in the second chamber, about eighteen paces square and a little taller. There was a gabled ceiling and unadorned walls. The only thing in the room was a table. This was the final station for the worthy pharaoh, and the sacred site. This was where Osiris and Isis would copulate to produce the future king. Yanhamu had been told that there were two shafts that pointed to the stars. When the alignment was right, the light of Sirius/Isis would meet the light of Orion/Osiris and Horus would be created.

That time was not now, but this was the holiest of holy places. This was the location that had been triggered in Yanhamu's mind when Sadhu had been discussing the Mansion of the Phoenix and sex. This is what it was all about. The proof of everlasting life; the proof that the gods existed was here. Horus had been created and ruled on Earth. And he would come again.

Yanhamu sat on the floor in front of the table and blew out his lamp. He closed his eyes and let his mind go free.

As it had been inside Tutankhamen's tomb, time became meaningless, life became something surreal. Yanhamu let go all of the negative thoughts of religion, the way it had been manipulated over the centuries by the priesthood. At first he tried to think through the problem and find the truth he could tell the deputy. Eventually he gave up and let his mind go blank.

It could have been hours or days that passed, Yanhamu had no idea. At one point he sensed eternity— as though being here was outside of time. He also felt there were spirits present and imagined the gods watching, although when he heard a voice, it wasn't one of them. The voice came from his sister, Laret, and he knew she'd been with him for a long time. She didn't say much but what she did say opened his mind. And then she was gone and the vastness of eternity was all around again.

When he was sure she wasn't coming back, he moved. His joints ached from sitting for so long. He stretched and then reversed the route he'd taken to get here. Of course, it was all downhill now and he was soon in the subterranean chamber. He snuck back out of the hole in the tunnel and made his way back to Memphis. Now he knew exactly what he was going to tell Ramses.

FIFTY-THREE

Through Special Agent Rebb's apartment window, Alex watched the sun go down.

"I have twenty-four hours," he said.

"We should talk to him," Rebb said. "Negotiate. If you wait until the dead-line, the evidence points to a lower likelihood of success."

"This is real life," Alex said and he heard the despair in his own voice. "This isn't theory. This isn't a training manual."

"I'm sorry, but you asked for help…"

Alex looked at her. What had he expected, realistically? Sure she was the FBI but she was on her own.

"I don't want the Egyptian police involved," he said quietly. "I don't know. I don't know what to do."

She closed the gap between them. She picked up the gun and put it in a drawer, then she sat close, her leg almost touching his.

"As I see it," she said, "we have two options. One, you bluff it out. You say you have the symbol and give it to him."

"I make it up?"

"Sure. The whole thing is made up anyway, isn't it? No way this whole resurrection thing by stabbing and tattooing some mystical sign works, right?"

"I guess." He nodded slowly. "What's the second option?"

"You give him the real symbol."

"Which I don't have and don't know how to find."

The special agent placed a hand on his arm. "So here's the thing: you try. You come up with a solution, whether it's right or wrong. The important thing is that you can convince the Surgeon that it's right. Can you do that?"

"I guess so."

"OK," she said. "First things first. We take back control."

"What do you mean?"

"We communicate with the Surgeon and we ask for proof of life."

"Proof Vanessa is alive?" Alex took a long breath. He'd been suppressing the idea that she could already be dead. Asking for proof of life could tell him the opposite. Was he prepared for that?

She held out her hand. "Let me have your phone and I'll message him."

"No," he said, watching her eyes. "I'll do the messaging." He saw a frisson of disappointment and then she smiled.

"Of course, but remember, I've had kidnap negotiator training. We have to say the right thing."

Alex opened up Telegram and messaged agent_k. His hand shook.

I'm working on the problem. First I want to know Vanessa is OK

There was no immediate reply. Then after five minutes the message was: **She's fine**

Rebb said, "Say you want proof."

Alex sent the message.

After a pause, the other person replied: You're in no position to make demands

"Tell him you can't work on the problem unless you know for sure she's all right."

Alex typed.

Then he said, Is she there, now?

Yes

Rebb said, "Ask for a photograph with today's paper."

But Alex typed, I want to hear her voice

He could see Rebb thinking. Probably that Vanessa's voice could have been recorded in advance.

The response from the Surgeon was immediate: No

Alex typed, Then I don't find your symbol. I need to know I can save her

He watched the screen, willing an answer. After a delay, the other person replied. Tell me what she has to say. Keep it short

Charlie said, "Ask for something you know will make her think. Like her middle name if she hasn't got one. That way she may give us a clue."

Alex thought then typed, I want her to say her name and that she's unharmed. I also want her to say the name of her first pet.

Alex followed up by sending his phone number.

Time ticked slowly until his phone rang. Number withheld.

Rebb said, "Record it!"

Alex hit *record* and answered. "Hello?"

Without preamble, Vanessa started to repeat the required statement. "Hello, Alex. My name is Vanessa Vance although you know I use other names."

She paused.

Her voice sounds off, maybe tiredness, possibly drugs, Alex thought.

She said, "I am tied up in a cage but I am unharmed." Another pause. Alex heard the call for prayer on the phone and through Rebb's window. The timing was slightly off. There was a noise, like wood on metal, maybe the Surgeon encouraging Vanessa to speak.

She finished: "My first pet was a cat called something like Anar. It's hot."

The call ended.

Rebb was almost leaning on his shoulder. She said, "Is that right? She took a long time to say the pet's name."

"I don't know."

"Then why the heck...?" She reached for the phone.

Alex shook his head. "Your objective—your priority—is not mine. You want the Surgeon. I want Vanessa back safe."

"I wouldn't be doing my job—" Rebb started to protest but then stopped, and he could see he was right. She said, "Tell him twenty-four hours isn't long enough."

"How long do we want?"

"As long as possible," she said. "No deadline at all would be ideal, but for now any movement is good."

Alex sent the message.

The reply was an emphatic: **No negotiation!**

"Don't give up," the FBI agent said.

Alex typed, I need longer to solve this

Then you'd better get cracking, hadn't you?
There was no further communication.

Alex paced the room. "We learned something," he said.

"I thought you didn't know her cat's name."

"She had a dog, never a cat. Cat was her undercover name. She was sending a message. Anar means something."

She looked at him expectantly.

"I don't know what it is. I can't think. But what I do know is there was a timing difference between the call to prayer here and on the phone."

She shook her head, not understanding. "But the phone call must have been live... unless..."

"It was live," he said smiling. "Because of the racket caused by so many muezzin competing to be heard, a law was passed in Cairo forcing the use of a centralized call. Some mosques defy the ban for a while. This tells us she's near one that's not using the recording."

He knew it wasn't much but the small knowledge gave him a little hope.

FIFTY-FOUR

McCubbin looked through the signs that Zart had used. The Seventh Hour had a team of smart people trying to solve the problem. He provided Zart with their output but the man was a creative, free spirit. Sometimes he used the suggestions, oftentimes he tried his own.

It was a weird set-up they'd created for him. This was the main room with Zart's working area, but he'd also continued painting and there were canvases all around. There were two more rooms, both underground: a garage containing an unmarked van and the fake paramedic's vehicle. And then the room where the bodies were kept. They'd bought him three chest freezers just in case.

On the wall over his desk, Zart had painted "God of Confusion" on a wide canvas. Was he referring to himself? Did he think of himself as the god Seth now? Did the power of resurrection make him a god? McCubbin closed his eyes. Had he created a monster or was Zart a monster before all of this? Did the end justify the means?

"Let's pray," he said.

Zart knelt on the floor, prostrate before McCubbin.

"We come to God in prayer for a variety of reasons," McCubbin began, "to worship Him, to thank Him for

His blessings, to confess our sins and ask for forgiveness."

After he'd completed the standard prayer, he went on to quote from the scriptures: those that spoke of the resurrection. The true story, passed down from generation to generation, not the confused ones of the Bible. The truth that told of the spear that pierced Jesus's chest to stop his heart. The Sign of Seth—the Mark of Cain—that would show him worthy. And then the dimensions—the Tree of Life. How God's energy was focused through the tree, through the four universes and into the body.

McCubbin ended it with: "He embraced them both, possessing the humanity and the divinity, so that on the one hand he might vanquish death through his being Son of God, and that on the other through the Son of Man the restoration to the Pleroma might occur; because he was originally from above, a seed of the Truth, because this dimension had come into being. So says the secret book of John."

"Jesus appeared before him and gave the secret to John the Apostle," Zart chanted, the standard response.

Then McCubbin broke bread and they drank wine in memory of Christ's body and blood.

A telephone on the desk pinged with a message. Zart picked up the phone as soon as McCubbin gave him leave.

"I didn't know you had a phone," McCubbin said as Zart stared at the screen.

"It's not mine, Master. I took this from Salam—the kid involved with Tomasz Schwartz. He was using it to communicate with Alex MacLure."

McCubbin nodded.

Zart said, "MacLure wants proof of life."

"Tell him he's in no position to make demands."

Zart exchanged a few messages and then said, "He's not backing down. He wants to hear her voice."

"Is she conscious?"

"Should be."

McCubbin considered the options. MacLure wanted control and could have it. If he could get the correct symbol on time, it would be worth the risk.

"All right, fine. Agree to it, but as a prepared statement from him. Short and no clever stuff."

Zart returned to the message and then told McCubbin what she was to say.

"Fine," McCubbin said again. It was almost laughable. Such a puerile question.

Zart hurried away, lifted the hatch and descended into the basement. While he waited, McCubbin heard the call for prayer, a cacophony that in his mind was anything but religious.

Zart returned. "It's done," he said, "Although the idiot asked for more time."

"How long did you give him? You know the perfect confluence is tomorrow tonight."

"Until 7pm—sunset—tomorrow. That gives us plenty of time."

"Then we stick with that. No negotiation."

Zart sent a message and tossed the phone onto the desk.

McCubbin walked over to the hatch and down the stone steps. The air was warmer down here and he figured it must be the freezer's heat exchangers and lack of ventilation.

He went through into the rear room and regarded the girl in the cage. She looked up with eyes full of hate. But there was no fight in her, the drugs would see to that.

McCubbin patted Zart on the arm, something he'd never done before, and said, "You've been resourceful."

"Thank you, Master. I am here to be the servant."

Good, thought McCubbin. Perhaps he's not as arrogant as I feared. Perhaps he does appreciate that he is purely a vessel.

Zart passed water into the cage. The girl drank hungrily and within seconds passed out as the drugs quickly took effect.

Zart stood, head bowed, awkward. "Master, may I ask a question?"

"Go ahead."

"What if MacLure doesn't deliver the sign on time?"

"We've waited 2,000 years. If it doesn't happen now, waiting another year is nothing," he said, although he knew everything was different. The FBI knew who they were now. The plan would have to change.

"And the student?"

"His body is in the first freezer."

McCubbin nodded. Good. "Then I'll take it with me," he said.

FIFTY-FIVE

Special Agent Rebb asked Alex for the recording and she sent it on to her partner in the States.

"We'll get it analysed," she said after convincing Alex that searching the streets near the mosque was pointless. Then she picked up an iPad and asked, "What am I looking for?"

"The symbol," he said. "I can't say more than that. If I knew—"

"But the Surgeon seems convinced you do know. Perhaps you have the knowledge but don't realize it."

He shook his head, although it was a possibility. "When I was at Giza, Salam talked and talked about the Sphinx and how he believed it to be a dog and representative of Seth. But the Surgeon had Black/Schwartz so he was telling me what the Surgeon wanted. I can't trust what he said."

"It doesn't matter if you trusted him. You learned the importance of Seth in finding the symbol. The same as the Mark of Cain. Doesn't matter whether it was the Salam kid or the Surgeon. That's what he needs."

As she said it, Alex wondered about the similarity in the name Cain and Canis Major—canine. Seth the dog. However, he said, "There has to be more. Salam was going to take me into Khufu's pyramid. He wanted to show me something there—even though I'd been inside many times."

He shook his head. It felt full of random thoughts that made no sense. She was looking at him, perhaps expecting great insight, but there was nothing.

He said, "So where do I start, Agent Rebb?"

"You start by calling me Charlie."

He smiled for the first time that day. "And next?"

"Find out what you can about Seth, I suppose."

They sat in silence for ten minutes, Charlie on her iPad and Alex on his phone. He was reading a paper called *Seth, God of Confusion: A Study of His Rule in Egyptian Mythology and Religion* when she spoke.

"Do you mind me interrupting you?"

"No," he said, looking up.

"This god Seth seems to have been called various things, mostly Set, but also"—she read—"Setesh, Sutekh, Setekh, and Suty."

"The main problem is that there are many forms of his name partly because of other religions merging, which resulted in the names Sutekh and Setekh but also because of the script or ideograms used. Seth was most common in the New Kingdom."

"New Kingdom?"

"The period of interest. It includes the Nineteenth Dynasty of Pharaohs Ramses I and II as well as Seti I and II. Ramses I became the pharaoh in the ancient story I translated."

Alex put down his phone and rubbed his eyes. It was hard work reading on the small device.

"I keep thinking I'm missing something obvious," he said.

"In the paper I'm reading, it suggests his name can mean multiple things and be broken down to mean more."

"Such as?"

"*Overmastering and overpowering.* Sometimes *Turning back* and *He who is pleased with desertion. The instigator of confusion,* and another one of the alternatives is *Beer.*"

"Beer?"

"Being a play on his mischievous nature, adding to the confusion by getting someone drunk."

"He seems related to many things. Chaos, darkness, storms, the desert—although I haven't seen anything about drunkenness."

"I'm not even sure he was the alleged incarnation of chaos. Maybe that came later when he fell from favour. You see, the serpent Apep was chaos, death and disorder."

She said something more but Alex wasn't listening. He'd seen something in the paper he was reading. "Hold on," he said, scrolling back and reading it again.

"What?"

He said, "There were also many ways of writing the god's name, and as the animal it could be in four positions, from lying down like the Sphinx to sitting like a man. But the most interesting is this…"

He used two fingers to zoom in on his phone and showed it to the agent.

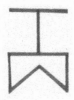

"It's from the coffin texts," Alex explained. "They used this to avoid using the name Seth because he was the instigator of confusion."

Charlie sat back, eyes wide. "So that's our symbol!"

"Maybe," Alex said slowly then shook his head. "It doesn't feel right. Surely we're looking for something hidden. I didn't know about this hieroglyph but I found it on the internet. The Surgeon has been searching for years."

"Because you know what you're looking for," Charlie said with hope in her voice.

"Maybe," he said, still unconvinced. "Let's keep going."

Alex thought about the name and wondered what he could find out about the worship of Seth. It didn't take him long to discover everything had been destroyed. There had been temples at Kom Ombo on the Nile near Aswan and allegedly temples at Oxyrhynchus and in the Faiyum area, although nothing remained. Sepermeru, a town connecting the Nile to Faiyum seemed the most encouraging. According to Fourteenth Dynasty documents, there had been a temple called House of Seth, Lord of Sepermeru. A twin temple was referred to as being developed by Ramses II. So there was a connection with one of the Ramses pharaohs although there were no statues or carvings to help.

Later he came across new research into Ramses I and a temple dedicated to Seth within an ancient fortress at Tell Hebua. It was south of Port Said on the edge of the desert. He found the image of a stele showing Ramses I with arms aloft, worshipping Seth. Seth held an ankh and *was*-sceptre. Disappointingly, the god's name was clearly written with no obvious hidden symbols.

"What's up?" Rebb asked.

"There's just nothing to go on. There are clear links with Ramses and the worship of Seth but nothing to indicate a secret symbol."

She was looking at his screen again. "I know that's an ankh in Seth's right hand but what's the staff?"

"It's called the *was*-sceptre—a symbol of power."

She was looking at him curiously. "What are you thinking?"

"I just remembered there's a plaster cast from Seti I's tomb. The sceptre is clearly a representation of Seth: not just the two-pronged tail but the head looks like Seth."

"And that helps us how?"

He shrugged. "I don't know, I was just remembering. However, the *was*-sceptre is often featured even when Seth is not. Despite his demonization, I think Seth consciously or unconsciously was a major force in ancient Egypt."

"OK…" she said optimistically.

He shrugged again. "It's too obvious. I need a secret sign, not something so blatant. But it does make me think of tombs rather than temples."

FIFTY-SIX

1307 BCE, the bank of the Nile opposite Giza

The royal boat moored after its short journey from Memphis. Ramses stood on the prow of *The Strength of Hapi.* He was still Pharaoh's deputy but had also taken the title Justice of Ra.

Yanhamu stood beside him and both men looked towards the pyramids.

"So we have arrived. Now tell me why we are looking at the pyramids, Khety." His voice sounded rough, and for the first time Yanhamu wondered about the deputy's health. Pharaoh Horemheb was dying and maybe Ramses had the same condition.

"Your Highness," Yanhamu began, "this is not about the pyramids. I wish to speak about the statue of Horem-Akhet."

Sirius was no longer in the night sky and it would soon be the New Year again. The priests of Horem-Akhet held a service every night, although they were quiet now in the heat of the morning.

"Tell me what truth you have learned, Khety? And remember, the crocodiles will be fed if you have been of no use."

Yanhamu ignored the threat and spoke with confidence. "As you know, I have travelled the length and breadth of the land. I have found out things that no ordinary man will discover."

"With my gold."

"Yes, and with wine, but also with guile. I got priests to share their secrets and when they did not, I would find the truth in other ways. I will be honest, Majesty, I became disillusioned with what I found. Since Thebes became the southern capital, the priesthood has gained in power and secrecy. I have found that they manipulate the truth and con the masses. I became cynical that they perpetuate myths in order to line their own pockets and strengthen their control."

Ramses said, "Don't think I don't know their power games. That is why the pharaoh must come from the military. Horemheb was commander and I was commander. My son, Menmaatra is also strong, and he will soon command the army. We are bound together by our worship of the gods, Khety, but Pharaoh is the master."

"Of course, Majesty. All I am saying is that I became disillusioned by their trickery. I have learned that the statues of gods only fly because of the metal B'ja. The priesthood has always forbidden its gathering and use. The reason is that they don't want others to learn the truth."

"What else?"

"They hide inside temple walls and pretend to speak for the gods. They have tools and tinctures that heal people and pretend there has been a miracle when the person is cured."

"Perhaps it is."

"I have learned of gods and demons that have been created—not by the gods but by man. The people want

317

more and are willing to pay for more, so that is what they get. I have also seen the creation of papyri purporting to be the Book of the Dead. Some are poor copies and others are just nonsense. Some are pure fantasy and some only partial. It seems to depend on how much you can afford."

Ramses hawked and spat phlegm into the slow-flowing river. "This is not sounding very good, Khety. I think I can see the crocodiles circling."

"I agree, Majesty. I can also tell you that Pharaoh Horemheb has an incredible tomb that penetrates far into the hill, but its depth will not help him. I noticed that he has the Book of Gates painted in his burial chamber."

"You told me this before—the instructions for the passage for Ra through the night."

"However, I didn't tell you it is incomplete but I will come back to that. First, I would ask Your Majesty to look at the statue of Horem-Akhet and tell me what you see."

"I see Pharaoh Khafre's face on the body of a great beast, looking east to where Ra will rise."

"And the stele between its paws?"

"The plaque that tells us Pharaoh Thutmose IV excavated the site because the statue had been buried. The old temple of Horem-Akhet was also uncovered."

Yanhamu nodded. "Because we had forgotten. The sands had blown over and buried most of the statue and temples."

"Because they are ancient."

"Perhaps they are even more ancient. Imagine you commissioned your own statue. Would you, Your Majesty, have a head so small on the body of the animal?"

"I would not."

"Before Pharaoh Meni reunited the Two Lands, there were two religions. In the south there was the Horus King. And in the north...?"

"Seth." Ramses hawked and spat again.

"The evil one? We use his name to scare our enemy."

"Of course. The Seth army and many of our border forts are named after him."

"And yet he is of the Ennead—one of the nine. In fact, he has great power and Ra relies on him. Now look again at the statue. Ignore the face and think about the worship of Ra before the lands were reunited."

"Tell me what I see."

"A dog. It is Seth waiting for his master to rise on the horizon. Seth who defeats the terrible Apep during Ra's journey. Seth who defeats his enemies and leads the way to the horizon." Yanhamu paused, hoping that the message was sinking in. "Your Majesty, you asked for the second truth. The first truth is Horus, and you will become Horus one day, joining the others in the sky, helping Ra in his transition. But the second truth is that Seth has two faces. It has been forgotten, and as pharaoh you will be stronger by recognizing him. When you have your magic bricks inserted in the cardinal points of your tomb, ensure that the western one is for Seth. When you have your murals designed, make sure you include Seth, and when you have shabti made, include one of Seth. He will give you strength in the afterlife and he will show you the way to the Field of Reeds. Through him, you will guarantee immortality."

"But I cannot openly worship Seth. Ptah has the power."

Yanhamu intoned the standard phrase, "In all his forms, Ptah has the power."

Ramses did not respond for a long time. He seemed to be staring at the Great Sphinx and processing what

319

Yanhamu had said. For anyone other than Pharaoh, such a thing would be heresy, and yet it would give him power over the priesthood. Yanhamu had looked beyond his disillusionment with religion because he still believed. He had sensed his sister so he knew the Field of Reeds was real. It was just the corruption of the message and the worship that was not.

"Majesty," he dared say. "All I ask is for the return of my wife."

Ramses turned and looked at him long and hard. "Perhaps," he said, his voice thick with the phlegm. "But you still haven't given me that second truth. I need detail."

"Of course, Your Highness. You need to know that by this mark you will recognize him—a secret sign."

Yanhamu picked up a stick and drew something in the dirt.

FIFTY-SEVEN

Charlie went on the phone with Zhang and gave him an update on the case.

"I received the proof-of-life recording. It's already with forensic audio."

"Great. Did they tell you how long?"

"They're on it. As fast as they can—through the night, Charlie."

"OK."

"Are you all right?" he asked, concern in his voice.

"I'm fine."

"And you're sure this guy MacLure is trustworthy and not a risk?"

"I'm fine." His concern was touching. She hadn't seen this side of Peter before.

"About the girl..." he said.

"What about her?" Charlie whispered back. She was in the bedroom, but if he listened hard, MacLure would surely hear her. She didn't want to worry him by talking loudly about his girlfriend.

"The Surgeon only takes males."

"And?"

"Just thinking out loud. Maybe she could be a victim too. Maybe he's getting desperate."

She finished the thought: "If he knows we're on to him, he might be afraid to abduct another man."

"Right."

She took a breath. She knew the odds of getting someone back alive. They weren't good, and this was no ordinary kidnapping.

"I hope you're wrong," she said.

"Me too." He paused before saying, "The LEGAT, Graham, called me. Did you say I'd give him updates?"

"No. Did you tell him anything?"

"Not me—in fact, no one here. That's up to you."

"Good," she said. "Keep ignoring him. He's just a glory hog getting in the way."

"Sure," he said. "A quick update for you then: the police are questioning Piccard again. In fact they've taken all of the CRC pastors in for questioning. These guys clearly believe the Second Coming is about to happen but were not so sure they're part of the Seventh Hour group. It looks like it was just McCubbin and probably the other two directors of the church."

"And what do they say?"

"Nothing—they directors have also disappeared. Documents were burned but the cops have found references to the seventh hour and secret gospels."

"Secret gospels?"

"Ones that allegedly didn't make it into the New Testament, but believed by this group. Remember the one Professor Suza mentioned—the Gospel of Nicodemus?"

Charlie didn't but her partner continued before she could respond.

"Apparently there was a secret book of John the Apostle. It's full of weird stuff about resurrection and dimensions."

"That fits," Charlie agreed.

322

"And one other thing. We've also failed to trace that roving pastor—the one on the hill—Robert Kingren."

"Maybe he's one of this inner circle too, this Seventh Hour group."

"Like before, we're checking manifests and airport CCTV footage. We know McCubbin is in Egypt. Working theory is they're all headed there."

They went back to discussing developments in Cairo and MacLure's search for the symbol.

Then Zhang said, "How long have we got?"

"Until 1pm tomorrow, your time, 7pm here," she said.

Charlie listened to dead air for a moment and wondered what he was thinking.

"Take care, Charlie," he said. "Don't do anything foolish."

Alex heard most of what the Charlie had said in the other room.

When she came back into the room, he said, "Your partner?"

"Yes. He's got the specialist audio forensic guys analysing the sounds on the recording. They'll work through the night if necessary."

Alex nodded. "Your partner... he's worried about you?"

She smiled. "He doesn't like you being here. Funny," she said, "I didn't realize he could be so protective. How are you getting along?"

Because of the plaster cast, Alex had been looking at images from Seti I's tomb, the largest in the Valley of the Kings. He'd remembered that there was a replica in Basel, Switzerland and had speculatively emailed the Antikenmuseum wondering if they could give him access remotely. They must have every single niche mapped out and recorded to the finest detail.

He told Charlie that he'd seen nothing that had caught his attention so far and was now about to look at Ramses I's tomb. As he talked he noticed her eyes closing.

"Tired?" he asked.

She nodded. "I need to go to bed."

Alex couldn't sleep, not thinking that Vanessa was in a cage somewhere. He looked at the time: already approaching 1am. "The seventh hour," he said automatically and then realized the significance.

"What?"

"The seventh hour is 1am. The Surgeon gave me a deadline of 7pm tomorrow. The day after is the vernal equinox." He shook his head with the sudden insight. "The day after tomorrow, the sun will rise in the east—precisely the east—and the Sphinx will be looking directly at the sunrise. We've been given a deadline on the evening before the big night. Whatever the Surgeon is planning will conclude at 1am tomorrow night."

Using Charlie's iPad, Alex found a computer-generated tour of Ramses I's tomb on YouTube. He was going through the burial chamber images, frame by frame, when a text message interrupted him. Andrew wanted an update. The last time they'd communicated was just before Alex had slipped out of his hotel and evaded the police tail.

Alex called him, keeping his voice low, hoping he wouldn't disturb the sleeping FBI agent.

"You're where?" Andrew exclaimed.

"I need help and can't trust the cops." And then Alex told him about Vanessa.

"But you knew before… why didn't you tell me?"

Alex said, "I wanted proof that she's alive first."

Andrew wasn't happy, which Alex found ridiculous, since it was his girlfriend who was being held by a serial killer.

"Give me something to work on," Andrew eventually said after a few terse words between them.

"I don't know…"

"Precisely, that's why I want to help."

"You could look through the images from the tombs of the Ramses and Seti pharaohs, I suppose."

"Is that what you're doing?"

"Yes, but—" Alex began.

"Give me something different. You're the expert on the images. How about sending me the list of symbols the Surgeon has used. Maybe there's something in that."

Alex agreed, and after snapping photographs and sending them, it was a relief to get his little brother off the phone.

But minutes later he got a text asking for the images from the five bodies in Cairo they knew about. Alex photographed and sent them.

His brother rang back.

"Already?" Alex said, exhaustion edging his voice.

"Two of the latest ones feature the same image."

"A djed," Alex said. "One on its own and one with an ankh. Both were objects given to the dead to aid their journey in the afterlife."

"I know the ankh is the life force," Andrew said, "but what is a djed?"

Alex looked at it.

"It's symbolic of Osiris—god of the afterlife—supposed to represent his backbone. However, personally, I don't see it. As a hieroglyph it means stability."

"OK," Andrew said. "One last thing, the helicopter hieroglyph at Seti I's tomb—"

"It's not a helicopter."

"Are you so sure?"

"It's a nice conspiracy theory but the effect is caused by hieroglyphs being plastered over and re-carved. Part of Ramses II's hieroglyphs have fallen away to reveal Seti I's originals. The effect is some odd-looking images that look like modern-day craft."

"OK," Andrew said before he ended the call. "All I'm saying is don't dismiss these things."

With his head down, Alex didn't realize how much time had flown until he heard Charlie showering. Twenty minutes later, dressed and with her hair wet again, she came into the living room with two cups of coffee.

"How's it going?" she asked, handing him a cup.

Alex showed her the pile of notes and sketches he'd made. "I've looked at lots," he said with a shake of the head, "but I don't know if I've got anywhere."

She pointed to a djed that he'd sketched. "Why that? It's in some of the tattoos."

"I was intrigued by Ramses I's tomb. There are surprisingly few paintings, and the Amduat—"

"The what?"

"Sorry. The Amduat is what we were talking about. It can be translated as *That which is the afterworld* and represents the sun's twelve-hour journey through the night."

"Oh, right." Charlie finished her coffee. "Go on, you were saying…"

"Ramses' burial chamber only has hours three and four of the journey, which struck me as odd since Yanhamu—my ancient Egyptian storyteller—definitely explains its importance, and the importance of Seth. However, there are portals that clearly relate to the hours, and my theory is that the full Amduat was painted on but then plastered over to hide the secret truth. My brother made me think of it when he asked about the famous helicopter hieroglyph that appears because of plastering over previous writing."

She said, "And you were explaining why you were interested in the djed?"

"Again because Andrew asked about it. But in Ramses' tomb there's a large painting of the pharaoh with the god Ptah. He's holding a *was*-sceptre and behind him is a giant djed."

"Which means?"

"I don't know. I also spent a lot of time on Seti I's tomb. His is the longest and most elaborate one in the Valley of the Kings. Ptah has a *was*-sceptre with an ankh on top of the head and a djed as the neck. There was

327

also the pharaoh addressing Osiris, who had a djed in place of his head."

"Alex."

He looked up at her. "Yes?"

"You're rambling. You look and sound exhausted. Use the sofa and get some sleep."

"How can I possibly—?" For the first time he noticed his hands shaking.

"Take a break," she said, like an admonishing school teacher. "Lie down and rest. Give yourself thirty minutes at least. Then you'll be fresher and maybe think more clearly."

He nodded despite thinking the opposite. "And you?" he asked.

"I'm going into the office. If I don't then Detective Shafik may come looking for me. And you don't want that, do you?"

"I don't want you to say anything to him about me."

"Of course not," she said. "Get some rest and then crack this problem. Let's get Vanessa freed."

FIFTY-EIGHT

Charlie marched into Shafik's office. "You let him break into my apartment and did nothing!"

He gave her a dismissive look. "You weren't worried about him. You were certain of his innocence."

"But... breaking and entering!"

"We were monitoring the situation. And you can take care of yourself. I remember you telling me that."

"You're an asshole!"

"And you're tired, Special Agent Rebb."

"What's that got to do with anything? I spent half the night going over maps and images. There's something..."

Shafik smirked. "You're getting too involved. This isn't about finding the symbol, it's about catching our serial killer."

She sat down, still angry. "So what's your plan?"

He shook his head. "Tell me what happened after MacLure arrived."

She told him about the communication with the person they assumed was the Surgeon. She concluded by opening her phone and played the proof-of-life conversation and statement by Vanessa.

While Shafik took a copy, she said, "We've got our audio forensics guys analysing it. Also, MacLure pointed out the delay in the call for prayer on the recording. You can hear the one near my apartment and the one where the girl is being held."

Shafik was on his computer. "Mustafa Mahmoud Mosque," he said with a grin. "Yesterday, that was the muezzin breaking the law." He showed Charlie the mosque on the map of Cairo. It was on the other side of the river. He clapped his hands.

"Yes!"

"What is it?"

"Within a few square miles there are four hospitals. What better disguise for a man pretending to be a paramedic?"

Charlie sent a message to Zhang so that the FBI sound analysts had something to go on.

"We need to flush the Surgeon out," Charlie said.

"Then MacLure tells him he's solved the problem and will deliver the symbol in person. We tell him where to meet and are waiting."

"What if he picks his own location?"

"Not a problem. We'll still be tracking MacLure. Better still if you stay with him and ensure we're kept up to speed."

"What if he goes out alone?"

"Like I said, providing he keeps his watch on, we'll be tracking him."

Charlie said, "But this isn't just about flushing out the Surgeon. There's another killer: the one who killed the Salam kid."

Shafik smiled. He'd clearly thought of that.

"We'll flush him out too, won't we? Trust us, Special Agent Rebb, we know what we're doing."

She shook her head. "If MacLure gets killed by the other man, we won't save the girlfriend and we might not get the Surgeon."

"Then I suggest you go back to your apartment and help Mr MacLure."

Alex stared at his notes. Charlie was right. He couldn't think. Even if he'd seen the right symbol, he might not know it.

Before she'd left, she'd told him to help himself to any food or drink he could find.

He splashed his face with cold water and made coffee and toast. Sitting away from his phone and the iPad felt better. Maybe a break would do him good. Maybe he should stop trying to find the answer and consider what he already knew.

What had Yanhamu written? Mahmood had translated it as *Seth has two heads* but it was actually *Seth has two faces*. But he didn't. He had one face. He wasn't like the Roman god, Janus, looking two ways. The god of beginnings and endings, passageways and gates.

The ancient Egyptian *Book of Gates* had developed over time to become the *Book of the Dead*. Could there be a connection? Were the gates of Janus the gates to the afterlife?

Alex shook his head at himself.

What else had Yanhamu said? *In all his forms, Ptah has the power.*

Ptah featured in Ramses' and Seti's tombs. And yet he wasn't one of the Ennead. As far as Alex knew, Ramses hadn't built temples to Seth; he and his predecessors built them to worship Ptah.

Ptah has the power.

Ptah held the *was*-sceptre, the symbol of power but also of Seth—the Seth animal-like head and the forked tail. The sceptre also had the djed. What did that mean?

And then in a flash of clarity, Alex realized his mistake. Yanhamu wasn't saying Seth had two faces, he was saying he could take another's form. *And by this mark you will recognize him.*

With his heart racing, Alex called up the image of Ptah in Ramses' tomb. Something had bothered him but it had lingered in the periphery of his consciousness.

There in the picture was a faint symbol. A part circle maybe like the letter C. He zoomed in, but the pixilation made it impossible to see clearly. Another mark could have been a less-than sign.

He searched for other images of Ptah associated with Ramses. Nearly every time, he saw a mark. Sometimes it looked like a smudge, a mistake, other times he saw it as circle.

In his excitement he picked up his phone and sent a message on Telegram.

I know, he typed.

You know the sign?

I know part of it and where to find it. But it's at the other end of the country. More than twelve hours away

Where is it?

You think I'm stupid?

I think you want your girlfriend back alive

I want proof she's still alive. I want to hear her voice again

The Surgeon replied, No

Alex needed the dialogue with the Surgeon to ensure Vanessa's survival. He was sure the FBI agent would agree that he should try. And maybe he really was close to finding the answer.

He typed, Ask her what her favourite ice cream is

There was no immediate response, so Alex felt hopeful.

Then: She doesn't like ice cream much but if she did she'd choose an orange one

That was correct, although he wondered why she added the second part. *An orange one.*

He decided to give something in return for the proof of life and messaged that the answer was in Abu Simbel.

The deadline would pass before he got there by car or train. He could fly to Aswan and then onto Abu Simbel but he needed to be back in Cairo for Vanessa's release.

"I need more time!" he yelled at the phone. "I need more bloody time!"

He took a calming breath and typed, I need more time. Please

You can't have any more time, the Surgeon replied, and ended the conversation.

Alex looked at flight times. Could he risk giving the Surgeon the answer and not be in Cairo? He put his head in his hands. The only way that could work would be to trust the police.

He paced the room. He trusted the FBI agent maybe eighty per cent. But he couldn't trust Detective Shafik. Could Charlie handle things for him?

Andrew rang for an update. "Any news?"

Alex felt his chest constrict. Less than ten hours to go. He took a shuddering breath.

"You OK?" Andrew said. "Has something happened?"

"No, sorry. Just…"

"I get it. You must be going crazy with worry."

"Worst thing is," Alex said, blinking back the tears, "I can't think straight."

Andrew said, "Where are you with your thinking?"

"That Ramses and Seti hid their secret knowledge. They knew of Seth's importance but disguised it. Maybe even the artisans who decorated the tombs didn't know. I've started to think that they also used the god Ptah in his place—used the symbol to secretly recognize Seth."

"The Sign of Seth."

"Right. But even that seems hidden. The only place I can think might tell me more is Ramses' temple at Abu Simbel."

"Wasn't that Ramses II?"

Under different circumstances Alex would have said how impressed he was with his brother's knowledge. Not now though. Now, all he could think about was finding the sign in time.

He said, "It always bothered me why Ramses II put Ptah in his temple at Abu Simbel. Horus—representing Osiris—is on the pharaoh's left. On his right is Amun-Re and then Ptah. Twice a year the gods are illuminated by a shaft of light—all except Ptah who is in eternal darkness. Like Seth."

"And?"

"The Ptah statue had his head knocked off in antiquity—which is unusual. Seth became the vilified God not Ptah." He took a long breath. "Anyway, I've looked at photographs and I think the symbol is there. I think Ramses II also used Ptah in place of Seth. His secret—although someone found out and damaged the statue."

"Great, then go to Abu Simbel."

"Even if I'm right, then we're talking many hours. Abu Simbel is at the other end of the country. I might find it before sunset, but…" Alex choked.

"Bro, you all right?"

"No way could I get back in time."

"Then delay the exchange."

Alex said, "Tonight's the deadline because the Surgeon needs it before sunrise. It's the spring equinox, and I think it's all happening between 1 and 2am."

The line was quiet for a while.

"Alex?"

"Yeah."

"You know people all over Egypt don't you? Other archaeologists? Don't go to Abu Simbel, dummy, get a contact to do it for you!"

His brother was a genius! Of course, that was the solution. Although he didn't have friends in the area, he certainly had contacts. After ending the call, he hastily messaged everyone he knew who could possibly get to the temple in time.

FIFTY-NINE

Alex was pacing the room when Charlie returned.

"How are you doing?" she asked.

He sat down and clenched his hands like in a desperate prayer. "I think the answer might be in Abu Simbel. The Ramses II temple there has a statue of Ptah who I think represents Seth. If the symbol is anywhere, it's on that statue."

"You're sure?" She was looking at her phone as she spoke.

"No."

"It's miles away! It'll take us all day to get there."

"We're not going," he said. "I've found someone who's in the area. They've promised me pictures within a few hours."

"OK," she said hopefully.

"The waiting is killing me."

She said, "Shafik knows you're here."

"You told him?" Alex shook his head, disappointed. But then maybe she was just doing her job. He shouldn't have expected any less.

But then she said, "No. He already knew," and pointed to Alex's watch. "They put a tracking device in your watch. They've known you were here from the start."

He pulled the watch off and tossed it aside. "Then why…?"

Charlie shook her head. "Yes, he knew you broke in here last night. He was expect—" She stopped abruptly as her phone rang.

"Peter?"

Alex couldn't hear the other person but Charlie became excited.

"Right… right? Yes!" she said before ending the call.

Alex could barely contain himself. "Good news?"

Charlie blew out air. "There was another sound on the recording. Forensics isolated it. Gunshots. Not a gun fight, the sound of regular shots, like on a firing range."

"And?"

"We now have two reference points. Shafik knew the mosque was Mustafa Mahmoud. There's a shooting club about five hundred yards south of there. The analysts think Vanessa was somewhere between. If they could get a third reference…"

Alex was on his feet. "Let's go!"

"You're joking."

"Do I look like I'm joking?"

"We're talking about an area of forty football pitches."

He shook his head. "I don't care. Either you're with me or I go alone. All I'm doing here is waiting and fretting. I need something to focus on and I can think of nothing better than searching the streets."

On the phone, the Surgeon said, "MacLure says he knows where to find the sign."

"Excellent!"

"He also asked for an extension of the deadline."

"You know we can't do that," McCubbin said.

337

"I know."

"Keep the pressure on him."

"Yes, Master."

McCubbin said, "Our friends say they will be ready in time. They will close everything off so we are not disturbed."

"Shall I go now?"

"Not yet," McCubbin said. "We need to wait. I don't want you on the streets until you have to be."

SIXTY

Searching such a wide area was pointless and it potentially placed MacLure in harm's way. Charlie knew that.

"Fine," she said. "We'll go together, but you put the watch on. Detective Shafik needs to know where we are."

"No."

"You're a stubborn idiot," she said.

"I'll take that as a compliment."

"Don't. If you want Vanessa back then you need all the help you can get."

He was about to argue but she cut him off. "We should also tell the detective why we're there. If he knows where we think Vanessa's being held, he can have men looking out for the Surgeon's paramedic vehicle."

"Paramedic?"

"Yes, why?"

"I saw a yellow paramedic's car on Eza Street, when—"

"The police know. The Surgeon pretends to be a doctor or paramedic. We tell Shafik the area and we have a chance of spotting him."

He shook his head but she could see him processing the idea.

"We need him," she said.

"Do you trust the Cairo police?"

"I trust Detective Shafik. That's why you wear the watch or do this with FBI help."

He bit his lip, probably weighing his options.

"Put the watch on, Alex. I'm taking a risk here too. There's a killer out there and I want Shafik knowing where we are."

"Fine," he said, clipping it back on.

After calling a cab, she wore her gun under a loose-fitting jacket and put on a headscarf.

She gave a scarf to MacLure but he didn't wear it.

In the taxi, she said, "It's not just the Surgeon you need to worry about. What about the man who killed the Salam kid?"

"Before he was working for the Surgeon, he told me there was another group involved. Ansar Beit al-Maqdis—the Champions of the Holy Site."

Charlie nodded. "But how do they fit in?"

"I've no idea."

"Well," she said, "they killed Salam and maybe they intended to kill you too. Maybe you got lucky at the pyramids."

He looked at her with bloodshot eyes. He was exhausted and addled. Roaming the streets for the Surgeon's safe house was insane, but perhaps the air would clear his head. Maybe he'd think more clearly and realize what the symbol was. Then they could start the real job of negotiating Vanessa's release.

Finally he nodded and covered his head. He'd clearly done it before because he wrapped it over and around his face like she'd seen locals do.

At Mustafa Mahmoud Square they got out opposite the mosque. Buildings on either side dwarfed the religious building except for the minaret, where the vital

340

call for prayer had come from. Early afternoon heat blasted off the pavement. People stood or sat under the line of trees in the centre of the square.

"Where do you want to go?" she asked.

He used his phone and showed her a map. The shooting club was almost directly south.

"We walk that way," he said and set off.

The roads were mostly in a grid but at an angle north-south. So they followed the main road south-west and then south-east, down a long avenue.

She looked at every building and saw Alex do the same. Clean streets, some nice offices. Lots of limestone and good architecture. Blocks of residential apartments, a government building. A reasonable neighbourhood.

They reached a roundabout and she figured the quality had gone up a notch or two. More greenery and an embassy.

"The shooting club is over there," she said, pointing across a large open space, mostly shingle but with areas of green and low-lying properties. "We're now too close. The gunshots would have been more distinct."

"OK," Alex said turning away. "Then we go back up, parallel to the road we've just been down."

They repeated the pattern over and over until Charlie was too hot and her feet hurt.

"I need a break," she said.

There were lots of cafés around and they just chose the next one they came to. It wasn't a franchise, but it wouldn't have looked out of place in any Western city.

"You should eat," Charlie said, ordering a sandwich.

"I can't eat. Just coffee will be fine."

Charlie sent update texts to Zhang and Shafik. Zhang replied that the sound guys were working on the intonation of Vanessa's message. They thought *It's hot* was a code for something, although they had no idea what.

Shafik replied that they'd stopped more than twenty ambulances and paramedic vehicles but all were legitimate. All were associated with local hospitals.

Charlie noticed MacLure staring out of the window. In her experience he'd gone past desperation and was entering a phase just before resignation. He'd stopped blinking. He looked numb, shell-shocked. The foolish hope of finding her in this vast area had finally sunk home.

She left him to his thoughts and then jumped as his phone pinged loudly.

Suddenly he was animated again.

"Photos from Abu Simbel," he said breathlessly. His hands shook as he opened up an image.

She scooted next to him.

"Slow down!" she said as he flicked through picture after picture. "What are we looking at?"

"These are close-ups of all the hieroglyphs around the four statues," he said, and zoomed in above the broken one on the left.

"That's this Ptah guy, right?"

"Yes, next to Ramses II. Damn!"

"Nothing?"

"I can't see anything unusual. Nothing suggests it's Seth."

"I'm sorry," she said.

He breathed in and out. "Maybe all the Seth symbols are hidden. Or maybe the symbol was destroyed along with the head. One thing though…"

He zoomed into an area below where the head would have been.

"What?"

He showed her the picture.

She said, "What am I looking at?"

"It's what's not there," he said shaking his head. "It looks like Ptah was holding a *was*-sceptre. Look here," he said pointing to a hollowed-out section. "Someone deliberately removed the staff as well as the head. And based on the outline, I'd say it had the djed symbol."

He sat back, hands together tapping his upper lip, thinking.

She waited for him to say something.

Eventually he said, "The sign we're looking for can't be the djed, but it keeps cropping up."

"Why can't it?"

"Because the Surgeon tried that tattoo."

She let out a little laugh. "You don't believe this stuff, do you?"

He looked at her for a moment and the desperation was back in those bloodshot eyes.

"I don't know what to believe, Special Agent Rebb. I just want Vanessa safe and sound."

"Charlie," she said.

"Yeah, sorry."

They sat in silence for a while.

Her phone rang and she snatched it up without checking the caller display.

"I want an update." It was John Graham. *Damn!* She'd expected Peter or Shafik and hoped for new information, not bureaucracy.

She said, "Sorry, John, I've just been busy."

"That's OK, Charlie." He was immediately less angry, smooth like the diplomat that he was. "All I ask is to be kept in the loop."

"Sure," she said, not meaning it. "It's all happening today. The Surgeon has MacLure's girlfriend as a hostage and he's been told to find the symbol that the Surgeon wants to tattoo on his next victim."

"Where are you?"

"In a café with MacLure. He's trying to work it out."

"Where?"

"Between Mustafa Mahmoud Square and a shooting club. We're also looking for where his girlfriend might be held."

"And the Surgeon might be there too?"

"Maybe."

"OK, good. What about Detective Shafik?"

"At this moment I don't know. He's waiting for us to come up with a symbol. Then we can arrange an exchange."

"So he's not with you?"

"That's what I'm saying."

"Make sure you get back-up if you suspect anything, Charlie."

"Of course." Charlie rolled her eyes. Alex was getting impatient. When he stood, Charlie quickly ended the call, promising to provide an update should anything happen.

Alex nodded to the door. "Break time over," he said. "I'm going back on those streets until I find Vanessa."

SIXTY-ONE

Alex looked at the map on his phone. They'd walked towards the shooting club again and come across a road they'd already covered.

"Maybe we should try another tack," Charlie said.

"What's your idea?"

"Where would you hide if you were the Surgeon?"

He shrugged.

"Somewhere you could come and go without too much attention."

"A side road?"

She nodded. "A quiet side street. Non-residential. Probably offices. Maybe a disused warehouse?"

He'd not seen any disused properties but there were plenty of side streets. Nothing quiet. Nowhere was quiet in Cairo but some were less busy than others.

She pointed to the map on his phone. "Let's try this block."

They walked in a square without seeing anything of interest. "OK, next block," Charlie said, and they repeated the pattern.

"Who was that on the phone back there?" Alex asked.

"Our main liaison in Egypt. A bureaucrat and a pain in the butt. He got all bent out of shape because I wasn't updating him before. Turns out the British Embassy were looking for you. They were probably putting pressure on him so he put pressure on me."

"Oops!" Alex said. "Vanessa reported me missing when I was first arrested. We never got back to them. Sorry."

"Don't worry about it," she said, looking in through a dusty window and then moving on to the next property. "Maybe it's time to start thinking about the other option."

"The made-up answer."

"Yes. Can you come up with a symbol we could tell him?"

He nodded. The idea made him feel sick. What if the Surgeon could tell whether it was right or wrong somehow? And then he realized the guy wasn't letting Vanessa go until he knew for sure.

"He will release her, won't he?" Alex asked.

Charlie said, "Yes," but she didn't look at him.

Oh God, I can't save her!

"Alex!"

He had staggered and she caught his arm, stopped him falling. Suddenly his legs were weak. He couldn't breathe.

"We need to get you back," she said. "This damned heat…"

And then he saw it. One second his vision was blurred and the next there was absolute clarity.

"*Something like Anar*," he said.

"What?"

"Vanessa said her cat's name was something like Anar." He pointed, his finger shaking. "El Manar Hotel! Don't you see?"

Charlie said, "My God, *It's hot* was a clue. She was telling us it was a hotel."

"And it's bloody well orange! Like she said. My God, we should have been looking for an orange hotel all along!"

The hotel name was written on a curved frontispiece above the entrance. Charlie looked at the hotel and then opposite. She said, "Vanessa could see the name, only not all of it... There!"

Charlie ran to the other side of the road and pointed to a window low down. She lay on the pavement and scrubbed at the glass then rolled and looked towards the hotel. She jumped to her feet and pulled out her phone.

"It's here, Detective. We've found the Surgeon's place. We've goddamn found it!"

SIXTY-TWO

Alex scrabbled on the ground to see inside. It was dark. He could see shapes, bulky objects, but nothing clearly. Easier to see outside into the light than into the darkness.

Armed police arrived within ten minutes. They came in silently and blocked off the road. Two men with a battering ram waited at the door to the building as Shafik jogged up.

"Any sign of life?" he asked Charlie.

"Nothing," she said. "The only window we can see into is the small basement one. The others are all whitewashed. There's this one door that looks reinforced. And I figure the up and over garage door belongs to this place. No back entrance."

On the right was a travel agency, although it was closed. On the left was a stubby office block with the name of a weird-sounding foundation on the door. Shafik sent policemen inside to clear it. Four bewildered people came out and were ushered down the street.

Shafik gave the signal and the door was pounded. It took three blows before it crashed open. In the UK, Alex guessed they'd have used teargas. Probably in the US as well. But here, the armed police just charged in. He and Charlie were being held back.

"I need to get inside," he said.

But she shook her head firmly. "We need to wait. What if—?" She didn't finish the sentence and his mind raced with the possibilities. Not so much, what if the Surgeon was in there, but, what if Vanessa was dead?

Shafik must have received an *all-clear* message because he went inside. Two minutes later he waved Charlie over. Alex followed.

"No!" Shafik said as Alex approached.

Alex kept walking.

"Let him," Charlie said, and Shafik hesitated before stepping aside.

After a short flight of stairs, the first things Alex noticed were a kitchenette and toilet and a strange smell.

Then the room opened up and he saw paintings on the walls with others leaning against them. The smell came from the oil paint. There was a large table with paints and brushes and cloths all neatly arranged. Precise and clean. There was another desk with a computer. The machine was open, the hard drive removed. There was also a camp bed with a pillow and sheet.

"He's gone," Shafik said unnecessarily.

The air was cooler inside and Alex noted a rattling air-conditioning unit. He kept on walking towards a door at the back.

"What's in the basement," Charlie asked, following.

The three of them descended stone steps into a garage area. Thick warm air rose up to meet them.

At the bottom, there was a yellow VW estate with a green, paramedic stripe. There were panels on the walls, tools arranged neatly on pins and clips.

Shafik spoke to a policeman who was pacing the room.

"It's big enough for two cars," Charlie said, maybe thinking out loud.

Shafik nodded. "Fresh oil on the floor. Best estimate is the paramedic vehicle hasn't been used for at least a day. My man thinks another vehicle was here until recently. Maybe very recently—within the hour perhaps."

Alex clenched his teeth. They'd just missed him.

He glanced around, saw the garage door. "Where's the basement window?" he asked.

Charlie worked it out the quickest. She must have figured the layout of the place because she started banging the right-hand wall. One of the panels moved.

A hidden door.

She snatched it open. Shafik held Alex back as one of his men entered, checked it and called them inside.

Inside were four large objects. Three chest freezers and a cage, a cage big enough to crouch in. Maybe designed for a large dog. Definitely used to hold Vanessa.

SIXTY-THREE

Alex woke up in a police car with Charlie beside him.

"You fainted. This police officer is taking us back to my apartment," she explained, handing him a bottle of Coke. "Here, this will improve your electrolyte levels. Make you feel better."

"Thanks."

"As soon as we get back you are eating something."

"I can't..."

"No debate," she said.

Ten minutes later he was eating falafel and bread. At first he stared at it but she stood over him until he put some in his mouth and chewed. He washed it down with water and took some more.

"It's good news, isn't it?" he said when he'd finished. "Not finding Vanessa there."

"Yes. If he wanted to kill her she'd be dead. No point in moving a body at this stage. So yes, it's good news."

"What about the freezers?"

"The police will check everything for evidence, but the freezers were all empty. However, it looks like the Surgeon stored bodies in them."

"Empty?" Alex repeated.

The Seventh Hour needed a body for their ceremony. Had the Surgeon taken one with him or was Vanessa the intended victim? Surely the Surgeon needed a man? They'd been so close. They'd found where Vanessa had been held but got there too late.

Alex tried to shake the negative thoughts from his mind.

She said, "We need to plan the end-game."

His focus snapped back into the room. "End-game?"

"You exchanging the symbol for Vanessa."

"I don't know the symbol."

She smiled kindly. "You're going to invent it, remember."

"But he'll know."

"We need to hope he doesn't."

Alex checked his watch. "I have over two hours. I'm going to keep trying."

"But have a contingency," she said. "Be prepared with a fake one."

Alex went back over the pictures from the Abu Simbel temple, willing something, anything different. Could he have missed it?

He found nothing. If there had been a sign, then it had been removed with the statue's head and the *was-sceptre*.

After that he went back to the computer videos of the tombs, backwards and forwards over images he'd checked and double-checked. The back of his mind shouted that he was being a busy fool. He needed to think, and yet he couldn't just stop.

Charlie was on the phone. First she called her US partner and gave him an update. Alex heard her mention "meet" and "exchange" and guessed they were debating the end-game. Then she got on the phone to Shafik and asked about the Surgeon's place they'd found.

"They're still gathering evidence," she said, frustrated. "But the bodily fluids have been confirmed in the freezers. They've also found long brown hairs in the cage—which I..."

Alex nodded. "Vanessa has brown hair."

She said, "I think it's just a matter of time before the Cairo police confirm the presence of Tony Zart's DNA."

"Is he the Surgeon?"

"We're pretty sure," she said, nodding. "Shafik said there are lots of fingerprints. Multiple people, so maybe that'll lead to others."

"Victims?"

"No. It's very clear that the Surgeon has needed a lot of help with this. He didn't set that place up alone. Someone also got him that paramedic vehicle—which by the way is a fake. A good fake. So someone created that for him."

Alex said, "Right. We know it's not just one man, it's an organization. Maybe they've been planning this for years. The Surgeon's probably just the man who does the dirty work."

They said nothing for a minute, Alex watching the FBI agent.

He said, "I'm all out of ideas, Charlie. What's the FBI play here? What do we do to get Vanessa back safely?"

She sat down and looked earnest. "We have to assume he's got Vanessa somewhere safe, ready for an exchange."

"Wasn't the place opposite the hotel safe?"

"No. It always needed to be somewhere other than his hideout. He didn't know we'd find it. Maybe he planned to return. If we weren't operating under a deadline we could have staked it out. But we don't have the time."

"No we don't," Alex said emphatically.

"We pick a location and we get prepared."

Alex took a long breath as his chest constricted. "We can't have their SWAT team—or whatever they call it here—I've seen enough of the local news to know how that will go down!"

"Agreed," she said. "This is a unique situation. The play is that you do the exchange, we ensure Vanessa is safe and we follow Zart."

"Because he has a ceremony to perform."

"Right. We think he's meeting McCubbin somewhere for this Seventh Hour ritual."

"OK, what's the location?"

"I've let Detective Shafik choose it." Alex moaned and she held up a hand. "He knows Cairo better than us. He's experienced. And… he's promised to play this our way. No SWAT team. A clean exchange with the objective of getting Vanessa back alive and then following Zart."

Alex closed his eyes, worried about the Cairo police involvement. But what choice did he have? They were almost out of time.

"Fine," he said.

"Then we need that symbol."

SIXTY-FOUR

Alex and Charlie walked along a path with walls on one side that reminded Alex of a ruined Scottish castle. Bile kept threatening to come up and his legs wobbled with the anxiety.

They were here to meet the Surgeon.

"Last night," Charlie said, "you accused me of having a different priority. That's not the case. Vanessa's safety is number one. It's an FBI principle: save the hostage because we can catch the criminal another day."

"Thanks," he said, although she'd said something similar earlier. Then Alex had messaged the Surgeon that he was ready to exchange.

Shafik had proposed they meet in the Arab Contractors Stadium. He could have undercover men on the ground ready to follow the subject. He'd also have aerial surveillance with high-powered scopes trained on the area.

Charlie was happy. She wanted control of the situation and she made Shafik promise there would be no SWAT team.

But the Surgeon had flat refused. "I choose the location," he'd said. "Or no deal."

Alex had tried to argue. After all, the Surgeon needed the symbol as much as Alex needed Vanessa free. There

355

was stalemate until Charlie told him to accept. That's when she'd first said Vanessa's safety was the priority.

Alex had immediately messaged the Surgeon. **Accepted. Where do we meet?**

You have the symbol?

Yes

Have it on your phone and send it to me

Alex had screamed at his phone as he replied: **Not before you release Vanessa**

Al-Azhar Park. 7pm. Any police and your girlfriend dies. Any plane or drone and she dies. You do exactly as I say and she will live. Agreed?

Of course, Alex had agreed, and now they were approaching the park. There was an ambulance behind them waiting for Vanessa but there was no sign of Shafik's men.

The Surgeon messaged: **Walk around. I want to see you are alone**

Alex showed Charlie.

"Your call," she said.

He messaged: **I'm with a friend. She stays with me. Neither of us is armed.** It wasn't true but he figured the Surgeon wouldn't know Charlie had a gun—providing she didn't pull it out.

To Alex's surprise the Surgeon didn't argue.

"A small victory," Charlie said to Alex. Then into a microphone she whispered, "Contact. Going into the park."

They kept walking and the setting sun burnished the sky and ruins.

Alex's phone rang. A number was displayed and Alex almost didn't answer thinking it couldn't be the Surgeon. But it was.

"One rule," the Surgeon said. "Don't call this number. Now walk towards the centre of the park." He ended the call abruptly.

Charlie spoke surreptitiously into her microphone and relayed the phone number used. As she finished, they started along a rising path through a sparse line of trees. Beyond was a grassy hill and they walked around it.

There were other strollers enjoying the final rays of light before sunset. Two men passed coming the other way. Another man sat on a bench. Maybe these are the undercover officers, Alex thought.

His phone rang again.

"Keep going round. You'll see a lake from the other side. Stay on the path around it." Again the abrupt end.

On the far side was an avenue of palm trees and a marble thoroughfare that wouldn't have looked out of place in any first world country.

Alex found himself studying every face they passed. Could one of them be the Surgeon in disguise? Was he on this path? And if so, where was Vanessa?

They followed the path around a featureless lake until it reached a Moorish-style building: a restaurant with people sitting outside beneath red parasols.

"Restaurant," Charlie whispered. "This doesn't feel right. He won't do it here, surely."

The evening call to prayer began. Alex looked at his watch. 7pm. Time was up. The adhan seemed like a Pied Piper lure as it reverberated off the walls and over the hills.

Charlie held Alex's arm as his legs began to give way.

"He's not here," he said, weak with worry.

"He's not got us this far for no reason," Charlie said, and he saw the logic in it.

They kept walking. Now they were going west. The sun had fallen below distant buildings. The sky rapidly darkened.

The Surgeon rang.

"Turn left. Go down the slope to the wall. Turn right, find the broken section and climb over."

"Is that—?" Alex started to ask if they were meeting there but the line was already dead.

Charlie whispered, "Directed south. Down the hill."

Alex had seen a mosque on the hill opposite but had thought nothing of it. There were mosques everywhere he looked. However, as they descended from the park, he realized he was now looking at a massive cemetery.

Charlie spoke into the microphone. "Cemetery."

Compared to the lush park, the site ahead was a harsh landscape: no grass, no trees, just a disorganized mass of tomb stones and mausoleums.

They found the broken section of wall and clambered over. There were people living here. These weren't just tombs but also makeshift hovels.

"Which way?" Alex said quietly, as though Charlie would know.

A child in dirty rags approached. She held out her bony hand, begging. But then the gesture changed. She beckoned and then began to slowly walk away.

Alex glanced at his phone. No call from the Surgeon.

"We follow," Charlie said.

The Haris al'Asrar answered his secure line. "Yes?"

"The police are closing in around the Bab el-Wazir cemetery."

358

"Where else?"

"I have no other information, sir."

The Haris al'Asrar said nothing as he wondered why they were there. Surely they'd made a mistake.

Or was this a diversion?

The other man said, "The police have a tracking device on MacLure."

"Good," the Haris al'Asrar said. "Get access to it and keep me apprised."

"Of course."

He ended the call and rang someone. "Your team is tracking MacLure. I need to know where he goes." He didn't wait for a response, ended the call and speed-dialled another man. "Close the Holy Site immediately," he instructed. "And double the guard."

SIXTY-FIVE

The urchin led them on a circuitous route, twisting and changing direction until Alex had no sense of where they were exactly.

The girl stopped and looked at Alex with thousand-year-old eyes. She held out her hand.

The phone rang.

"Give the girl at least ten pounds," the Surgeon said, and stayed on the line.

Alex pulled out his wallet, handed the girl a few notes, and watched as she stuffed them under her dirty blouse. Then she turned and fled.

"It's done," Alex said. "Where's Vanessa?"

"The FBI agent stays there. You continue alone. Agreed?"

"Agreed."

"If the agent moves, your girlfriend dies."

"I understand."

Alex held up a hand to Charlie. "You have to stay here."

Her eyes widened with concern but she nodded acceptance.

"Right," Alex said into the phone. "Where is she?"

Keeping his phone to his ear, Alex was directed through the maze. He saw no one else but heard scurrying, scrabbling sounds. Maybe people, maybe animals. The sky was rapidly turning to ink and he began to fear the dark spaces between mausoleums. The call to prayer continued and he felt it bounce off the walls.

His hand shook as it pressed his phone against his ear.

The Surgeon's voice was suddenly loud. "Stop."

Alex froze. He'd come out of a long corridor. The ground ahead was more open; the mausoleums more scattered between a confusion of tombstones.

"Look right. The mausoleum with two Roman columns. See it? Don't move."

Alex peered through the grey light. He could see the tomb. He could also see something between the pillars. Human in shape. Long dark hair. Tied to the pillars.

"Vanessa!" His voice caught in his throat.

"Stay there!" the Surgeon commanded, and Alex realized he'd started towards her. "Another step and she dies. I have a gun trained on her."

Alex's hand shook violently now, his breathing rapid.

The Surgeon said, "The symbol is genuine, right?"

"Yes!" Alex had almost convinced himself it was true. Charlie had made him practice over and over until she was happy.

"Good," the Surgeon said. "This is how it works. You send the image to this number. As soon as you do, you can rescue her. Understand?"

"Yes."

"If you are lying about the symbol, I shoot her. If you move before sending it, I shoot her. Understand?"

"Yes."

"If the police appear, I shoot her. Understand?"

"Yes."

"Good. Now send me the image."

The call ended.

With trembling fingers, Alex opened the photograph of the symbol and sent it.

He counted to ten. How long before he was sure the Surgeon had received the image? Tentatively, he took a step forward. His phone didn't ring. He took another, then another, and then he was running to the mausoleum.

"Don't shoot her!" his mind screamed as he ran. And then out loud he shouted, "Vanessa! Vanessa!"

The call to prayer ended with a fading echo and Alex could hear blood pulsing in his ears.

"Vanessa!" he shouted at the top of his lungs.

She was struggling against her ties. He was thirty paces away, stumbling over scattered stones and graves. Almost there.

She was in a black gown, her arms looking thin under wide sleeves. And then she raised her head, her long hair falling back. She was gagged; a thick band over her lower face. Her eyes...

Alex staggered and vomited.

It wasn't Vanessa.

SIXTY-SIX

The Surgeon dropped his binoculars and stepped back from the window. He looked again at the image MacLure had sent him. It looked good. It could be the one.

He deleted the image and pulled apart the single use phone before disposing of it. He could hear the Imam's chant. A building full of people, but they were too focused on their prayers to notice him.

Then he slipped out of the mosque, into the night filled with the sound of police sirens.

Charlie gave Alex a cup of coffee. They were back in her apartment.

Alex said, "He must have known it was fake."

"He never intended to do the exchange."

"Who was the girl?"

"I don't know," Charlie said. "Just someone he found. Probably just someone living in the cemetery. Shafik's men will question her, but he doubts they'll learn anything."

Alex didn't say anything for a while. He tried to sip the coffee but everything tasted of acid and his hands trembled. He felt his nerves jangling, like he was wired up to the national grid.

"I failed her," he said in a quiet voice.

Charlie put a comforting hand on his arm. "You did your best."

"I failed." He took a tremulous breath. "Why hasn't he released her?"

"Because he wants to know the symbol is real?"

Alex shook his head. "Or she is the next victim. You thought of that, right?"

"We've considered it. But she's... well the Surgeon has only taken men before."

"Maybe that's why he failed. Maybe..." Alex said trying to breathe more calmly, "maybe he's also learned that it needs to be a woman. Or it could be either."

Charlie didn't comment.

There was another long silence before she said, "You told me it would happen at 1am. We're not out of time."

He looked at her like she was insane. He'd tried everything. Twenty-four hours and he had nothing except for certainty, in his mind, that Vanessa would be dead in about five hours.

"We're not giving up," she said in a firm voice. "Take a shower, clear your head and let's get back to work."

When Alex got out of the shower, he found clean clothes on the bed.

"Thanks for the clothes," he said, joining her in the living area. She was reading the FBI files again.

"Do they fit OK? Look all right? Not the best style since I grabbed what I could from a shop downstairs."

"They're great," he said, and forced a smile. "And thanks for being positive. My head is clearer and I do need to get refocused."

"Good," she said in the same firm no-nonsense voice she'd used before. "Now get to work."

"What am I looking for?"

"Main priority has to be a location. Quantico is on it, as well as Shafik's guys. He'll be in a specific place at 1am so tonight is our main chance of stopping him."

"And rescuing Vanessa."

"Of course!"

Alex nodded. He believed her.

She said, "Go back over everything you know. The advice is to try and think like them—think like the Seventh Hour guys. They needed the symbol, but our working theory is that they also need a location."

Alex said nothing.

Charlie added: "The Quantico guys have highlighted his use of cemeteries and religious places. The American cemetery where we found four bodies. The cemetery where he took us this evening. Of course, there's also the churches in Georgia. But there's one key location—when the Surgeon was disturbed before completing his ritual. The ancient site—the temple in Abusir."

"Which one?"

Charlie checked her notes. "Ramses II, temple to the sun god."

"It's a total ruin," Alex said. "Discovered only a couple of years ago and there's not much else been found. Just two fragments: one with the names of Ramses II and another stone including Ra's name." He shook his head. "Doesn't mean it was actually a temple to Ra. It could have been any God."

That set Alex off, thinking about Seth and Ptah. *Seth has two faces.* Could this have been a temple to Ptah or Seth? Could the Seventh Hour know this?

Charlie said, "Shafik's men are guarding the whole necropolis in case the Surgeon goes tonight."

Alex returned his attention to what he could find out about the temples. There was nothing useful about the destroyed Seth temples, but maybe Ptah would yield something. The *Creator god* interested him because he wasn't one of the Ennead—the nine main gods. The Great Ennead of Heliopolis. Seth had been one of the Ennead and Ramses I had been a high priest of Seth. Why then was he building temples to Ptah?

Alex had a growing conviction that Seth could take the form of Ptah. He reviewed the pictures from the Ramses II temple at Abu Simbel. Had he missed the symbol?

Nothing new.

He realized he'd been distracted by the symbol again and went back to thinking about locations. Could it be a temple to Ptah? Is that what the Seventh Hour believed?

"Tell Shafik to have men at all temples dedicated to Ptah," he said, and listed those he knew. "The three nearest Cairo—in old Memphis—seem the most likely. And then there's the recently discovered temple of Seth in Tell Hebua."

Charlie called Shafik and relayed the message.

Alex took a break. He prowled around the room like a lion stalking its prey.

"Mortuary temples!" he suddenly exclaimed.

Charlie was still on the phone with Shafik.

Alex said, "Tell him to get people to the Ramses and Seti mortuary temples. If I was to pick any I'd choose Seti I's temple in Abydos." Then the realization struck him and he shook his head. "It'd take too long to get there." The Surgeon had less than five hours.

Charlie said, "Detective Shafik says they're looking at a radius of under two hundred miles, assuming he's driving."

"Still a lot of country," Alex said, "though only as far as Amarna to the south. But it rules out the mortuary temples in Karnak and Abydos."

Alex went into his email and messaged all the colleagues he knew, asking about mortuary and other temples of the Nineteenth Dynasty or suspected as dedicated to Ptah or Seth.

He was about to leave the email account when he noticed an email from the University of Basel. The message was from a research fellow who had worked on the replica of Seti I's tomb at Antikenmuseum. Alex had forgotten all about contacting them since he'd found the simulation on YouTube.

He sent a short message thanking the person for responding. He'd been interested in finding a symbol, possibly associated with Ptah that couldn't be explained. While he waited for a response, he carried on checking temples.

After an hour, another email arrived from the research fellow. The lady wanted to know what sort of thing he was looking for.

Alex responded by describing the circle-like mark he'd seen near Ptah in Ramses I's tomb. He included his phone number and immediately got a text.

I saw the same in Seti I's tomb. Though it's not in the reconstruction. We thought it was a mistake

Alex noted the past tense and replied, Thought? Did you investigate?

We think it might be something underneath. A mistake plastered over. It shows up under infrared. We're planning to rescan the whole tomb next year.

Alex's heart leapt into his throat. *A mistake plastered over.* Something hidden.

He replied, I don't suppose you took a look at the circle-like mark under infrared?

Alex tapped his fingers. Why was the girl taking so long to reply? And then he discovered the reason. The research fellow had attached an image to his next email. Alex clicked on it and zoomed in. It wasn't a circle.

"Oh my God, Charlie," he said. "I know what the secret symbol is!"

SIXTY-SEVEN

Charlie picked up the piece of paper that Alex had drawn on. "Is this it?"

"I'm ninety-nine per cent sure." He watched as she put the paper down. Casually. "You're not excited?" he asked.

"Does it help with the location?"

"No, but—"

"We need a specific location, Alex. Great that you worked out the symbol, but it doesn't help." She gave him a placatory smile. "We have just over three hours. Focus on the location."

Alex clenched his fists and stared at the symbol.

"We could negotiate."

"With the Surgeon?"

He nodded rapidly. "Yes. Don't you see? With the true symbol he might really let Vanessa go this time."

Charlie said nothing.

"It's worth a try," he said.

"All you'll do is let him know the other was a fake. Do that and we don't know how he'll react. Plus, we can't trust him. He said he'd trade last time, but he tricked us."

"It's worth a try," Alex said, although the conviction ebbed from his voice.

"No," she said firmly. "We keep searching for the location."

Sometime during the following hour, Alex received an email from an archaeologist who was working on a site in the Sinai Peninsula. A giant fortress had been discovered at Rafah, close to the Gaza Strip. Alex knew about it. A statue of Ramses II had been discovered there. As he read through the research he learned that there was evidence of Ramses I and Seti I. The contact also believed that there had been a temple dedicated to the god Seth.

Alex told Charlie and pointed to Rafah on the map.

"About two hundred miles," he said. "The Surgeon could have made it in time."

Charlie got up and touched the map, checking the distance. "You don't sound convinced."

"If you needed to be at a specific location at a specific time, would you risk it? What if there was a problem with the traffic? If I'm right about the spring equinox and the seventh hour, then I wouldn't risk it. I'd pick somewhere closer. Maybe half the time—which could still mean most places in the Delta and south, which would include the necropolis at Saqqara."

Alex drew circles on the map showing historical sites including Saqqara. He said, "Everyone knows about the Step pyramid of Djoser, but there is a massive historical site there."

"Temples?"

"Of course," Alex said, checking the details on his phone. "Temples associated with Djoser himself. The Temple of Heb-Sed. Unas Valley Temple and Serapeum."

"And?"

"Nothing I can find about Seth or Ptah."

"But anything interesting?"

Alex didn't think so since most of the Saqqara site dated back to the Fifth Dynasty and earlier, but they both started browsing the internet for information.

He said, "I didn't know that Unas had his own cult and was worshipped long after his death. A lot of the complex was demolished but there are still walls and corridors."

Charlie grunted, maybe only half listening. Then she said, "What about this? Serapeum was a combination of Osiris and Apis. Interesting, right? Didn't you tell me Apis was the snake?"

"Apis or Apep was the serpent speared by Seth during the seventh hour."

"Exactly!" She jumped up with excitement. "Don't you see? It fits. Osiris, god of the dead... The serpent which connects him to Seth—"

Alex shook his head. "That was much later... the Greek period. I don't think—"

But Charlie was already on the phone. "The temple of Serapeum in Saqqara," she said breathlessly to Shafik. "Osiris and a snake. I wonder if it's like the... what's it called..? ... the Staff of Hermes—the medical symbol?"

She listened for a second and then confirmed, "Saqqara," before ending the call.

"Shafik is sending people. You're not convinced, are you?" she asked Alex. He had his head down considering other sites.

"It can't hurt," he said. "Although the Surgeon isn't actually medically trained, is he?"

"No." She seemed deflated all of a sudden and then snapped out of it. "All right, which site do you think is most likely?"

"Any one of the three Ptah temples close by. At a push I'd also include the complex at Tell el-Daba." He pointed to a circle he'd already drawn on the map about halfway between Cairo and Port Said. "It's now believed to be the place once called Hut-waret, Pi-Ramses or Avaris."

"I can feel a *but* coming on."

"Probably about two and a half hours drive. My feeling is it's too far."

"For us," Charlie said, "but Shafik will have a local force cover it."

"I'm going to keep looking," Alex said, and put his head down again.

Charlie called Shafik. No answer. She tried repeatedly and finally left a message that the Tell el-Daba site was worth investigating.

Thirty minutes later Alex got a text from his brother asking for an update. He didn't reply. He didn't have time to update people. It was a distraction from the papers he was reading.

And then Andrew called.

Alex let it go to voicemail.

Andrew called again.

"I'm busy," Alex said, unable to mask the irritation in his voice.

"I've got something for you. Maybe it'll help." Andrew paused. "You know I asked about the djed symbol."

"Right." Was it a coincidence that it had been so prominent in Ramses' and Seti's tombs? Alex thought probably. When you're looking for something, that's what you see, right? A self-fulfilling prophesy.

"I asked the gaming community and you won't believe what's come up." Andrew paused again.

"What? Just tell me, don't draw it out."

"A connection with the Tree of Life. Osiris was placed under the Tree of Life and was reborn. The djed is the tree. It's not Osiris' backbone."

Alex wasn't convinced. "How does that help?"

"The Great Pyramid," Andrew said. "It's going down at the Great Pyramid!"

SIXTY-EIGHT

Alex got Charlie's iPad and found a cross-section of Khufu's pyramid.

Andrew said, "Take a look at the Kings Chamber in the Great Pyramid. What's overhead?"

"The..." He stared at the King's Chamber. "My God, four stones above the sarcophagus!"

"Yeah, officially there are five relieving chambers. But that's about the space. The real purpose relates to the four stones. Ignore the supporting roof at the top. It's basically a lintel. The four stones beneath it represent the four universes. It links the Jewish Kabbalah, the Tree of Life and the djed to the pyramids."

The word cloud had included the Tree of Life.

"I see it," Alex said, hardly able to breathe. "Oh my God I see it!"

"Charlie," he said, "it's the Great Pyramid. We've got to get to the pyramids in Giza."

Charlie took him into the basement garage where she had a rental. Minutes later they were forcing their way through the congested streets.

Alex gripped the door handle as she squeezed through barely visible gaps, raced into spaces and drove on the brakes. On the misnamed ring road—because it mostly ran straight, east-west—traffic flowed and Charlie settled into a smoother rhythm.

She got on the phone and left a message on Shafik's phone letting him know about the Tree of Life and pyramid connection.

Fifteen minutes later she pulled off and took the road towards the famous necropolis.

The traffic stopped and they crawled for a few minutes. They could hear the screech of car horns ahead.

"An accident?" Charlie said.

"Whatever, this is too slow," Alex said. "We need to get out."

Charlie glanced left and right, looking for somewhere legal to park, then gave up. She pulled out of the queue and bumped onto a side road's pavement.

They bundled out and started running towards the pyramids.

Just short of the necropolis entrance, police had barricaded the road, turning cars away. As Alex and Charlie ran towards him, a policeman raised his gun, his meaning clear: *Approach and I will shoot you!*

They backed off.

Alex led her around the side street to approach the ticket office another way. They ran until they turned a corner and saw more barriers ahead. This time there were no cars blocking the road and the police looked more relaxed.

Charlie held up her badge. "I'm with Detective Shafik," she called as they walked up.

An English-speaking policeman was waved over.

"What?" he snapped.

"I'm with Detective Shafik," she said again. "US Liaison."

"I don't know anything about—"

"Is Shafik here?" Alex interrupted.

"I don't know any Detective Shafik."

Charlie said, "Murder Division. El Khalifa police station."

The man's eyes narrowed. "Not here."

"Surely this is his operation."

"Tourism and Antiquities," the policeman said although Alex noticed the man's unit appeared to be "Security", and in his black cap and uniform he didn't look like either the tourist or criminal police.

The man must have seen him look, because he said, "Special Security. Now what are you doing here?"

Charlie raised her hands in a placatory gesture. "Just looking for the homicide detective." She stepped forward like she had a right to pass.

The security man brought up his pistol. "You cannot go any further." Two other nearby guards became more interested and raised their rifles.

"Why?"

"The pyramids are closed. Special order. Even your murder division detective couldn't get past me."

Alex said, "The whole area?"

"Yes."

The two other guards closed in.

"So nobody can get to the Great Pyramid?"

"Why are you so interested?" The man's eyes narrowed again.

He pulled Charlie's arm. "We were just looking for the detective. We were told he was here. Sorry to have troubled you."

They backed off and rounded a corner before stopping.

Alex said, "He was becoming suspicious of us."

Charlie raised her phone and dialled Shafik. "Still going to voicemail," she said. "What do you think's going on?"

"Either Shafik has instructed another police unit to protect the pyramids or—"

"Someone else knows what's going on!"

"That's my thinking."

They started walking back to her abandoned car.

Charlie said, "There's another possibility. What if these people are protecting the Surgeon? Maybe he's already here."

"I don't think so. He'd need a lot of power and influence." Alex walked a bit further before the realization struck him. "This is the other group! This is Ansar Beit al-Maqdis. My God it makes sense. This is the Holy Site."

Charlie was turning towards her basement garage when her phone rang. Shafik came on the speaker.

"We've got something," the detective said. He was driving and they could hear his siren. "I'm on my way to al-Matariyyah district—to the obelisk there."

Alex said, "The other group—those who killed Salam—Ansar Beit al-Maqdis. They've closed down the area around the pyramids."

Shafik said nothing for a moment. "Mr MacLure... Agent Rebb, I want you to bring the young man with you."

Alex interrupted. "The pyramids are the Holy Site. We need—"

"It's not happening at the pyramids, Mr MacLure." Shafik was shouting now. Partly due to the background noise and drowning out Alex's voice. "It's happening in al-Matariyyah. The obelisk area."

Charlie turned the car around. Alex opened his door.

"What are you doing?" she asked, shocked.

"Not coming."

"What?"

"One, I don't trust Shafik, and two, it's not right. It's not happening there."

"Shafik thinks so."

"It's too early!"

"Maybe it's not 1am tonight. Have you thought about that? We should go."

"You go," Alex said firmly. "I want to keep looking."

Charlie hesitated then handed him the door key. "Stay inside and don't go anywhere. If you get any inspiration then call me. And I'll call you once I know what's happening at this obelisk."

Alex sat in Charlie's apartment with her iPad. Dedicated to Pharaoh Senuset I, the obelisk in the al-Matariyyah district of Cairo was the oldest in Egypt. He was Twelfth Dynasty. Nothing about the obelisk or ruins was linked in any way to Seth or Ptah.

He checked his watch. It would be midnight in a little over half an hour. It wasn't happening yet at the pyramids and it wasn't happening yet at this obelisk.

He was ninety-nine per cent sure.

But what if this was the one per cent? He shook the thought from his head. The police were dealing with it. He would be better focused on finding the true location.

Charlie battled through traffic with Google Maps instructing her which way to turn. The female electronic voice stayed calm despite the chaotic traffic and terrible driving. Things eased along a stretch of dual carriageway and then clogged up when she had to leave it. After a total of five miles, she knew she was close. The sky lit up and buildings pulsed blue. And then the road was blocked by police vehicles and armed officers. Straight away she could see these men looked different to the men at the pyramids, more like standard Egyptian police officers.

She got out, and held up her FBI credentials.

"Detective Shafik?" she asked as she approached a barrier.

No questions. The police waved her straight through.

To her left she could see an open space, a massive site of ancient ruins. Detectives were crawling all over the place, mainly around and behind the obelisk, which flashed blue like a weird kind of lighthouse. In a square beyond, arc lights were being set up, and then she spotted Shafik directing the operation.

"You said it was happening," Charlie said when he acknowledged her.

"Happened," he said, and started walking. "Follow me."

The crowd parted and she saw something pale perched on top of the stone ruins. Twin spotlights burst on and she gasped.

Of course, she'd seen plenty of dead bodies before, but it was the sudden reveal: a naked body, spread-eagled on a stone slab, a stick jutting from its chest.

"It's a spear," Shafik said, leading her closer. "Initial assessment is the blade had punctured the heart."

She was three paces away now. "No blood."

"Already dead," Shafik said.

"The MO is different."

"Not much. White male, early twenties." He pointed to the chest above the spear. "A tattoo. A circle with a triangle and a line through it."

She said, "That's the symbol."

"From MacLure."

"That's what he gave the Surgeon."

"Different MO, but I'm sure it's the Surgeon's work." Someone spoke to him and he apologized to Charlie.

She pulled out her phone to call Alex and realized she'd missed two calls. There was also a text from Zhang. She dialled voicemail and was told she had two messages.

The first was also Zhang.

"Charlie, the Quantico boys think you're making a mistake. Not the pyramids but the rock tombs. Two possible sites: A huge area near Saqqara or—more likely—there are rock-cut tombs known as the North Cliff Caves. They're just west of the pyramids. I'm sending you an image."

Shafik was back at her side full of information. She held up a hand as she checked the text—a satellite image of the pyramids and red arrows to their left pointing to a cliff edge.

Shafik looked at the image. "Not very exciting," he said. "But I have more interesting news."

Charlie looked into his eyes. "What?"

"Visual ID of the dead man. We have a photograph of the missing man. It's the computer student, Tomasz Schwartz."

SIXTY-NINE

Alex knew exactly what he was going to do next, and he knew the FBI agent wouldn't agree.

He sent a Telegram message and prayed the Surgeon was still accessing Brown's messages.

I made a mistake. I now have the true symbol

He waited. His palms became damp and he repeatedly wiped them dry. Finally a response came back.

What is it?

How can I trust you? You didn't release Vanessa

I said I would release her. I didn't say when

I want to hear her voice

You can't. She's not here. She's safe. If the symbol is true then I will tell you where she is

Alex paced the room and then typed, **Call me. I want to hear you say it**

His phone rang.

"I'm telling you the truth," the Surgeon said. "It's your choice whether you trust me or not. It's your choice whether Vanessa lives or dies. Give me the true symbol and she lives."

Alex thought the man's voice sounded different. The same man but with a slight echo. Probably where he was.

"This is the true symbol," Alex said. "Seth could take the form of the god Ptah. It was his secret sign. The Sign of Seth."

The Surgeon said nothing.

"What if it doesn't work? It's the true symbol, but..." Alex tried to control the tremor in his voice. "It's not my fault if it doesn't do what you expect."

"We'll see," the Surgeon said. "I'm not an unreasonable man."

Alex swallowed. His hands were dripping again. "You're a murderer!"

"I've had a purpose. I've never killed unnecessarily. Send me the symbol and Vanessa will live."

The call ended and Alex was left holding the phone to his ear wishing he could talk more, be convinced more.

A text arrived. A new phone number for the image. Alex took a photograph of what he'd drawn earlier but then hesitated with his finger over the send button. His hands shook and acid burned his throat.

Press.

It went and he collapsed into a chair.

His hands were still shaking when he answered a call from his brother.

"The pyramids are closed off," Alex said.

"Tighter than a gnat's arse. I know. It's all over social media. No one's getting into the Great Pyramid tonight. Not unless it's the police."

Alex said nothing. Where the hell was the Surgeon and where had he taken Vanessa?

Andrew said, "Any other ideas?"

"Nothing," Alex said, his voice weak.

"Are you OK?"

"Just about coping, but not well."

"I don't know if it helps, but one of the gaming guys mentioned a different conspiracy. One about the Seth papyrus."

Alex said nothing. His mind wasn't working right. He remembered something about a papyrus being found at a pyramid but it was the wrong age.

"I'd not heard of Pharaoh Senusret," Andrew said.

Alex's mind turned to fire. Charlie was on her way to Senusret's obelisk. Different place, but hell of a coincidence.

"It was found in Senusret's pyramid in Lisht," Andrew was saying. "It's south of those pyramids at Saqqara."

"What about it?"

Andrew started to explain that it included a lengthy prayer by Seth that was said to invoke the appearance of God.

"I remember," Alex said. "It's the wrong period. The papyrus was written in Coptic script."

"It also refers to the mountain of the murderer, Alex."

Alex took a long disappointed breath. "It dates to five hundred years after Christ. Much too late."

"Fine." Now Andrew sounded disappointed. "My guy thought the whole Cain and Seth thing was mixed up. Why would Adam and Eve have a third son and call him Seth after a god associated with the same story? Cain killed Abel. Seth killed his brother Osiris."

Alex thanked his brother and decided the only thing he could do was wait. Wait until after the Surgeon's ceremony and pray that Vanessa would be set free.

And then it struck him.

The obvious thing that he kept overlooking. This was as much about the resurrection of Christ as it was about Osiris. There wasn't a pyramid in Jerusalem. Christ was placed in a cave after he'd been taken from the cross.

Cave.

Coptic papyrus.

Coptic cave.

Alex ran outside and hailed a taxi. From the backseat, he called Charlie, got voicemail and left a breathless message. "Oh my God, Charlie. It's the Coptic Cave Church. The Monastery of Saint Simon. Mokattam cliffs. I'm going there now."

Charlie cursed the traffic and the fact she was effectively doubling back. She was heading to the rock tombs on the far side of the pyramids—she'd been so close less than an hour ago with Alex.

Alex!

She'd forgotten the second voicemail. She listened to Alex's excited message then immediately called Zhang.

"The Monastery of Saint Simon," she said. "Ask the Quantico guys if that could be the place. I might be headed for the wrong caves."

She'd already stopped and put the monastery into Google Maps when Zhang called back. "Yes, Charlie. That's a yes!"

The monastery was only half a mile from the cemetery where they'd gone to rescue Alex's girlfriend. The Surgeon hadn't gone far.

"Come on! Come on!" she shouted as the satnav cut her a zigzag route through the city. The time was going too fast. It was half past midnight as she rounded the Al-Azhar Park. Then down past the cemetery and off east into a suburb that gradually rose through twisting and turning streets.

And then the satnav failed her. Each time she came to a road it had told her to turn down it jumped. They weren't roads, but narrow tracks. Outside, the air was hot and thick with bad odours. It smelled like a garbage dump. Her headlights picked out what looked like stacked trash—giant piles of bound-up cardboard and blue sacks on both sides of the road, closing it in, impossible to pass.

The satnav jumped again and showed a route that took her around before climbing the hill. She went around a sweeping bend and she saw the cliffs outlined against the star-speckled sky.

After the road opened up onto a plateau, Charlie found herself in a parking lot. She drove past dark round huts that wouldn't have looked out of place in Hawaii. Vendors, she guessed, although devoid of custom now.

Behind them was a church. Only, as she stopped and looked closely, she realized the twin towers were just a façade. There wasn't a building behind, just a cliff face.

Everything was in darkness. For a moment she sat wondering if she'd come to the wrong place. Apart from a handful of cars around the parking lot, this area was deserted.

Well, I'm here now, she decided, and got out. There was still a faint whiff of garbage but also warm rock. It was like the cliff radiated heat despite the darkness.

Charlie walked towards the twin towers. Now she could see carvings in the rock face. To the right was a huge statue of Jesus on the cross. Ahead was the entrance.

She took a step towards the towers and jumped. A man stepped from the shadows.

"God you scared me!" she said.

John Graham held up a shushing finger.

"Have you just got here?" he whispered.

"Yes."

Despite Graham being a bureaucratic irritation, she was relieved to see a friendly face, relieved she wasn't here in the darkness alone.

"Is the Surgeon definitely here?" he asked.

She raised her palms: I don't know.

"Have you got your gun?"

She nodded.

"Good. Get it out, ready," he said, then pointed forward and started walking.

There were notices and barriers up, blocking their way.

"Closed for urgent repairs," he said.

"How did you know?" she whispered, walking right behind him.

"Know what?"

"That I'd be here."

He hesitated and looked at her, a frown on his face. "I didn't. I knew MacLure was."

He started walking again and they reached a flight of steps up to the entrance.

"How did you know—?"

"Charlie! What's with the questions?" He kept walking and sounded irritated. "You told me we were tracking his phone. Now let's go get this bastard, OK?"

They reached the top of the steps and he slunk to the side wall, looking ahead. The floor sloped downwards. Twenty yards later it opened out into a vast cave. In front of them was an amphitheatre with concrete pews descending into a stage. Candles around it provided a dim light she hadn't seen from outside.

The stage was empty. She looked around. The pews, thousands of them, were empty. Intricate carvings on the walls flickered gently, seemingly alive. They told stories from the Bible, and on the right-hand side, half way up the rock, was a rock-cut tomb. A round stone leaned next to it, like it had just been rolled aside.

Charlie followed Graham down the steep slope and then across towards the tomb. He pulled out a flashlight and held it, classic-style, under his gun.

Above the tomb was Arabic, and then in English it said: *He is not here; he has risen, just as he said.*

"Up there?" Charlie whispered.

Graham held a finger to his lips again, listening hard.

Then Charlie heard it too. A faint chanting had begun.

She pulled out her phone. The time was 1am.

"He's here," Graham whispered.

She was still looking at her phone.

You told me we were tracking his phone, of course.

She frowned at Graham. "We weren't tracking Alex's phone. And I didn't tell you."

Graham blinked, thrown by her comment. "What?" Then: "Keep your voice down."

"How did you know he was here?"

"Shush!"

"How did you—?"

Graham leaned in. "Charlie, Charlie, Charlie."

She didn't see what happened, but suddenly she couldn't breathe. Her body convulsed and she felt like she was falling, falling forever through the darkness. Then she was in a playground, pushing her sister Liz on a swing. She'd been six. A happy time just before Mom had died. Then Liz was suddenly an adult and pushing a little boy on the swing—her own child. Their dad was there, and then Mom, arm in arm with him, alive and smiling at her until it all went black.

SEVENTY

Alex's taxi driver stopped in the streets below the mountain. Ahead the road was blocked by small trucks on either side. They could get through but not a full-sized car.

The driver said, "Quicker for you to walk. Straight up there."

Alex didn't quibble at the extortionate price quoted. He stuffed a bundle of notes into the man's hand and hurried out. The smell of rotting vegetation in the warm night made him gag at first. But he put one hand over his nose and mouth and just ran up the hill.

At the end of the street the houses ended and he scrambled up a stony path. Without street lights he struggled to see by the light of the stars. Then he was at the top and after a bunch of shrubs and trees he burst through onto the plateau.

He kept running, past huts and towards what looked like a church in front of a mountainside.

Was Vanessa here? Was the Surgeon here? Last throw of the dice, he said to himself. He didn't have a plan. He didn't have a weapon. But he had hope and he needed to save Vanessa. Somehow.

He stopped by barriers. The place was closed and in darkness. He recognized the Arabic for danger written on signs and he almost laughed. "You're right," he said out loud. "But danger's an understatement."

He leapt the barrier and at the foot of a stairway into the church he pulled out his phone. Twenty minutes to go. Had Charlie got his message? Was she on her way? He went to try her number again but there was no signal.

He ascended the steps. Behind the church façade was the gaping maw of a cave. He could hear his own breathing, loud in the otherwise silent space.

A metal gate barred his way but was easily jerked open. Passing beneath the entrance and down a corridor, he saw a faint light ahead.

A hundred candles burned in the darkness, lighting an incredible cavern.

Where do I go? he wondered. The place was deserted, although he sensed more than an empty cave. If he'd been religious he'd have believed a thousand souls were here, silently praying to the Lord. Or maybe it was just the ominous weight of rock arching around and above.

Alex went all the way down to the stage. Despite the ancient feel to the amphitheatre, there were projectors and projection screens down here. He looked up and could see spotlights set to illuminate the centre and sections of wall. He also spotted a rock-cut tomb, presumably representing Christ's own tomb.

He was almost below it when he heard the scrunch of stones. Feet. On rock maybe. He peered up. And then something rushed in from the side—a dark shape that smacked into the side of his head, plunging him into oblivion.

Alex was swimming through a tunnel, only it had swirling patterns on the side and it was getting wider. Angels were singing in the darkness.

And then the fog of unconsciousness lifted and he became aware of hard ground. He was on the floor, his hands and feet bound with duct tape. The whole of the right-hand side of his face burned. Pain throbbed below his eye socket and above his ear.

He looked around. This wasn't the cavern he'd entered. The seats here were wooden chairs, not concrete pews. He could see light between them and then a stage. A different stage.

Above the stage was a structure suspended from the ceiling. Four sections. Like the djed. Like the four stones above the King's Chamber, Alex realized.

What he'd thought of as singing angels was in fact a single chanting voice.

Alex shifted until he could see a man in a white gown standing on the stage. He recognized him from a picture in Charlie's apartment. Not identical but similar, like he'd had plastic surgery. Tony Zart. The Surgeon. And in his hand was a spear.

The Surgeon wasn't chanting. That must be someone else. Or a recording.

Alex shifted again, rising up to see what the Surgeon was looking at. On the ground was a table and on the table was a body in a shroud.

Vanessa! Alex's mind screamed.

He struggled against the restraints but couldn't move more than a few inches.

The Surgeon pulled something out of a bag, flung it down and then stabbed with the spear. When he raised it again, Alex saw a snake writhing, pierced by the blade.

Then the chanting swelled, the spear was stabbed into the ground and the man now held a sword. The fine metal gleamed orange in the candlelight.

The sword was raised over the body.

Alex struggled, the duct tape tearing at his skin.

The chanting built to a crescendo and then abruptly stopped. Down flashed the blade, hovering over the body's chest.

With care, the Surgeon pushed the blade into the body.

"Vanessa!" Alex screamed.

And then the cavern boomed with a single gunshot and the Surgeon was blown sideways.

Alex could barely breathe. He squirmed around to see who'd fired the shot. Had the police arrived? Was Charlie here?

But the man walking rapidly towards him wasn't either.

"Thank God!" Alex said, but the man's expression made his heart freeze. "Who the hell...?"

The other man stood over Alex with a clenched-teeth grin. "Sorry," he said, pointing the gun at Alex's face. "I have to do this."

SEVENTY-ONE

The man standing over Alex aimed his gun and looked like he was about to say something else. Instead he was thrown aside as a volley of shots echoed through the cave.

Running feet seemed to be everywhere, and then Alex saw police rushing down the aisles. One reached him, pulled his trembling body up and slit the duct tape.

Weak though he was, Alex pushed through the chairs and clattered to the stage. As he stumbled up the steps, he saw Detective Shafik coming the other way.

Alex felt like his chest was empty. He couldn't speak, he couldn't breathe. Vanessa was dead.

Like walking through water, he staggered towards her.

He couldn't see her face. A trickle of blood and liquid ran over the shroud onto the floor.

Shafik was there, beside him now, and caught his arm as his legs gave way.

Alex reached for the shroud, his hands trembling. "No," Shafik said, restraining him.

"I have to."

Shafik eased his grip and Alex lifted the cover from the body's face.

"Sir," a voice shouted from high up in the amphi-theatre.

Alex hesitated and turned with Shafik to look. By the entrance corridor was a policeman supporting a woman.

Vanessa? "Vanessa!" Alex shouted. Despite the pain in his head and the ache from the bindings he found the strength to rush up the aisle towards his girlfriend.

SEVENTY-TWO

Vanessa lay asleep in a hospital bed. She'd been found in the rock tomb, unharmed. Charlie had been found too. She'd been rendered unconscious by a Taser and abandoned in a corridor above the smaller cave church.

She joined Alex and Detective Shafik outside Vanessa's room.

"How're you feeling?" Alex asked.

"Like a fly on an electric bug catcher," she said. "Now I know how the bad guys feel."

"Who was he?"

"Who?"

"The man who Tasered you and then shot the Surgeon."

He saw Charlie make eye contact with Shafik before saying, "We don't know."

Alex guessed she was lying. He said, "Was he the Haris al'Asrar—the Keeper of Secrets?"

"Unlikely," Shafik said. "Probably worked for him."

"So you have no idea who the Keeper of Secrets is?"

"No."

Alex turned back to look at Vanessa through the window.

She was comfortable, dehydrated, suffering from excessive use of anaesthetic used by the Surgeon to knock her out, but otherwise fine. The doctor had said that after a day's rest and observation she should be able to go home.

She hadn't recognized Alex yet and he'd been told to let her sleep.

Shafik said, "Be grateful they didn't kill her."

"I am. Believe me!"

Shafik said, "I don't understand how he could have killed so many men and yet kept her alive."

"And didn't kill me either."

Vanessa started to stir and Alex pressed closer to the window. Then she opened her eyes and smiled at him.

Charlie waited a minute after Alex rushed into the private room. She watched him embrace his girlfriend.

"They'll be all right," she said, but Shafik was already walking away.

She caught up with him.

He said, "You didn't want MacLure to know about your LEGAT."

"No," she said. "Would your people want to announce something like that?" Graham had been with the FBI for eighteen years. Had he always been working for the Haris al'Asrar? Or maybe he didn't know who he was working for. Maybe it was all about money. There would be an investigation and they'd find out either way. She realized when he'd known where Alex would be but not how he'd been tracked.

And she should have guessed earlier. He hadn't been interested in MacLure for bureaucratic or embassy reasons. The Arab murdered in Schwartz's apartment had been working for the Champions of the Holy Site too. Graham had become interested when he discovered the Surgeon's connection. He knew someone wanted the secret, just hadn't immediately figured they were the same case.

"So who is the Keeper of Secrets?" she asked Shafik.

He said, "Someone capable of mustering the Tourism and Antiquities police as well as other special services. There's a deputy minister... Whether it's him, I don't know. However, I can assure you there'll be no direct investigation."

Charlie nodded. She could guess how things worked here. Shafik needed to file it away and hope that one day direct evidence would materialize.

Charlie said, "How did they know?"

"To go to the church?"

"Yes."

"Someone was feeding them information. Someone with access to the tracking updates. One of my men was working for them. Don't worry I'll find out who."

She had no doubt he would. Investigating your own people was a different matter from exposing a deputy minister.

Shafik asked, "What will you do now?"

"Go home. Go and see my sister and father. Spend some quality time with them. My sister had some good news and I was unreasonable. We need to reconnect... I need to apologize."

Shafik nodded. "You'll write a report before you go?"

"Of course."

"I know you recognized the body in the shroud. You'll give me a name?"

"I knew him," Charlie said. "Kingren. Robert Kingren. One of the pastors of the Church of the Risen Christ. In fact, they openly treated him like a latter-day Jesus. The plan must have been to resurrect him all along."

They were outside now and he flagged down his driver. "This is where we part," he said, holding out a hand.

She shook it.

He said, "It's been a pleasure."

"Really?" she said sceptically.

"No, but I've come to appreciate you."

She smiled. "I'll take that as a compliment."

"It is," he said, getting into his car. "We cracked the case and it's over."

Charlie watched Shafik drive away. "Except we don't know where McCubbin is," she said to his retreating car. Someone other than the Surgeon created the diversion with the body at the obelisk. Someone left Schwartz's body there to distract them and she bet that was McCubbin.

They hadn't found anyone else at the monastery, although someone had been recording it. There had been no evidence of McCubbin, but it didn't mean he hadn't been there. He had been controlling all of this and he wouldn't have missed the ultimate ceremony, the resurrection of Kingren.

"No," she said, still talking to herself. "McCubbin is still out there."

Over two thousand miles north, Governor McCubbin stepped off a plane in Helsinki. Only he wasn't McCubbin on his passport anymore and he'd changed his appearance.

So much time had gone by, so much effort had been expended and they had failed. Zart and Kingren were dead. Despite all of the deaths, they had been necessary sacrifices. He knew his heart was still pure, that God understood. The world needed a new Christ, a new saviour. And he had prevented Zart from killing MacLure and his girlfriend.

What's more, the whole thing hadn't been for nothing.

He got into a cab and headed for the rendezvous. The two directors of the Seventh Hour would be waiting for him. And he had good news as well as bad.

He pulled MacLure's phone out of his pocket and looked at the image.

They would set up a new church here. They would find their new candidate and this time there would be witnesses. Their preacher would be killed in public—in some way that would capture the world's attention. And then they would see the resurrection broadcast live on social media. The world would go crazy for the man who had died and was brought back to life. They would know the new Christ had been among them, and observe the ascension to Heaven. He smiled to himself. He, the head of the church, would be responsible for the Second Coming.

SEVENTY-THREE

1306 BCE, Thebes

Yanhamu watched his wife from a distance. She was as beautiful as she was wise and their years apart hadn't dulled their love for one another. Perhaps it had even strengthened it.

She sat under an awning like a magistrate, but instead of a crowd she had a queue of people. Instead of guards she just had a slave and there was no scribe. And the people weren't summoned. They came forward in an orderly fashion and told Nefer-bithia their dispute or issue. She wasn't a woman assuming a forbidden role; she wasn't an official magistrate. She was just a wise-one offering advice and solutions.

Yanhamu heard her discuss a dispute between two brothers. Their father had left them land and they couldn't agree the split. They both wanted the fertile land. But they had assumed half each. Nefer-bithia told them to split it so that one had a smaller portion with fertile land and the other had some fertile land and the larger portion of desert.

"How do we do that?" one asked.

"Divide it up, and the point at which you feel you would benefit from either package of land then that is the fair split."

The men agreed and made a payment—not a fee, but a gesture of thanks.

The next case was a woman who was unhappy about the new woman her husband had brought in as a concubine. Yanhamu wondered if his wife used her own experience from the deputy's palace when she told the woman that there were two choices. She could resist and become bitter, and in the end her heart would be heavy. Or she could find commonality with this new woman, perhaps because they both loved the same man, or maybe not. Perhaps they would find agreement in despising his foibles. Perhaps they would become friends.

After that, there were people who felt unlucky and asked Nefer-bithia to offer an alternative patron god. She asked questions, made suggestions and the people left contented.

When she was faced with a case of theft, Yanhamu was shocked that this hadn't gone to the magistrate. An owner accused his baker of taking bread. Surely, if guilty, the thief would lose a hand? But the men were reasonable, and after Nefer-bithia found the accused guilty of taking flour for his own purposes, they asked for her solution. She told the baker to work extra days without pay. Then she asked the owner if the baker could in future also be allowed one sack of flour per month. The men agreed.

Afterwards, Yanhamu walked back to their house. It was the old magistrate's house where Lord Khety had first taken him in. And where he'd first seen Nefer-bithia, the young girl he'd been told not to look at, the girl he'd fallen in love with and the one he would never leave again.

They'd extended the house with the money he'd received from Ramses. Horemheb had been buried in his deep tomb across the water and the old man was now Pharaoh. He'd appointed his son as commander of the army for the Two Lands and renamed him Seti.

They changed and a slave gave them a package of food for later.

"Don't you miss being a magistrate?" Nefer-bithia asked Yanhamu as they strolled through the temples and pylons of Karnak. Heat shimmered off the stone.

"One magistrate in the family is enough," he said with a laugh. They'd discussed this many times and he knew she didn't consider herself to be a magistrate any more. She was better than a magistrate. But if he took the same role, it couldn't be in this nome. He'd probably have to go to Elephantine, and then they wouldn't be together.

They kept walking until they came to a grove of sycamore fig trees on the edge of the city. They found the tree where they'd carved their initials and promised undying love. How old had he been then, twelve? She'd been two years younger and yet here they were, twenty-four years later.

He spread a blanket in the shade of their tree and she unpacked their food and drink.

It was a tranquil spot, away from people. Even the sparrows and goats were sleeping in the heat of the day.

She leaned over and kissed him as he took bread from her. "So what are you going to do Yan-Khety?"

"I've been a slave, a scribe, a magistrate and a soldier, isn't that enough for one lifetime?"

"You could have been Pharaoh's Keeper of Secrets."

"And lived in Memphis? You'd have hated Memphis, my love."

He could tell from her look that she didn't believe him. She knew he'd turned down the job and suggested Sadhu. He'd told Ramses that his assistant knew as much as he—and was much younger and less cynical.

"Tell me what you told Pharaoh Ramses," she said.

"I am sworn to secrecy."

"Just imagine I am the wise-one and you need to unburden yourself."

He grinned. "No need to imagine. You are wise. The people love you."

"You're deflecting. Talk to me, Yani."

"Ramses wanted the Two Truths and I told him. The first is the resurrection. Horus was born as Ra on Earth and that each pharaoh becomes the new Horus, one day joining with Ra to ensure He rises each day." He took a breath and checked for sparrows. When he was sure none were within earshot he said, "I told him about the old religion, the one that had been corrupted and also forgotten. I told him about Seth on the right hand of Amun-Ra."

"And Horus on his left in place of Osiris."

"Yes. I told him about Seth's importance and strength. For the northern land He was critical to the rebirth of Ra. He is not the serpent, He destroys the serpent with His spear and He shows the way to the new dawn."

"And that is why Ramses set me free?"

"Almost. He wanted one more thing so I showed him the most sacred, forgotten symbol. The Sign of Seth. The way that Seth could be disguised as Ptah but that he could still be recognized. In this way Ramses could be reborn and live forever like Osiris."

"You discovered an ancient symbol?"

Yanhamu put his finger in the dirt and drew a figure of eight on its side.

"This is the loop of eternity. Like a ring, it does not end, but this symbol has a twist. It goes round and round but also down through the underworld. Only the pharaoh can know this and use it to guarantee his immortality."

She blinked. "So that's why you didn't tell me. You really shouldn't tell anyone."

"No," he said, "that's not the secret."

She leaned forward.

"I needed something to ensure your release. It had to be good." He paused and looked around again but now he was grinning. "So I made it up!"

At first she looked horrified, but then her stern face cracked as she started to laugh.

He said, "Ramses wanted to know the second truth. But he didn't want what I learned from my sister. Ramses was a soldier, all he knew was strength. If I'd told him the real truth he'd never have released you. I didn't lie about the history and misunderstanding of Seth. And Ramses wanted to believe it. He also wanted to believe there was a symbol."

"And the real truth?"

"You know I went into the Great Pyramid. I don't know how long I was there but I sensed eternity. Time means nothing outside of this realm and the sacred site is a portal to that Field of Reeds."

"Yes," she said, her eyes full of wonder.

"I sensed a thousand souls and the gods themselves. And among all those voices, I heard my sister's. And Laret made me understand the second truth. A truth that Ramses could never appreciate."

"What?" Nefer-bithia asked breathlessly.

Yanhamu pulled his wife in and looked into her pretty eyes. "The second truth is love," he whispered. "It's as simple   as   that."

Acknowledgements

A number of experts provided help and debate in the creation of this story. In no particular order, they were: Simon Lewis, Professor of Forensic and Analytical Chemistry, Curtin University; Dr Aidan Dodson, Senior Research Fellow, Department of Archaeology and Anthropology, University of Bristol; and, SSA Jeffrey P. Heinze from the FBI Office of Public Affairs for advice on FBI practices. I was also provided expert help on medical issues from Dr Kerry Bailey-Jones, and thank John Alexander ThM for discussions on theology and the resurrection story. I am grateful to them all and must point out that the views expressed within the story are mine and do not necessarily reflect the experts' opinions.

I am grateful to Mike Baker from The United Grand Lodge of England for the tour of the building and discussion of conspiracy theories.

Alex JJ Mynette inspired the character of Andrew MacLure and deserves a shout out. It is my hope that this story promotes awareness of the genetic disorder, Duchene muscular dystrophy, and the plight of those who suffer from it.

Thanks once again to my official editor, Richard Sheehan and my unofficial ones: Pete Tonkin and Dustin White. The final word of gratitude must go to my wife, Kerry, my lodestone, my B'ja.

murraybaileybooks.com

IF YOU ENJOYED THIS BOOK

Feedback helps me understand what works, what doesn't and what readers want more of. It also brings a book to life.

Online reviews are also very important in encouraging others to try my books. I don't have the financial clout of a big publisher. I can't take out newspaper ads or run poster campaigns.

But what I do have is an enthusiastic and committed bunch of readers.

Honest reviews are a powerful tool. I'd be very grateful if you could spend a couple of minutes leaving a review, however short, on sites like Amazon and Goodreads.

Thank you
Murray